the difference between you and me

the difference between you and me

A NOVEL

Kathleen DeMarco

miramax books

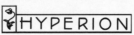
HYPERION

This book is fiction.* This is probably obvious to people who work in the film business—lucky people, they already know that the kind of lying, cheating and airs of self-importance depicted in this novel would not be tolerated in their industry. Still, to those who wonder, all characters and events are the product of the author's imagination, and any resemblance to anyone living or dead is coincidental and unintentional.

For information address:
Hyperion, 77 West 66th Street,
New York, New York 10023-6298.

ISBN: 1-4013-5191-3

FIRST EDITION

Designed by Christine Weathersbee

10 9 8 7 6 5 4 3 2 1

*Well . . . it is true that my brother's roof did collapse in Manhattan during the month of October 1987, but it has since been fixed and he doesn't live there anymore anyway.

For my father,

Mark Anthony DeMarco

Or maybe it's curiosity I mean. You don't ever see or notice anything important that goes on. You never watch and think and try to figure anything out. Maybe that's the biggest difference between you and me, after all.

—Carson McCullers,
The Heart Is a Lonely Hunter

Josephine

Twenty-eight. Daughter of Paul and Isobel Hibberd, from Portland, Oregon. Granddaughter of Paul Hibberd I, otherwise known as "The First Dentist in the Family." Best friend of Rebecca Mosely, mother of two in Beverly Hills. Married to Mike O'Leary, her college sweetheart, even though she cheated on him four times, once with Derek Hutton, who went on to be a much-loved soap opera actor on *Guiding Light*. Forced Mike to move to Los Angeles so she could become President of a Movie Studio, just as her father, Dr. Paul Hibberd, big-toothed and fleshy lipped, told her that she could.

Carla

Forty-one. Daughter of Candace (alive) and John (deceased) Trousse, from Wilmington, Delaware. Niece of Paulette Giberson, the long-faced but handsome woman featured in both *Vanity Fair* and *National Geographic* for feeding famine victims in Ethiopia while financing children's vaccinations in Accra, Ghana. First cousin of successful Hollywood lawyer, Phillip Giberson, product of Paulette's brief attempt at wedded bliss with British scholar E. Rupert Giberson. Never married, in debt, and fired from her last job four months ago. B.A. from Lehigh, M.F.A. from NYU, and a Ph.D. from Columbia just as soon as she turns in her dissertation. In love with David Stegner, who lives in Pasadena, and who has slept with her approximately once, at cousin Phillip's wedding nine years earlier. She cannot remember her father, John Trousse, who died of acute heart failure when Carla was three. Carla is sure that if she had a father she could remember she would be able to figure out that most arcane of equations: Having x (intellectual scholarship) and y (verbal fluidity), she wants to solve for z, that as-yet-abstruse combination of personality traits that would finally push her from her rotting apartment in Greenwich Village and onto the world stage, under hot and deserved bright lights.

Part One

Chapter One

The distraction for Josephine O'Leary on this spring morning in Los Angeles was not her disintegrating marriage but the fact that she had not been invited to her (ex-) friend Juliet Eckhardt's thirtieth birthday party.

She drove on Wilshire Boulevard, west of La Cienega, under a strong morning sun and beneath blinking traffic signals, past car dealerships and sleek restaurants, past expensive retail shops with red awnings stretched trampoline-tight, past architecturally assured modern buildings signifying trendsetting and trendbusting people inside, working to push and prod and wrangle money and ideas from "talent," the way old-time farmers used to work their plots of land.

She was one of those people now. It was her destiny, heralded by her father, Dr. Paul Hibberd, Portland's most esteemed dentist. "You are my princess!" he would tell her. "You'd be a far better sight in that movie president's seat than the bozos that are there now." Law school had given her the imprint of credibility; as much as her parents supported her decision to go to Hollywood, they also were firm believers in the side benefits garnered from an advanced degree. "We're not saying that you have to be a lawyer, honey," said Isobel Hibberd, her new face-lift healing seamlessly, "we're only suggesting, *suggesting*, sweetheart, that having something to fall back on makes sense. With your intelligence and your looks, *and* a law degree, there's just no end to what you could do!"

Paul Hibberd's best friend from the country club had a brother who was on the board of trustees at U. C. Berkeley's Law School, and Josie—scoring in the ninety-second percentile on her LSATs after only four tries and five sessions with the Princeton Review—was accepted just two years after she received her B. A. from the University of Oregon.

Throughout her academic tenure, Josie studied the men and women of Hollywood from afar. She read biographies and autobiographies of the wildly successful and the disastrously unlucky; she learned about Sam Cohn and Darryl Zanuck and Sherry Lansing and Dawn Steel; she studied *People* magazine, *Us Weekly*, and *InStyle*. She examined how celebrities spoke, what they wore, and who they married. And she learned, after lengthy and deliberate study, that while her list of goals (successful career, gorgeous and rich husband, instant seating at a crowded restaurant, and never having to wait in line) was essential to her everyday well-being, what would set her apart would be to attain an image of *not caring*. Indeed, to project an image of *not caring* had become Josie's personal Mount Everest. To not care—or to seem to not care—would mean that she (like her idols) had cleared her mental palate of troublesome insecurities (like not being invited to a silly party) so that she could concentrate on noble, more admirable pursuits, like, say, world peace and campaign finance reform.

And it was this *not caring* that brought Josie back full circle to the person of her (ex-) friend Juliet Eckhardt, the woman whose precocious ability to trust in herself had propelled her to the head of her magazine's masthead, not to mention bold-printed mentions in gossip columns.

It had never occurred to Josie that she wouldn't be invited to Juliet's annual bash. Instead, when Josie didn't receive an invitation, she assumed that Juliet had decided to do away with her lavish birthday party because of her fear that terrorists would choose Spago as their next target.

And then—this morning—Josie saw the photograph on page seven of *People*. Juliet, it seemed, not only had thrown herself a party in the style of Nero but had also pruned her invitation list to make way for the prosperous new growth.

Josie knew that being upset was silly—she had foolishly trusted Juliet the way a child trusts a friend who throws rocks, and she shouldn't feel hurt now that one had been hurled metaphorically at her. Her husband, Mike O'Leary, was always in this kind of predicament, surprised and sensitive that his big bad colleagues at the bank could misrepresent him, or hold grudges, or else belittle him for "not playing the game." In the early days of their marriage, Josie had taken time to comfort Mike, to assure him that the others were "bad" and that he was "good." After time, Josie had resorted to her more pragmatic nature. "What do you expect?" she would admonish. "Stop acting like a child."

But Josie wasn't Mike, and she wouldn't be bamboozled again. Furthermore, there was no need to fret, because Juliet's rejection would soon be righted. For just as Adam Smith believed an invisible hand guided a nation's economy, so Josie believed that an invisible hand managed a nation's social hierarchy.

Right now, for example, the Hand had decided to flick Josie off her plinth of complacent trust into this muddle of insecurities and rejection. It was up to Josie to pull herself up by her invisible bootstraps and begin anew. But the Hand was fair—inevitably it would push Juliet off her perch too. It would be at that precise moment that Josie could overtake her in their race for status.

Josie envisioned a scene from the future. Juliet would call, perhaps after Josie had produced some noteworthy, critically acclaimed movie with an unknown cast and a salt-of-the-earth director who told anyone who would listen that he flew coach. Josie would look at the caller-ID and recognize Juliet's private cell number. Josie would motion to

Nadine, her sweet-faced but big-legged assistant, to answer the call.

"One moment," Nadine would say, none-too-cordially. She would pause and then grin at Josie watching in the main office. Then Nadine would say, "I'm sorry, Josephine's not available. Perhaps I can help you?"

Juliet, of course, would not rise to the bait; she was entirely too adept at professional politics to behave rashly. Juliet's inheritance—a sum that ranged anywhere from fifty to five hundred million dollars—gave her a psychological suit of armor that repelled even the most acute of attacks. Her aim was self-preservation, and she was able to sustain this through her own signature blend of limited emotion and sharp social judgments. So when Nadine politely spurned Juliet, Juliet would bubble a response of *Yes, oh, just tell her it's been too long and I can't wait to see her!* Then, Josie knew, Juliet would hang up the phone and immediately propel Josie forward onto the list of people for *her* to snub when the roles were reversed.

But that was a long way off. Josie's practicality infused even her fantasy life; Juliet's payback would occur after Josie's payback, and it was imprudent to dwell two fantasies in the future. Instead, Josie chose to linger in the steadying triumph of fantasy number one.

She pulled into the driveway of her office building and grimaced.

"Goddammit." Her space was already occupied by a little off-white Toyota Corolla. It was a car with no personality, a car that signified the driver knew nothing about the rules of Hollywood. She was going to have it towed. But then the thought crossed her mind that the car may be evidence of a peculiar Hollywood condition Josie called the Reverse Affect: when a successful person feigned a lack of pretentiousness to achieve the same veneration as the ostentatiously successful. She would not help herself by raising a fuss. Moreover, during the last five seconds she had morphed her nagging hurt from Juliet into a benevolent mood toward the efficacies of the Hollywood system. She decided she would alert Nadine about the offending car and insist that it not be towed, only that it be moved as soon as possible. As she turned into a visitor's parking space, she congratulated herself on her aplomb.

She stepped out of her forest green Saab convertible. She had dressed carefully today. She was having lunch with Seth Levin, her mentor from her early days in Los Angeles, when she had worked at Y&W, one of Los Angeles's largest entertainment law firms.

It was one of her biggest missteps—she had arrived in L.A. full of vigor and optimism, but within five minutes knew she needed to have a career strategy in place. She was going to be President of a Studio, yes, but how? She had been tempted to call her father and say, "I'm here, now what?" Instead, she had called acquaintances from Berkeley who were similarly destined to conquer Hollywood.

Nell McKnight, a bone-thin reporter for one of the entertainment networks, told her she should be a producer. "Let's simplify, shall we? If you're not talent—talent with a capital *T*, talent as a noun, not an adjective—you have to work with talent. How do you that? You agent, you manage, you produce. Actually, managers now produce, which has aggravated everybody in town, but that's another story. Agenting's a good gig, once you put in the time, but everyone says it's grueling—I know people who were afraid to leave the office for weeks at a time, afraid to miss something. You'd learn the business cold, but I think maybe—I don't think it's for you, Josie, no offense. The grunt work is kind of demoralizing, especially at your age. No. I think you produce. Anyone can do it—you simply say, 'I'm a producer.' "

"Right," Josie had said. She had paused. "There's got to be more."

"Sure. Depends on what you want. You could be a creative producer, a producer-producer, or a glomming producer. The easiest is glomming, but you don't know any talent well enough, so it's gotta be material. Find good material—a book or an article, anything, then buy it, and say you're producing it. Done deal."

Catherine Von Hauptman, a publicist with curly brown ringlets, had told Josie she should be a manager. "Look, I'll be honest with you, no one cares unless you're someone—are you sure you can't write? Not at all? Well, then, here's the thing. I'll swear I never told you this, but here's the word you need to know. Glom. As in 'I glom, you glom, everyone gloms.' Find talent—an actor, a writer, if you're lucky, a director—and weld yourself to their hip. I'm talking *weld*, as in, attached in steel. Do not let go. Become their *manager.* Then you can make a commission off their fee *and* demand producing credit and money. It's the best gig in town, by a long shot."

Jonathan Sachs, a short, pudgy man who wore starched white button-down shirts, told Josie that he was a producer who, at that very second, was working on "several projects." He had appraised Josie thoughtfully and said, "Listen, I'm the type of guy who follows his gut. I'm in need of—let's say a *confidante* for lack of a better word. We should work together." He couldn't offer her money, but he could get her an invitation to the next party at the Playboy mansion, and he told her he'd be happy to give her assistant-to-the-producer credit if anything ever came of their relationship.

It was Seth who had finally advised her properly. Seth Levin had been a friend of her favorite law school professor's, and one of the first people Josie had called when she moved to L.A. He was also the only person on her list of career counselors who had actually become both respected and rich. "I'll be honest with you, Josie. I don't know if I'd jump headfirst into producing. I'd use some of that chutzpah in a field you know—it'll give you time to learn the ropes, get your feet wet, the whole thing. If you still want to produce after that, go right ahead. I know there's a whole Habitrail out there of so-called producers and representatives claiming to be the hottest things in town, but my experience is that the truly successful people don't have time for all the bullshit. They have to be on sets, they have to set up budgets and arrange financing and make sure distribution is figured out, and most of all, they have to be involved *up here.*" Seth had tapped his head. "The best producers are like smart military men— *women*, excuse me—attuned to every possible disaster, large or small. Contrary to popular belief, there are real producers out here who work

8

really hard. You've got to see both sides. For the time being, come work with us."

Since Josie was reasonably sure she wasn't Talent with a capital *T*, and since she hadn't found anyone to glom on to, the decision had been simple. Managing, agenting, and producing would not pay her a decent starting salary, and Josie's need to keep Prada on her feet was too important. Her mother had been right—it was essential to have something to fall back on. More significant, Josie's ability to practice law when her peers were stuck lying about fake friendships with movie stars would help her maintain her sense of superiority over the rest of the strivers.

This had meant accepting a position at Y&W. Seth had convinced the other partners that Josie would tire of her aspirations to be a producer and become one of their very own professional barracudas. Before the year was through, however, it was obvious that the opposite had occurred. Everything Josie had learned in the six months since she had arrived had corroborated the advice of Nell, Catherine, and Jonathan. She was a producer at heart, she was sure of it.

"You know what you're doing?" Seth had asked.

"Yes."

"You know the saying? When a movie fails, it's the producer's fault, and when it succeeds, it's because of everyone else."

"I've heard it. I don't care."

"Listen to me, Josie. This is your career we're talking about, not a temp job. You should wait to get your name up there, as you call it. It takes time. Contacts. Relationships. Right now your goal should be to make everyone like Josephine O'Leary. The first-class tickets will come later."

"No, Seth," she answered. "With all due respect, you're wrong."

"Wrong?"

"I don't care if people don't like me. Until I have enemies, I'm nobody. So if people don't like me, great. Perfect. It's the way I can get people talking—get that buzz started. I don't write, Seth, and I don't act. But I want my name in big letters. My only chance is to produce."

"Good producers work hard."

"I'm not going to be *that* kind of producer. Come on, you hire people for that. I'm going to be a "creative" producer, it's another thing entirely."

"It isn't." Seth paused. "Aw, what the hell. You know everything, right, Josie? Far be it for me to tell you otherwise. But I will say this—you could be a very good lawyer."

"I know. But when was the last time you saw a lawyer stand up and accept the Academy Award?"

Surrendering, Seth had gotten Josie a job at Unforgettable Films Inc., a (hopelessly old-school) film production company run by his old friend Wallace Pickering.

Wallace Pickering had been clear to Josie at the time of her hire that what he needed was someone to read scripts and meet with writers, and that in no way, *I want to be clear about this,* would she be entitled nor should she expect to receive the perks and advancement inherent in the position directly above her in the hierarchy, the position called Director of Development. That position was currently held by Wallace's beloved niece, Priscilla, who had recently moved to California from New York City because she had (in no particular order) decided she hated working at a magazine, hated her boyfriend of seven years, hated the apartment they had bought on the Upper West Side, hated the entire knee-jerk liberal hypocritical pretentiously intellectual Northeast. She had decided that she needed to stop the sludge of bad movies clogging up theaters and help out the movie business through her superior intellect and her unique grasp of mainstream America's entertainment wish list. That Priscilla could immediately be hired by her uncle Wallace, a former Hollywood player, was a transition so easy that whenever Priscilla read sob stories about people who couldn't get a job in the film industry, she assumed it was because they were not talented, disciplined, or aggressive enough to be hired.

Priscilla Pickering was Josie's boss. She was younger. She was prettier. And of course she was the boss's niece. Her attitude toward Josie, then, was one of patronizing benevolence. Priscilla knew that any lawyer worth his or her salt would not leave a law firm like Y&W— she knew that there was something askew in the person of a young woman who left a stable, high-paying job to go and work instead at a basically entry-level position. Priscilla was inclined then to be solicitous toward Josie, within reason, until of course Josie's attitude expanded beyond her skills and/or experience, at which time Priscilla would polish her firing skills. (Priscilla envisioned the wording of her future biography: *a tough boss who handled difficult matters with grace and strength.*)

On this day, Priscilla had watched Josie drive into the parking lot from her seat in the reception area. She checked her watch.

"Morning," Josie said, as she walked through the glass door.

Priscilla checked her watch again, dramatically lifting her wrist to her eye.

"It's nine-thirty," she said, as she replaced her wrist to her lap.

"Right," said Josie.

Priscilla folded her issue of *Daily Variety* neatly. "I don't mean to be harsh, Josie, really. But I can't have you coming late to the office. It's an issue of respect."

"Excuse me?" said Josie.

Priscilla, all eighteen pounds of her, winced. "Please," she said, as if Josie were about to embark onto a chain of worthless excuses.

"I didn't know—" When Wallace had hired her, he had said office hours were nine until six. But Josie had never abided by time clocks; she wasn't a salesclerk.

"Listen, Josie," Priscilla resumed. "It's important. It's important to be here on time; this town will kill you if you let up for a second. I told him I wouldn't tell you, but Uncle Wally notices. He didn't say it exactly, he just echoed my own opinion that there's a need to be as professional as possible because we're such a small office, and knowing you're a lawyer and all, I think he just expected that timeliness wouldn't be a hardship for you, but if it is, you should probably figure out a way to start your day earlier. Maybe set the alarm clock a half hour ahead?"

When Priscilla spoke, her head jerked, perhaps because it was so much larger than the rest of her body and talking for so long expended much of her body's energy. Thus Josie stared at the movements of Priscilla's skull, jabbing the air with each third word, as in "if it *is*" (jab) "half hour *ahead*." (jab).

"I can be here at—" Priscilla was feeling threatened, Josie thought, and in her gracious mood she acquiesced. "I'll be here at nine," Josie said.

"Obviously, if there are extenuating circumstances . . ." Priscilla turned back to *Variety*.

"Do you know whose car is parked in my space?" Josie asked.

"Excuse me?" Priscilla snapped her head upward, blonde hair swinging back. "*Your* space?"

"Yes." If she didn't have her own parking space, she might as well quit right now and move back to Portland.

Priscilla chose not to fight. "I don't know," she said. "I've been here since eight-thirty and you're the first person I've seen."

"Wallace?"

"In a Corolla? Never. Plus he's never here before nine-thirty."

But then the door to Wallace's office opened. Wallace stepped out first, tall yet hunched over, a sunflower about to break. There had been rumors that Wallace was suffering from some kind of cancer, but his demeanor in the office had never changed from one of benevolent but stern man in charge, so Josie had assumed the gossip was false until a moment like this when she saw him from a bit of a distance and it was obvious that ordinary movement presented a physical challenge.

"Hello, girls," he said. "Here early?"

"Not as early as you," said Priscilla. "Aren't you the eager beaver?"

"Hi, Wallace," Josie said quickly, trying to atone for Priscilla's silly phrase. Priscilla, for all her iciness, spilled words like used cough drops.

Someone walked out of the office behind Wallace. Josie turned.

There was Henry Antonelli.

Henry Antonelli. As she subconsciously took a step backward, blasts of his public persona punctuated Josie's mind. Horse trainer turned movie star. Action-adventure movie star. Romantic lead movie star. Legendary blue eyes. Handsome at sixty-two or seventy-five or whatever his age. Humble. Charming. A man who seemed to shun all of Hollywood's wannabe behavior; the man who had scaled and triumphed at the top of the *not caring* mountain while performing the added feat of seeming humble at the same time.

America loved him, old, young, white, black, male, female. He was like the comfortable but slightly more noble member of one's family— always eagerly embraced, always one you were sad to see go.

Josie stared Henry in the eye. Forgetting she was practically the lowest member of Wallace Pickering's Unforgettable Films Inc. staff, she strode toward the movie star.

"Josephine O'Leary," she said, extending her hand. "I'm a huge fan."

Priscilla Pickering had not moved. She seemed glued to the leather seat in the waiting room.

"Priscilla," Wallace said, "come and meet Henry."

Priscilla stood, the issue of *Variety* falling to the floor. Josie knew she was flustered, because Priscilla didn't kneel to retrieve the paper, although from appearances, she was as inscrutable as ever.

"Hello, Henry," she said. Josie watched Priscilla and sensed that her behavior was as much for Josie's benefit as her own. Priscilla was battling Josie in one of those private internal wars about gaining the edge in the all-important millisecond of first meetings. She was acting the role of the "steely-eyed movie executive" while Josie had donned the role of "overeager, too-deferential striver." This kind of self-knowledge tempted Josie to alert everyone in the room to their silent drawing of swords. But then Henry spoke to her.

"Josephine, you said?" Henry asked her. "My grandmother's name was Josephine."

"I was named for my father's girlfriend," Josie said.

Henry smiled. "Understanding mom," he said. He closed his lips in the tight smile that had charmed thousands of movie audiences.

Henry Antonelli's fee for movies hovered over the twenty-five-million-dollar mark, but this fact was deemed almost irrelevant in a media coverage that described a man whose acting prowess was matched by his legendary kindness. He had been, before September 11, the nation's most glorious and revered star, and he only reinforced notions of his humility when he willingly stepped aside at the mass benefits with the comment "We're just entertainers, *they* are the heroes."

"You must be the person who parked in Josie's space," Priscilla said to Henry.

Josie flinched. Priscilla had thrust her invisible épée into Josie's side.

"I don't think—" Josie began.

"A dirty Corolla?" Henry asked Josie. He smiled, and Josie knew she was winning.

"Not so dirty," Josie replied, "and the perfect camouflage car." She was right! The Reverse Affect!

"Yeah," said Henry, "but don't give me false credit. My Mercedes is in the shop."

"Mine too," said Josie. They both laughed, while Josie considered what it would be like to sleep with Henry Antonelli.

"Josie's brand-new convertible Saab is exactly like your Corolla, exactly," Priscilla smiled through small teeth that she gnawed at night despite her retainer. "Corolla and Saab, no difference whatsoever."

"What are you talking about?" Josie spoke as politely as she could. "Of course, there's a difference between those two cars—oh, I see. Henry, Priscilla wants me to tell the truth. I don't have a Mercedes. I have a Saab."

Priscilla glared.

"I have a Saab too," said Henry. "Great car."

Josie felt the exhilarating rush of an exquisite female triumph, not because of Henry's love of Saabs, but because of the way his eyes raked over her perfect size-six, Pilates-trained, fat-free body.

"Well, then," Henry said, walking over and shaking Wallace's hand. "Thanks. As always."

"No problem," answered Wallace. "Glad you thought of me."

Henry nodded to Priscilla and Josie and walked out of the reception area. Josie, emboldened by her encounter with Henry, and angered by Priscilla's attempt at tacit humiliation, spoke. "If you have a problem with me, Priscilla, I'd prefer you say it directly. I don't think that you were helped by your petty little commentary about cars."

"Excuse me?" answered Priscilla. "Excuse me?" Her voice grew louder; Wallace tilted his head.

"Is there a problem?" Wallace asked.

"That's what I want to know," said Josie.

"No problem," answered Priscilla. But she looked at Josie with problems flowing through her cheeks, her ears, her mouth, and Josie, temporarily mollified, opted for a graceful exit.

"I'm going to move my car," she said, grabbing her keys.

As she descended the steps, Josie congratulated herself for not stooping to Priscilla's level. Priscilla was destined for mediocrity, Josie thought, a bit player. She was not worth Josie's ire.

Again, Josie felt she was reaching a new peak of emotional maturity. It was relatively effortless to stay unperturbed by Priscilla, despite her petty thrusts, and this Josie attributed to some greater, innate sense of her own future place in her chosen industry, if not the world.

She reached her car and was about to get inside when she saw the slip of paper wedged underneath the windshield wiper. She picked up the scrap. As she read the inky letters, she trembled. The flimsy white paper in her fingers, so insignificant in tangible mass, so delicate in heft, bestowed onto Josie a change of stature so sweeping and mammoth that she took a moment to close her eyes and inhale a gust of

Southern California's springtime air, forgetting she was in an entry-level job with a mediocre company, forgetting she was standing in an unremarkable parking lot behind Wilshire Boulevard.

When she opened her eyes under the bright pre-noon sunlight, she saw anew the remarkable words, and her whole body shuddered in glorious, soul-stretching triumph.

310-655-2341. Please call. H.
p.s. Nice car.

Chapter Two

Carla Trousse slotted New Yorkers into two categories—those who, if you went on a car trip, dropped you off at your apartment (a "Door" person), and those who dropped you at the nearest subway station to their own apartment (a "Subway" person). The man to whom Carla was now speaking, the man who was interviewing Carla for her first job in four months, was without question a Subway. This was not a compliment. Still, she persisted; she needed the job.

"It has been a continual observation, and source of my own distress, that universities are not teaching their students how to write. And I find that abominable, really, truly almost sinister. All great societies are governed by their citizens' ability to communicate. And how can they communicate if they can't write? How?" Her cheeks flushed, her thoughts poured through her lips, unfiltered. "Truly. It's an abomination. The absolute disregard for writing at even our most prestigious institutions. I know. I mean, I was accepted to Harvard but my mother wouldn't—well, that's another story. But I've been writing my entire life. I began when I was three."

"Three?"

"Three. My mother, she was, well, she was very committed to her causes, which did not always include me, but—well, you learn from everything, and what can't kill you helps you, right?—my mother is a nurse, a nurse with a master's degree from Penn, she's an activist, she brought me and my cousin Phillip to all kinds of protests: civil rights, anti-abortion, you name it, she was there, and she took us, and really, there's no better way to encourage children to pay attention to what's going on around us. And really, that's what it's all about. Paying attention. That and being able to *communicate*. Communicate in the written word, much the same way they did pre-e-mail, pre-Internet, pre-computer, even pre-typewriter. Is it a coincidence that the quality of writing has plummeted alongside the advance of technology? I don't think so. I often think how much better as a society we would be if we could just, all together, stop typing and pick up a pen."

Carla Trousse stopped, struck by the fear that she had spoken too much, but pleased that she had been able to bring her disparate thoughts back to the issue of writing. It was, after all, the subject of this interview.

"Well," uttered the man across the desk from her. "Well." Carla stared at him. He was balding, skinny, middle-aged, and he wore glasses. His skin was reddish, and his clothes were ironed, both his button-down shirt and his jeans. On his feet were Gucci loafers. He was snivelly, she decided, snivelly, like Templeton the Rat from *Charlotte's Web*.

"Do you think it might be an issue for you then, writing marketing briefs for a company whose business is the advance of technology?" The man, George Schmidt, smiled at her.

"Well, no." She paused, unsettled. "No, not at all. I didn't mean to deride the advance of technology, far be it from me, technology is fabulous, it's pushed America to the forefront of the globe, not that we haven't been there for a while, of course, even if you do, as I, take some issues with the Republican mandate. I mean, think about it, should we really be forcing countries around the globe to adhere to all of our policies when everyone knows it isn't for the good of the world, only the good of some people, and all these people are, sad to say, white men, even if women aren't much better, some women, but I mean to say that I can write anything you tell me to write, that's the long and short of it. The too long of it, probably."

Carla covered her mouth, silently admonishing herself for chattering. She did this when she was nervous. George Schmidt said nothing. The silence was protracted.

"The bottom line is I need a job," Carla declared, as submissively as possible.

"Yes," said George Schmidt. "Thank you for coming by. We'll be talking to you."

She left the wood-paneled office uneasy. She had been out of work for four months. She had been fired from her job as a copywriter for business manuals because she had fought with her boss when she defended her choice to change the text—*Are we all monkeys? Is that why we have to keep printing inaccessible pamphlets that a graduate from MIT couldn't decipher, when all the user wants to do is burn a DVD? Why can't we change things, why can't we be known as the one company to have understandable manuals?*

Her boss had shaken his head and said, "Pack your things and get out. Now."

A week later, the editor of the Greenwich Village literary magazine, *AEIOU*, for which she wrote book reviews at a rate of fifty dollars apiece, had told her she should look elsewhere for more appropriate employment. It had been determined by the editorial board that Carla's reviews were too nasty. Carla had protested. *The book was bad. B-A-D. Of course I said it was forgettable, because it WAS forgettable. I have not studied Proust and Flaubert for ten years just so I can write sugarcoated reviews of incomprehensible novels written by people who are published simply because their sole talent is to be photogenic. I want to make them feel bad! Maybe then they'll stop writing and leave room for those with true talent!*

The editor had listened to her politely and then said evenly,

"Clearly you'd be happier elsewhere. No hard feelings. There's room in the world for everyone who loves books."

Since then, no job, no income. Phillip, her cousin, had come through as usual, paying her rent, giving her a spending allowance that supplemented her unemployment pay. But that was running out, and in times like this, leaving George Schmidt's office with a nauseous feeling in her stomach, she felt worthless.

She decided to go to Riverside Park, up on the Upper West Side to do some writing. The budding flowers, the mothers with their children, the bike riders, the young lovers—all of this could invigorate her. She thought she could be inspired by the mighty Hudson River, and she wanted to finish her thirty-third short story about the Tribeca "artists' salon" where neophyte writers with long hair and skinny hips smoked and drawled about their privileged pasts, all the while calculating how to marry the richest man in the room. They weren't writers, they were *aggrandizers*.

Fifteen minutes later, on the subway ride uptown, a man wearing a Jets cap and a bulging black backpack stood in front of her. She was sitting uncomfortably on the front of the seat, certain that if she pushed back, wedging herself in between the imperious-looking African American woman and the equally imperious-looking man in a business suit, she would not fit, her hips too big. Carla reasoned that they were on the train first, so it was only fair that she should perch herself unsteadily on the edge of the orange plastic seat.

The subway rattled and swerved up the tracks and then came to an abrupt stop at Ninety-sixth Street. Carla held on to the silver bar in front of her, her arm sticking through the thighs and hips of the standing passengers. When the train stopped, the man with the backpack swung around fast, smacking Carla's face with his bag.

"Excuse me!" Carla yelped. "Excuse me!"

"Huh?" said the huge man.

"Your bag is a menace."

"What?" he said, as he stepped out. His strides matched his

height—he moved quickly ahead of Carla. But Carla's cheek hurt, and she was peeved. So she ran after him, in shorter, quicker strides.

"Hey!" she hit him on his shoulder.

"What is with you?" He planted his feet firmly on the ground. A little boy, running, collided with his knee.

"Mom!" the little boy cried, and the mother grabbed her son by the elbows and glared at the huge man and Carla, who were now staring directly at each other.

"Sorry," the man said to the mother and the little boy.

"It's his bag," offered Carla.

"His bag?" said the mother.

"My bag?" said the man.

"That!" Carla pointed to the offending backpack. "It hit me on the cheek twice, twice! On the train. You should be more careful. You could hurt someone."

"You've gotta be kidding," said the mother. "You did hurt someone." She pulled at her son's arm. Carla thought that if she had a son, she would never pull at his appendages as if they were made of rags.

"You're telling me I can't wear a backpack on the train?" The huge man wrinkled his lips and cheek together, as if there were something about this altercation that emitted an odor.

"Look at my cheek!" Carla persisted.

"Looks fine to me," said the mother, who turned toward the stairway, yanking her son with her by her free arm.

"There's nothing wrong with you. You should watch where you're going. It's a crowded train, New York City, right? Don't you have anything better to do?" The man rubbed his cheek with his hand. Carla noticed it was strangely small for a man of his size. He looked at her one more time, no doubt taking in her red eyeglasses and the orange sweater that fell off her left shoulder in some *Flashdance*-tribute, her jeans faded by wear, not by intent, and her size-fourteen shape (just like most of American women, she reminded herself).

"You gotta have something better to do than harass me," he muttered. Then he turned and walked up the gray concrete steps, leaving Carla alone in the dank subway tunnel.

She didn't have something better to do. That was the truth. The allure of Riverside Park suddenly faded, and for the next six hours, Carla sat underground on a wooden bench at the Ninety-sixth Street subway station.

She watched people depart and board trains, envisioning their lives, inspecting their clothes, examining the way they stood and leaned and paced. Movement and desperation she saw, herself deadened to anything but the minute perusal of these New Yorkers, rushing, thinking, forgetting as she watched.

When she finally stood, boarding the downtown train to return to her home, she saw that she had chosen one of the modern subways slowly replacing the older cars. It was brighter and cleaner, and Carla believed that this indeliberate choice was an omen that better things would come.

Perhaps she had needed the day underground to assemble her thoughts, to rearrange her life.

She departed the subway at Fourteenth Street. Her apartment was located in the midst of the West Village, on a tree-lined street with tall brownstones and thick buildings made of crimson bricks. Her apartment building was the sole exception—the white paint had chipped, and the purplish-gray steps on the stoop had broken edges. When she walked through the front door, the broken hinge on the top gave way and the door scraped open, and then stayed there. Carla didn't bother to pull it shut behind her—she would appreciate the drama of an intruder and did not much care if the other tenants didn't.

Her ability to endure the vagaries of New York illegal subletting gave credence, she felt, to her unsung gifts of temperance and composure. She paid an extorted fee to Tommy Quickly, her landlord, so that she could stay in this fourth floor walk-up rent-controlled apartment. The extorted fee was still less than market rate—at sixteen hundred dollars a month, Carla had a bargain. That she had no money coming in, and that her unemployment was running out, and that her cousin Phillip had already bailed her out of seventeen thousand dollars of credit card bills were cudgels constantly smacking at her. She avoided their impact only by a series of mental bobs and weaves, assuring herself all the while that her intelligence and big heart would win out over the indelicacies of modern Manhattan economics.

She unlocked her apartment door and pushed it open. Inside the two rooms twilight streamed in underneath the sills of brand-new windows, incongruous in this apartment of plaster walls and slanting floors. Carla figured that the last time the building was maintained was circa 1927, when no doubt the "prewar" features of a built-in bookcase and wobbly French doors were pristine and appealing.

The saving grace of the apartment was access to the slanted, silver-painted, unsafe roof. Most of the other tenants did not take advantage of the roof, but Carla, already living on the top floor, used it during the summer months whenever she could. She'd sunbathe nude and feel quite modern, even when the graphic illustrator who lived below her had barged in through the roof's door and, seeing Carla, had shaken his head and gone back downstairs.

The worst aspect of the apartment was that it had one sink, for both her dishes and her toothbrush. The last man she kissed, Paul Zeig, had taken one look around and said *that has gotta be depressing.* To Carla, that pronouncement indicated a lack of empathy so extreme that she considered it vindication when Paul told her he had begun dating a woman who had just been made partner at Goldman Sachs. Paul had left her his watch, a Timex Ironman, and still Carla wore it every day, even after the battery stopped working.

There was one mirror in Carla's apartment, a squarish pane of glass the size of a wedding album adhered to the front of her medicine cabinet. Carla spent the first half hour of every morning staring at her face. Her ritual was the same every day: the careful tweezing of eyebrows; the microscopic examination for black hairs squeezing from her chin and upper lip; the searching for indentations more pronounced than before; and, upon finding such impressions, the undiluted, healing gaze she'd apply. She would stare at the offending part of her face for so long that the area would soon seem inoffensive, and bland. Carla's skill at looking at her face was practiced and comprehensive. She knew from experience that nothing but pain could be gained by ruminating on misshapen lips and small, deep-set blue eyes. But now, as Carla stood in front of the mirror, her idea of herself jolted with the image she saw before her. That woman with the glasses, the wide face, and the vivid stretch of extra chin? *Who* was that?

She abruptly turned and walked from the bathroom to the wooden desk she had placed between the two bookshelves. The novel she was reading, *Grotesques* by her favorite living writer, E. R. Robin, lay splayed open to her right. The laptop computer Phillip had purchased for her last Christmas was dozing—she pressed the spacebar and the screen lit up. She decided that she would definitely not get the job she had interviewed for with George Schmidt, and she saw the dwindling balance in her checking account as a rapidly depleting IV bag. She went online to check her email.

There were three: 5.25% 30 YR FIXED RATE MORTGAGE! ACT NOW!, PENIS ENLARGEMENTS—CHEAP!, and FROM PAULETTE.

Carla hesitated before opening her aunt Paulette's e-mail. Carla could not remember which organization Paulette was currently using to save the world, but she was sure it was something appropriately noble and appropriately selfish. There was nothing as disconcerting to Carla as the righteousness of women who used their chosen vocation as a reflecting glass to those who were not so visibly altruistic. The last time they had seen each other, two Thanksgivings ago, they had argued.

At the time, Carla had been working for a television commercial producer and had been telling her family about the producer's newest hire, a woman named Dawn who had long legs and no brain.

"She's a first-class idiot, but Linus doesn't care." Carla had become angry just thinking about Dawn.

"You know, Carla," Aunt Paulette had interjected, "there are women who manage to be intelligent and attractive at the same time."

Carla said sharply, "Of course, but this isn't one of those times."

"Maybe."

"No maybe, definitely. I'm there, I've talked to Dawn. Really, I'm not sure she can read."

"I'm sure she can read."

"I'm exaggerating, but I can promise you she isn't smart, and that he hired her for her looks."

"Maybe." This time Paulette had smirked, or Carla had thought she had smirked. It infuriated her. Why couldn't Paulette just agree with her? Why was this so hard?

"You're wrong," said Carla.

"Maybe."

"Why do you keep saying that? How do you want me to prove it? SAT scores? An essay?" Carla's face had become sweaty, and she had felt attacked.

"It's not a question of wrong or right."

"It is."

"Carla, sweetie, what are you really angry about?"

At this, Carla had stood up, irate and hurt. "This isn't a therapy session. I'm angry because you're deliberately ambivalent over something abundantly clear."

"Well, Carla, I don't think the way you do. That isn't a crime, is it?"

"You don't think that some men hire some women on the basis of their appearance?"

"I think that you have some great need for me to agree with you, and given the evidence presented, I can't."

"Why can't you?" Carla had yelled.

"Carla, calm down," Phillip intervened.

"I won't calm down! Why can't she agree with me? Even if I'm wrong, even if Dawn is a rocket scientist, why can't she just say for once that Carla Trousse, her niece, is right about something? Why is that so damn hard? Why can't she just lie?"

Paulette, sitting across from Carla in a perfectly arranged cashmere sweater and tweed pants, drop earrings dangling with two tiny topazes, and gray hair hanging long and straight and glamorous, tried not to smile, but she did anyway. Anger stirred Carla's breath, it roiled her blood and seemed ready to foam from her mouth. There was nothing she hated more than when someone was so close-minded they couldn't even permit their own views to flirt with someone else's. It was a mark of the truly selfish—a mark of people who used the excuse of honesty as a way to make them impervious to criticisms of superiority. "I'm just being honest," Paulette would say. "I don't have to agree with her, do I, just because she wants me to?"

So Carla had fled the room, unable to hide the sound of her tears but at least able to conceal the sight of them. She heard Paulette say "She's so sensitive, how did she get so sensitive?" and Carla had locked the bathroom door, hurt and embarrassed.

They had not spoken since. And now Carla had this e-mail. She pressed "open," and sat back.

> Hi Carla. I'm sure you're surprised at this letter. I won't pretend that I don't know you've hit a proverbial rough patch in New York City; I do speak to Phillip at least once a month. I'm writing to ask you to come to Los Angeles— Phillip & Samantha have offered their home for you to stay, but moreover, there's something I need to discuss with you in person. It's important, or I wouldn't ask you to come. Please think about it, and don't refuse just to prove your inimitable intransigence.
>
> I think of you often, and wish we had a better relationship.
>
> Love,
> Paulette

Carla turned from the computer and looked out the window. Her apartment faced north, and she could sometimes see inside the bedroom of the people who lived across the street from her. Tonight a woman sewed at her kitchen table, a retro-sewing machine nailed to a board, the woman's brunette head bent under a neon kitchen light. The tablecloth under the board was red-and-white-checked. In the other window, a balding man with black glasses sat on a white couch and stared at the other wall—Carla could see the reflected light of a television image emanating from the space behind the window.

She was not curious about the information Paulette seemed to need to impart to her. She was only mildly riled by the dig at her "intransigence." Mostly, Carla felt . . . bland. Bland and flabby, a fleshy blob with eyeballs and fat fingers. She saw the woman sew, and the man watch television, and she thought she did not ever need to leave her apartment if she could just watch these people live their lives and learn from them. She did not need to listen to her aunt Paulette, she did not need to find out whatever it was Paulette wanted to tell her, she was perfectly fine in New York City, in her Village apartment, watching her neighbors. Los Angeles was a terrible, terrible place full of shallow, illiterate, knee-jerk fools with no real thoughts and no conviction.

Except, of course, for her cousin Phillip.

And Nadine Dillenberger, her old assistant at the commercial producer's place. Nadine could be tiresome, but she wasn't shallow. And she loved to read.

And there was also Jimmy Stigwood, an NYU classmate with flaming red hair who had gone on to be a big reporter for one of the entertainment newspapers. Carla had read some of his articles and had even sent him a note telling him how much she enjoyed them. He had not responded, but she remembered how he kept himself busy (with golf, cigars, and the purchase of bow ties) even before he became a celebrated journalist.

There was also someone else in California, someone not in Los Angeles, but in Pasadena. A man named David Thomas Stegner, a lobbyist for the energy commission of California. He had gone to Dartmouth with Phillip. He was under six feet tall, had lost most of his hair, and looked at the world through intense brown eyes and an exacting brain. He was an expert on everything scientific, but also considered himself a gifted writer and was easily annoyed if people assumed that because he was versed in the sciences he could not be creative.

He had slept with Carla on the evening of Phillip's wedding to Samantha Sellers, the daughter of one of Los Angeles's most fearsome agents. Carla and David had bonded over the topic of Samantha's intelligence. "Let's face it, not the sharpest knife in the drawer," David had said, and Carla had agreed, as they watched Phillip and Samantha swing together on the dance floor. "Some men don't need to be challenged all the time," Carla had opined, and after more wine, and more music, and more revelations that the two of them agreed about practically everything, including the need for American students to study abroad, the supremacy of NPR, and the love of any film with subtitles, the two of them had tumbled into one bed.

On that night Carla had felt more calm than she would have expected, calm and contented. David had tried to impress her by quoting poetry and short stories, and she had felt this as sweetly as if she had been eating jam with her fingers. Feeling calm amid David's attentions had led her to believe that David Stegner was more important to her than any other man in her life, as all of the rest (including Paul Zeig) had left her a frightful, neurotic wreck.

Moreover, Carla had been sure that their union at the wedding validated the saying that soul mates appeared in your life just when you least expected. She had gone to Phillip's wedding alone and unhopeful of any romance of her own. The receptionist, the dimwitted Dawn, had said that it was okay for Carla to be jealous of Phillip and Samantha's happiness. But Carla had protested. She was not jealous but thrilled.

Dawn told Carla she was just fooling herself—all women would be jealous, and Carla wasn't any different. Carla had kept her mouth shut, because she knew that Dawn assumed that all women were focused on the game-playing competition of ensnaring mates. Carla knew that it was a widely held belief that single women were jealous of married couples until they themselves were married, so Carla had waited, expecting a blade of envy to plunge into her heart, making her want to rip the veil from Samantha's head. But it had never happened. At most, Carla had been amused at the way some of the idiot bridesmaids (friends of Samantha's, of course) focused on makeup and men. She had not told anyone about her absence of jealousy, however, certain it would elicit the same kind of response that Dawn had given. "Oh, come on," Dawn had said. "Carla, it's okay to admit it. It's normal. Anyway, I don't believe you. You're no different from the rest of us."

Carla had wanted to say, *I am, I am different.* She knew herself well enough to wonder whether she had repressed her jealousy, certain she could never attain the happiness expected by all these other women. But she doubted it. She was just lucky, she thought, that she could selflessly celebrate true love.

Later, when she and David had held each other in bed, David snoring and Carla wide awake, she felt that God had given her David as a gift for being so guileless, so trusting in the course of true love. She was sure that the fates had aligned themselves and that she too was going to be able to fill the slot of "boyfriend" as effortlessly as it seemed other women did.

Only David had never called her. She had called him, four distinct times, and had stopped when he mentioned the name "Eve" in a way that did not connote "Mom." She believed she had been successful in ridding her mind of him completely, of stomping and killing all the sprigs of hope that kept telling her how perfect they were together.

Yet here was hope again, not dead at all, but as alive as ever, popping up and blaring at her. *David's in Pasadena. David's in Pasadena.*

She closed her computer and returned to the window. The night was dark, and underneath her, the light green foliage formed such a thick barrier to the sidewalk Carla thought it looked like a quilt of leaves, flung wayward over the tops of the branches.

A *proverbial rough patch in New York City.* Was that how she was perceived, by her beloved cousin Phillip and her least favorite relative Paulette?

She closed her eyes and saw herself alone on a sheet of ice, surrounded by thick trees like the ones she saw right now, her heels skidding on it like wet tires, flung around, broken, amid the greenery that promised new and exciting Manhattan lives.

And then she saw the same ice melted, an ocean of blue foaming water, crashing onto the shores of Los Angeles, a continent away, where she found herself standing upright and expectant.

If she didn't hate Paulette so much, she would go.

Chapter Three

During lunch with Seth, at a place on Sunset called Balboa, Josie saw the men who worked with Henry Antonelli at a nearby table. Rather, she saw the three men and one woman who worked with Henry Antonelli. The men were his two agents and his one lawyer; the woman was his business partner at his production company, New Jersey Thoroughbred Films, or as it was commonly called, NJTF. Josie had heard about this woman when she worked at Y&W. Her name was Esther Rodriguez Rabinowitz, and depending on who was talking, she was a true creative producer, a fickle, supercilious woman who didn't return phone calls, and/or Henry's lover, despite Henry's long-term marriage to Cecilia Rosenberg, a psychiatrist, and Esther's own long-term marriage to Aram Rabinowitz, a heart surgeon at Cedars-Sinai.

Josie examined Esther when she walked by—she was a petite woman, with dark hair and dark eyes and full lips. Her nose was rounded into a ball, her eyebrows were thick, and her eyes were shaped like teardrops. She dressed in a sophisticated casual way, the kind of woman who bought the most expensive bag at Barneys on the condition it did not have a label. Josie decided that while Esther optimized whatever beauty she had, she could not be having an affair with Henry because, at the end of the day, Henry was spectacular-looking and a movie star, and Esther, while attractive, was fundamentally ordinary.

But Josie didn't doubt that Esther was powerful. She was Henry's partner, which meant that even though she didn't have to do anything, she'd still have sycophants telling her how smart she was just so Henry would be in their movies. Josie didn't believe the stories about Esther being the best creative producer in town—what the hell did that mean, anyway? What Esther was, Josie thought, was lucky. She had glommed on to Henry long ago and had held tight. Her "success" was inextricably tied to his, and if he ever cut the strings, she'd be forgotten in two seconds.

The same was not true for the two agents and lawyer sitting with her—they had other clients than Henry, although Henry was responsible for the majority of their commissions, and hence probably did occupy the majority of their day-to-day work.

Josie understood that the people working on Henry's behalf were, in effect, no different from the advertising companies that focused on a single account, or the small-town company that employed most of the town's population. That these people worked for one person in the aim of casting him in a movie was no different from a legion of lawyers, businesspeople, politicians, and lobbyists working to push ahead the interest of one pharmaceutical company, say, or GE. Henry could generate fifty million dollars himself, just in fees in one year, at a minimum.

The only difference Josie could see was that in Hollywood, charm was as valued a premium as intellect. And the people at Henry's table were, by reputation, the most charming of the charmed. Henry wasn't there, of course. The percentage of Henry's salary earned by each of the men at the nearby table (and the producing fee earned by Esther) assured Henry of their dutiful effort without necessitating his presence. They were the best and the brightest of Hollywood. When Josie walked by them, she suppressed the urge to wave Henry's phone number at them.

"Josie," said Seth. "If I invite you to lunch, I expect you to find me irresistible."

Seth Levin was tall and thin, with an angular face and deep-set gray eyes. He wore wire-rimmed glasses and his hair was wavy and dark, with abundant white and gray streaks. He walked with his shoulders back and the gait of a champion tennis player, which in fact, he was, on the weekends, at his club.

"I do," Josie answered. "Of course I do." Seth, happily married for ten years to a high school teacher named Nancy, was one of the people in Hollywood who did not subsist on meetings. He was one of the "truly assured"—and he had parlayed this relaxed confidence into a charm that guaranteed him entry into every major event Hollywood hosted. That he almost never attended only bolstered his reputation and increased the number of invitations. Seth's dismissal of the Hollywood games would have typically confounded Josie, but she had been able to qualify his behavior under a term she called the Brilliant Eccentric; the kind of person, male or female, who marched to the beat of their own drummer *(or so they said)*, people who were so blasé about their achievements that Josie was positive they acted like this deliberately, so people would be doubly impressed when their achievements became known.

"Do you think Esther Rodriguez Rabinowitz and Henry Antonelli are lovers?" Josie asked.

Seth spit out a laugh. "Christ. No. N-O. Esther's husband's my heart doctor. Where'd you hear that?"

"You know . . ." Josie's voice trailed off because she didn't want to say "my gossipy friend Nell."

"They work together."

"Okay," Josie shrugged. "Just wondering. She is the only woman over there."

"I know," Seth interrupted. "Listen, honey, do me a favor."

"What's that?" Josie replied.

"Read this," Seth tossed her a large envelope. "He's a kid who Marcus hired to walk his dogs."

Josie took the package from Seth. "Don't take this the wrong way, but what are you doing reading scripts?"

"Marcus put the kid on the phone, and he begged me, and he's a nice kid from Florida, and I told him that I personally was too busy but that, lucky for him, I knew the most powerful woman in Hollywood."

"You jest," Josie said. "But just wait."

"No doubt," said Seth. "But I promised Marcus I'd get someone to read it."

Josie examined the package.

"If it turns out to be an Oscar winner, all I ask is that you thank me in the speech," continued Seth. "Otherwise it's all yours, free and clear, do with it what you will."

"Really?"

"Really. 'Course, if the kid's any good, maybe you could pass him my way for legal representation . . ."

"For you, okay," said Josie.

"Do it for Marcus, not me," replied Seth. Marcus Hernandez was one of Seth's highest-profile clients, a man who had worked his way from a KFC in Miami to the sobriquet of the Latino Woody Allen. Josie's husband, Mike, was one of Marcus's biggest fans—to see Marcus perform, Mike had told her, was like watching Bruce Springsteen live in concert, or Tiger Woods at golf.

"I love Marcus," said Josie to Seth.

"You and everyone else," said Seth. "Get in line."

The waiter approached. "We'll have two Caesar salads, no cheese for her, all of the cheese she didn't use plus the usual on mine, and two Pellegrinos. Thanks." He turned back to Josie. "That's what you wanted, right hon?"

"Does this guy have an agent?" asked Josie.

"Honey, he lives in Florida. Flor-i-da. Does that sound like he has an agent?"

Josie put the script in her purse. "Seth," Josie said, head raised, "I have to ask you something."

"Yeah," Seth said. "What is it?"

"You've got to promise not to judge me."

"What is it?"

"It's—I shouldn't say anything—I shouldn't—"

"C'mon, Josie, spit it out."

"It's Mike."

"Mike what?"

"Mike and me."

"What about Mike and you?"

"It isn't working. It hasn't been working."

"Oh, grow up, Josie. This is life. Marriage is hard."

"That's why I'm talking to you. I don't want to be married anymore. I want a divorce."

The food arrived, and Seth pointed to Josie's portion. "I love croutons. I tried that Zone thing, no carbs, whatever, maybe it's true, maybe it isn't, but the bottom line is I love croutons."

"I'm not joking," Josie said.

"I'm not either. I love croutons, French fries too, although they're killing me." Seth punctured the leaves of his Caesar salad with his fork.

"I'm asking you first."

"Asking me what?" Seth jammed a handful of leaves into his mouth. "Asking me for permission to leave your husband? No way, Josie. This is serious."

"I know that," she snapped. "Don't you think I know?"

"No." He ate some more salad. "If you did, you wouldn't be tromping in here talking about scripts one second and the state of your marriage the next. No. I don't think you appreciate the seriousness of divorce."

"Well, I do," Josie put her fork down. "I do, and I've thought about this, and it's the right thing to do, for me and for Mike. For both of us."

"Really?"

"Yes."

"Then let me ask you this. One thing."

"What?"

"What does Mike say?"

"What does Mike say to what?"

"Your divorce."

Josie met Seth's implicit challenge. "He doesn't know."

"Bingo," said Seth. "Bingo bingo bingo."

"Are you going to help me?"

"I'll help you with a lot of things, but divorce is not one of them. Especially not before you've talked to him." Seth sat back in his chair, chewing, rubbing his hands on his napkin, uncomfortable.

"He won't care," Josie said. "He doesn't care."

Seth shook his head. "Don't try that, Josie. I know Mike. It won't work. He's a good guy."

"There's someone else." Josie blurted out the words, shocked to see herself naked under Henry Antonelli's gaze in her mind. She wasn't lying. There was someone else.

Seth flushed, but then chuckled. "Of course there is, honey. There's you."

"That's not what I meant. I mean—"

"No no no," Seth shook his head. "No. Not one more word. I don't want to hear it. I'm not helping you on this one. Come back when you've had a full conversation with Mike, and when you've gone to counseling or whatever the hell therapy is available, and then we'll talk. But I'm not going to talk to you seriously about a whim. Trust me on this, I've been there. Divorce is not easy."

"You're not even listening to me. I have thought this through. I haven't talked to Mike yet because I know it's going to hurt him too much—"

"Oh, good Lord, don't even start this." Seth pushed back his chair. "Josie, listen. I don't want to know about the other guy, I don't want to know about your and Mike's troubles, what I want to know from you is that you will make an honest effort at figuring out your marriage. After that you can tell me anything, I promise."

36

"What if I don't read this?" Josie pulled at her purse, and while doing so, recognized it was an infantile response. She put the purse back down.

"You'll read it, don't annoy me," Seth answered. At that moment, two of the members of Henry Antonelli's team approached the table.

"Seth," said the startlingly handsome man who, unlike most Hollywood power players, had grown up in Mississippi with no ties to the entertainment business. He had moved out to Los Angeles and worked his way up from the mailroom to his present position, the agent to the most handsome and most affectless Hollywood stars. "Eddie Cleveland, remember?"

"Yeah right, Eddie, funny." Seth shook his hand. "This is Josephine O'Leary." Josie looked at Eddie Cleveland directly in the eye. She wanted him to remember her.

"Hello," she said.

"I think we met, didn't we?" Eddie asked. "You were a lawyer with this guy, right?"

"I'm telling you, Josie, this one doesn't miss a thing, not a blessed thing." Seth spoke while Eddie shook Josie's hand. He was blond, with cropped hair that stood straight (thanks to pomade), and he spoke with a raspy undertone, as if the words were being run through a woodcutter. He had dimples, broad shoulders, and white glistening teeth. He spoke to Josie as if he were about to propose. And then she realized that this man, this Eddie Cleveland, was one of the best talent agents in town precisely because of this quality.

"I'm Gordon Kelly," said the other man, with an unassuming air that belied the roster of his clients: the top comedians in the country, including the one who just signed a contract for a million dollars an episode. Gordon was balding and the kind of man who would pat at his slight paunch to prove he was appropriately self-deprecating, but Josie could tell that he would lash out like a slingshot if anyone underestimated his ego.

"I'll see you at the game?" Seth asked.

"We're going to the Lakers," Gordon said to Josie.

"Let me guess," Josie said. "Courtside, right?"

"Well . . ." Gordon grinned. "What do you think?"

"Of course courtside, honey, it's a job requirement," said Seth.

"Well, nice meeting you," said Gordon.

"Bye Seth," said Eddie. "Good to see you again, Josie."

"She likes to be called Josephine," Seth called out to the departing men. Josie watched them leave. "Get that out of your mind. Gordon's happily married, and you don't have a chance with Eddie. So forget it."

Josie dreaded the end of the lunch, mostly because she knew that she had to abide by Priscilla's time clock. She had already been gone forty-seven minutes, and she had to get her car from the valet.

"So I can't tell you about who I met—" Josie asked.

"Not one word. Not one syllable. Nothing," Seth answered. "And go on, get out. I know you've got time pressure."

"How'd you know that?" Josie asked.

"Do you think Wallace is as out of it as he looks? Come on, sweetheart." Josie leaned over to kiss Seth on the cheek. "Damn," Seth said. "If you'd just do it on the lips, it'd do wonders for my reputation. I promise. Nancy won't care."

"Bye Seth," Josie said.

"Bye," Seth answered. "And get back to me on that script, okay?"

Josie walked out of the restaurant slowly. She resented returning to the office; she resented that even Seth knew that she was being held to a time clock. She put on her sunglasses, pulled out her wallet and looked at Henry's note again.

The piece of paper was imprinted with Josie's fingerprints; the number and message were still legible, but terror struck, and Josie considered that if she didn't immediately write the number in a separate place, she would be tempting the fates to lose the paper altogether. She stopped, found her Palm Pilot, and carefully etched in the numbers on the electronic scratchpad. When she was finished, she was calmer, and put both the scrap of paper and her Palm Pilot back into her purse. She checked her watch. She was definitely late, inexcusably late.

But still she sauntered in languidly, as if she were staring at a flower garden. She would soon be in contact with Henry Antonelli at his behest; she had met Gordon Kelly and Eddie Cleveland. Priscilla Pickering, her no-talent boss, had probably never left the office.

"Hello," said Priscilla, when Josie passed by her open door on the way to her own office.

"Hello," said Josie.

"Uh, Josie," called Priscilla. "Could you come in here for a minute?" Josie stopped, and lackadaisically but with deliberate intent pulled out the script from Seth.

"What?" asked Josie, now standing in Priscilla's doorway.

"What's that?" Priscilla asked.

"What do you need?" asked Josie again.

"Is that a script?" asked Priscilla.

"Do you need me?" asked Josie one more time.

Both women refused to respond and Josie felt the impasse as if it were a truck too tall for a tunnel. She was feeling reckless, however, and met Priscilla's gaze, which was a mistake. Priscilla had the good looks of a doll from FAO Schwarz: the round blue eyes, the long eyelashes, the pursed pink lips. Her body was a living, breathing stick, and her hair was long, curly, and blonde. If she hadn't been such a socially awkward person, Josie would be jealous.

"Where were you?" Priscilla choked out the words.

"Lunch," said Josie.

"With?" asked Priscilla.

"Seth Levin," said Josie. "From my old office. And Eddie Cleveland and Gordon Kelly. I asked them if they would send us any projects they thought Wallace would like. That's okay, right?"

"You had lunch with Eddie Cleveland and Gordon Kelly?" Priscilla had the demeanor of someone who was unimpressed, but Josie guessed

39

that Priscilla's mind was convulsing over the idea that Josie knew such stratospheric players.

"Lunch was with Seth," said Josie. "Anything else?"

Priscilla picked up a pencil. "Let me see that," she said. Josie gripped the envelope.

"See what?" Josie spoke nervously; if Priscilla asked to read it, Josie might have to give up her Academy Award. It was that simple.

"I want to read it," said Priscilla.

"No," Josie said.

"No?" repeated Priscilla. "No's not an option."

"I want to read it first. It's a favor to Seth."

"Seth won't care."

"Yes he will."

"Josie," said Priscilla.

"My name is Josephine," Josie responded.

"Josephine, don't make me have to pull rank," Priscilla said.

"I'm not," Josie repeated. "You're doing that. Fact is, Priscilla—and you know this very well, since you're the one who recited it to me seventeen times—my job is to read scripts and meet with writers. You bring me submissions. I don't have to bring them to you." Josie stopped. "Unless you and Wallace want to promote me?"

Priscilla's face contorted; Josie was right.

"Well, don't read it on office time!" Priscilla finally snapped.

"No problem," said Josie, who turned and left Priscilla's office.

The package had gained a weight in Josie's hand, and she fantasized that some alchemical sprite had turned the white pages into gold. Certainly that was the "gold" in Hollywood—good material, or rather, the impression that something was good. Once the latter happened, Josie thought, the sky was the limit. She thought she had better contact the writer and immediately option the screenplay herself. If she owned it, or at least owned the rights to sell it, then she could control the project and no one could tell her what to do.

She went to her desk, shut the door, and looked at the package.

Ordinary, a golden-colored legal-size envelope. She pulled at the flap with her fingers and extracted a sheath of papers connected by a gold brad. The fact that all the appurtenances were of a gold hue was not lost on Josie; she believed in omens, she believed at that second that there was no possible way this was not, no pun intended, a golden opportunity.

The Bear That Saved Christmas was the title. Joshua King was the writer. Josie sank back in her chair. *The Bear That Saved Christmas?* She already knew she'd hate the script. She pictured those three animated bears in that summer movie that had just tanked. Bears and Christmas. Maybe there was a chance she could sell it for television.

She picked up the script and turned to the first page. She had to read it before Priscilla had a chance to sneak into her office and steal it. She began to read.

An hour later, Josie's assistant, Nadine, buzzed her. "Mike's on four," she said through the intercom.

Josie jerked her head up. She put the screenplay down. She spoke to the telephone unit.

"What's that?" Josie asked.

"Mike's on four," said Nadine.

"I'll call him back," Josie said. "Take a message."

"But he said—" Nadine persisted.

"No." Josie pressed the intercom button off and was about to pick up the script again, when she heard someone approach her door. She quickly picked up a Wallace-owned script.

"Josie?" Priscilla stood in the room. "Josie?"

"What?" she murmured, as she emphatically turned a page.

"I was talking to Nicole Jexson," snarled Priscilla, "who said you didn't have lunch with Eddie Cleveland today."

"She's so astute, that Nicole," Josie replied.

"You're not reading that script, are you?" Priscilla asked.

"Nope. I'm reading the one about sitars," Josie said, waving the screenplay. *The Bear* was safely turned upside down on her desk.

Priscilla stood there for a moment, fuming, and then stomped from the office, slamming Josie's door shut behind her. Josie waited until she heard Priscilla's footsteps fade, and then, quietly, she placed the script on her desk. She dug her cell phone out from her handbag. She dialed a number.

"Joshua?" Josie spoke into her phone. "Joshua King?"

Chapter Four

Carla had gone outside, believing it would help her think if she took a nighttime walk alongside the Hudson River. The Village streets were filled with people—springtime had allowed for leisurely walkers and lovers to leave their overheated apartments and come out to breathe in the fresh air. Now, at eight-thirty in the evening, as she walked north on Hudson Street, Carla felt part of the vibrant Manhattan populace, and was soothed.

At Twelfth Street, Carla turned left. The river was visible in front of her, a sparkling horizontal line intersecting the high vertical planes of the high-rises on both the Manhattan and New Jersey sides. The city had built a pathway all along the West Side, and one of these days, Carla was definitely going to walk the entire stretch from Battery Park to the Upper West Side. She saw herself ambling alongside the river against the moonlight-suffused blue twilight, and was sure this activity would lead her to her decision about whether to go to California or not. But then she spotted the lights of the meatpacking district, and walked there instead.

The look of the people had changed—here, amid centuries-old warehouses that had sides of beef hanging from the ceiling, were stiletto-wearing women, pink newsboy hats perched on their heads.

The men's hair was greased and upright, and most wore formfitting crewneck sweaters. Carla thought for a second about her own black oversized pants, and her own black oversized shirt, and was happy she had put on the silver rope necklace she had bought for herself when she turned twenty-five.

She walked inside one of the new restaurants, a combination Asian-Italian-themed business that served osso buco mignon with pad thai. Two huge tusks of some hairy animal jutted from the wall above the heavily stocked bar; Carla sat down on a stool and waited for the bartender to approach her.

"Hey," said a voice.

"Scotch," Carla said, unwilling to raise her head.

"Yeah?" the man said. "Well, we'll see about getting you some, then."

Carla looked up. The man who spoke to her sat by her side. He was chubby, this man, with thick dark hair and black-rimmed glasses. His face was ruddy and round, skin forming a perfect semicircle underneath his chin. His white-collared shirt was open three buttons down on his chest, but Carla couldn't tell where the chin ended and the neck began. His shoulders sloped and sweat stained the outskirts of his armholes.

"I'm Carla," she said.

"I'm Clive," he replied. Carla waited for him to ask to buy her a drink. He didn't.

"Hi."

"Hi."

Carla curled her fingers under the bar; the cuticle on her left ring finger was bleeding, and she didn't want Clive to see it.

"I don't know many Clives," said Carla.

"Yeah, I know. It's an original name. My parents are original." Clive turned to Carla. "So, do you like it?"

"What?"

"This place."

She turned her body around on the stool to look at the space. She turned back. "A little pretentious maybe, but okay."

"Right," said Clive. "Right."

"Not that pretentious," said Carla.

"No, I want to own a pretentious place. That way more people will want to come here."

"You own this?" Carla asked. Clive nodded. Carla looked down at her finger. She had pinched the cuticle with the fingers of her right hand and it seemed as if the bleeding had stopped. "You don't look like an owner," she said.

"What's that?" Clive spoke through thin lips pried apart only a half of an inch, so his words skimmed through the space as if they were being strained. "You here alone?"

"No," Carla said immediately. "I'm waiting for someone."

"It doesn't matter if you are," he said. "Alone, I mean."

"I'm not," Carla answered testily.

"Some women are afraid to come out by themselves, that's all I'm saying. I wish they were all as brave as you. I bet right now there's a thousand girls in New York just sitting at home tonight and here you are, out here." Clive put his back to the bar and cased the room. Carla turned too, and watched as he waved to an incoming patron, as he smiled at the table of two to her left.

"You own this by yourself?" Carla asked.

"I have investors, of course," Clive said. "But it's me on the line, that's how this business works."

"Did you own a restaurant before?"

"Nope," he said. He motioned to a mosaic on the other side of the tusks. "That's from before Christ."

Carla hesitated. Was *Before Christ* the name of some artisan she should know about?

"That one's worth over seven hundred thousand, can you believe it? People want their stuff displayed, and one of the investors loaned it to me to spruce the place up. I don't care what the hell's up there if it brings people in. All about the show, that's what it is, you know? All about the show. That's why what you said—the pretentious part—is good."

"The lemming-like quality of the masses," said Carla, taking in the design of the mosaic, which she thought resembled two gray-toned women lying prostrate on a coral-colored ground, bits of concrete and black stone embedded in their knees, their foreheads, their elbows. "One person announces a masterpiece, and the rest follow. Kind of destroys one's faith in intellectual conviction, doesn't it?"

Clive blinked. "I'll get you your scotch," Clive said. "When your date comes, I'll make sure you get a good table." Clive motioned to the bartender. "A Macallan for the lady," he said. "And get the two at the end whatever they want."

"Thank you," said Carla. The bartender gave her a scotch. Clive was still standing next to her. She tapped Clive on the back.

"I'm not brave," she said.

"Huh?" asked Clive.

"I'm not brave," she repeated. "You said that before, and you're wrong."

"Sure you are, honey," Clive told her. "Bravest girl in the world. Out here all alone, biggest jungle, you're here, and I thank you, I really do, I wish there were more girls just like you."

Carla nodded thoughtfully; perhaps he had a point. She envisioned herself in bed with Clive, her hands pulling at his shirt, his hands on her back. "You really think so?"

"Nowhere else on the globe would a woman like you just show up and sit at the bar alone."

"I'm waiting for someone," Carla repeated.

"Right," said Clive.

Carla saw herself in the mirror across from the bar. She wondered if she was indeed brave, or whether Clive said that to everyone so they'd come back. She saw in the mirror that Clive's forehead was sweaty. Her finger ached. "What do you think of California?"

"What's that?" asked Clive.

"California. I may move there."

"You're breaking my heart."

"Seriously, what do you think? Should I move there?"

"Whoa, Nellie, or Darla, whatever your name is, we just met." Clive grinned, though, and it made Carla feel reckless. She drank from her glass.

"I know we just met, but I need advice. You're the one who said I was brave."

Clive appraised her again. Carla looked at his eyes through his glasses, the shadow on his cheeks.

"All right, then. Why do you want to go to California?"

"I'm not sure. I've lived here twenty years."

"That's a long time."

"I know."

Neither said anything.

"You like New York?" asked Clive.

"I love New York," answered Carla. But even as she spoke, she wondered if she was telling the truth. What did she love exactly? Sitting underground at a subway station for hours?

"Sounds like your decision's made." More people were coming into his restaurant. Carla sensed his attention waning and wanted to shake free this one response from him, certain, suddenly, that it would tell her what to do.

"But—"

Clive clinked her glass with his own drink. "You gotta do what you gotta do. Follow your gut." Clive patted his stomach. "Cali's a nice place, New York's a nice place, I think Iowa's a nice place. You're a cutie, you'll make it work."

"But—"

"I gotta go, sweetheart," he said. "Good talking to you, Marla, come again. We'll set you up." Clive patted her shoulder. A tall woman had entered the restaurant, a woman over thirty, with a mile of space between her skinny legs and her brown hair in pigtails. Carla watched

Clive greet the woman as she drank her scotch, all of it, in four consecutive gulps. Then she saw Clive was kissing the pigtailed woman, whose chin was as sharp as Clive's was flabby. They seemed like a strange fleshy sculpture, in the middle of the restaurant, tusks and mosaics above them, people milling about. Carla examined all of them, her mind racing. Would it be different in Los Angeles?

She left a dollar for the bartender and stood. The scotch affected her immediately; she pushed her glasses up on her nose and centered herself before she took a step. This was a productive evening, Carla thought. She had talked to someone else, and she had not paid for a drink.

"Darla!" Carla turned. It was Clive.

"No date, right?" Clive had one arm around the shoulder of the pigtailed giantess. "I knew it."

Carla stood where she was, positive that all of New York City, all of the Northeast had heard this strained voice, over the tables of meat-eating men and women, all of whom now knew she had said she had a date and did not. Perhaps they fed on these nightly scapegoats—perhaps providing an object of scorn was one of Clive's responsibilities to his investors.

"My name isn't Darla," Carla said back to him, loudly. "And your restaurant is pretentious and you're a creep." Carla then pointed to the woman next to him. "And you shouldn't be wearing pigtails!" She turned and took a step, the scotch pushing her out the doors, people staring at her from behind, and she didn't care. An older couple stood outside looking at the menu encased in glass.

"They just found salmonella," Carla whispered to the potential patrons. "They'll be evacuating the place in a second."

The two people looked at her and then turned to go to the adjacent restaurant. Carla saw Clive watching this through the glass doors, but he just shrugged and turned back to the dining room.

Carla stood alone on the street. The lights of the trendsetting neighborhood shone down on her as she walked on the cobblestones, on the slanted pieces of concrete that made it easy for steel trucks to unload their red slabs of cow and pig and bull. Was she brave, or was she just pathetic?

A short man ran out of the restaurant, carrying a vinyl bag. He looked to the right and left and spotted Carla. "Hey, lady, here's your bag."

Carla stared at the man for a second, unable to focus. But then she saw he carried her handbag, the one she had filled quickly with a wallet and a book before leaving for her walk.

"Thanks," she said. "Thanks." She felt her eyes water, and was grateful that it was dark.

"Don't let him bother you," said the man, as he lit a cigarette. He smiled kindly at her. Carla nodded to him, afraid that if she spoke, she might cry.

Minutes later, as she walked home, she considered the sweaty image of Clive telling her to follow her gut, and decided that it was an omen that she had met someone as shallow as anyone she might find on the left coast.

Chapter Five

Josie's assistant, Nadine Dillenberger, pushed through her closed door.

"Mike called again, he said it was important," said Nadine.

"I'll get to him," said Josie. That Josie spoke from a yoga pose prevented Nadine from hearing clearly, so Nadine stepped around the desk. Josie was bent over from her waist, her legs in a deep "V," her head between her knees.

"Are you okay?" asked Nadine.

"I," began Josie, as she swept her head up to a standing position, her face flushed with blood, her eyes popping from her head, her highlighted hair in great tangled outstretched pieces, "I have never, ever been better."

"You look crazy," said Nadine.

"That, Nadine," said Josie, "is a compliment. Crazy with luck, crazy with potentiality, crazy is the name of the game out here. Crazy is good."

"Yeah, well, Mike sounded crazy too, and not crazy good. Crazy-upset."

Josie heard Nadine say her husband's name and wondered briefly who she was talking about.

"This," Josie picked up Joshua's script. "This script holds the key to my dreams."

"What script?" replied Nadine.

"This one," Josie continued. "This script is so good—this script—I promise you, this is the one."

"Who's the writer?"

"A new guy, from Miami. Wait!" Josie stepped toward Nadine, putting both of her hands on her assistant's broad shoulders. Assuming seriousness, Josie looked deep into Nadine's eyes. "You cannot say anything about this. You cannot say one word. Promise me."

"Say what?"

"Please, please, don't tell Priscilla I called Joshua."

"Who's Joshua?"

"He's the guy from Miami. Wallace and Priscilla can't get their greedy hands on it—it's mine, all mine."

"You sure about that?"

"Priscilla's own fault—she told me over and over again my job was to read scripts, not get scripts."

"What's the story?" asked Nadine. "Why's it so good?"

"It's just—it's just, I can tell, I know it, the idea is so good."

"So let me read it."

"No!" Josie yelled. "I mean, not yet." Josie put the script into her purse. "I've got to go."

"Josie—" Nadine held on to the back of a chair, as if she were ready to bring it up and fend off Josephine the Attacking Lion. "Josie, you know how Priscilla is . . ."

"Tell her Mike's sick," Josie answered. "I'm not lying. He could be sick."

"You're kidding, right?" Nadine asked.

"No." Josie pulled her purse straps onto her shoulder. "You told me Mike was crazyupset. I have to go to my husband. Tell her that." Josie thrust herself through the doorway with a sense of purpose—she needed to tell someone, anyone, about her good fortune. It was all too much for her today, Henry and Seth and Eddie Cleveland and Joshua King. She needed to think, and she needed to get some good advice, neither of which she would accomplish in the treacherous confines of Wallace Pickering's film production company.

"Jose—" Nadine began.

"Nadine," Josie snapped. "It's better for you, for us. Really. Tomorrow I'll tell you more. But trust me, trustmetrustmetrustme." Josie grinned at Nadine. "You'll be happy about it, I promise."

"Okay," said Nadine thoughtfully. Josie walked down the hall in front of her. "Call Mike on his cell," Nadine yelled. "He's not at the office."

Josie heard Nadine, but faintly, and her information about Mike was instantly forgotten. What Josie was thinking about, as she raced to her car and started the engine, was the immensity of opportunity that had just plopped into her lap.

Josie drove only one block out of Wallace's driveway before pulling to the side of Wilshire. She sat motionless in her car for a full five minutes before turning down the visor to avert the glare of the sun.

She was exhausted and exhilarated simultaneously; she felt her life clicking into place—two shifting plates, coming back together, in the opposite way that the continents broke apart. Opportunity, with resolve; an idea with ambition. Hollywood fed on ideas—it was one chomping mouth, devouring creativity and mediocrity with equal justification, gorging on fast food and luxury cuisine with the same ravenous appetite.

But Joshua's idea—the story behind *The Bear that Saved Christmas*— was fabulous. His script was a combination of two masterpieces: *Trading Places* and *It's a Wonderful Life*. It was a high-concept idea, with a lead role that was perfect for one of Hollywood's A-list stars. And it was a Christmas movie, appealing to everyone—men, women, and children. Josie recalled Nell McKnight's advice—*Find good material—then buy it and say you're producing it. Done deal.*

She imagined herself at the premiere, being interviewed by Access

Hollywood and explaining how this movie was entertaining for all ages, how it was a morality movie without being preachy, how it was an important movie, and how, yes, the script just sort of landed in her lap and she knew just what to do with it.

Only she didn't. Not at this second. She knew what *not* to do: She could not show Priscilla. She could not show Nadine. She could not tell Seth. She probably shouldn't even have called Joshua, but she had acted impulsively and couldn't retract it now. The conversation had gone swimmingly, however, and Josie congratulated herself for achieving the correct equilibrium of interest without assurance of money. But now she would have to consider her options.

She could try to sell the project without telling Joshua anything. Then, once she was assured of her own six figure deal, she could call Joshua and offer him a thousand dollars to buy it free and clear. He'd probably jump at the chance—most writers would, so eager for outside approval—but there was the risk he'd find out she had presold it for a lot more money.

To avoid this Josie could pay him a couple of thousand dollars to "option" the script—to own the rights to the story for some period of time. It would, however, take precious days to negotiate this with Joshua.

Suddenly, the paranoia of the film industry infected Josie; she had something that other people would want, which meant by definition that they would try to steal it from her, ripping the project from her long tapered fingers and shouting from the rooftops *"This is mine, this is mine!"*

But what if she were wrong?

For a brief moment, she thought of other people who genuinely did not have any interest in the entertainment business. She thought of her father, a dentist, drilling into people's teeth, and her mother, carefully arranging placards at charity dinners. There was her friend Rebecca, a former studio executive who had specialized in marketing but who was now a housewife and mom in Beverly Hills, raising two children and happily married to Johnny, a tennis pro. And she thought of Mike, her husband, a commodities broker with a love of poetry who had played football in college and loved beer on draft so much he had insisted on a tap in their kitchen.

None of these people, despite her history of intimacy with them, could understand the explosion of emotion she felt holding this script in her hands. It symbolized everything to Josie: money, success, power, ambition, and pride.

She checked her watch. It was five o'clock. She remembered that Rebecca took her children to Roxbury Park. Rebecca, stolid, practical, unexcitable Rebecca, would orient her.

Plus, Josie remembered, she had wanted to talk to Rebecca about Mike.

She turned the key in the ignition and pulled back onto the road. The sun was waning, a stream of violet and orange running through the April sky. She heard the children's cries before she parked her car; she imagined a future with her own rose-cheeked children, straining in their car seats to be released into this, their universe of pleasure, on the corner of Roxbury and Olympic. This was a vision for the future, after she had gotten rid of Mike. The idea of having two toddlers in five years with a different husband nicked at Josie's imagination for just a stressful moment, but she pushed it away, as she did not like to consider the reality of timing in her calculations for her imminent perfect life.

"Rebecca!" Josie saw her best friend near the swingset.

"What? What? Hey—oh, no—no no no! Amelia! Stop it, stop it. I'm so sorry, really, she doesn't know that they hurt—stop biting, Amelia, right now!" Rebecca lifted a red-haired child by the armpits, hugging her close.

"I give it two minutes," Rebecca said to Josie. "Two minutes before she pounces again. Of course she doesn't understand what I'm saying. She's one and a half. One-and-a-half-year-olds do not understand."

Rebecca sat down suddenly, in the sand. She pushed her bangs from her forehead, a useless gesture, as her fine, blunt hair moved back exactly where it had been, joining the strands stuck to her forehead in sweat. Rebecca was one year older than Josie, but she was wider, more pronounced, somehow; where Josie was slight and wispy, Rebecca was solid and dense. Rebecca was tall with a pug nose and as much as Josie loved her friend, she felt Rebecca should do something about her appearance. In college, Rebecca had been svelte and stylish. Now, dressed in a navy blue peasant dress with no discernible shape, Rebecca looked like a San Francisco organic-eating, figure-concealing former hippie.

"Where's Roman?" asked Josie.

"Probably about to fall to his death because his mother isn't watching him."

"Why aren't you watching him?"

She nodded over to where Amelia was playing nicely with a brunette youngster. "Roman's basically an adult, I figure."

"He's six."

"Six. Almost old enough to vote." Rebecca shrugged.

"Hello, Amelia!" Josie gushed as she reached for the little girl. Amelia began to cry immediately, her hands flailing about for her mom.

"She has this thing with other people—" Rebecca took her daughter away.

"Listen, Rebecca," Josie began.

"Oh, sweetie," Rebecca interrupted, as she knelt down to keep Amelia from putting sand in her mouth. "I told you—"

"Can you just listen to me for five seconds?" snapped Josie.

Rebecca looked up at her in bewilderment, but then, after cleaning up her daughter, rose back to her full height. "Sorry, Josie," Rebecca said, an amused smile playing on her face. "What's the matter?"

Josie smiled back, even though she remained resentful. It was not a fait accompli that women with children could no longer pay attention to their single friends—it was a choice, a way to prove to women like Josie that children were more important than anything Josie could be doing.

But she needed Rebecca's advice.

"Two things," Josie began. "One business, one personal."

"I'm ready," said Rebecca, who was doing her best not to look at Amelia, who was pouring sand into her diaper.

"I read this script today that was utterly, totally fantastic."

"Amelia, please—" Rebecca glanced at Josie. "Great. You found the Holy Grail. Congratulations."

"I don't want to make any mistakes," Josie said. "Luckily I don't have to give it to Wallace. But I've been thinking. I could sell it first . . ."

"No," Rebecca stated. "No."

"Just listen," Josie began.

"No," Rebecca continued. "Amelia! Please keep the sand . . . Josie, don't sell out the writer. What if someone else sells it in the meantime?"

"Can't happen. The guy's a dog-walker from Miami. I'm sure I'm the only person who has the script."

"You're not sure. That's the beauty of this business. No one knows anything, remember? This dog-walker may have it out all over town."

"No way," said Josie, but she wondered. Joshua King had seemed exuberant over the telephone, but maybe he was lying?

"If the studio finds out you don't own it when you say you do, you'll spend your career atoning. Plus, it's just not fair to the writer."

"That's the least of my worries. He should be grateful anyone out here is even reading the thing."

"I don't know," said Rebecca. Amelia stood up, tottered, then fell back down in the sand.

"I'm telling you, that's the case. I'm not worried about him. It's me I'm worried about," said Josie.

"I'm truly shocked," Rebecca said. Josie ignored the sarcastic tone.

"The question is, should I pay money out of my pocket to option the script so that I don't have to worry about Mr. Florida selling it to someone else, or should I go the more risky, but potentially more lucrative route, of selling it to a studio first?" Josie asked.

"Easy," said Rebecca, now turning around the playground. "Oh, good Lord, I don't see Roman anywhere. Amelia, do not throw sand in that girl's face. Do not!" She spun back to Josie. "Option the script. Not because you're scared. And not because it's the right thing to do, which it is, but as you said, that's not your worry. You should do it because it would make you take yourself seriously as a producer, and that's what producers do. You reduce the risk of losing the project, and you can sell it the way you want without worrying. So it's better for you. Roman!" Rebecca screamed suddenly, jarring Josie. Amelia stood up again, covered with sand. She walked toward Josie.

"Look at her," said Rebecca. "Headed straight to you. Maybe she's changed her mind."

Josie instinctively put out her arms, grabbing Amelia. The sand got on Josie's white shirt, but more powerful was the feeling of holding the precious flesh of this little girl. Josie felt moved suddenly, as if a wind had knocked down a building she had thought was indestructible. She lifted Amelia up.

"You know how good I am with kids," Josie said to Rebecca, as she turned Amelia toward her and lifted her up and down, up and down. "She just has to warm up. I just took a bit of getting used to. I like that about Amelia—she doesn't let just anyone in, you have to prove your worth."

As Josie spoke she began to toss Amelia just a bit, applying a scant bit of pressure to the armpits as she lifted her upward. Amelia giggled, and Josie threw her higher. This time, Amelia opened her mouth wide, in glee. Josie looked at her, throwing her high above her own head. Amelia was a beautiful child, fine red hair standing straight up, big almond-shaped brown eyes, and right now, at this second, a huge smile on her face, so happy with Josie, and Josie smiled an open-mouth smile back at the little girl. This *is* a goal, Josie thought for a moment before she took notice of Amelia's change of expression.

"Agh!" Amelia came down and Josie caught her, just as a stream of vomit poured from Amelia's mouth onto Josie's shirt.

"Dammit!" Josie cast Amelia from her arms to Rebecca's. Vomit had spattered her favorite Marc Jacobs shirt from shoulder to waist.

"Gotta avoid those projectiles," smiled Rebecca, as she threw Josie a cloth napkin. Josie gritted her teeth and smiled back at her friend, as she swore to herself that her child would never vomit.

"Amelia, hon, tell Aunt Josie you're sorry." Amelia spun the spoon on the ground, covered it with sand. Then she picked it up and put it in her mouth. When she looked up at the adults, she smiled. "Can't wait to have children, can you?" Rebecca pulled the spoon from Amelia's mouth, wiped off the sand with her shirt, and then gave it back to her. "Mike wants a kid yesterday, right?"

At first Josie wanted to respond, "Mike who?" But then she remembered. Mike. Her husband. The man she had promised to love and honor till death did them part—the man who she swore would be the father of her children. But what did she know then? She had been twenty-five, a baby herself.

She imagined a big playpen with a baby and her hulking husband, a suit jacket rumpled among the stuffed animals. The vision terrified her, and while she knew it was politically incorrect, she admitted to herself that she wanted a husband who wouldn't crawl on all fours or change diapers. She wanted a husband who would willingly hire a nanny, who would snort at the idea of waking up with his wife to feed the child. Her husband, her future husband, a man like Henry Antonelli, for example—would understand his mission was manifold, it was a macro-mission, not a micro one. Mike O'Leary was many things—he was kind, he was big-hearted, he was humorous, and he was athletic. But he wasn't going to be ruthless. She had not known when they married that this was what she wanted. Now she did.

"I, uh—" Josie answered. "I wanted to talk to you about that."

"About what?" Rebecca asked.

"About—look at this," Josie turned to her bag. She pulled out the scrap of paper and waved it to Rebecca. "This was left on my car. Now guess. Just guess."

"Guess what? You do have a nice car."

"Guess who the 'H' is."

"No."

"What do you mean, no?"

"No. I will not be a party to this."

"To what? A party to nothing? A party to finding out that this little piece of paper may be the most exciting thing to happen to me since I moved here, a piece of paper that the *Enquirer* would *die* to have in their little hands . . . why won't you be a party to it?"

"Who is it?"

"Guess."

"Josie, please, I have two children, and a husband. I don't have time to guess."

"Henry," Josie said. "There's a clue."

"Henry," Rebecca repeated. "I don't know any Henrys."

"Think big."

"Big."

"Real big."

"Henry Higgins? Henry Antonelli? Prince Henry?" Rebecca rattled off the names as she scanned the playground. "Do you see Roman anywhere?"

"Yes! Yes!"

"Where?"

"Where what?"

"Where's Roman?"

"Why aren't you listening to me?"

"I am listening to you, I just have kids now."

"You said it."

Rebecca stopped looking around the playground and for the first time considered Josie as she might have long ago, pre-children, when they were both sharing cafeteria food. Josie spoke slowly.

" 'H' is for Henry Antonelli."

"Come on."

"Really."

"Why is Henry Antonelli leaving his phone number on your car?"

"I don't know."

"Call him," Rebecca pulled her cell phone from her pocket. "Call him right now." Her expression had changed from smiling mom to intrigued voyeur. "I want to watch."

"I'm not calling him now. I may not ever call him. I'm just basking in this moment."

"Then I'm calling him—"

"Mommy! Mommy!" Rebecca turned. A boy with thick yellow hair and deep blue eyes ran toward her, holding a soccer ball. "Mommy! Catch!" The boy's feet suddenly planted themselves to the ground and he hurled the ball as hard as he could at the two seated women. "Catch!"

Josie saw the ball coming at her and froze. Rebecca reached in front of her and caught it. "Roman, you know better than to throw balls!"

"He's a killer."

"I know," said Rebecca. "Sometimes Johnny and I think about killing ourselves in a suicide pact, just so you and Mike will know what you're getting into."

Mike's name felt incongruous in this playground. Josie thought about forming the sentence "I think I want a divorce," to her best friend. But Rebecca wasn't paying attention—Roman was pulling at her to push him on the swings.

"Beck—" Josie started, "Beck, I need to tell you—"

"Not now, Roman, not now!" Rebecca glared at her son. "Tell me what—you've got three seconds before this one starts up." She motioned to Amelia.

"I think that Mike and me, Mike and I, I mean, I've been think-ing—"

"Mom! Please, I *need* to go to the swings. I *need* to." Rebecca looked to Josie to her son and back again.

"Go ahead," said Josie.

"You sure?" asked Rebecca.

"Yes," replied Josie.

"We'll finish the talk soon," said Rebecca. She leaned in and kissed Josie on the cheek. "Don't leave Mike until we talk," she whispered into Josie's ear, then took Roman by the hand. "You gotta sleep on it, Josie, what's a couple more days before you hook up with the world's sexiest man?"

Her voice grew fainter as she walked away, although the snappish sounds of "Roman, leave your sister alone!" and "Amelia, please, no biting, please baby, please!" pierced the air. Josie stayed where she was, sniffing her shirt.

After she had left Rebecca and her little monsters in the park, Josie walked slowly to her car. She turned the key in the ignition and looked at her face in the mirror. Reality again, reality. She must concentrate. She had a lot to accomplish in Los Angeles, a lot to accomplish with her life. A baby threw up on her, so what? She was going to hurt Mike. Well, that's how life worked. It was painful, but it was better in the long run. She had Joshua's script and Henry's phone number. People survived divorces all the time, every day. Thank goodness there were no children. She would be just fine.

Chapter Six

Carla slept on her back, with her down comforter pulled tightly to her neck. The sweet air of the spring evening had vanished; clouds had amassed over Manhattan at midnight and Carla had gone to sleep with the drumming sound of rain showers on her roof.

She had been dreaming about her first love, Marty Malone. He had been Carla's first boyfriend. In the dream, Marty was asking Carla to move to Alaska with him, and then, suddenly, had taken a straw and blown on it, releasing diamonds.

Later, Carla would remember that she had woken up first, before the collapse. Her mind heavy with sleep, she thought she saw the diamonds from her dream crystallizing on her ceiling. Her eyes were fluttering open when she heard the first crack. She thought: *This is a very strong rainstorm.* Then there was a ripping sound. At this she had sat up, shaken, acutely aware that someone might be breaking into her apartment and that she might soon be killed. She reached her hand underneath her bed and pulled out her best steak knife, which she kept there precisely for this type of emergency. If someone came near her, she'd stab first, ask questions later.

The second crack was louder. The third was thunderous. The fourth, fifth, and sixth combined in a blast as loud as jackhammers, as loud as rioters.

Her roof was collapsing.

From her bedroom, Carla watched as the ceiling in her living room gave way, thickets of soggy wood and nails and plaster and white-painted floorboards plummeting to her carpeted floor. Rain poured through the hole in her ceiling; the debris from the roof shifted and slanted itself with loud, splattering, abrupt noises as if she were using a saw to crack a rib, or cranking up the engine to a motorboat. She pulled the comforter tighter. She checked Paul Zeig's watch, which was stuck permanently at 10:42 P.M. She looked at the alarm clark near her bed. It was 4:43 A.M.

Strangely, in a way that surprised her, in a manner of someone she did not know, Carla laughed. She watched soaked beach towels fall heavily to the ground, amid the wreckage, and she laughed. She laughed and laughed and laughed, all the while putting on her glasses, pulling on a sweatshirt, prying new jeans onto her unmuscled body. She walked into the living room and leaned onto the leather Restoration Hardware chair, pushing it out from underneath the hole in the ceiling. For a brief second, Carla stopped laughing and looked up through the mess. Rain fell onto her head, spotting her glasses.

She found trash bags in the kitchen and stretched them onto the rug, the coffee table, the hundreds of pens, and the off-colored couch, all of which were covered, to some extent, with the sopping debris of the roof. She grabbed her laptop, and she grabbed a picture of her mother and father, and she took a stone that was engraved with the word OPEN. She worked steadily, but not for long. She was finished in barely twenty minutes. She backed into the archway leading from the living room to the door. She watched it rain inside her apartment. And then, grabbing her umbrella and a Red Sox baseball cap, her handbag and her wallet, she went outside.

She scurried down the stairs as fast as she could—already envisioning the water soaking through her living room floor and then through the ceiling of the tenant underneath her. A long time ago, that tenant had taken her *New Yorker* magazine, and she had not spoken to the man since. She did not want to talk to him now.

Instead she ran outside, to streets that were now empty, to rain pelting the ground. She ran to a public telephone platform across the street from her building. Looking up, she could see no evidence of the roof's collapse from the ground, but in her mind she saw the gaping hole in the roof as if from up above. She dialed a phone number and asked the operator to say it was a collect call from Carla.

"One moment, please," said the operator.

"Carla? What is it? Are you okay?" Her cousin Phillip sounded tired, but concerned.

"I'm going to do it," said Carla.

"Do what?" he asked.

"Come to L.A.," she said.

"I'm asleep, Carla, I don't understand."

"Paulette e-mailed me. I'm coming."

"She didn't say anything about it to me."

"Whatever."

"Are you sure you're all right? You sound funny."

"I'm fine, fine, superb actually." Carla took a step backward and closed her umbrella, happy with the way the rain was bouncing off of her hair, her body. "I was waiting for a sign and it just happened."

"Wait a second, Carla, what's going on?"

"My roof fell in," she said. "But don't worry. I'll call you tomorrow." Carla hung up the phone, soaking wet, smiling, alive.

She had no apartment. It was now so clear. This was nothing less than an emphatic signal from Those Above to *get out*, move forward, begin life! The e-mail from Paulette was just a catalyst. What was important was that tonight Carla had glimpsed the future through a hole in her roof at the same time that dream diamonds were forming on her ceiling. The world had opened up to her in a cataclysmic way, and she would take this chance—as she would take all such chances in the future—holding on with exuberant fingers as she was tossed across the country, alighting with outstretched toes on the shore from which she would embark on her own expedition.

She waved down a cab. "Newark Airport," she said.

"Cool," said the driver.

Carla got in the backseat. The clock in the car said it was 5:32 A.M. She could be in Los Angeles by noon.

Chapter Seven

Josie pulled into the driveway of her Beverly Hills home at 7:35 P.M. Mike's car, a Ford pickup truck that Josie had allowed him to purchase under the Reverse Affect rule, was already parked. Despite her desire for a divorce, she wanted to tell him about Joshua and his script; she wanted him to be happy for her.

She walked inside and found Mike in the living room. He was sitting in the chair, reading the newspaper.

"Hi," said Josie. She put her bag on the counter and kicked off her shoes. Mike didn't answer her. She looked over at him; his thinning black hair was too long in the nape of his neck, and she saw that he was wearing the blue DKNY shirt she had given him last Christmas.

"Hey," Josie said again. Mike looked up at her. One leg was crossed over the other at the knee. He looked strangely graceful for an ex-football-playing athlete; he looked almost regal.

"What's going on?" asked Josie. She walked over to the chair where Mike was sitting and turned on the light. "You can't read in the dark." She had begun to feel nervous, as if Mike knew everything she had been thinking during the day. She was too present in the moment to consider ways to quell her fear—or even to soothe her anxiety by remembering she was the one calling the shots.

"I called you today," Mike said.

"I'm sorry," Josie said immediately. "I was in meetings all day. I saw Seth for lunch—he said hello—and then I stopped to see Rebecca. I've got vomit all over my shirt and—"

"Right," said Mike.

"You knew I had vomit on my shirt?" Josie answered.

"I knew you must have been busy," Mike replied. He stood up. She saw there was a duffel bag near the chair. "You must have been busy because I called you five times. I called you at the office and on your cell."

"Don't start this with me, Michael," Josie said. "I can't be at your beck and call every time you ring. I have a life too."

"They're going to test for testicular cancer," said Mike. "The doctor's appointment today. That's why I called."

Josie turned her back to Mike, even as she knew that this was the wrong response. She folded her elbows to her chest. "Are you trying to make me feel guilty?" she said.

Behind her, Mike O'Leary laughed, the laugh of the quietly resigned. This was his wife, and not to have recognized her supreme self-absorption was as much his fault as hers.

"No, Josie," Mike said evenly. "I'm not trying to make you feel guilty. Here's the report." He handed her a manila file. "The doctor's going to get back to me next week." Mike picked up his bag.

"What—oh don't play the martyr, don't do it. I screwed up. I'm sorry," said Josie.

"You're sorry because you screwed up, or because I may be sick, or because you're just trying to make everything okay?" Mike didn't sound angry. He sounded curious.

"Mike—Jesus, do they really think this?" She was not used to the cloudy feeling in her head; she did want everything to be okay.

"I'm going to a hotel tonight," said Mike.

Josie stood in between him and the doorway. "Why?"

"I'll call you, leave a message where I am." Mike looked at her, his eyes blinking, but dry. "I just have to think, Josie. I have to think." He leaned in, kissed her on the cheek. "I know you've been busy," he said. "But tonight I just can't hear your excuses."

"Mike—" Josie heard desperation, and anger, and terror in her voice. She wanted her knees to buckle, or to faint; she wanted to do something that would distract them both from Mike and this terrible news; she wanted to be free of this guilt that was lowering itself upon her like a thick curtain; she wanted to start the homecoming scene all over again and have Mike pretend to be interested in her recounting of her day.

"Mike, don't go," Josie said.

"Yeah, this isn't—this isn't, I don't want to be a martyr, Josie. I'm not one, you know that, or maybe I am, I don't know, I just have to get out of here right now. I've been here for two hours, just waiting, and it's killing me more than any cancer. Or maybe not. Maybe this is cancer talking—how crazy is this, Josie? Maybe I have cancer? I'm thirty-three years old!" Mike's face contorted, and his shoulders raised and his elbows lurched forward. Josie instinctively moved toward him and put her arms around his waist.

"Mistake, Josie," Mike said, as he pulled away from her. He stepped toward the doorway.

Josie looked at him, her husband, a man six feet one inch tall, dark straight hair, handsome and tormented. There was a force within her pushing her toward him, willing her to unleash all of her emotions to bind him to her, to make him see that she cared for him, that she would take care of him if this news were true, to assure him again and again, that she would never leave his side.

But she didn't move. Nor did Mike. They just stood and looked at each other.

And then Mike broke the gaze, and left. Josie didn't move until she heard his car ignite, until she heard him pull out of the driveway. She stood in their living room, amid their life together, summoning up the requisite emotional fortitude and finding herself bone-dry, as if someone or something had drained her pump of emotions without her knowing. She wanted to feel for her husband, and she did, she *must*, but right now, she was empty.

And then she sat where Mike had been sitting, underneath the bright light. The telephone was on the side table. She was by herself, completely alone with her thoughts, and she knew that if she had a different temperament, she would be calling family right now, in distress. If she were different, she would have never allowed Mike to leave; if she were different, she would have been with Mike at the doctor's.

But she was not different, and she was sick of apologizing for herself to her husband, to anyone. It was not cruel to be true to oneself. Mike might not have cancer, but if he did, she would do anything she could to help him, even if that meant divorcing him quickly so he could resume his life. She was not heartless, she was not without emotion.

But she would not feel guilty.

And she would not shortchange herself, not anymore. She picked up the telephone. She had memorized Henry's number. She trembled as she held the receiver. Again, she felt that strange sense that life was finally making sense; suspending judgments, that this was the right thing for Josie to do.

"Hello," she said into the mouthpiece. "I'm looking for Henry?"

Part Two

Chapter Eight

Long ago, Henry Antonelli had learned the value of nurturing a habit. People disparaged habit as the murderer of free thought and all things spontaneous, but Henry knew they were wrong. The trick was developing a habit that would serve you, not one that would sabotage you.

For Henry, this habit was horses.

As a young child, Henry had worked at horse farms throughout New Jersey, rushing to the area racetracks and Thoroughbred farms whenever he was free. He had been born in 1940 in a small southern New Jersey city called Vineland, and—like every one of his peers—had worked for one of the local farmers until he went to college. But unlike many of his peers, Henry had the guidance of his uncle Angelo Falcinelli, a state supreme court justice, revered for his scholarly mind and mischievous wit. Angelo loved horses and began buying Thoroughbreds after he left his lucrative private law office to become a judge. For Angelo, the appeal of Thoroughbreds was not gambling; for Angelo it was the horses themselves, the majestic animals that could race around the grounds with their manes soaring behind them, their bodies flush with light and power. He housed his horses at a stable near his hometown, where all of his children, as well as those of his sister, Antoinetta, worked during their summer breaks. When Angelo saw that his nephew Henry would always lag behind his siblings at the shed, combing the horses with the thick handbrush, talking to the horses as if they were his confidants, Angelo introduced him to his horse trainer, Dennis Novak, who taught Henry everything he knew.

When Henry graduated from Rutgers in 1962, he followed his uncle's lead yet again and applied to law school. He was accepted, and Henry's mother, Antoinetta, wept because her oldest son was going to become a lawyer like her brother.

But Henry, a diligent but uninspired law student, could not divorce himself from his first love, the horses. He had the opportunity to travel to Santa Anita in Southern California with a group of Thoroughbreds he had raised since they were yearlings. The rich owners, another farming family from New Jersey, had pleaded with him to come for the racing season. This meant that Henry had to defer his admission to law school, and Antoinetta sobbed again, louder, this time in disappointment.

Even now, after Henry had won two Academy Awards, after he had begun his own world-famous film production company, reverentially called New Jersey Thoroughbred Films (NJTF), and after he had been lauded around the globe for his benevolence and humanitarianism and prowess, Antoinetta Antonelli, eighty-four years old, lamented he had not ever returned to Vineland, New Jersey, to become a lawyer. *Make-believe, you live in make-believe and I live in reality. Hocus-pocus, movies, don't tell me, I know what it is, it's a business of kooks!*

Henry's wife, a child psychiatrist named Cecilia Rosenberg, tolerated Henry's passion, just as he tolerated hers: antique quilts. The two had tried to have children of their own, but after seven miscarriages and years of in vitro attempts, they surrendered to their bodies' limitations. Henry's five siblings had a total of twenty-eight children, and Cecilia's two siblings and three best friends had another eight, so their days were filled with youth, even if they didn't bear Henry or Cecilia's DNA. Antoinetta lived with them in Malibu, developing her own passion: poker. It had become part of Hollywood's lore that the best card-playing in Los

Angeles—the tables with the most celebrities clamoring to get a seat—was in Henry's sunlit atrium, next to Antoinetta, no smoking allowed.

He had fallen into acting in the most facile of ways. After he decided not to go to law school, he remained in California training Thoroughbreds. One of his clients was a Hollywood producer whose daughter believed herself to be in love with the young New Jerseyan and pursued him relentlessly with phone calls and flowers and beef chili from Chasen's. Henry, flattered but uninterested, had dissuaded her with grace and conviction. At night, he and his girlfriend—an accomplished equestrian—would laugh at the relentless arrogance of the young heiress.

But despite Henry's rejection of his daughter, the young woman's father (who was well aware of his daughter's shortcomings) had been impressed by the young trainer's composure and intelligence. He had been casting a film set in the late 1800s. He had Henry play the part of Gangster #3, the man who took the bullet for Gangster #1, dying ignominiously in the desert of New Mexico, held by Gangster #2.

Gangster #3 became Policeman #2 and Taxi Driver #1, until eventually Henry was scoring lead roles in movies. He became a prolific actor, loyal to his representatives, composed to his fans, and insistent upon maintaining a sense of dignity in his films. He cared little for the pomp of the industry; just as he had formerly disdained racing galas except as a meeting place where he could discuss what he truly loved, the horses. Other people in Hollywood, he knew, affected a similar disdain for the parties and the glitz, but, unlike Henry, they were acting, and even the best of them could not maintain the resolve needed to ignore the schemes of a power-hungry publicist or money-seeking manager. Henry could, because fundamentally he did not care.

What he did care about—what he could not help but be intrigued by—were the women in Hollywood who wanted more than anything to be as powerful as the men. He had never been truly attracted to the actresses; unlike his peers, he rarely mistook the energy and intellect of "spitfires" as evidence of anything other than selfishness. But when he thought about women other than his wife, he always found himself drawn to the women who wanted, as their life's goal, to be powerful and rich. Like Schulberg's Sammy Glick, they wanted power, and money, and the adoration of idiots.

He knew that women had the right to be as shortsighted as men; that if women wanted to be Sandy Glick, for example, then God bless them. It was not up to him to tell these women that they had life by the balls, so to speak, because they could bear children and be nurturing and be brilliant and be creative and make money and be respected *all at the same time.* There were all kinds of examples of this in Hollywood—the studio chief who demanded day care on the studio lot so she could work on her projects and spend time with her children; the senior vice president who, while masterminding the rise of her cable company to be one of America's most admired corporations, also managed to be a terrific wife and mother and friend.

But women who push hard, who don't care about the product, who just want money and fame? What made them tick? What made women like Josephine O'Leary want to run in a race that had no end, an exhausting, frenetic, terrifying race that was comprised of people flashing their heads left to right to make sure that no one got in front of them? Why?

He wanted to ask her. He wanted to sit down and figure out what had led her to become this kind of person. He wanted to know her life story, her childhood dreams and wishes.

And, of course, he wanted to sleep with her.

He had had one affair in his past. Her name was Rhonda and she had been an agent back when most women were secretaries. She was determined to run a movie studio and could rationalize any unseemly behavior that helped her on this path. Rhonda told Henry that she had studied great leaders and their one similarity was that once they got to the top, they could say to anyone who judged them, "Talk about me all you want. I'm here, and you're not."

But Rhonda had eventually bored him, and he had ended their

relationship. Years later, she gave up the business and was now, he heard, an organic farmer in Eugene, Oregon.

Henry had admitted all to Cecilia, thus initiating the worst phase in their marriage, but this was many years in the past, and since then he'd been able to keep his fascination with Sammy Glick–style women in check.

Until now, with the arrival of Josephine O'Leary, whose appearance happened to coincide with the aftermath of Henry's sixty-second birthday. Turning sixty had not been traumatizing, but turning sixty-two had been. He was still handsome—his navy blue eyes as clear and large as they had always been, his body as taut as a marine's. But he was restless. He had just heard that Harrison Ford was going to receive a fee in the "thirty million" range. The most Henry had earned was twenty-five (and, while an astronomical amount, was considerably less once the 10 percent agency fee, 5 percent lawyer's fee, 2 percent accountant's fee, and taxes were deducted). But the money itself was not the issue, not anymore. It was the competition. Harrison's good fortune came at the exact time Henry began to see himself as an old man. Was he skidding on the slopes of his career? Had he been oblivious to his own obsolescence?

Petulantly, Henry believed that Cecilia had not been sympathetic to his worries, offering pseudo-comfort in the way of one brief sentence, "We don't need the money." He felt like he asked for a towel, and she had given him a Kleenex.

"I'm not talking about money," Henry insisted. "I'm talking about credibility. About maintaining my stature."

"You're talking about a competition between little boys," she replied instantly. "And I'm not going to listen to it."

Henry had gone to his old friend Wallace, believing Wallace would commiserate, assure him that he too would soon be garnering quotes in the thirty-million-dollar range. Instead, Wallace had told story after story about "the old times," and moaned about how the studio president was passing off his phone calls to underlings. Suddenly Henry felt like the character he had portrayed in *The Last Counselor*, his most recent movie. Henry had played a successful lawyer who discovered, after forty years of practicing law, that he was increasingly archaic and that his clients were leaving him to go with younger, flashier colleagues. Could this be what was happening in real life, after an illustrious career, to Henry Antonelli? Was he the last one to discover that his career was over, and that before he knew it, he would find out he had prostate cancer and be dead?

Was it the beginning of the end?

This was the mood he was in when he met Josie O'Leary, a woman unafraid to meet his gaze, and a woman who was in that final glow of sleek, healthy, fearless youth.

The day after he had received her first message, he reconsidered the whole situation. It had been an insane thing to do, to leave his number on the windshield of a car—it was the act of a brazen man, someone who engaged in extramarital trysts as a matter of course. Moreover, he was a busy man, someone whose schedule was meticulously arranged every day, every hour. Henry had enough difficulty scheduling the meetings and plans that didn't necessitate secrecy. Just yesterday an old girlfriend had called him to plan a dinner. He had had to shuffle six meetings and force a charity to change the day of their benefit, and in the end had had to invite her to dinner before the premiere of *The Last Counselor*, six weeks away. And this was for dinner with an old friend. An affair required strategic planning, subterfuge, and covert operations. Was it worth it?

He didn't know if he would call her back. He did know she was only interested in him because of his fame—if he were still a horse trainer, Josie would have found his number on her car and called security.

Still, he was the one who had left the number. And still, he was the one worried about becoming obsolete. And still, he was the one driving around Los Angeles in a dented Corolla, wondering whether he'd call a young woman back in order to pursue an affair, making him as predictable and mediocre as the rest of his male peers, scurrying around the country, attracted to a pretty girl, and hoping he didn't make a mess out of everything.

Chapter Nine

Phillip Giberson was a generous person. If he had not been able to earn a lot of money, this personality trait would have caused him many problems. But he was Head of Business Affairs for Studio X, which meant he was the lawyer who negotiated the biggest deals, the most profitable ventures, the most creditworthy acquisitions. This also meant his annual salary and bonuses were enough to keep him and his family in a big home in Santa Monica, close enough to the beach and far enough from Hollywood to believe he was still the same old Phillip from Long Island.

He wasn't, of course. He knew that. He was a man who knew his strengths and weaknesses and had decided that when measured against each other, his strengths outnumbered his weaknesses, which then led him to conclude that whatever his bad habits were, he was going to keep them.

This meant golfing one day a weekend, tipping too much, spending too much, and smoking too much. This meant leaving dirty clothes on the floor before he went to sleep. He knew he should restrain himself—he knew that better men than he could be disciplined and sensitive and expert clothes-folders. Maybe, when he was older, when his son Christopher had gone off to school, he would change. But for now, as he told Samantha, what she saw was what she got.

And right now, what Samantha and Christopher got was Carla Trousse, Phillip's cousin. She had shown up one day, wearing a ratty orange sweater and jeans, her short red hair gelled upward in tufts. She was wearing bright red glasses with pointed edges, and she wore no socks under brown clogs.

Eight-year-old Christopher had not remembered her at first. Phillip had been surprised to see how much she had changed since the previous year. Carla had smiled brightly, and Samantha had immediately told Carla how well she looked. Carla had rolled her eyes and, looking at Phillip, had said, "I look awful. I've gained a ton of weight, my skin's broken out, and I think I have bad breath."

She had breathed on Christopher to prove her halitosis, and Christopher had nodded yes, and added, as nicely as he could, that her breath smelled like a dog's.

"A nice dog?" Carla had asked.

"Uh-huh," Christopher agreed.

Samantha had led Carla to the guest room, where she had a queen-sized bed, her own washer and dryer, and, if needed, her own Pilates machine.

"I don't think I'll need that," Carla said dryly. "Unless I'm torturing someone."

"It's up to you," said Samantha. "Make yourself at home."

Later, after Carla had unpacked and showered, she returned downstairs and showed Phillip and Samantha the e-mail she had received from Paulette.

"I don't know anything about this," Phillip had said.

"She didn't say a word," said Samantha.

"Well, I certainly don't know," said Carla. "I didn't even know she was living here."

"She isn't, she's in Santa Barbara," said Phillip.

"You're kidding," Carla said. "I come all the way here so she can tell me about my proverbial rough patch—"

"Doesn't sound like that's what she wants to talk about," said Phillip.

"Thanks, by the way, for telling her about my desolate life in New York."

"I never used the word 'desolate.' I think I said 'miserable.'"

Carla flushed. Phillip prepared himself for one of her bristling rejoinders, but instead she looked directly at him and said, rather gently, "It was that obvious?"

"No," said Phillip. Carla raised her eyebrows. "Well, yes," Phillip continued. "I just told her that you weren't working. That's it." He paused. "Did you even tell her you were coming?"

"No," she answered. "You're the only one I told. It was kind of spur of the moment anyway."

"Well, I think she's away for the next couple of weeks. But she did drop a bombshell the last time we talked."

"She's finally solved the crisis in the Middle East?" asked Carla.

"No," Phillip smiled. "But she did use to date Henry Antonelli."

Carla and Samantha stared at him. "That can't be true," said Samantha.

"It is," Phillip answered.

"You're kidding. Please, Phillip, tell me you're kidding." Carla pushed her glasses up onto her nose.

"She's coming to L.A. to have dinner with him, and he's taking her to the premiere of *The Last Counselor*," Phillip answered.

Carla and Samantha exchanged a long, bewildered glance.

"I know I'm in the minority, but I've never liked him much as an actor. Do we really need to see another movie with a sixty-year-old man and a twenty-five-year-old woman hooking up together? I bet he's older than sixty. Like sixty-five, at least. He's probably not even Italian—his publicist probably just came up with that, just so he could be perceived as a 'man of the people' like De Niro. Please. He's as

81

blond and blue-eyed as they come." Carla looked around to see if either Phillip or Samantha agreed. "Basically, he's a hack."

"Only you would call one of America's favorite actors a hack," commented Phillip.

Samantha turned to Phillip. "Paulette dated Henry Antonelli?"

"Guess so," Phillip shrugged.

"Maybe that's what Paulette wanted to tell me," Carla said.

"I'm not sure she even knows who he is," Phillip answered. "She got annoyed when I tried to tell her what a huge star he was. 'He was a horse trainer when I knew him, and far as I'm concerned, he still is.'"

"When is the premiere?" asked Samantha.

"A month or so from now?" guessed Phillip. "I don't know. Sometime in June."

Carla gazed around the kitchen—it was spotless, with dark gray marble countertops and sleek silver appliances.

"Fancy," said Carla. "A Sub-Zero refrigerator and everything."

Phillip heard the contemptuous tone in Carla's voice. So did Samantha, who responded icily. "You should see the Lamborghini."

Phillip chuckled.

"Do you really have a Lamborghini?" Carla asked Phillip.

"Are you out of your mind?" he replied. "Sam's just stopping you before you go off on your conspicuous consumer rant."

Phillip knew that when Samantha had first met Carla, she had been intimidated by Carla's extensive academic credentials. Phillip had tried to tell Samantha that there was no one on earth more insecure than Carla, but Samantha was certain that her own B.A. from USC did not stand up next to Carla's numerous degrees.

The tension had culminated at their wedding, when Samantha had told Phillip during their honeymoon that she had overheard Carla and David Stegner, a friend of Phillip's from college, talking about how stupid Samantha was. Phillip had told Samantha she must have heard incorrectly, but privately he knew all too well that both his cousin and his friend were only too apt to judge people on their academic credentials.

But now, nine years later, Samantha had grown more confident. Phillip watched her from the couch in the great room off the kitchen. She was smart, she was a good mother, she was funny, and she was pragmatic.

Carla, meanwhile, was still staring at Phillip, fumbling for a response to his accusation. "I don't have a rant about conspicuous consumerism," she began. "I just think that when people are lucky enough to have a lot of money they should—"

She stopped. Phillip and Samantha looked at each other.

"Never mind," Carla said, before she began to smile. "You know, I used to think Sub-Zero meant that the food was kept at that temperature." No one said anything. "Sorry, Sam. Your house is gorgeous," Carla said in as contrite a tone as Phillip had ever heard. "My entire apartment would fit in here."

Samantha brightened at Carla's compliment. "The benefit of Los Angeles. Space."

Carla walked over to the refrigerator, where Samantha had arranged photographs on the door. "Who's this?" she asked. "With David?"

Samantha walked behind Carla. "Eve. Eve Marvell."

"Right," said Carla, remembering David's tone when he mentioned "Eve" during one of their long-ago phone calls.

"She's wonderful," said Samantha. "You'll love her. But I don't know what she sees in him."

"Samantha . . . ," warned Phillip.

"What do you mean?" asked Carla.

"Eve's one of the nicest people I've ever met. But there's got to be something wrong with her," Samantha said. "Otherwise she wouldn't be with him."

"Why?" asked Carla. "I don't understand." She looked utterly perplexed.

"Because David . . . David is . . ." Samantha looked around for a moment before she responded, ". . . charmless. David is utterly charmless."

"He isn't that bad," said Phillip.

"He is the rudest person I have ever met. And I live in L.A."

Carla turned her head from both Phillip and Samantha, giving Phillip a chance to glare at his wife. *Stop it*, he mouthed. Samantha looked at him questioningly. Phillip shook his head.

Carla returned to the great room. She took off her glasses, rubbing her eyes.

"So what's up with New York?" asked Phillip.

"I spent my last day there sitting underground at the Ninety-sixth Street subway station." Carla was tired, and blurted out her first thought.

"I'm sure that's a good distraction—" Samantha began, but allowed her words to trail off.

"I'm tired of it." Carla spoke quietly, resolutely. "I know I'm supposed to love it. I'm the quintessential New Yorker, bitter, lonely, overeducated, highly critical." She paused to smile at Phillip. "I know it, don't worry." She scratched her jaw absentmindedly. "But I think it's enough. New York City, center of the universe. Twenty years of pushing and scribbling and begging for people to pay attention to me. I'm so tired of it, buoying up my spirits with fake hopes and stupid trite sayings and of course—my own specialty—ripping apart anyone or anything who succeeds." Carla again paused, wiping her hands across her face. "I know it. I've become some kind of hyper-garrulous monster. I think I can literally talk people to death. I'm not kidding. It's like some affliction. I need to go to TA, Talkers Anonymous, but the only reason I'm like that is because I'm so rarely with anyone." She closed her eyes.

She put her hands together and bowed her head. Phillip appraised her silently.

"I'm sure it isn't that bad," offered Samantha.

"It is," said Carla calmly. "Don't worry. I'm admitting it all here, in your private confessional. I know it's true."

"It isn't," said Phillip, none-too-convincingly. Carla smiled at him, the smile of the skeptic. "Have you talked to Candace?" Phillip asked.

"My mother?" Carla now laughed outright. "My mother is very

very busy. And she has no time for my hysterics. 'Carla, you must calm down. Life isn't easy, I've always told you that. Stop thinking about yourself. There are people in this world with diseases riddling their bodies, people who have machetes at their throats. You are very lucky. I love you unconditionally, as Jesus wants me to, but I think it's high time you stopped relying on me for so much emotional support. You are an adult, you realize.'"

"She didn't say that," said Samantha. "Jesus wants her to?"

"Oh yes. She did. She's on some radical Catholic bent of late. Jesus died for our sins, have faith, trust in the Lord, protest outside abortion clinics. You know how it works. I asked her what she said to the girls she blocked from the clinic. She said she counseled them about the sanctity of life. I told her I'd go with her on one of the protests if I could tell these girls what a loving, supportive, generous mother she was." Carla grinned. "Well, that didn't go over very well. She left for some Catholic Charities trip soon afterward, saying she'd see me at Christmas." Carla's eyes lit up. "Maybe she called Paulette and told her she was worried. Maybe that's why she contacted me?"

"You have to admit, 'inimitable intransigence' is a great phrase," opined Phillip.

"Paulette's a smart woman, no question about it. No emotions to speak of, but she's definitely smart," Carla replied.

Phillip was acutely aware that Carla's version of her life story was less melodramatic than normal. This was a sign of promise.

"Can't choose your parents," he said. "God knows what we're doing to Christopher right now."

Carla surveyed the great room. "Seems like you're killing him with toys."

"It's all Phillip," said Samantha. "I've tried. He never listens. The one rule is there are no rules. Anything Christopher wants, he gets."

"And he isn't a spoiled brat?"

"You'll see for yourself," said Phillip. "He's not that kind of kid, I don't think. Maybe another kid would be. Listen, Paulette was my mom, and she isn't much different from Candace. Maybe even worse—she wasn't around much at all. Doesn't matter. They're both selfish people, she and Candace. Maybe it was in the water, who knows why? You deal with it." He paused. "And you do what you want to do when you have the chance. If the worst thing I do is give Christopher too many toys, I'll take it."

"So you don't know what she wants?" asked Carla.

"Nope. No a clue," said Philip.

Carla wandered over to the refrigerator again. "David and Eve have been together a while now?"

"I don't know, a couple years," answered Samantha.

"You're not thinking of him, are you?" asked Phillip. "Tell me now."

Carla glared at him. "I forgot how utterly ridiculous it was for an old friend to comment upon a mutual acquaintance. Forgive me."

"Don't fool yourself, Carla," said Phillip. "He loves Eve."

"As much as he can love anyone," murmured Samantha.

"He isn't that bad," Carla said. "He can't be."

"What do I know?" Samantha relented. "He thinks I'm an idiot."

"Why aren't they married?" asked Carla.

"I hope it's because Eve's smart enough not to ruin her life," said Samantha. "So, Carla. What do you think you want to do out here?"

"Do?" Carla considered. "I suppose I'm a little old to get the ingénue parts."

"You know," smiled Phillip. "I think you should think about staying for a while. This is the place for creative people."

"Right. All those geniuses who put American entertainment at the forefront of the culture wars."

"So do something about it," said Phillip.

"I told you, I'm a much better criticizer. It's the only thing I'm good at," Carla replied.

"Seriously," said Phillip. "You should think about it. I can hook you up with some people. Do you know anyone out here besides us?"

"Yeah," said Carla. "My old assistant Nadine works somewhere.

And there's a guy from NYU who's a reporter out here. I can call him."

"Sounds good," said Phillip. "Before you know it, you'll be just as shallow as the rest of us."

"One can only hope," said Carla. "I'm going to bed, okay? I'm still on East Coast time."

"Sleep well," said Phillip.

"Our house is your house," Samantha called out to Carla. "Remember that."

Carla left, and Phillip lit a cigarette, breathing the smoke out in perfect circles.

"She's tough," said Samantha. "Tougher than I remembered."

"She's a complete marshmallow," said Phillip. "Complete and utter marshmallow."

Samantha sat on the couch opposite her husband. She fiddled with a framed photograph of their son, taken on Christmas Day.

"How did you two come out of those women?"

"We did okay. They're not evil. They're just cold."

Samantha moved to sit behind Phillip, on top of his desk. She began to massage his neck.

"But I was able to get out," Philip continued. "Carla got stuck."

"I don't know about that. She's gotten so wrapped up in herself she can't even take a step out—she's afraid. And entitled. You can't have sixteen academic degrees like her and spend all your time criticizing, doing nothing. Like being all dressed up with no place to go. What's she going to do?"

"I have no idea, Sam. You heard her tonight. She can't keep a job, she can't keep a boyfriend, I keep bailing her out—I don't know. Do I stop? Do I keep going?"

Samantha smiled before she kissed Phillip on the forehead. Then she rose and took a step toward the archway leading to the second floor. Phillip pulled her back. "Where are you going? I asked you a question."

"Look at all these toys," Samantha said, gesturing around the room.

"What does that mean?"

"It means you couldn't stop if you wanted to."

"So you want me to stop?"

She took the first step toward their bedroom. "Can't fool me. I know what you're trying to do. You're trying to get me to give you an order, so you can blame it on me. No way. You're going to keep supporting her, which is exactly what you should do because no matter what, she's family. And yes, it's going to be a drain, and that's about the size of it." Samantha left the room.

Phillip stayed at his desk, looking out the window. He had a conference call at seven-thirty in the morning, and Simon, his personal trainer, was coming at six to cajole him into trotting on the beach. A movie was about to fall through, and another one was rumored to be hitting three times the original budget. Christopher had a tennis match over the weekend, and Samantha and he were supposed to host a dinner party on Sunday for twelve. Now, with Carla, it would be thirteen.

She could be difficult, but she was also his oldest friend, the one who surprised him with quirky letters and sudden moments of great insight. She was as loyal and trusting as a person could be. As a child, she had told the most original and creative stories—she could keep him laughing for hours. Maybe Los Angeles was going to wreak a miracle—maybe Carla was finally going to use some of her abundant potential now that she was in this nexus of ideas. Samantha was right. It was futile to think about doing anything differently. He might golf on Sundays, and he might keep the toilet seat lifted up, but he wasn't going to bail on his cousin, and if that was a weakness, so be it.

Chapter Ten

Josie entered her office carrying a new Hermès bag. She had bought it at Barneys with money she had received from Mike. Mike refused to speak to her, which made her more determined to talk to him. He was living with his best friend Anthony out in Hancock Park. Anthony was one of the most respected literary agents in town, but it seemed to Josie that his favorite pastime was belittling her. "Oh, is this the woman who walked out on her cancer-stricken husband?" "Hmmm. Josie O'Leary, can't quite place it. Let me think. The bitch who abandoned my best friend? Does that sound familiar?"

Josie finally gave up, which Anthony had predicted as well. "I'm making it easy for you, Josie. You can say that his prick of a friend kept you from assuaging your guilt. It's a perfect alibi." She had slammed down the phone.

Her new tactic was money. Mike was going to have to deal with her—she would force him. But whatever she asked for, he gave. She would submit the request through Seth, her lawyer, who gave it to Mike's lawyer, and money would go into her account, no questions asked. Mike's parents were multimillionaires, and they disliked Josie, so she guessed that they were handing him money just to get rid of her. Or maybe it did just come from Mike, since he himself had garnered a small fortune from his own ten years as an investment banker. Either way, the fact of the money's easy concourse to her bank account proved her suspicion that Mike and his family were trying to hurt her. This was why she was justified in asking for more.

She knew nothing about his diagnosis, nothing about his treatment. She had been upset for at least three days, until her publicist friend, Catherine Von Hauptman, had convinced her that Mike was being passive-aggressive. It wasn't Josie's fault that Mike acted like a child. Josie had told Catherine she suspected Mike was deliberately keeping Josie in the dark so that she would seem callous when she couldn't answer people who asked her about his condition. "Cancer or no cancer, men are spoiled brats. You weren't the demure little wife. Tragic. Some men cannot accept ambitious women. That's Mike's problem, Josie, not yours."

That Catherine's assertion about ambitious women had explained the demise of her last twenty-seven relationships was a fact Josie ignored. She also ignored the fact that Mike relished her take-charge nature. She needed Catherine's interpretation to make her own behavior understandable. So naturally, Catherine was right.

Josie resolved to take as much money as she could, and then lie, lie, lie. She worked in the business of fiction—when someone asked her about Mike, she'd make up something. She didn't need to know about his cancer treatments; she no longer wanted to know.

"Nice bag," said Priscilla, who was sitting in the lounge when Josie entered.

"Thanks."

"No, I mean it. Nice bag."

"Thanks."

"You and Mike back together?"

"What gave you that idea?"

"Oh, nothing." Priscilla smiled. "Just thought he might have gotten you that."

Josie stopped walking. "That's none of your business," she said. Priscilla stepped over to Josie.

"You're right," she said, sweetly. "Sorry."

Josie threw her bag onto an armchair, her irritation now a full-fledged storm. Priscilla's sweetness was like a pretty river with nitrates flowing underneath. Josie hated her, hated everything. Her new apartment in the flats of Beverly Hills was unfurnished because she couldn't decide what kind of image she wanted to project—shabby chic or western—and Henry Antonelli hadn't returned her call.

"Hi, Josie," said Nadine through the door.

"Hi," said Josie, as she sat up and pasted on a fake smile.

"How's everything?" asked Nadine.

"Everything's great," Josie said. "Really fabulous."

Nadine nodded. "Cool. Listen, there's something weird going on."

"What?"

"I don't know, just something weird. Priscilla actually told me I looked pretty."

"You do," said Josie, thinking how she might politely mention liposuction to Nadine without offending her.

"No, I'm telling you, there's something going on. Wallace was in before me."

"Probably someone canceled his lunch. Now he'll have to pretend he has plans and stay in his office smoking his pipe."

"Whatever," said Nadine. "Just wanted to warn you."

Nadine left, and Josie sat down in front of her new iMac computer with the seventeen-inch flat screen.

"Nadine—wait. No one called?" Josie spoke loudly from her desk toward the open door. "Nadine?"

She waited for Nadine to return, but she didn't. She looked at her phone, and wondered who she could call, but no one came to mind. Her call sheet was completely blank. Josie heard a noise and looked up at her doorway.

"Nadine, finally—" But it wasn't Nadine. It was Priscilla. Josie hadn't noticed earlier that Priscilla was dressed like Little Bo-Peep, replete with a garish pink flower stuck in her hair.

"Josephine?" said Priscilla.

"What?"

"Wallace and I need to speak to you," said Priscilla.

Josie flashed her eyes up to her nemesis. "Sure," she said. She picked up a script. "After lunch okay with you? I'm meeting—"

"Josie," said Priscilla. "Sooner is better."

"Fine," said Josie to herself. "Fine."

When Josie walked into Wallace's office, she found Wallace behind his desk and Priscilla in an armchair directly in front of him. The surprise was Nadine, sitting on the couch. Josie looked at her, and Nadine shrugged.

"Well," Josie said. "Here's sooner. Like Priscilla said."

"Josephine," Wallace said, coughing. He looked up at her, and smiled kindly. "We have some bad news."

Josie peered over to Priscilla, who preened in such a way that Josie thought for a second her skinny neck would snap and her big head would loll about the floor, pink flower and all.

"We?"

"Well, I just wanted to be direct with you," said Wallace.

"What's going on?"

"Well," Priscilla began, "the bad news, the *very* bad news, I assure you, is that we're letting you go."

The words hung in the room. Josie's eyes narrowed, and she turned to Nadine.

"Why is she here?" Josie asked, pointing to Nadine. "Did she know about this?"

"She?" Nadine asked, affronted.

"Now, Josie," said Priscilla, "there's no reason to be snide. Nadine is going to be your replacement—"

"I'm what?" blurted out Nadine.

"Although it will be very difficult to replace you, my dear," Wallace said to Josie.

"I don't understand," said Josie. She looked at Nadine, infuriated. "And I fail to see why you are needed in this room."

"Josie, shut up. I don't know about any of this either," Nadine responded.

"The bad news," interrupted Wallace, "is, as Priscilla said, you'll be leaving us. But wait. The good news is that I've already written a stellar recommendation on your behalf." Wallace sat up and smiled at her, as if he were giving her a golden parachute worth millions of dollars instead of a piece of paper.

"What?" Josie held on to the edge of a chair. "What?"

"I'm very sorry, dear," said Wallace again. "It's just—"

Priscilla stood up near Josie. "The thing is, our deal wasn't renewed."

Josie shot a glance toward Wallace. This was more than just bad news. This was as if Wallace had been spit upon by the industry he had ruled.

Wallace's deal had never been questioned. Even when most production companies were shutting down because of the horrible economic climate, Wallace's stayed afloat, if only because of the fact that Wallace had earned so much money for the studio in years past.

"But—" Josie stammered. "They're really shutting you down?"

"I'm afraid so," Wallace said. He looked kindly, like Santa Claus, and sad that he must give this young woman a lump of coal.

"It's terrible," said Priscilla. "It's disloyal. I mean, who do they think he is?" She shook her head. The pink bow wavered. "Their *lawyer*— not even the president—called us on Thursday and said Monday was the last day we would be funded. I thought she was joking. Then the president hemmed and hawed when Wallace called—but he didn't change his mind. I have half a mind to call him myself."

Josie considered, briefly, the fact that Priscilla had only half a mind.

"Sweetheart," said Wallace to his niece, "that won't be necessary. I've had a great run. I could fight it in court, but frankly, I don't have the stamina. The business is changing. The people in charge have different priorities, the president over there doesn't care about movies, only money. It was only a matter of time before I was shut down."

For a second, Josie thought Wallace was sincere. But then she remembered the recent Hollywood business magazine that listed his fortune in the hundreds of millions of dollars.

"But surely you can keep this company going yourself?"

Immediately, Wallace sat up straighter. Priscilla glared at her. Josie remembered the Hollywood rule: *Never, ever, use your own money.*

"I can't," said Wallace. "I really can't afford to keep you. I'm not even sure how much longer we'll be able to stay on our feet."

"But you're worth—"

"We're really sorry, Josie," Priscilla interrupted. "What with your marriage going under and everything—"

"Priscilla!" Wallace reprimanded.

"I'm sorry, I didn't mean to pry," said Priscilla. "But I've heard that Mike is sick and, well, this must be awful to hear on top of everything."

"Thank you for your concern," said Josie.

"There's no reason to be nasty," opined Wallace.

"Of course she's nasty!" Nadine spoke loudly. "You're firing her."

"Nadine, we'll talk to you later," said Priscilla, who then turned to Josie and talked to her soothingly, as if she were comforting a toddler.

"Come on, Josie, think of this as an opportunity. The entire city awaits! Think of it that way—you're actually very lucky. Don't you just want to pinch yourself?"

No, Josie thought. *I want to pinch you.*

She stood up and looked around the room, at the piles of scripts with titles scratched onto the bindings, names like *Imagination* and *The Happy People* and *Demonseed* blurring into one eddy of black scrawled letters. It was hard to remember that an actual human being had sat down and poured his or her heart into these indistinguishable packets of paper.

"When should I leave?" asked Josie.

"Take your time," said Wallace.

"Well," started Priscilla, "staying too long would probably only put off that *exciting* job search—"

"Fine," snapped Josie. "Fine."

She turned to leave.

"Wait a minute," said Nadine. "Wait, Josie." Josie turned back. Nadine was standing, one hand gripping the heft of her hip, the other waving about. She turned to Priscilla and Wallace. "Don't you think you should have asked me if I wanted this job first?"

"No," said Priscilla sharply. "No. That never occurred to me. This is a coup for you."

"Really," said Nadine. "Really."

She shook her head. Josie stared at her, this overweight girl with thick blonde hair, her clothes wrinkled and her glasses on her nose. "I suppose I should be happy," said Nadine. "I guess I'm being naive. But this just isn't the right way to treat people. Josie, hold up. I'm coming with you."

"Priscilla," said Wallace. "Will you please *do* something?"

Priscilla glared at both women. "No," she said. "They can leave. We'll be fine." She turned her back on Nadine and Josie, who watched this all from the doorway.

"Thanks, Wallace," said Nadine. "If you find time, could you write me one of those recommendations too?"

Wallace beamed. "Certainly," said Wallace. "I'll do it today." Priscilla kept her back turned. Nadine picked up her bag and joined Josie in the hall. Josie pulled the door shut behind her.

"Thanks," she said to Nadine. "Never would have expected that."

"You're a jerk," said Nadine.

"What?"

"You heard me. Jesus, you acted like I put a knife in your back when I didn't know a thing."

"You can't blame me for that. Think of what it looked like."

"Yeah, well you should have thought about what it was, and about who was involved." Nadine turned toward the exit, then stopped and

95

looked back at Josie. "There's nothing I hate more than people who assume that because they're spineless, other people are too." Nadine spun back toward the exit.

"Wait—Nadine, wait!" Josie stood perplexed in the hallway. "Aren't you going to get your things?"

"Nope," said Nadine. "I have my bag. They own everything anyway, it wouldn't be fair." She turned back, ready to trudge to the door.

"Wait—" said Josie weakly. "Wait."

"What for?"

"I—"

"Forget it, Josie. Just forget it. I'll see you around. It's a small town, remember?" Nadine smiled and walked to the glass door at the end of the hallway, a door where the afternoon sun shone through blurred streaks.

Josie stood for a second, and hearing the door to Wallace's click, and unwilling to have another confrontation with Priscilla, she hurried to her office. Her mind recited a list of to-do's even as she moved feverishly: E-mail client list to herself, then delete it. E-mail coverages to herself, copy development files, e-mail telephone numbers to herself, *Bear* script is at home—thank God. She threw heaps of files into a shopping bag she had in her bottom drawer. A picture of Mike and her, hiking in Telluride, glared up at her as she rifled through the manila files and white pieces of paper on her desk. She tossed in her Rolodex, her favorite pens, paper clips, and legal note pads.

Before she left, she picked up the photograph of Mike from Telluride. She tossed that into the bag too.

Chapter Eleven

When she was young, Carla assumed that the Brothers Grimm and Hans Christian Andersen not only told the truth about how someday your prince would come, but were also strict interpreters of the passage of time. How fast would Pinocchio's nose grow? In the instant he lied. How fast would it take Beauty to make her Beast a prince? In the time it would take to kiss him. And how long would it take Cinderella to transform from scullery maid to belle? One night. One small night.

When Carla had arrived in Los Angeles, she had hoped that one exchange between the sun and the moon would be enough time to transform her. But it wasn't.

To begin with, she hadn't seen David. This was because she hadn't called David, of course, and he had no idea she was even here. Carla recalled Samantha's comments about David's girlfriend, Eve. *She's wonderful. You'll love her.* Carla knew already she would not love Eve; she would hate Eve. She already hated her. Eve, the temptress; Eve, the destroyer of men; Eve, the bane of human existence. She supposed Eve was the pseudo-perfect L.A. woman, with straightened teeth and fake appendages. If Eve were a Barbie doll, Carla would rip off her head.

She wouldn't have expected David to be with a Barbie, but many years had passed, and Los Angeles had an insidious way of working its values into the ethics of even superior beings.

But this is what scared her. She hadn't admitted this to anyone, but she was falling in love with Los Angeles. So far, she loved everything about it—the driving (despite the accident with Phillip's Volvo), the weather (even though her skin was red and blotchy from her first suntanning session in Phillip's backyard), the freewheeling attitude (which came into question when the next-door neighbors called the police because Carla had been lying outside naked for the aforementioned sunburning incident). Something clicked for her, and while no major changes in her life had occurred, it seemed as if the incremental changes were having an effect.

Like last night. During an otherwise inconsequential conversation about the movie business, Samantha had unknowingly set Carla on a specific career path.

"If you want to write," Samantha had said, "what's stopping you?"

"You seem to think it's so simple," Carla snapped.

Samantha was unperturbed. "I don't care what you do. But you said you like it, and Phillip says you're talented."

"It doesn't work like that," Carla protested.

"All right," Samantha said. "Forget I said anything."

But this morning, when Carla walked on the beach, she relived the conversation. Samantha was no great intellectual, but she was eminently practical. Carla had not applied herself. She was not even sure she knew what that meant.

She strolled alongside the Pacific Ocean, walking south toward Venice. She had begun walking almost as soon as she had arrived. Every day it surprised her that more people were not out there, partaking of the sunrise, the birds, the water that seemed too vigorous not to have its own heart beating deep within. In New York, she had convinced herself that it was bourgeois to get up early and look at the sunrise; she had to force herself to rise before dawn to go and sweat with all the drones.

But here, on this coast, Carla found that she could quiet that critical voice. It was still there, pushy and thrumming, but it wasn't keeping her from doing what she wanted. She could walk to the beach from Phillip and Samantha's architecturally renowned home in the Santa Monica Gardens, and she could stride directly to the water's edge. She could walk north or south, toward Malibu or Venice; she could lie down in the sun or just walk, wherever she wanted, whenever she wanted. It was trite and predictable, but she felt as if she had reduced her philosophy of life to a Nike ad: *Just do it.*

But it worked.

Memorial Day had just passed. Carla and Samantha had gone to a spa in West Hollywood. Samantha had urged her to step on the scale, certain she had lost weight. And she was right—Carla had lost eight pounds. Samantha had also encouraged her to dye her hair dark brown and had taken her shopping at the boutiques on North Robertson Boulevard and at Barneys on Wilshire. She felt healthy, as if the weight of New York City itself were falling from her small-boned shoulders.

Over the years, Carla had convinced herself that it was okay to think and talk about herself incessantly, provided it was all negative. She used to call it her reverse narcissism. Out here on the beach, she saw now why a therapist had told her this was the same self-absorption that prevented her from truly engaging in life. It never allowed her to step outside her own mental cage, to see what else might be out there.

Carla reached the Santa Monica Pier. She touched the wooden stake with one of her fingers. The air blew sand everywhere, and the ocean swept near her feet. She turned around, and began her walk back.

A woman jogged toward her. She appeared different from the other people on the beach, who were, to varying degrees, skinny. This woman was chubby. She didn't wear the typical half-top and spandex attire of the bony people—she wore a long T-shirt and baggy sweatpants.

And she was smiling.

The woman ran slowly, in the deep sand. As she passed by Carla, she put up her right hand and said, "Hi."

Carla turned around. The woman was plodding along, and Carla saw that she waved to everyone she passed.

Carla resumed walking north and this time looked out to the ocean. She was so enthralled with the sweeping water she tried to swallow the sight of the Pacific in her eyes. She considered the friendliness of the woman who had just passed her, and without thinking, began to walk faster. And faster. Soon she was—well, if not jogging, exactly, moving more quickly.

Life was not perfect. She did not have a job, and she felt horribly guilty about accepting Phillip's handouts. She still did not know what Paulette wanted. There were an amazing number of people in Los Angeles who talked in exclamation points—"hi!" and "fabulous!" and "can't wait!" She remained, she knew, critical and too talkative. And she had not gotten up the nerve to call David.

But she had lost eight pounds and she did have some new clothes and she did walk on the beach every day because *she liked it.*

Maybe she could write. Maybe she could decide, for a minute, for an hour, that she should take herself seriously as a writer and see what happened.

When she returned to Phillip and Samantha's house, she took off her sneakers and drank the orange juice Samantha had left for her on the counter, with a note that said "Be back at lunch! Have a great morning." She then marched to Phillip's office, where she determinedly picked up the phone and dialed a number.

"David Stegner, please. Yes. That's okay. Could you please tell him Carla Trousse called? Yes. Trousse, T-R-O-U-S-S-E, rhymes with grouse, 310-888-2938. Thank you."

She hung up the phone and then congratulated herself in the mirror, happy with the way her blue eyes and red cheeks jumped out from the glass. She was going to get LASIK surgery, she decided, and she was going to get a job. And she was going to write. She didn't know what form it would take, a short story or a novel, a poem or a screenplay, but she would begin, today.

And then, when she finally did see Paulette, she would not forget to thank her. For no matter what reason Paulette had for urging Carla to come to Los Angeles, it would be dwarfed by the immensity of what Carla now believed was going to be her complete personal transformation. For this she had Paulette to thank, and whether Paulette was gracious (unlikely) or glacial (more likely), it didn't matter at all. What mattered was that Carla was already different from the woman she had been in New York, and that meant that little by little, she was becoming who she was meant to be in Los Angeles.

Chapter Twelve

Nadine Dillenberger drove to her job interview with one hand on the wheel and the other on her cell phone. She was talking to Ernie, her boyfriend of seven months, a man who loved hamburgers and wearing baseball caps, and who was a sports documentarian for one of the cable channels.

"Just be yourself, Nadine, you know that," Ernie was saying.

"I'm allowed to be nervous to you, right?"

"Of course."

"So then I'm nervous."

"He's supposed to be a jerk, if that's any consolation."

"I know."

"I heard he used the word 'humbility' in a meeting."

"Come on."

"No, really. Reed told me that he called this big agency meeting, and he started telling everyone how calm he was. Reed swears he said, 'Now that I'm older, I'm learning about humbility.'"

"That's unbelievable."

"So think of that during your interview. Humbility, Hollywood's newest ethos . . ."

They clicked off, and Nadine drove down Santa Monica Boulevard toward the studio lot. She had interviewed for three jobs since leaving Unforgettable Films, but none had worked out. She was running out of money and was determined not to use her credit cards. Ernie was always offering to pay, as if he were a big-time movie producer rather than the guy who did all the work for none of the money. But that was Ernie's Achilles' heel, and Nadine was damned if she was going to give up the kindest man she had ever met because he couldn't stand up to the assholes who paid him.

In fact, that was just another good thing about Ernie. He wasn't an asshole. He was great at what he did, he loved sports, and the people with whom he worked adored him. It was only his boss who abused him. Ernie's friends would tease him, telling him that his boss was walking on him like a bad masseuse. Nadine would have to convince him later, as he persisted in describing to her what a first-class wimp he was, that he wasn't a wimp, he was a filmmaker. A good one. She had met Ernie's boss and disliked him on sight. He was a former All-American swimmer and a retired investment banker, two distinctions that seemed to make him believe he had earned the right to be respected as a producer. Nadine did respect him for being pushy and for being politic, but she had seen the films, and she knew that without Ernie's input, they would have failed.

One day it would turn around for Ernie. Just as it would for her, perhaps even today.

Her cell rang again. JOSIE blinked on the display. Nadine opened up her phone. Her favorite feature on her cell was the "ignore" button, a tab she could press that would shunt the caller to the voicemail system as instantly as if she had ignored her in a restaurant. Nadine loved pressing "ignore," especially with someone as offensive as Josie.

Her old boss had called her almost every day since she'd been fired. Nadine hadn't spoken to her once. It wasn't that she disliked Josie—she understood her, and was typically more amused than angry. But Josie deserved to be on the bitter end of the pile for once in her life. She might even see that she shouldn't be such a bitch—that it had consequences. But even as she pressed "ignore," she knew that Josie would never, ever learn that. Josie didn't care if someone confronted her on her behavior; no matter how egregious her actions, Josie would saunter on, unaffected. She didn't care, and she liked that she didn't care.

Nadine's cell rang again, this time with a name and number she didn't recognize. P. GIBERSON blinked at her. Nadine was twenty minutes early and the lot was right in front of her. There was a long line of cars waiting to pass by the security gate. She pulled up behind a black BMW and took the call.

"Nadine?"

"Yes. Who's this?"

"It's Carla. Carla Trousse."

"Carla?" Nadine almost drove into the BMW. "Carla from New York?"

"Yes, Carla from New York. But I'm in L.A. now. Carla from L.A. What do you think?"

"I think—I think—" Nadine considered saying what she was thinking, which was *I think that you in L.A. is a complete and total disaster.* "I think that's great. Just great."

"You know I love New York. Love it. But—and I know it's a surprise—but I actually think I like it here. Yep. Assuredly. I like it here."

"What?"

"I do. I like L.A. Who'd have thought it, right?"

"Right." Nadine pulled up to the security gate. "Hold on one second, will you?" She told the guard her name and was directed to her parking spot. She drove to her assigned place while she talked. "So what brought you out here?"

"My cousin. My aunt. My roof. It's a long story. I've been here for about two months. Can you believe? I'm sorry I haven't called before now. I've been figuring things out, you know? It was hard at first, but my cousin's a peach, and I'm loving the beach and—"

Nadine remembered Carla's discourses, talks that went on and on and on. When they worked together, Nadine would literally hold a book in front of her face to give Carla the message that she wasn't interested.

"Did you say peach?" asked Nadine, as she parked her car.

"I did. Guilty as charged. It's the sun out here, I think, the sun or the people or the coffee, the coffee, thank God for coffee, if this place were caffeine-free I think I'd have to leave."

Nadine checked her watch. "Listen, Carla, I've got a meeting—"

"Right. Of course you do. I was calling for a reason." Carla hesitated.

Nadine knew she could alleviate some of the older woman's discomfort by chiming in with *Want to have dinner?* But Nadine stayed quiet. She hadn't seen Carla in more than four years, and over that time she had learned the importance of deliberate silence.

"Would you want to have dinner or lunch or something sometime? I don't have a job, and I'm still figuring things out, so I made a list of all the people I knew and—"

"Sure, Carla," said Nadine. "That would be fun. When's a good time for you?"

"I don't know," Carla paused. "I'm kind of free. Like always. I mean, I do things with Phillip and Samantha, and I'm starting yoga classes, but basically—"

"I can do Thursday night. How about eight o'clock at the Ivy?"

"Sure."

"Great."

"Where's the Ivy?"

"On Robertson. It's easy to find. You'll figure it out. It's a good first-time-in-L.A. place. Call me if you have any problems."

"Sure. Thanks." Carla still did not hang up.

"Carla?"

"Yes?"

"Are you okay?"

"Yes."

"Are you sure?"

"Yes."

"Then why aren't you hanging up the phone?"

A pause. "You've changed, Nadine. You sound much more grown up than the girl I remember from New York."

"That was four years ago. Sorry. I just have this meeting."

"Right. No problem. See you Thursday," said Carla, who this time hung up.

Nadine looked in the rearview mirror. Carla Trousse in Los Angeles. In some ways it was the perfect place for her—she read every book she could get her hands on, and she was a fine writer. She was also an impossible person, one who was adept at getting in her own way. Nadine saw Carla suddenly as she had been in their long-ago office days—a woman with strangely dyed hair and stranger tie-dyed shirts. She could be pretty if she'd stop dressing in what she thought of as "quirky" attire and pay attention to her shockingly beautiful blue eyes and fair skin. Carla used to talk about her mother and her aunt all the time, alternately proud and disgusted by them. Nadine had not liked the sound of them—righteous women who had obviously seen Carla's neediness but not her intellect. On her more sympathetic days, Nadine had felt sorry for Carla, unappreciated even in her own family.

Nadine's family was different—they supported her wholeheartedly, even if they had no idea what she did. Her father ran a restaurant in Ohio, and her mother did all the cooking. Neat and simple, no hysterics, no drama. Nadine had loved movies since she was a kid, and never even contemplated trying to get a job in another field.

She had worn her best black skirt and pulled her long hair into a ponytail in the back of her neck. She wasn't a hipster and she wasn't a waif. She looked like what she was—a healthy German girl from Ohio.

But she was passionate about movies. And if Mr. Humbility, aka Roland Starr, could get beyond himself for a couple of minutes, maybe he'd see that and hire her, knowing that for the time being, she could work tirelessly for him, and he could take all of the credit.

Chapter Thirteen

Josie lied to everyone. "I'm fine," she told Catherine Von Hauptman. "Fabulous," she said to Nell McKnight. "Superb," she said to Rebecca.

She was not a victim. She was not a crier. And now—even though she was alone in an apartment in Beverly Hills, an apartment with one couch and three emptied bags of microwave popcorn arrayed on the floor, jobless and husbandless—she would not let herself be childish. Sometimes, at night, she missed Mike so much she hugged her pillow like a little girl. But in the morning, she'd erase that memory, certain it was the fault of an errant strain of sentimentality that sometimes reared its ridiculous head. Rebecca had given her an update on Mike's condition. His prognosis was excellent. The doctors had removed the cancerous testicle and expected Mike to make a full recovery. Josie waited for Rebecca to tell her that Mike missed her, or that he hated her, or that he wanted to talk to her. But Rebecca hadn't said anything, and finally Josie had asked.

"What did Mike say about me?"

"Nothing," answered Rebecca.

"Nothing?"

"Not a word," said Rebecca. "It's better that way, right? He's getting over you cleanly, just as you said you wanted."

"I miss him," she had admitted to Rebecca. "I really do."

Rebecca's lips pursed into a smirk. "Don't pretend, Josie. I know you hate people who wallow in sentimentality. You're hurt he didn't ask about you, but you don't miss him. Don't confuse the two."

Rebecca was right. Josie detested displays of emotion—her father often joked that if he and her mother died suddenly in a car crash, Josie would arrange the perfect funeral, wear a designer black suit, and cry exactly one tear that would not ruin her makeup. Josie had wittily (she thought) told her father she would wear waterproof mascara. But of late Josie wondered why she couldn't shake an overall feeling of dread. She would rectify everything. It was just a matter of time.

When her doorbell rang, Josie was sitting on the couch, reading the *National Enquirer.*

She sprung up, alarmed. No one dropped in to visit in Los Angeles. Moreover, no one knew she was home. She went to the intercom.

"Yes?" she called through the intercom, as she conjured up visions of killers dressed as deliverymen. "Yes?"

"Is this Josephine O'Leary?" It must be a florist, she thought. It sounded like a florist. Someone was sending her flowers. Henry Antonelli was finally sending her flowers, apology flowers, for taking so long to return her phone call! Finally!

"Yes," she answered, sure the glee was seeping through the intercom. "Leave them at the door and I'll be right down."

"Leave what?" queried the voice. "What are you talking about?"

"You're a florist?" she asked.

"No," said the man's voice. "Hey, Josie. Open up. It's Joshua King."

Josie took her finger from the buzzer. Joshua King, the screenwriter of *The Bear That Saved Christmas.* The dog-walker from Miami. What was he doing in Los Angeles?

The last time they had spoken Josie had offered him three thousand dollars to option his screenplay. He had almost leaped through the phone—*You're not kidding? You're telling me the truth? Option, you want to option this? You want to option this? Wait'll I tell my mom. My friends. You're not kidding me, are you?*—and Josie had felt like a queen, benevolent and virtuous.

But now Joshua was on her doorstep. She no longer had the job with Wallace Pickering, a name she had freely dropped in their telephone conversation. She looked out her window to the sun shining on the rich green of the eucalyptus tree leaves. Did he know she was fired?

He buzzed again. Josie pressed LISTEN.

"Did you hear me?" Joshua yelled. "Did you hear me? Because I flew in today—"

"You what?"

"I flew in today. To see you," Joshua said decisively. "I'm waiting."

"You can't come in." Joshua King might be a crazed lunatic. Josie looked around the apartment for a suitable weapon, in case he persisted and she was forced to defend herself. She didn't worry much about security—Beverly Hills was safer than Fort Knox—but a stranger appearing on the doorstep of her home terrified her. She had seen *Clockwork Orange*.

The doorbell rang again.

"Joshua, if you want to make an appointment, please call . . ." her voice trailed off as she remembered she no longer had an office.

Luckily, Joshua had not listened. "Aw, come on, Josie, I flew all the way here from Miami. I'm beat."

"That's your problem."

"Josie—please! Look, I'm just going to wait here, downstairs. In public. Just come down and talk to me, then, if you're scared."

"You can't just show up at someone's home," Josie insisted.

"I just did," retorted Joshua.

"Obviously."

"Josie, I did this to show you how much this means to me. I had to wait till school was over, and I took the first plane I could. Please, just have coffee with me."

"I can't."

"Why?"

"I just can't."

"There's a Starbucks down the street. I just walked by it."

"You walked here?"

"Not all the way. I took a cab from the airport, but I wanted to walk around a little to get my bearings. We can walk there."

"No we can't," said Josie.

"C'mon, Josie," Joshua pleaded.

Josie hesitated. "One second," she said. She left her apartment and walked down the carpeted hallway to the apartment of the only other tenant she had met, a screenwriter named Casey Cortellessa.

"What?" Casey asked, pulling open her door. She glared at Josie. Josie hadn't read Casey's script, *Life Is Not a Pizza*.

"There a guy downstairs who I'm going to let in, but I was hoping you'd just keep an eye or ear out for me, in case he's a criminal."

"So don't let him in."

"I have to. He's a client."

"A writer?"

"Yes."

"Fuck you, Josie," said Casey, and stepped back into her apartment.

"Casey—wait." Josie's voice stopped her from shutting the door completely. "Here's what I haven't told you yet—it's too early, and I didn't want to raise your hopes. But I read your script over the weekend, and now it's sitting on Priscilla's desk. I told Wallace and Priscilla it was the best thing I'd read in years." She paused, building to her brilliant finale. "You're such a good writer Casey. I'm so impressed."

Casey had opened the door again, maintaining her expression of chilled stone. But she couldn't hold it—when Josie said she was impressed, Casey's lips broke apart into a huge, gratified smile.

"You are?"

Josie nodded.

"Okay, I'll keep an eye out. Who knows—you could get lucky. He may be cute."

Back in her apartment, Josie looked at herself in the hallway mirror as she buzzed Joshua inside the building.

Seth Levin used to tell her that the "talent" were like game pieces. *At the end of the day, Josie, we're the ones who are left. We're the ones making the deals, putting the movies together. Think about it. Ryan O'Neal was as big as Tobey Maguire is now—and today's kids don't even know who he is. You couldn't name even one writer from the seventies, the eighties. They can have their moment in the sun, but you know, they need us, not the other way around. Sure, I go along with them, let them think they're the necessary ones. But I've been here for thirty years. Which one of them can say that?*

Joshua needed Josie. It didn't matter if she had a job—what mattered was that Joshua thought Josie could get the movie made.

Josie could see the elevator bank far away at the end of the hall, and heard the lift stop at her floor. The doors opened, and Joshua emerged. The hallways converged at the elevators at right angles, and the minute Joshua spent orienting himself toward Josie's apartment allowed her to inspect him, as if seeing him through a telescope.

He was tall. Tall and sloppy, a baseball hat and Teva sandals, wide shoulders and straight hair that stood out from his balding scalp as he walked. He wore wrinkled khaki shorts and a bright blue T-shirt.

She kept her eye on the peephole and watched him so intently that she didn't have time to pull away when Joshua bent down in front of the peephole and stared back at her.

"I knew you'd be doing that," he said through the door. "Whattya think?"

Josie opened the door. Joshua King, six feet six inches tall, stood in front of her. He took off his baseball hat (Florida Marlins) and gave a facsimile of a royal bow to her.

"Joshua King," he said. When he rose to his full height, she was startled by the warmth of his smile. His eyes were deep-set and wide apart in his face; they were the color of his shirt, a kind of blue found in Italian pottery. He had about three days' growth of beard. Sunburnt, his skin was white around his small eyes. He was young, in his mid-twenties. And his arms were strong.

"I've been thinking about who should play the lead, like, what do you think about Michael Douglas . . ."

Josie moved aside as Joshua entered. She was processing his appearance because she saw immediately that there was something askew. When he turned back to face her, she realized what was wrong. His head was too small for his body; he had the delicately constructed face of a small boy atop a behemoth body. He was like a good-looking brontosaurus.

"What?" he asked.

"Nothing," she replied. "I'm just thinking about what you said."

"I'm not messing around," he said.

"Hold on one second," she said. She walked out of her apartment and back to Casey's. Casey was standing there, one slim leg and one strand of blonde hair visible from Josie's.

"He's okay," Josie said.

"I know. I saw the shoulders."

"So thanks."

"Not a bad stalker to have," said Casey, as she shut her door.

When Josie reentered her apartment, she heard Joshua in her kitchen. "Josie?" Joshua called. "I wasn't sure what to bring." Joshua kept talking from the kitchen. "But I'm in California. So I brought some blueberries, almonds. And brussels sprouts." She walked into the kitchen. He was unpacking a bag of groceries she hadn't even noticed he was carrying. "I don't like to come without a gift. And I don't know you, so I had to guess."

"Right," she said, nonplussed. "Could you come in here, please?" Josie walked to her living room. Joshua followed her.

"Just moved?" he asked.

"Yes," she said. She motioned to the couch. "Sit there."

"That's kind of rude, right?" Joshua answered. "Where are you going to sit?"

"I'm fine," Josie said. Joshua sat down and then reached over to the floor to pick up the partly hidden tabloid. He looked back at her, approving.

"Well," he said.

Josie took it from him. "I read it for work," she said.

"Right." He sat back, quiet.

"So what are you—"

"I know this is unorthodox," he began, "but I figured I should just show up. You liked my work, I liked the way you sounded, so I flew on instinct."

"But—"

"I was going to call, but I thought it would be more impetuous—daring—if I just showed up."

"What if I wasn't here?"

"I took a shot. Anyway, I was always going to come out here, I told you that."

"No. No, actually, you didn't."

"Well, I had to finish school. Last year, you know?"

"You're in school?"

"Don't you listen? I know, you're probably doing a million things. Last year of law school, University of Miami."

Josie stood in front of Joshua, uncomfortable. "I know you didn't tell me anything about law school." But she was not sure.

"Whatever. I just figured, why wait?"

"Wait for what?"

"Wait for anything. It's the work that's important. And most of all," he paused, "I wanted to meet you."

"Terrific. I wanted to meet you too. But not like this. We don't even have an agreement in place."

"Yeah, that'll happen, but why should creative people like us wait for the robots to do the paperwork?" Joshua crouched forward, as if to sprint into Josie's arms. Energy clenched and unclenched in his skull; veins defined themselves like gopher's tunnels in his forehead.

"Let's stop a minute. I don't appreciate you showing up here, uninvited. It isn't impetuous. It's rude."

Joshua raked his eyes over her. "Sorry," he said.

She was flattered, but cast her eyes downward so Joshua couldn't tell. Someone knocked on her door.

"This never happens," she said to Joshua, walking to the door. "Who is it?"

"It's Casey." Josie opened the door a crack.

"I told you I was okay," she said. Casey poked her head through.

"You sure?"

"I'm fine."

"Who is it?" asked Joshua.

"Who is it?" Josie echoed. "Why do you—it's my neighbor." Casey pushed open the door.

"Hi," Casey said. "I'm the neighbor." Casey was about five feet five and had a perfect, Halle Berry–like body. Josie, the perfectionist, found Casey a bit déclassé. But judging from Joshua's reaction (as well as the mailman and the apartment supervisor and the man who lived in 4E), Casey was stunning.

"I'm the stalker," said Joshua.

"Nice to meet you," Casey said, walking over to him. The two shook hands. Josie remained near the door. Casey sat next to Joshua on the couch. Josie had the sensation that she was the uninvited guest, the third wheel.

"Casey?"

"What?"

"I'm meeting with Joshua."

Joshua sat back, spread his arms on the back of the couch. His head looked even smaller this way, perched like a little boy in a big man's outfit.

"She's optioning my script," said Joshua. "Called me herself, raved about it, and now she's going to buy it."

"She's what?" Casey asked.

"She's optioning my script. You love it, right Josie?"

Josie saw Casey's eyes flicker. "Yes. I am optioning his script."

"Right," said Casey, whose eyes left Josie's as she glanced about the room. Joshua wore a trace of a smile, and Josie was instantly peeved, as if he had seen her undressed.

"Casey, would you mind leaving?" asked Josie.

"Leave?" Casey stood.

"Yes," said Josie. "I'd prefer for you to not be here." There was a moment in law school when Josie had absorbed the crushing power of stating exactly what she wanted. It had been uncomfortable at first to storm into the confrontation, loudly asserting her position, but that had gone away when she realized how effective this strategy could be.

"Please go, Casey," Josie repeated.

Casey stood up. "Fine," she said. She stood up, alert to Joshua's appraisal. She turned back to him. "Knock on your way out," she said. "I'm a writer too."

Joshua nodded at Casey. Then he sat back in the couch, pulling a square of white gum in aluminum wrapping from his pocket. His eyes were close to the line of his brow. His lips had stretched into a smile, without any show of teeth.

But as Josie watched Joshua, she was not paying attention to Casey, whose blue eyes were scanning Josie's apartment. Josie caught the problem too late.

"You liar," Casey muttered, as she walked over to a stack of screenplays. She extracted one from the pile. "Did you make a copy of mine, because this looks like the one I gave you."

Casey wore a tank shirt, and Josie concentrated on the composition of Casey's skeleton—she was so taut that her arms were like white stalks of bone, fitting perfectly into the bulb at the top of her shoulders.

"I can't believe you," Casey said. She clutched her screenplay close to her chest. "You fucking liar."

"Casey—" Josie began.

"You just lied to my face. I bet Wallace hasn't read a thing, has he?"

Casey turned to Joshua. "Hollywood 101. Don't trust anyone. If I were you, I'd make sure that option agreement was reviewed by the Supreme Court." She looked back at Josie. "I can't believe I fell for it." She turned again to Joshua. "Make sure you stop by after you leave this viper's den. I have lots of stories to tell." She left, slamming the door.

"Nice girl," Joshua said, after Casey's exit. "Is she any good?"

"Good at what?"

"Is she any good? She said she's a writer. You're a producer. Kind of perfect access if she's good, and if you're good, for that matter."

"I don't know," Josie admitted.

"It's like one of those E! stories. Two hot women, living next door to each other in L.A., one writes, the other produces, and the rest is history. See it on *Entertainment Tonight,* live at eleven."

"You've read too many fairy tales," Josie answered. "It doesn't work that way."

"Aw, don't go dashing my hopes. I'm expecting everything, I'm too smart not to have it all happen." He paused. "You're welcome to come with me." He reclined fully onto Josie's couch. "What's her script about?" he asked.

"Whose?"

"Your next-door neighbor's."

"I don't know. You're trying to change the subject. The fact that I don't know is a case in point. You're lucky I even read your script. Not for you, but for Seth."

"Who's Seth?"

"Seth is Marcus's lawyer."

"You know Marcus?"

"No."

"You should. Great guy. One thing you gotta know, his career comes first. Nothing would get in his way. He'll sell out anyone, do anything, for his career, for his ambition."

"How would you know this?"

"We're friends."

"You walk his dog."

"Dogs. Plural. You know how to hurt a man when he's down, don't you? You sure you don't want to sit here?"

"I'm sure," Josie answered. She remained standing.

"So tell me. What do I do?"

"About what?" Josie asked.

"The script. How does it become a movie?"

"It doesn't work like that."

"Josie. This isn't brain surgery. A script is written, a script is produced, it happens all the time."

"Not just like that."

"Of course just like that. You surprise me. I'd have thought you'd have gotten this moving already." Joshua looked toward the kitchen and coughed. "Could I have some water?" He put his elbows on his knees. "Okay. I'll get it. Want any?" Joshua then stood and traipsed to her kitchen. "I'll find the glasses, I'm great at other people's kitchens. Glasses over the sink, almost always—and yes, ladies and gentlemen, here they are. So what do you think of the budget? Probably not more than ten million." Joshua stepped back into the living room, and offered Josie her glass.

"And listen, don't get nervous, but I think I could direct it."

Josie snorted. Up to now, Joshua had been unpredictable, and therefore of interest. With his latest pronouncement, akin to a young boy saying he wanted to be president, Joshua became—in an instant—mediocre. "Of course you could," she said. "In fact, you may get an Oscar nomination on your first try."

"I know you're laughing, but I'm not joking."

"I'm sure."

"I'm a director," Joshua said.

"Good," Josie replied. "Good for you."

Joshua leaned back in the sofa. "Listen. About my script," Joshua began. "I think—"

All of the irritation Josie had stored for the past month blew through its restraints and pointed straight at Joshua.

"Yes, the ten-million-dollar script that you think someone should not only buy but invest all that money in with you at the helm. That script." Josie felt blades turn, cutting into Joshua's hubris, and was suddenly very pleased with herself. "The script that one person in town read because you're a friend, no, a dog-walker of a famous person, and the script that you think entitles you to a full-fledged Hollywood career, do not pass go, do not put in your drudge time, leapfrog over all the stupid people, and go right to the top." Josie went to her piles of scripts. She pulled out *The Bear That Saved Christmas.* "Here," she said. "Take it. Good luck."

Joshua didn't move. Josie held out the script. "Really, take it. I have no claim on it."

Josie remembered the idea of the story and suffered a lapse of confidence. But if she were going to continue with this project, she needed to crush Joshua King at this moment. Crush his fantasies, his delusions, his confidence.

"What makes you think I'm just starting out?" Joshua asked. "Why do you think I don't know anything?"

"I don't know what you know or don't know. I don't think about you at all," said Josie. She felt as if she were in an athletic bout, a match she needed not just to win, but to win convincingly, without any potential for doubt. Suddenly her ownership of this material, and dominance over Joshua, were more important to her than life itself.

"I'm asking for your help," Joshua put his hands under his chin, knuckles clenched, his face studious and pleading. "You can think what you want about me. I don't care. But I know you liked what I wrote, and I know you want—wanted—to work with me. I'm here, and ready to work. Right now. This second."

"I said it doesn't work that way."

"You're angry because I'm not listening to some arbitrary set of rules? This is Hollywood. This place survives on breaking rules."

"That's where you're wrong—so wrong. You need to play the—" Josie stopped. She still held on to the script because Joshua had never taken it from her. On the couch, Joshua closed his eyes. When he spoke it was with a different tone, the voice of a resigned lawyer unhappy he's been pushed to say exactly what he thinks.

"Listen, let's just talk about this later. We'll agree to disagree on my arriving today."

"You can't tell me—"

"And then, if we continue to disagree, no hard feelings, but I'm going wide with it."

"Going wide?" He was from Miami, how did he know Hollywood terms? Joshua now stood up and looked down on Josie. He was so tall she pushed her head back, as if she were staring at a burning cloud. Joshua looked back at her, and she felt small. She had—perhaps—played this entirely wrong.

"My mom worked in films, about twenty years ago. Moira MacDougal. She had a couple of movies under her belt before she got married and moved to South Beach. I know a little something about the business." His voice changed to a place where his charm stiffened into strength.

"Like I said, take it."

"I won't have to do that if you will just do what you said you were going to," Joshua answered. "And anyway, I had hoped—I had wanted for us to work on it together. That's my first choice."

"You don't even know me," she said.

"Yeah, but you called. You want to option it. That means you want it, no matter what you're saying to me right now. Who are we kidding? It's like dating. I see a girl I want to date, I call. If I'm not interested, I don't. But if I do go to the trouble—if I do pick up the phone—then it means only one thing. Interest. So don't pretend. I was so excited when you called me. Let's make it work." He stretched out his hands, splaying his fingers. "I'm here to do your bidding."

"Have you given any thought to what you will do if I'm not ordering you around?" Josie asked.

Joshua chuckled. "Well, Mrs. O'Leary, I've done some checking too. And I haven't lived in Miami all my life. A bunch of friends moved here after college. Nicole Jexson? She works at Disney. Or Armond Fellman? I forgot where he works. Anyway, I can hang out with them."

"You know Armond Fellman?" Josie asked.

"Yeah, sure," he said. "He dated my cousin. And Eddie Cleveland's a buddy of mine."

Josie inhaled quietly. "Funny, but if you know Eddie Cleveland, than I don't see why you need me."

"You like my script," he said instantly.

"Eddie didn't?" Eddie Cleveland must have turned it down—passed, in Hollywood lingo. A wave of fear struck Josie—was she wrong about *The Bear?*

"He never read it." Joshua picked at his fingernails. "I didn't send it, because I don't think it's cool to trade on friendships like that. Right? You get what I mean?"

"It's cooler to show up unannounced on someone's doorstep?" But as she spoke, Josie wondered if Joshua was telling the truth.

"Yeah, absolutely," Joshua replied. He looked at her, and she felt uncomfortable suddenly, as if she were the one who had intruded on his apartment. He continued. "You are a risk, but a calculated one. I give Eddie the script, he hates it, then we have a weird thing in our relationship. You and I don't know each other, so if something goes wrong, well, there's nothing really to ruin, so—" Joshua clapped his hands. "Over and done with, and moving onward, et cetera et cetera." He stopped, and then smiled. "Plus you loved it, you know you did."

"I thought there was a good idea, somewhere, amid writing that needs a lot of attention."

"A lot of attention," Joshua repeated. "You don't like the writing?"

"I didn't say that—"

"So you do?"

"I didn't say that either."

"I think the script kind of rocks the way it is."

"I'm not surprised."

Josie held on to the script as she stared at Joshua. He moved toward the door. "Where are you going?" she asked.

"I don't know. Armond's maybe."

"How are you going to get there?"

"How far is it to—" he checked the piece of paper he had in his pocket, "4375 Skylark?"

"You can't walk."

"I swear to God, I hate this place." He picked up his bag. "I only turn on my cell between six and eight at night, and ten and twelve in the morning, so call then if you want to talk to me. Otherwise, leave a message."

"Why only certain hours?

"I don't want to get brain cancer." Joshua was at her door. He turned. "You know, I think we're going to have a great working relationship."

"We don't have any relationship," Josie said. "Not yet."

"Details, details," Joshua said. "We've got a script, and that's ninety-nine percent of it." And he closed Josie's door behind him.

Ninety-nine percent of it. The product was the blood, yes, but without any other flesh it meant nothing, a useless pool of fluid.

After her door closed, Josie felt a gust of loneliness. Joshua had filled her empty apartment with energy—and she found herself adrift with him gone.

She peered through the peephole in her door. She saw Joshua standing in front of Casey's apartment door. The door opened and she saw one of Casey's long legs stepping out over the threshold.

How long had Joshua been thinking about meeting up with Casey? During their entire conversation? Was she not as attractive as

Casey? And then—another fear. Had Josie missed an opportunity when she hadn't read Casey's script? And then—would Joshua and Casey begin an affair, a physical relationship, under her nose, so she would be confronted by them every time she entered and left her apartment?

Josie knew Casey would be smiling, and remembered Mike telling her that any man worth anything valued a woman's smile above all else, more than breasts, more than legs, more than sex appeal and intelligence and humor. A smile, Mike had told her, could open the door to a man's heart so widely that it could break off as lightly as a twig, leaving behind a man eager to embrace all that the smile had to offer, grace and honesty and care.

She watched as Casey's door closed. She was flustered, sweating under her arms, in between her breasts. What afflicted Josie was a sudden desperation—the fear that what she held were stems and pieces of a whole she was not capable of seeing. The people in Hollywood moved fast, and Joshua would not wait for Josie to get back onto her proverbial feet. She had to be equally fast. She would get the option contracts drawn up immediately, and get Joshua his check. And then she'd do whatever it was producers did to get a movie made.

She stopped to consider her reflection in the mirror. She was smarter than most people—she was certainly smarter than most people in Hollywood. She thought of her father. "You're my girl!" he had exclaimed when she told him that Mike refused to talk to her. "Just remember that. He's going through a difficult time. But that has to do with him, not you. You're my masterpiece, sweetheart, you can do anything. Are you listening, Josie?"

Josie had grinned. Ever since she was a girl, her father had given her the same encouragement. "No one's better than you, sweetheart. You're better than all of them. Got that? I can't hear you . . ."

"I got it, Dad," Josie had replied. "I got it."

The phone rang. It had to be Rebecca, finally returning her call.

Josie couldn't wait to tell her about Joshua. She found the telephone nestled in between Joshua's blueberries and brussels sprouts.

"Hello?" Josie said, only slightly out of breath.

"Hello?" It was Henry Antonelli.

Josie recognized the voice immediately. She leaned against the counter, happy that he could not see her relief.

"Well," she said. "Finally . . ."

Chapter Fourteen

The traffic light at the intersection of North Robertson and Alden was taking an eternity to change. Carla wanted to be early for dinner with Nadine, since she had looked up the Ivy on Robertson in *Zagat's* and discovered it was one of Hollywood's most celebrated restaurants, both in terms of quality of clientele and quality of desserts. She saw the white picket fence lining the perimeter of the cottage-like restaurant, and watched the black Mercedes pull up by the curb. It thrilled her, that she was here, in the thick of things, with L.A.'s best and brightest.

But once she had handed over her car to the valet parkers in front of the Ivy, she moved more slowly, reconsidering her clothing choices: a flame-red blouse, a black skirt with red stripes, a red Fendi bag, (courtesy of Samantha) and red Converse sneakers. At the house, Carla thought she had achieved the perfect look—passionate and youthful, with a touch of whimsy. But now, emerging from the car, she hesitated. The other women were dressed in sleek, low-slung pants that hung on hipbones like towels on hooks. Presumably they ate here, at the Ivy, where some of the best food in town was reputed to be served, yet these women had no flesh on them. Did they not eat? Did they just smoke? She no longer thought she looked festive or whimsical. She thought she looked fat.

She walked up the brick steps and was told by the hostess she would have to wait until Nadine arrived to be seated. She ordered a glass of wine and looked around the restaurant. It was brimming with people, glossy-haired, casually dressed, talkative people. She heard scraps of conversation: *you have to give me something better to work with* and *can you believe she got billing above the title?*

Carla had written for two hours this morning, completing a short story about a middle-aged railroad station manager from Wilmington and a teenaged passenger. It was far from perfect, but she was pleased that her main character wasn't some facsimile of herself. That afternoon, when Carla had finished her story, she had felt confident, assured. Now she wondered if her story was any good at all.

She looked around the patio, focusing on the long brown curls of a particularly petite man, a man who was surrounded by smiling people and who looked, to Carla, like a male version of Shirley Temple. But then a commotion started—a commotion of nudges and stares. Along with everyone else, Carla looked toward the hostess stand.

Standing there, alone, was Henry Antonelli.

Henry Antonelli the movie star. Henry Antonelli, Carla's proclaimed hack. And Henry Antonelli, Aunt Paulette's erstwhile consort. She didn't pause to think as she leaped toward him.

"Hi," Carla said to Henry Antonelli, extending her hand.

"Hi," Henry repeated.

"I'm Carla," she continued. "Carla Trousse. I know you. I mean, everyone here knows you, but I, I mean, my aunt, knows you. Paulette. Paulette Giberson. She's a diplomat. You know."

"Nice to meet you," he said, uncomfortably. Henry believed wholeheartedly that since the public was responsible for his success, it was incumbent upon him to treat the public with great respect. Still, he was nervous about this dinner already, and he wanted just to be seated. He looked toward the hostess for support.

"I've never approached a movie star before," Carla continued. "Actually, I rarely talk to anyone new. Well, that's not true either. I just moved here from New York. Because of Paulette, actually." She spoke hurriedly, wanting to let him know she was not just another autograph seeker, a celebrity hanger-on.

Henry appraised Carla, and she saw his wrinkles, the rush of blood under his thin reddish cheeks. "Paulette? Really?" Henry released his hand from Carla's. "She's coming down here—just called me, a couple weeks ago."

"I know," Carla beamed.

Henry stared back at her. "Well," he started, "perhaps I'd better—"

"Do you know my cousin—Paulette's son, Phillip Giberson? You probably do. Everyone knows everyone out here, it seems. He works at Studio X. For a long time now. He's been out here for years, since Dartmouth."

"Nope," Henry shook his head. "I didn't even know she had a son."

"I think she forgets herself sometimes," Carla replied quickly, and then regretted it. She didn't want to disparage her aunt in public. "She's very busy."

"I remember. She was like that when I knew—"

"Mr. Antonelli?" asked the hostess. "Your table's ready. And your lawyer's tracked you down." She gestured toward a telephone.

"Duty calls," smiled Henry, as he nodded at Carla. "Good to meet you." He began to follow the hostess, but then turned to Carla once more. "Please tell Paulette that my wife and I look forward to seeing her."

"I will," said Carla. "But—" She didn't want him to leave. The fact that they could talk about Paulette made him accessible, and she liked that he was friendly. She had expected him to be a jerk.

Henry disappeared into the back room. Carla stayed near the archway. She suddenly felt the weight of eyes upon her. A waitress smiled sweetly at her as she balanced a tray on her elbow. A skinny woman with a long face and jutting jaw glared at her. The Shirley Temple man nodded. Carla walked back to where she had been standing, aware that people's eyes were trailing her body. She wished she were not wearing the red Converses.

"Carla?" exclaimed a woman loudly. Carla turned. "Carla?"

It was Nadine Dillenberger, rushing to hug her. Carla was smothered under bright colors and swinging hair. "You know Henry Antonelli?" Nadine was kissing her on the cheek as she spoke. "Is he as nice as they say? I can't believe you know him. I just can't. Wow. And look at you." Nadine took a step backward. "I love the hair."

"Thanks," Carla said. "I forgot I had changed it."

"So how do you know him?" asked Nadine.

"He used to date my aunt, apparently. Remember Paulette? The one who saves the world when she isn't emotionally destroying her children?"

"I remember," said Nadine, shaking her head emphatically. "Proves my point. Men like cruel women. Always have, always will." Nadine grinned. "Still. Henry Antonelli. That's very cool."

"I hardly talked to him."

"Right, but you did."

"This town is making me nutty." Carla gestured to a free corner in the vestibule. "Let's go over there till our table's ready."

When Nadine stood next to her, Carla studied the younger woman. She had remembered Nadine as an overeager, continually smiling youth who had eternally impressed Carla when she had announced that she was following her dream and moving to Los Angeles. Carla had smiled with all the other skeptical adults, thinking that hope in youth was like ice cream, fresh if consumed, otherwise a messy, unfulfilling disappointment. But now, here she was, obviously thriving.

"Carla!" Nadine gave an appraising look. "My God. You look great."

"Thanks," said Carla. "You too."

"I'm serious, you look amazing." Nadine assessed the restaurant. "This is a great place, one that serves real food."

"Not that anyone eats it," Carla said.

"I do," said Nadine, and Carla saw she was telling the truth. On Nadine the extra pounds seemed correct—she was as fresh-faced as she had been in New York, and she looked exactly the way Carla pictured the old-fashioned Swedes in Sinclair Lewis novels.

"This business is like high school," Nadine commented. "A high school where no one graduates. I bet everyone here is in the business." She stopped and looked up at Carla. "So. California . . . ?"

"California," repeated Carla. "The verdict is in. I like it."

"More than New York?"

"I don't know. Maybe." Carla glanced around the restaurant. "So far, so good. I'm still getting used to waiting at traffic lights and not jaywalking, but otherwise, this has been a great change for me." Carla took a deep breath. "It scares me. You know the saying that the older you get the less you know? That's what I feel like. Five years ago I'd have never let myself come here. But who knows? I may grow to hate it within a month. I've got a cushy setup—my cousin pays for everything and tells me I don't have to rush to get a job. And I didn't leave anything spectacular in New York, except for a collapsed roof."

Nadine chuckled. "That's an exaggeration, I hope?"

Carla shook her head. "No exaggeration. It collapsed during a rainstorm. Would make a great movie scene. Woman thinks someone is breaking and entering as the ceiling falls in. She begins to cackle maniacally and then heads to Los Angeles on the next plane."

"Is that what you did?"

"Yes," said Carla. "And now I like it. You have no idea what it does to a person to find out that a belief they hold as an absolute truth is absolutely wrong."

"Out here," replied Nadine, leaning back against the wall, candlelight illuminating her cheeks, "as I'm sure you've noticed—it's very trendy to put down L.A. and talk about how great everything is in Manhattan. Everything about New York becomes great—the cold weather becomes a mark of resilience, the nasty people become evidence of personality, the people in New York are all smarter, better, more sophisticated. Blah blah blah. I've thought a lot about it. And you're hearing this from the horse's mouth—I love everything about L.A."

"Even earthquakes?"

"Well," Nadine said, pursing her lips. "I've thought about that too.

First of all, even if you die, at least you've died in a momentous natural disaster. And second, if you don't die, then you've lived through a natural disaster. Either way, you win."

"One way, you're dead."

"Well, there is that, of course."

The hostess informed them their table was ready. They were seated outside, on the brick patio, cars moving by on Robertson. "So," said Carla.

"So," echoed Nadine.

"So what are you doing? Are you in the business like everyone else?"

"Well," Nadine took a sip from her glass, "today was something. Today I got a job. I just got the call this afternoon."

Carla attempted to ward off the envy that instantly swept through her—she insisted to herself that she was happy Nadine got a job. Happy happy happy.

"I'll be doing development again, but this time for a company on a studio lot. I don't like the head guy—he's a starfucker, glommed on to a movie star and now can do what he wants—but some of the people working there are pretty respectable."

"Who's the movie star?" asked Carla.

"You know. Mr. Action himself, Kirk Gordon. Actually, I've heard he's an okay guy, he's just never around. The starfucker—Roland Starr—is the one who's always there, playing chess with the other power brokers in town."

"Sounds very Machiavellian," commented Carla.

"You have no idea," responded Nadine. "One way of looking at this entire business is to believe everyone, and I mean everyone, the waitress, the patron over there, the man with the thing in his nose, is out to screw you."

"Lovely," said Carla. "Are you screwing them back?"

The waitress overheard Carla's remark as she arrived to take their orders. Nadine didn't answer until the waitress left. "No, not yet. Never say never, though. Anyway, they promised me that I'd meet with writers, and that if I brought anything in myself, I'd get a bonus, and maybe a promotion."

"Amazing," Carla said. "But what do you do, exactly?"

"I'm in development," answered Nadine.

"Me too," said Carla. "A constant state of development: emotional, physical, and mental."

"Exactly," said Nadine. "Exactly. 'Develop' is actually the right word. We get material and we make it better, hopefully.

"For example, I just found out we're doing a remake of *Sister Carrie*. Now that could get totally messed up, as you know. But if it's good . . . and if I get to work on it . . ." Nadine's face brightened.

"*Sister Carrie?*" Carla paused. "Please, Nadine, please. Don't ruin that book."

Nadine cocked her head. "Good to know. I'll make sure I tell those people who are determined to ruin the book to stop."

"That's not what I meant."

"No one wants to make a bad movie, Carla. Think about it. It isn't like someone sits around and says 'I want to make the worst movie ever.' Even the people who make the worst stuff—no one wanted that to happen."

"I just don't want them to ruin one of my favorite books."

"Mine too. But 'them' is 'me,'" said Nadine. She pulled a paper-sized bound script from her large bag. "Here. Read this."

Carla opened the front cover. *Sister Carrie*, based on the novel by Theodore Dreiser.

"I'm a Dreiser addict," admitted Carla. She put the script down. "This is what you do? Read?"

"The best job in the world," Nadine replied. "I read scripts all the time. Most of them are terrible. But some are amazing—it's just like reading a good book. And you get to read everything. Like with *Sister Carrie*, I'll get to reread the book. The guy told me today they're also planning to do something about William the Conqueror, so I think if I want to, I can do the research."

"Right," murmured Carla. "Who knew?"

"Who knew what?" asked Nadine.

"Who knew that there were jobs where you could read what you wanted to and get paid for it," said Carla.

"That's the secret," said Nadine. "People who grow up out here know. Otherwise, you're outta luck."

"You figured it out."

"I'm very smart."

Carla smiled. "Yes," said Carla. "You are." They looked at each other for a long moment. Nadine waited for Carla to launch into one of her run-on soliloquies, telling herself that this time she'd be very polite to Carla as she droned on. But Carla was quiet, drinking sips from her wine and tearing off a piece of bread from the loaf in the basket on the table.

"So. What are your plans? How's—Oh my God. Oh my God," Nadine repeated, her eyes focused on something behind Carla's back.

"What? What is it?" Carla turned.

"That woman," Nadine said, "the one coming through the gate." Carla looked at a sharply profiled woman with long blonde hair pulled into a ponytail, wearing slim dark jeans and a black jacket and very high heels. She could be Gwyneth Paltrow.

"What?" asked Carla. "Who is it?"

"My old boss," said Nadine. "Josie! Josie! Over here!"

The woman turned, and Carla watched as she regarded Nadine with large brown eyes composed in an expression of calculated surprise. She did not smile, or grin, or in any way return Nadine's pronounced warmth. "Josie!" repeated Nadine. Carla saw the woman's shoulder twitch at the sound of her name, yet again. She held up one finger, gesturing for Nadine to wait just a second.

"She doesn't look particularly welcoming," Carla said.

"She isn't welcoming. She's a jerk, but an interesting one. I haven't talked to her in weeks, but watch her be nice to me." Nadine nodded at Josie, who at this moment was walking over to their table. "By the time she gets over here, she's going to act as if she's meeting Prince William."

"Nadine!" exclaimed the woman, as if on cue. "Nadine Nadine Nadine. Where have you been hiding?" She bent down and kissed Nadine on both cheeks. "I can't believe I caught you!" she gushed. "Do you think you'll answer one of my calls these days? You're the hardest woman in town to get hold of."

"You called?" replied Nadine. "I didn't get a message."

"Right," Josie said. "Remember, Nadine. I taught you how to lie." She smiled, and Carla saw her perfectly formed, dazzlingly white, weirdly small teeth. "Hi," she said, as she turned to Carla. "Josephine O'Leary."

Carla extended her hand. "Carla Trousse."

"Right," said Josie. She shook Carla's hand limply as her head swiveled on its neck, assaying all the patrons of the restaurant. Carla pulled her hand away, aware that she was no longer of interest. She looked at Josie's pale skin and knobby wrist bones. Carla felt herself sinking.

"Who are you here with?" asked Nadine.

Carla saw Josie's eyes brighten as she grinned. "Why?"

"Just wondering," answered Nadine. It was just like a game beginning, as if Nadine had shuffled a deck of cards and was turning over the first one. "C'mon, Josie. Is it about a job?"

"Sort of," Josie said. "Maybe."

"Where?"

"Not where. Who. Henry Antonelli."

"Henry Antonelli!" Carla said, exuberantly. "I just talked to him. He's here."

Josie ignored her and turned to Nadine. "Remember when he was at Wallace's? He must have seen something he liked. He's the one who arranged this meeting. I don't know what he wants to talk about."

"If you get to work at NJTF, I will be the most jealous person alive," said Nadine.

"Well, let's not jump to—" Josie began.

"What's NJTF?" asked Carla. "What's—"

"I haven't even told him I'm out of work," Josie told Nadine.

"I'm talking to you," said Carla, more loudly. "Can you hear me?"

Josie stopped for a moment, turned to Carla, and nodded. Then she resumed her conversation with Nadine. "He just called me out of the blue."

"Why are you not answering me?" repeated Carla.

Josie turned. "I don't know you," said Josie. And then her lips shifted into a cold smile. Carla looked into her eyes and saw no warmth, no humor, no common thread. If she had wanted to hit her, it would have been like swiping at poisoned air. Josie returned her gaze to Nadine.

"As your friend said," Josie's smile was etched on her bony face, "Henry is here already. I shouldn't keep him waiting. Great to see you, Nadine. Call me!" She turned back to Carla. "Bye, Marla."

The other patrons stared as Josie joined Henry Antonelli at his table. Carla saw Josie beam as Henry stood, and she grimaced when she saw that Henry greeted her as if she were an old friend.

"She's odious," said Carla. "Is she always like that?"

"Yep," replied Nadine. "She likes when people don't like her. Loves it. Part of her strategy."

Carla was shocked. She was from New York; she knew rude people. But they were rude for a reason. Josie was rude just because she could get away with it, and because Carla was unimportant to her.

"This place is full of unlikable people," Nadine continued. She remembered the first time she was confronted with Josie O'Leary, and people like her. It had felt as if the Josies of the world knew a secret code of behavior, one that would garner money and happiness and dinners with Henry Antonelli. And the truth was, they did. But Nadine's code of behavior worked too, once it was refashioned for the peculiarities of the Hollywood social system. Keep your eye on the ball, Ernie always told her, remember it's about the work.

"I stay away from it all as much as I can," Nadine said. "I figure, I do my work well, everything else will follow. It'll be the same for you." Nadine suddenly felt awash with empathy for Carla, and knew she was speaking the truth.

"She wants you to call her," said Carla.

"No, she wants me to call her back so she doesn't have to respond," smiled Nadine. "You'll figure out the game soon enough."

"That doesn't make any sense," Carla replied quietly.

Nadine picked up her wineglass before she answered. "Welcome, Carla, to Hollywood."

Chapter Fifteen

Josie was sure she heard the steady thrum of a murmur—*who is sitting with Henry Antonelli, who is sitting with Henry Antonelli* . . . She knew her name was seeping through the restaurant and that people were saying "Josie Who? I think I've seen her before. I know her. I dated her. I met with her . . ."

She would be doing the exact same thing.

"Josie?" Henry tapped her on the shoulder, and as she lifted her head and tossed her long highlighted hair back, she felt as if she were being filmed in slow motion. Each frame of her movement would be spliced with a reaction shot of the other patrons: There was the young girl in the corner, gawking; there was Tess Johnson, a studio executive who had snubbed Josie at a party a month ago, looking first at Henry and then narrowing her eyes as she contemplated his dining partner.

Josie locked eyes with Henry. He was older than she had remembered, and his skin hung in slight saggy pouches under his chin. But those eyes . . .

"Well," she said, with the appropriate ease of someone deserving to be in celebrity circles. "This is certainly public, Henry. Isn't your wife going to be angry?"

Henry smiled with closed lips. "Going right to the crux of things, I wouldn't expect anything else. No. Cecilia won't be angry. She trusts me." And in truth, Cecilia had kissed Henry good-bye, wishing him luck fending off yet another Henry-Glommer.

"Should she?" Josie had decided while driving to the restaurant that she was going to say exactly what came to her mind, with no regard for the consequences.

"Yes," said Henry, as he coughed.

Josie had also told herself that she was going to appear 100 percent unmoved by Henry's celebrity. If she acted—if she believed—that Henry was any better than she, then she deserved to be treated like a low-level person, the kind who smiled too much and fawned too much and in general behaved like a sniveling child around these brighter lights.

When he had called her out of the blue, just after Joshua left, Josie had not lost her composure. The fact was, Henry wasn't superior to Josie, he was just famous. He could help her. And he was attracted to her. If she didn't use these components to advance herself in the business, she should get out right now and go back to Portland.

She had done her research. She had gone on the Internet for hours amassing information about Henry and his wife, Cecilia Rosenberg, the psychiatrist. Cecilia was a pretty, petite woman who looked a bit like Snow White. An *old* Snow White. Old for women was, simply, different than old for men, and feminists could rage about this all they wanted, and older women could point to Sophia Loren as proof of eternal sexiness, but Josie was nothing if not pragmatic. Young women were the prize and Josie was still young. She would not waste precious moments lamenting the consequences of a superficial culture. The truth was Josie was delighted when she was being ogled like a stripper.

"Have you ordered?" she asked.

"Just this," he said, pointing to his wine.

They ordered their meals, and Josie saw that Tess Johnson was still staring at her. She smiled at her, and turned to Henry.

"So . . ."

"So . . ."

"I'm sure you've never heard this before, but I have this script . . ."

"You do?" Henry laughed. "You have a script? I'm shocked."

"Right," she grinned back. "And I know—I know everyone says this, but this one's good. It's original. It's—"

"Extremely well written. Superb characterization. The role that will earn me my third Oscar."

"All of the above," Josie said. "And maybe even things you haven't thought of yet."

"I'm pretty much thinking of everything right now," Henry answered, and Josie pictured herself putting her own little Josie Flag right on Henry's head.

"And I need a job," Josie said. She surprised herself when she said it. The idea had begun forming when Nadine said something about Henry's company, NJTF. Then, when Henry flirted with her, she sensed the consolidation of a plan, the one where she could achieve her ambition and maybe latch on to a movie star.

"What?" Henry looked startled.

"I need a job," she repeated. "Wallace fired me. His deal wasn't renewed."

"Right," said Henry.

"In all honesty, I was a threat to his niece. But it doesn't matter, there wasn't any room to grow there. But your company—"

As she spoke, Josie calculated the benefits of her current strategy. She was using a professional tack, and she could see it had taken Henry by surprise. If she was just a sexual conquest, Henry could forget about her. This way, she could keep her leverage and maybe have her movie produced.

Henry laughed, the same laugh that was so genuine in the movie when he was president. It was honest, and she saw again why he was so admired by the populace. Most of the time, he played himself.

"That's pretty direct," he said.

"I know. Why shouldn't I be? I'm experienced. And I need a job. I—" Josie broke off her response and looked to the floor. Her mind raced—she had come upon another bit of information that could seal her fate with Henry, if she dared to play it.

"You what?" Henry asked.

"My husband and I split up."

"Oh," Henry said.

"It gets worse." Josie arranged her features into a composite picture of sadness. "He has cancer."

Henry paused before he replied. "I'm sorry."

"He won't let me take care of him. There may be someone else." Josie stared directly at Henry. "I've stopped being prideful about this. My mother tells me I shouldn't admit this to anyone—that it makes me look spurned. But the truth is the truth, and I'm not going to get anywhere by staying quiet. I've lost my job and my husband. You're my chance to start all over again."

She allowed herself to sound distraught, and assumed a disconsolate expression. "I've just had a tough time, and I'm doing whatever I can to get myself out of it."

The little scene had worked—she was a consummate actress. Henry believed her; she could see it in his face. She called "cut!" in her mind and looked to the table for her emotional denouement.

Henry was stunned. He had been completely wrong about Josephine O'Leary, and he was usually a terrific judge of character.

"Your family? Your friends?" he asked.

"Everyone's been terrific," she answered, looking up slowly. "But my parents live in Portland. They're supportive, of course, but I've got to move on."

As she spoke, Henry chided himself for thinking that Josie had been interested in sex with him. Sex was probably the farthest thing from Josie's mind. He saw her sleeping alone at night, clutching a pillow, tormented that another woman was nursing her husband in his sickbed.

"Here," Henry wrote a number on a napkin. "Call Esther. I'll give her the heads-up. It'll work out."

"Thanks," said Josie. "Thanks. I'll call her tomorrow."

"Excuse me, Mr. Antonelli?" A waiter was holding a remote telephone. "There's a call for you."

"Just when you think you've escaped . . ." Henry said. "This is exactly why I shut the cell off. I'll be right back." He left the table with the waiter.

Josie sat back, a closed smile arched on her lips. She forced herself to stay seated, to pick up a piece of bread, to drink more of her wine.

"Josephine, right?" Josie turned. It was Tess Johnson, the executive who had snubbed her.

"Yes," said Josie. And then, unable to resist, she continued. "I'm sorry, I've forgotten your name."

The truth was that Josie not only knew Tess's name, she knew that Tess had recently been promoted to executive senior vice president at Studio X, that she was from Sydney, Australia, and that she had posed for naked photographs for her last boyfriend, an actor from Sweden.

"Tess." Tess knew Josie knew everything about her, but she went along with the script, just like the millions of other Hollywood game players had done for the last hundred years. "Tess Johnson."

Tess extended her hand. After silently counting to three, Josie shook it.

Chapter Sixteen

It had been fate that Phillip had handed her premiere tickets on Wednesday morning before he left for work.

"I know you think you'll hate the whole Hollywood thing," he said. "But just in case you want to join me and Sam, and about a million others watching Antonelli's next movie, here's your chance."

"What's it about?"

"Think Willy Loman as an old lawyer, losing all his clients. The test markets are raving. Every studio in town passed on the project, but then Antonelli and his company jumped on it. Supposed to be good. Mom's coming down for it next Friday. Has she called you?"

"Nope," said Carla. "Not a word from my overly extended aunt. It's quite rude to tell someone to travel across the country and then to wait six weeks to divulge your secret. Can't be too important."

"Sure it can," said Phillip. "It just can't be more important than her." He was leaving for work. "So who do you want to take?"

"Take?"

"To the premiere."

"Right." Carla looked glumly out the window.

"You won't have any problem with this ticket—all the wannabes want to go. Want me to find someone?"

Carla glowered at him. "No."

"All right. Just trying to help."

"I can go by myself, right?"

"Sure, if you want."

"I may."

"Shame to waste a ticket, though."

"Good-bye, Phillip," said Carla, shoving the door shut. She knew she should be excited by the prospect of the premiere—and she was—but it was almost dwarfed by the anxiety she felt about finding a date for it. She was forty-one. Did this feeling ever change?

What was so wrong with going by herself?

This is exactly the question Carla asked Nadine, hours later, when the two of them met for lunch at a café called Urth, on Melrose.

"You can go by yourself if you want," said Nadine. "It's helpful, especially if you work in the business, because you can actually see and talk to people. The problem starts when people decide you're a loser because you're there alone."

Carla and Nadine were sitting outside eating a muffin made with brussels sprouts and walnuts. Carla watched the symphony of tanned arms raising and lowering their coffee mugs underneath the umbrellas. She could not see heads, but she saw the tank tops, the Oxfords, the T-shirts. Some of the tanned arms were old, frazzled from the bone like a dripping brûlée crust. But the majority were young, and their casual attire belied their conversation. Everything was about the industry: *We thought it would be good, but not seventy million good*, and *We're getting good response, but they're going to take it to an urban neighborhood for more tests.*

"So I have an idea," said Nadine. "Thank me later. But I've already got the okay." She sipped her latte from a bowl. "You should work for us."

Carla laughed. "I should what?"

"You should work with me. Us. With Roland Starr and Kirk Gordon. The Glomming Company."

Carla's eyes locked onto Nadine's; this was a development she had not considered. Suddenly, all of the clumsy odds and ends of their relationship—that she was the older one, that she had been Nadine's boss, that she was the one who was supposed to offer Nadine a job—melted in front of her.

"I think the rate's about one hundred dollars a script. Read it, write a coverage. We'll give you as many as you can handle." She paused for a moment, a faint look of concern. "You have a résumé, right?"

Carla nodded, still unsure what to say.

"Great." Nadine sat back.

"But—"

"Carla, it's the right thing. I just had this brilliant idea when I was doing yet another sloppy job—you're perfect for this. Really."

"But—"

"But what? What could you possibly 'but' about?" As she tried to convince Carla, Nadine saw the pile of scripts she could now pass off to her. She was tired of writing coverage. It was time for Nadine to ascend the development ladder herself. She had convinced Roland Starr that she deserved a promotion, and he had finally given his approval, provided that no scripts fell through the cracks, unread. The second-in-command, a skinny, curly-haired man named Gerry Simpson, was furious that Nadine had gone directly to Roland to wrangle herself an assistant. He had advised Nadine that all requests should go through him first, and then, in somber tones, warned her that she ignored the company hierarchy at her peril. Her only response had been to smile sweetly as she told him to relax.

"I'll be working for you?" asked Carla.

"Yes," said Nadine. "I guess. But there's no 'reporting,' so to speak."

Carla had felt the temptation of the entertainment industry hanging like thick and sugary grapes since she had arrived.

"You look so serious," said Nadine.

"I'll do it," said Carla. "I'd love to."

"I was hoping you'd say that," Nadine said as she reached into her bag. "Here. Use these as a guide." She handed Carla a voluminous pile of papers. "There are six scripts, two sample coverages, and a reader's report guideline. Should be all you need. Maybe you can come in on Friday?"

It was so easy. She had spent a professional career submitting résumés that failed to capture her capabilities and attending interviews so heavy with awkwardness she felt nauseous. And now she had a job—admittedly entry level, admittedly with her old assistant—where she could read and get paid for it.

Nadine gave Carla the directions to get to the lot where the Glomming Company had its office. She would arrange for a "drive on." Carla promised to be there by nine on Friday. Nadine told her that she could handle part of Nadine's "weekend read," the stacks of scripts slumped against every Hollywood executive's walls, sneakily hiding, perhaps, the one example of wit and vibrancy that would make a studio millions of dollars.

An hour later, when Carla was driving back to Phillip's house, she wished that all six of her acquaintances in New York could see her. She had not been this expectant of something good for a long while.

She pulled into Phillip's driveway, stopping the car before colliding with Christopher, who was riding his bicycle. The sprinkler system was on, scattering water in brief, sparkling arcs around the lawn.

"Hey, handsome!" Carla shouted. Christopher braked his bike. She jumped out of the car. "Come with me!"

She hadn't run through sprinklers since she was a child. She sprinted to the lawn, where she began to rush around in circles, getting wet. Christopher watched from his bike.

"We have a pool," he said.

"Try this," she replied happily. "Just try."

Christopher pulled his bike against the garage. He stood for a second in the driveway, his shoulders slumped, his face inscrutable as he studied his aunt.

"You're acting silly," he said.

"Aren't you hot?" she answered. He shrugged. "Please," she persisted.

Christopher walked to where Carla stood. He still wore his pointed blue bicycle helmet. But he closed his eyes as the water landed on his cheeks, and she saw him smile.

"Now run," Carla ordered, and the two of them ran in opposite directions on the lawn.

"Carla!" shouted Samantha from inside the house. "Telephone!" Samantha came to the front door and found her son and husband's cousin crisscrossing the lawn over the spinning pumps, increasingly soaked.

"Sudden burst of immaturity," Carla explained, as Samantha, amused, handed her a towel. Christopher asked his mother if he could invite friends over to play with him on the lawn. Carla stepped by him and went into the kitchen. She picked up the receiver.

"Hello?"

"Carla?" said the man. "Carla? It's David. David Stegner."

"David?"

"Hi, yes. I'm returning your call. You're in Los Angeles? I'm glad I didn't miss you."

Carla pulled the towel around her neck. She looked outside Samantha's windows at the green lawns, the perfect California sky.

"David," Carla repeated.

"Yes?"

"Want to go to a movie?"

Chapter Seventeen

Esther Rodriguez Rabinowitz was short, so short that one person, a producer from New York, had admitted he thought she was a "little person." Her hair was long, brown, and flyaway thin; she weighed approximately ninety-nine pounds, and she dressed simply, expensively. She had been working with Henry Antonelli for nine years, beginning as a low-level receptionist, working her way up to become his full-fledged producing partner at NJTF.

Their office was in Santa Monica, in a Spanish-style mansion that had been re-zoned for use as commercial space. Originally there had been six bedrooms and five baths, but Henry and Esther had fashioned work areas out of almost every possible living space, and the result was a comfortable, deep-cushioned, dark-paneled, and sunlit "fraternity house" for creative people. Haphazard children's paintings mixed with Lichtensteins and Pollocks on the walls; index cards were pinned up on various walls, and Apple PowerBook computers were positioned on desktops as well as on an old dining room table. Writers were invited to spend time freely inside the walls of NJTF rather than remaining at a safe distance. The only entry requirement for the writers was that Esther had to like them and, perhaps more important, trust them.

Some of their competitors thought them crazy, but Henry and Esther had a fiscal method to their madness—it was not as if they did not have expectations of the people who used their space. NJTF's mission was carefully predicated on Esther's principle of an Upward Spiral, which Esther had convinced Henry he could justify using the most quantifiable of economic measures—profit.

"Henry," she had said four years ago, after she had earned her M.B.A. from UCLA at night, and after she had confirmed her suspicion that what business schools taught best was how to use arcane economic euphemisms to describe basic human behavior. "Here's the thing. Businesses need to make money. Businesses make money when they supply a product the consumers demand. In show business, consumers demand an 'entertaining' product. People tend to create entertaining product when they work in a comfortable atmosphere. They do not enjoy being watched by a time clock, they do not want to be charged for every time they FedEx a gift to their parents in Missouri, they do not want to feel micromanaged."

Henry had said "So we pick up the cost of their phone calls and FedExes? My father always knew every dime he spent."

"Good for him. Maybe that made him money. But look at it in a *macro* sense," Esther confirmed. "And yes, 'macro' is one of my business school terms. Think about it. Even the most perverse person here— the real user, the one who abuses all our trust—how much could he or she cost us in petty office expenditures? One thousand dollars? Two? Now think about it. The potential profit of a movie written by one of them, or brought in by one of them, is at least six figures, hopefully more. Then there's the bonus that they want to be here—they want to come to work every day because we're not smothering them, because they're being treated well, because they're not being nickel-and-dimed. Instead, we take away every single impediment to their work. They can't complain because they're happy, they have a fair bonus system in place, they have one hundred percent medical, and every once in a while, if they want to FedEx a package to Topeka, Kansas, we don't say a word. They can be creative on their terms, and we benefit—by better product, and because we stand to profit with hundreds of thousands of dollars because they're happy and not running off with our competitors. Upward spiral. I don't understand why more companies don't employ it."

Henry had grinned. "I don't know what you're talking about. But you're in charge. Just don't throw money away."

"Trust people, they'll trust you back."

"Esther the humanitarian," he had said.

"Esther the connoisseur of human behavior," she had answered.

The Upward Spiral worked. Four of Hollywood's highest-grossing films in the last three years had been generated here, and only one of them starred Henry. The rest were movies written and directed by unknown talent that had broken through the studio films and earned millions of dollars. NJTF had recently closed a three-year revolving financing deal with Studio X; Esther had become one of the most respected producers in town; and Henry had added the desired "hyphenate" to his name, as in Henry Antonelli, actor-director-producer.

Esther did not spend much time congratulating herself. She knew she was truly blessed because of what she knew was her one special trait. She was not the prettiest, nor the smartest, nor the most gifted.

What she knew, and knew instinctively, was story.

Story as a stretchy, changeable, piece of material—story as a colorful, tentlike canvas, or story as a steel and white thin streak of metal. Story that could have the appeal of McDonald's; story that could be rarefied, like the one perfect pearl in the one oyster deep in the sea. Story that could be ruined by one errant thread of hubris; story that could be irreparably damaged by too many seamstresses. Esther had not expected to be so agile with movie scripts. When she had begun to read them years ago, when her main job was to say "NJTF, can I help you?" she had been very unsure of her talents.

But after reading more than five thousand scripts, after writing so many coverages she was able to finish one in an hour, Esther—an otherwise self-deprecatingly amiable person—was as confident as Michael Jordan with a basketball when she held a script in her hand.

What Esther Rodriguez Rabinowitz also did—when she wasn't with her husband, Aram, or her twins, Laura and Lisa, or at work at NJTF—was write. She had published four novels under a pseudonym, E. R. Robin, and they had all been critical successes. None had hit any bestseller list—her husband had joked that if she kept on giving her books esoteric names like *The Gloaming of Macallister* and *Grotesques* she was doomed to dank libraries—but the most upmarket publications had all raved about "Robin's ingenuity" and "original voice."

Not even Henry knew her secret. She had written the first one almost as a lark, and had given it to one of her best friends, a book agent. The book agent/friend, Lee, a woman whose taste ran from nonfiction stories of life with Hugh Hefner to commercial fiction about women in grief, was impressed, and urged her to continue. Esther had, and the result was E. R. Robin's status as one of the leading women of letters, even if no one knew who she was. She would write in the morning, when the twins were in school, and she would write on weekends, when she could.

Soon enough, Hollywood called. Lee had said that with the publication of Esther's newest novel, *Secrets My Friends Have Told Me*, she had received sixteen calls from Hollywood agents and managers, all pleading to meet with the reclusive E. R. Robin so they could help turn the novel into a film.

But Esther refused. She decided that until she wrote something she felt would be served well creatively by adapting it for a film, she'd stay quiet, and stay invigorated by her dual roles in the entertainment industry. She liked that she was known as Henry's unflappable business partner, and she loved that she had a following of intelligent readers out in the populace. And she was proud of NJTF, her innovative workplace environment that had established such a stronghold in Hollywood.

What she vociferously loathed, however, were the ungracious, unabashedly ambitious, crude people who formed so much of the Hollywood machinery. She had foisted her dislike even on the walls of NJTF, where she had commissioned a sign that listed the office rules:

1. Keep it clean.
2. Be respectful of others.
3. Be inclusive.

These were the rules for everyone: the writers, who were under no contractual obligation to NJTF, and the employees, who were. For the most part, Esther and Henry agreed upon their work staff—hiring respectfully ambitious, decent, intelligent people.

But in the beginning, Henry and Esther did have one major disagreement. Henry had insisted that NJTF hire at least some "barracudas," provided they were "barracudas with humanity." (That he said this with a straight face was impressive; Esther had wanted to laugh outright.) But Esther eventually was convinced. It would behoove NJTF to have some ruthless people in their midst to keep them aware of the machinations of the Evil Hollywood they both desired to avoid.

Heather Kavakos was the first hire under the barracuda banner: Transparently ambitious, Heather was entrenched in the movie business thanks to her family, and her network of close friends included at least three of Hollywood's most bankable actors and actresses.

Esther didn't tell Henry, but she was sure Heather's "humanity" was stuck somewhere in between her silicon breasts and reflexive self-absorption. Still, Esther had to admit that Heather's relationships in Hollywood did sometimes help them contact key people directly.

Esther had gotten her way with the hiring of her personal favorite, Danny Cohen. He was a former agent who spoke fast and loved to be a part of the conventional inner circle of Hollywood. *Esther, honey, get outta here, I'm talking like a tentpole movie, I've got the biggest people in town talking about this project.* He was handsome, and charming, and intuitive—Esther kept telling Henry that when he finally realized that he didn't need to be deferential to the mediocre people who formed most of the machinery of Hollywood, he'd be unstoppable. Esther had said this to Danny directly, and he had agreed with her, sort of; his reply was a typical blend of self-deprecation, flattery, and avoidance. *You're right, you know, you're right. What the hell do I know, a kid from New Rochelle? You're gonna run this town, Esther, I'm telling you, you're the real deal.*

There were others. By far, the majority of people at NJTF complied with Esther's mandate. But when Josie O'Leary walked through the doors, teeth bared, Esther knew immediately that Henry had commandeered the employment of yet another barracuda.

Henry had told Esther that Josie was intelligent, had an eye for material, and had an estranged husband with cancer. She was ambitious, he said, but he was sure there was a humanside to Josie that Esther would see if she could only take the chip off her own shoulder.

As Esther sized up Josie from across her desk, she felt herself stiffen: Any humanity this woman had was freeze-dried and stored, waiting to be released when she was an old woman in Rancho Mirage, playing tennis and tipping the help exactly 13 percent. But to Josie's credit, she did not put on any airs.

"When can I start?" asked Josie.

"Excuse me?"

"Can I start on Monday? I want to work. I need to work."

Esther had stepped back, examining Josie. Josie had unbuttoned her shirt to her sternum, and Esther could see Josie's black bra.

"Well, that's admirable but—"

"You don't understand. I'm chomping at the bit," said Josie.

"Henry says you may want to submit a script to us?"

Josie clutched her bag. She thought of all the writers in the world who didn't have access in Hollywood, people who couldn't just hand a script over to a powerful producer.

And yet, here she was, Josie O'Leary, about to give Esther

Rodriguez Rabinowitz a copy of *The Bear That Saved Christmas*. Joshua King should be at home right now lighting candles, praying to the altar of Josie O'Leary.

"You own this?" Esther asked her pleasantly.

"Yes," said Josie. "I do."

She lied easily, although her stomach contracted. Joshua had "forgotten" to sign the contracts on three separate occasions. He always had good excuses, but Josie was beginning to wonder if the delay was deliberate.

"I'll read it this weekend," said Esther. "Tell me. What is it you do?"

"Do?"

"Do. I mean, what is it you like? Are you a writer? A director? Do you have producing aspirations? Have you ever produced anything? Our business is so filled with people who like the gray areas that Henry and I pride ourselves in being more clear about a person's desires. It helps you too—that is, for example, if you want to be a writer, we can help you toward that as you work with us." She paused. "We like to have an awareness of everyone's predilections before they begin."

Josie was sure that Esther was being snide, already sensing Josie as her rival for Henry. Josie wouldn't succumb. She smiled breezily.

"I do everything," she said.

Esther stared at her for a long moment without speaking. "Yes," said Esther. "Of course you do." She turned around and selected three different scripts from her wall cabinet. "What about if you give me coverage on these three by tomorrow and we'll take it from there."

Josie took the three scripts. She counted to ten. She took a deep breath. And then, very clearly, she announced to Esther her feelings about coverage.

"Esther, I don't mean to be disrespectful, but I am well beyond coverage."

If Esther was not innately polite, she would have yawned. Josie's postures were boring to her.

"If you want to test me, fine," Josie continued. "I'll write one. But I'm not a development girl, sorry."

Esther had heard from Wallace Pickering himself that Josie was not a development girl, largely because Josie refused to consider "development"—that is, the process of editing a script—important.

"Like I said," Josie continued, "I'll write coverage this first time. But I'm not someone who's going to be proud because I wrote a good book report."

"To us, coverage is perhaps the most important component of the process."

"Come on," Josie rolled her eyes. "I'm not out of the gate."

"What is it you'd rather do than coverage?"

"Anything. Anything meaningful. Productions, script meetings, casting . . ."

"Right. I understand."

Josie felt Esther's sneer underneath her smile, and smiled right back. Josie felt sorry for Esther, so short, so plain-looking, so devoted to the boring world of scripts and "development" that she didn't see (or perhaps, didn't want to see) that what mattered in Hollywood was the production of film, the meetings, the contacts, the parties. Everything else was just coin trading, the handing of a penny back and forth between timid and polite women.

"Here it is," said Josie, as she handed the *Bear* script to Esther. "The writer's ecstatic. When I told him Henry's name, he almost jumped through the window." This was another lie, since Josie's protective antenna had cautioned her, and she had not mentioned Henry's name to Joshua at all. Joshua had become ensconced in Hollywood's nightlife— he had moved to the shabby but glamorous Le Deluxe apartment building in Hancock Park, where at least two B-list actors lived. But now she considered using Henry as bait to ensure Joshua signed the contracts.

"Thank you," said Esther. "I'm looking forward to reading it."

Josie looked around the room where they were standing. To her, it looked like Mike's old cluttered office. "Where can I sit?"

"Your desk, you mean?"

"Yes."

Esther pointed to an armchair on the side of a Shabby Chic couch. "What about there?"

"Where?" Josie looked to where Esther was pointing.

"For the first month, you can sit anywhere out here. Our other employees do have designated 'offices'—but they've chosen them after their own two-month acclimation period, after they've seen where they'd be most comfortable."

"What about phones? Faxes? Computer, the Internet?"

"They're all over the place," Esther gestured. "It's all shared."

"Shared."

"Yes."

"Right," said Josie, who had begun to walk around the room. "This is kind of unconventional."

"Well, creativity is unconventional."

"Right," said Josie. "What is my salary?"

"Excuse me?"

"Henry and I didn't discuss compensation."

"Nor did we," said Esther.

"Are you the person I should talk to?"

"Well, I think I can tell you what's available," said Esther. "We typically start people at forty-five thousand dollars a year, plus one hundred percent medical."

"I can't do that."

"Can't do what?"

"Forty-five thousand doesn't work for me. It won't work for you either, Esther, because I'll think you don't value me. I think one hundred is fair."

"Well, then you should go and find a place to pay you that."

"I really don't want to negotiate. I just want to start working."

"I'm not negotiating. We're kind of Communists around here. Everyone starts at forty-five thousand, and then every month we have a review. If Henry and I decide someone's deserving of a raise, we give it to them then. After a year, if you bring in a project, we discuss an appropriate division of back-end profits."

"Forty-five thousand dollars?" said Josie. "I earned three times that my first year at Y&W."

"It's your decision," said Esther. "Don't rush it."

Josie walked absently around the living room. She peered into a couple of doors and saw random men and women, some dressed in high-fashion skirts and casual shirts, others dressed in jeans and a T-shirt. One man had bells braided into his thick beard. A woman had an elaborate gray streak painted in the front of her black hair. A boy who looked about twelve played video games on the computer.

She was dismayed, but she would not exhibit this. She had expected Henry's coven of creativity to be more reflective of the society in which he had triumphed; at her old law office, the décor was sleek and silver; there were works of art, internationally recognized, in the *parking garage*. Henry's office was shabby, and intentionally so. It was unkempt, she thought, and the people looked as if they worked for Microsoft, not NJTF.

From her chair, Josie saw Esther stand in the threshold of a room, and inspected her Levi 501's, her small white T-shirt, her thin leather belt, her JP Tod's sandals. Her presentation was chic, according to reigning Los Angeles standards, but again it was not what Josie expected. She had seen executives at the biggest production companies—rather, she had seen *female* executives at the biggest production companies. Esther Rodriguez Rabinowitz, well-known and respected by people like Josie's mentor, Seth Levin, was nothing like them.

But Henry Antonelli was Henry Antonelli. And she had no job. She returned to Esther.

"I'll take it," said Josie.

Esther grimaced. She had hoped the salary would dissuade Josie from accepting Henry's offer. But Henry was too big a magnet, and Esther could not override him.

Esther noticed that Josie's wedding finger was bare.

"Henry said your husband was sick?"

"Oh," Josie paused. "Yes, he is. Thank you for asking." Esther waited to see if Josie would divulge any additional information, but she kept silent. Instead, Josie walked to the wide-backed chair and sat down in it. A PowerBook G4 lay on the end table. Josie glanced over to Esther, who was looking at her.

"Hey, Esther?"

"Yes?"

"Do you think you can get me two tickets to Henry's premiere? I've heard the movie's tracking through the roof, and that Henry's just fabulous."

That Josie wanted premiere tickets was not surprising to Esther. What was surprising was that this enterprising young woman had not already secured them.

"I'll see what I can do," Esther replied, already thinking about how she would get tickets for Josie that sat her way in the back, with the radio giveaways and promotional raffles. She knew that for a woman like Josie, the one thing worse than not having an invitation to a big premiere was going and having the worst seat in the house.

Josie was not thinking about the seating arrangement; Josie was thinking about her future. It was all lining up for her so perfectly: NJTF, Henry, *The Bear*. The air from her personal Mount Everest was so close and so exquisite that she felt she could inhale it from here—all she needed was a bit more time, and a bit more effort. But it was all within reach.

Chapter Eighteen

"Because, frankly, calling you was not the first thing on my list after I *closed a million dollar deal*," yelled Gerry Simpson from his office at the Glomming Company. "I didn't think, oh, let me close a huge deal with the network and then call only the least important person on my call-sheet."

Carla overheard Gerry's side of the telephone call, flinching when he slammed down the phone. On her first day last Friday, he had greeted her with the admonition *Remember, you are the lowest person here. You are lower than the assistants, lower than the receptionist.* Since then, she had avoided him as much as she could, although his office was within five feet of her cubicle.

She had set herself up in a space outside of Nadine's small office, which was on the other side of Gerry's. She had a computer, a telephone, and as many scripts as she could read and cover. In her one week she had, apparently, set some kind of record by reading thirty-seven scripts. At the end of each report, there was a comments section, where Carla found she could use her critical abilities to slam the scripts, if she felt it was appropriate. (Sadly, most were slammable, up to and including the screenplay *Life Is Not a Pizza* by a woman named Casey Cortellessa.)

The Glomming Company, or TGC, as it was called in the business, was set up so that the development girls, like Carla, sat outside the offices in cube-like, open structures. Bright flower arrangements blazed from the coffee tables; *Variety* and *The Hollywood Reporter* lay open next to *Gotham* and *L.A. Magazine.* The interior design was silver and black, with the odd purple streak painted in slashes on a gray wall. The assistants all were in their twenties, wearing identical headsets on attractively disheveled heads. Nadine had merited an office only because she had approached Roland about the empty room. Gerry had gone ballistic, fuming that someone so raw did not deserve her own office. Nadine held her own, and Roland acquiesced. Still, the battle between Nadine and Gerry raged, and Carla watched it toughen into formidable hatred.

"Mr. S. wants a meeting," barked a voice on Carla's intercom. "Conference room in ten." It was the receptionist named Magda, whom Roland was rumored to be romancing when his wife was out of town. Her voice sounded like James Earl Jones, however, and no matter how sexy she looked, every time she spoke Carla thought she was being asked to subscribe to Verizon.

When Carla joined the others sitting around the oval table, the chestnut wood shining under the overhead light, she found a seat quickly, determined to hide her shoe choice before Magda and the other receptionists noticed. The younger women didn't talk to her much at all, but when they did it was almost always to offer suggestions about where Carla could shop.

Gerry Simpson walked in the door with Roland Starr. Roland was dressed in a button-down blue shirt, so stiff with tight cotton threads it looked as if it could stand by itself. It was tucked impeccably into a pair of casual Armani trousers. He was tall and awkwardly shaped; he slicked his dark hair over to one side, and he had small shoulders that gave him the impression of weakness, no matter how much he strained for nobility.

"I don't say this lightly," said Roland, "but the work effort of late has been disgraceful."

Everyone in the room grew quiet. Magda pushed her chair from the edge of the table, and Carla bent her head down, beginning to scribble on her notepad. She had always doodled.

"Disgraceful," Roland continued, in an eerie, soft-toned voice. "If it weren't for the tirelessness of Gerry, I doubt if we'd have any projects going." He turned to Nadine. "Now, Nadine. You've recently been promoted. Did we get the script from Shep Adams?"

Roland was talking about the thriller that had just been submitted to the major production companies and studios around town. It was a road movie that led from Houston, Texas, to the desert of New Mexico, and at one point in the story an entire kickline of skeletons shoots Uzis at the transsexual behemoth and the aimless college student.

"We got it," said Nadine. "But I want to pass on it."

"Every studio in town is bidding on it," replied Roland. "From what Gerry tells me it could be a good film for us."

Nadine looked at Gerry. "It's a bad script."

"It's a great idea," replied Gerry. "We fire the writers and get new ones."

"I may be slightly off," retorted Nadine, "but I believe four hundred and twelve people and three dogs are killed during this one screenplay."

"It has a quirky kind of humor to it," said Gerry, "and the tone is surreal, so the deaths aren't really affecting."

"Do we have it or not?" asked Roland.

"Yes," said Nadine. "Do you want to make an offer?"

"Yes," he answered. "But I'll have Gerry do it. It seems to be out of your comfort zone, Nadine. *He* may be able to bring it in."

Roland stood up and began to stalk slowly around the table. "All of you are exceptional people. Every single one of you. I fully expect that one day I will be working for *you*." He paused, magisterially. "But if we fail to jump on new material as it is passed around this town, and if we fail to expand our creative parameters to expedite the limitations of our slates, and if we do not pursue projects with the speed of sound, and light, we will cataclyophically fall to pieces."

"You're absolutely right," said Gerry.

Carla and Nadine looked across the table at each other. Carla mouthed *cataclyophically?*

"We are a production company. We make movies. We are different. We are better." As he spoke, Roland's voice grew more strident. "We are creative, prideful people. We see dead on into the eye of the tiger and we're geared up for the challenge. Other people in this town want us dead. We must conquer them, we must vindalate." He smiled beatifically. "We must find projects quickly, and we must get them under our roof, and we must make them into the superb movies we are known for."

That TGC had distributed one movie that was a remake of a 1970s sitcom was a fact no one mentioned.

"But I am not finished," he continued. "I have an example for you all to ponder." He walked behind Nadine. "This weekend a movie called *The Last Counselor* will open, and predictions are it will be a great success." He crossed his arms in front of his chest, and smirked. "We had this script. We had it here in our hot little hands. We were in negotiations with the studio, we were ready to make this movie, and then because of Henry Antonelli, Esther Rodriguez Rabinowitz and Antonelli's agent, Eddie Cleveland, we suddenly were out of the ball-park." He put his hands on the shoulders of the person in front of him, who happened to be Carla. Instinctively, she put her hands over her mouth so she wouldn't blurt out something she shouldn't.

"Out of the ballpark." Roland repeated, lifting his hands from her shoulders and beginning to walk again. Carla sat back, relieved.

"This cannot happen again. We will compete vigorously and dominantly in this business for every project of merit." Roland had returned to the head of the table. His voice had settled into a low murmur that resembled the hypnotic drone of a cult leader. "Repeat after me. We are creative. We are different. We are," he put out both hands, a priest about to conclude his sermon. "We are better."

Carla and Nadine looked at each other. They were the only two not chanting.

Roland stopped and looked down to the ground. "Please," he said, "let us all take a moment and consider that it is not too large an assumption to make that what we do influences not just the town but also the state, and yes, I may be stretching, but also, maybe, California too."

He left the room quietly.

Carla whispered to the person next to her. "Was he serious?" The person, a woman who had renamed herself Rilke when she moved to California from Baltimore, looked at Carla with venomous eyes.

"What exactly are you saying?" she asked in a portentous voice.

Carla backpedaled. "Just, just asking if he is always so serious."

"Well, when we fail someone like Roland, we should take it seriously." Rilke pulled her shoulders back and strutted out of the room.

Nadine reached Carla's side. "This was a joke, right?" Carla asked.

"He's legendary," Nadine replied, as Gerry pushed by them.

"I just don't believe it. Are these people for real?" Carla repeated.

"Yeah. He's got a movie star like Kirk by his side, so he's untouchable. For now," said Nadine. "But here's the problem. Roland thinks he's creative. He isn't. He's a cheap bastard whose only concern is making money, no matter how much he goes on and on about a creative community. He wouldn't know a good script if it hit him in the face. It's pathetic."

The room was empty except for Carla and Nadine. "I have a lot to learn," said Carla. She couldn't wait to tell Phillip about her day at the office. Ever since she had begun to work for TGC, Phillip had grilled her for information about the company. Up to now, with the minor exception of Gerry's phone calls, she could not offer Phillip any stories of interest.

"So did you get someone to go to the premiere of *The Last Counselor* with you?" Nadine asked.

Carla nodded. "David Stegner."

Nadine cocked her head backward, as if attempting to hear a faint sound. "Did you say David Stegner, as in the guy you've thought about since I lived in New York?"

"Yes," Carla could not help smiling. "Yes."

"Oh baby—after all these years. Have a great time. Guaranteed if you see either Roland or Gerry there, they'll be all over Antonelli and Esther, telling them how terrific they are, even though they thoroughly despise them."

"Answer me seriously. Is Roland truly someone who moves in the highest echelons out here?" Carla asked. "For real? Not a joke?"

"Absolutely real," she answered. "His business partner makes thirty million a movie."

"Thirty? I thought the ceiling was twenty-five," Carla commented.

Nadine walked toward the door. "Someone's been reading the trades."

Carla followed Nadine. She had been reading the trades, every day, cover to cover. She had also begun to read the gossip columns from L.A. and the New York tabloids. Yesterday she had subscribed to *Entertainment Weekly*. Carla was counting the minutes until the premiere of *The Last Counselor*—and not only because of David Stegner. She wanted to see the business in action; she was eager to observe the people whose jobs were so coveted, whose creative choices so influential.

"I've got a lot to learn," Carla repeated to Nadine. "And I've always been a very good student."

Chapter Nineteen

To Esther's surprise, she loved *The Bear That Saved Christmas.* So did Henry. They wanted to move ahead, with NJTF producing and Henry starring. They were going to tell Josie the news this morning, and hopefully go straight to Studio X, where they had their deal, and get the paperwork started.

Josie didn't know any of this yet. She crouched deeply in the chenille-covered sofa in the "meeting center"—another cozy room without any pretension to hierarchy. She pulled a throw pillow over her lap to hide her tension. She did not know why Henry and Esther had called her. Business tenures shrank and expanded in Hollywood like the most elastic of rubber bands. She had not seen Henry since their dinner at the Ivy, and she knew she had succeeded perhaps too well in making Esther dislike her.

The door opened.

"Josie," said Henry. "Congratulations."

Josie pushed the throw pillow to one side and sat up in the sofa. "Thanks. For what?"

"Your script. We love it." Esther followed Henry inside. "Clearly, you have a good eye for material."

"Really?" Josie beamed. She felt her ego swell, in a wise but prideful way. And then, just as quickly, she felt nauseous. *Joshua King still hadn't signed the option contract.*

"We wanted to talk about the next step," said Henry.

"Next step?"

"How to meet with the writer, how to get the paperwork done. We have a deal with Studio X, and our lawyer will need to get involved."

"Fine," said Josie. "That's fabulous."

"Do you think he can rewrite it?"

"What?"

"Depending on your deal with him, we could either hire him to do the rewrites, or else find someone we think would be better. It's a good script, but it needs work."

Josie mentally replayed Joshua's words: *I think it kind of rocks the way it is.*

"What I think is the best scenario," said Esther, "is to give Joshua the chance to rewrite it first. We'll give him notes, and then see what he does."

"And about my deal?" asked Josie.

"What's that?" asked Esther.

"My deal," she repeated. Henry glanced at Esther with a paternal smile.

"We'll protect you, of course," said Henry.

"I don't doubt it for a second," Josie said, "but I think we'd all be more comfortable if we spoke about it now."

"Fine," said Esther. "What do you have in mind?"

"Credit and money, that's what all the deals boil down to, right? I have a lawyer, Seth Levin, and I want to pass to him all the negotiations, but I just want to make sure of one thing."

"What's that?" asked Henry.

"That I'm a producer," said Josie. "Not co-producer, not executive producer, not co-executive-associate producer. Producer."

"Producer," echoed Henry.

"I own the project," declared Josie, by this time believing her lie. "I mean—"

170

"I know what you mean," said Esther. "We'll protect you."

In her as-yet-unsigned deal with Joshua, Josie was to pay him one hundred thousand dollars if a studio bought the script from her. She would then control the material, and the cost of this to the studio. Josie began to smile. Henry Antonelli was very rich. Studio X was a mega-corporation. She would negotiate that she and NJTF would jointly produce the movie, and that Studio X would finance the whole thing. The money supply could be substantial—and better yet, she could buy a Porsche.

But best of all, one producer credit on one Henry Antonelli movie meant she not only had opened the proverbial door for herself but had shoved it aside, torn it off its hinges, and sauntered in like a rightful occupant should.

But she had to get Joshua to sign.

"It's your script, it's your movie," Henry commented, interrupting Josie's thoughts.

"Well, we'll be producing it with you," said Esther, glaring at Henry. "Since of course, as you may recall, you've never produced anything before."

Esther hoped, for a second, that Josie might admit she needed help. Instead, Josie laughed.

"C'mon Esther, it's the *game*," smiled Josie, digging into her bag for lip balm. "I don't pretend to be the person who made the rules. I just listen to them. Making movies. You hire someone to do that."

Recently Josie had been at a party where she met members of a production "crew"—those men and women who put film into cameras, who connect power lines to generators, who paint actors' faces and curl their hair. She knew they were the people who "made" movies—they were the people who put the pieces of the film together, in the same way that assembly-line workers in Detroit "made" a Ford Taurus, or the children in Thailand "made" a Nike sneaker. And while occasionally one of these people made some impression on Josie—a pink streak in their hair, perhaps; an impressive grasp of the French language—she still relegated them to the "other" side of moviemaking, the side in which she had no interest, the side that wasn't, right now, meeting with Henry Antonelli and his business partner.

"Some producers like to stay involved," offered Henry. "You may like it." He grinned at Josie, and Esther looked down at the table, wanting to smack him in the head for glaring male stupidity.

"The studio lawyer's going to call you," said Esther. "His name is Phillip Giberson. You should send him all the paperwork. And we'd love to meet the writer." Esther looked at the script. "Joshua King?"

"He's a law student from Miami."

"Well, he's a writer now," said Henry.

"I'll give you a set of notes by next week," said Esther. "And we'll set up a meeting with Joshua and give them to him."

"Perfect," said Josie. "Perfection."

She thought ahead to the *Variety* press release. She would want final approval on the article. But maybe she should hire Catherine, her publicist friend, so that she too could have a full-page spread in *Vogue* or *Bazaar*. *Josephine O'Leary is a woman of many talents, finding films and practicing yoga with equal aplomb. Henry Antonelli says he doesn't know how he managed before Josie came along . . .*

"Josie?" asked Henry. "I don't want to bring up a sore subject, but how's your husband?"

Mike. Josie's last update from Rebecca was that Mike was feeling much better and that he had, in fact, begun dating "someone special." Josie believed that Mike had forced Rebecca to say this to her, so that she would be jealous. Josie wasn't, of course—she reminded herself that she was the one who wanted the divorce to begin with—but her emotions were agitated when she thought about Mike, and it allowed her to carry off another brilliant acting performance.

She shrugged her shoulders in what she hoped was an appropriately *"I'm uncomfortable with that question"* reaction. The time span allotted for properly acknowledging the illness of your sick husband who was nonetheless now healthy and happily dating someone else was about one minute, sixteen seconds. Josie waited, concentrating on a spot on the glass table, a fingerprint. Then she pulled her head up and with as much appropriate emotion as she could muster, she answered Henry. "His doctors tell me he's doing very well."

"I see," said Henry.

Josie moved off the couch, marched her legs up and down to shake her skirt back to its position, and stepped toward the doorway.

"Wait—" called Esther. "I almost forgot."

When Josie turned, she envisioned all of the ominous bits of information Esther could say that could turn this triumph into a tragedy.

"Here," she said. Esther handed Josie an envelope. Her name was handwritten on the outside. Inside, in the lavish script of a Los Angeles graphic designer, were two invitations to the premiere of *The Last Counselor.*

"Thank you," said Josie, who put the invitations back in the envelope. Esther waited for some broad overture of appreciation. But if Josie proffered that to her, then she would always have to be obsequiously grateful for perks to which she was entitled. So she didn't say another word.

As soon as she walked out of the office, she called Joshua on her cell.

"Joshua, it's Josie. You need to come to my office. Today. Now. Don't bother to call, just come."

Up to now, Josie had not let Joshua know how angry she was that he had not signed their agreement. Instead they had become "friends"— and nothing more than that, since he had quite openly begun an affair with Casey, her *Life is not a Pizza* neighbor. He was charming, always, very funny, and quick-witted. He was also elusive. It was clear that he had never had any doubts he was going to make it in Hollywood, with or without Josephine O'Leary.

Josie poured herself a cup of coffee and went to her room, and instead of sitting at her desk, she chose the deep-cushioned chair where she liked to sit when she read scripts. An assistant walked over to her, handing her a telephone message from the studio's lawyer, Phillip Giberson. Her eye began to twitch.

"Hey," said a raspy woman's voice. Josie looked up and saw Heather Kavakos. She was Josie's closest ally at NJTF, even if her long nose and small blue eyes, which almost seemed to be set at each of her temples, made Josie think of a particularly mean pigeon.

Heather was smart, but she held no respect for the creative process; actually, she had no respect for anyone, except herself and the jeweler, Harry Winston. Heather was unafraid to ask her assistant to feed her dog or pull the lint from her sweaters, she was unafraid to yell about missed deadlines to blocked writers, and she was not above sleeping with the most aggressive of agents if it meant she could receive the newest, most sought-after script, despite her dazzling engagement ring.

"Sophie and I are going to dinner at Ago. Want to come?" Heather asked.

Heather's best friend was a literary agent at one of the big three agencies, a pushy, unattractive, and insincere red-haired woman from Maine named Sophie Bendix.

"Can't make it tonight," said Josie. "I'm waiting for someone."

"Do tell," said Heather.

"This writer," she replied. "The one who wrote the script Henry's going to do . . ."

"Henry's going to do your script? No fucking way. When did he tell you this?"

"About an hour ago."

"You are the luckiest girl on the planet. The fucking—wait till I tell Cohen. He's gonna flip out, just go off the fucking charts."

"Josie?" The two women turned. Joshua King stood there, expansive and broad like one of the young trees grappling for root space in the Santa Monica terrain.

Heather leered. "Are you the writer?"

"I direct too," Joshua said.

"Of course you do, handsome," Heather said, walking away and winking at Josie as she left.

"Where have you been?"

"Hey, hey, simmer down. What's the problem, sunshine?" His eyes raked over her. "I came right away. Lucky for you I was already in Santa Monica."

"Lucky me."

"Hey—is he here? The big guy? Or that woman—the producer woman, Esther? I heard she's hot." Josie grimaced. "Oh, come on," he continued. "I just wanted to meet her. Everyone says such great things about her."

"Everyone says great things about everyone out here. It's called *fiction*."

"You're so cynical," he said, sitting across from her in one of the thick-cushioned sofas. "This is a sweet place—you must rate, Josie, to get a room like this."

Josie nodded, unwilling to yield to the truth of Henry and Esther's determinedly democratic seating system.

"So what's the problem?"

"Not a problem at all." She removed contracts from her bag. "Here. Sign."

"Whoa, where's the fire?"

"Sign," she repeated.

Joshua took the documents from her and paged through them with a grave look on his face.

"Can I just—"

"No," she said.

"Don't do this," he said, and she saw that he was tired. "If I don't sign, you have a problem. You and I both know this. So listen to me for a second."

"Okay, Joshua. I'm listening."

"I don't like signing documents. On principle."

Josie smiled as sweetly as she could all the while envisioning Joshua's body being ripped apart by sharks.

"Life's full of surprises, right, and how can words, mere words, encompass everything you want? Everything you need? The blunt instrument of the law . . . how can it really protect you?" Joshua put his hand on Josie's knee. "I should have told you this before. Don't worry, though. I trust you. Let's just keep things as they are."

"Okay," she agreed. "I guess you don't want to go with me then."

"What?"

Josie picked up the envelope Esther had given her. "I have two tickets from Henry for the premiere tomorrow night. I thought you might want to go with me."

"I do!" Joshua grinned. "I'd love to go with you. I'm flattered."

She opened the envelope. "Here they are," she said. "Here they are, two tickets, two VIP party passes, two all-entry access passes." She looked at him. "It's okay. I can find someone else."

"Josie, I said I'd go."

"I know." She put the tickets back in their place. "But I'm not going to take you until you sign this contract."

Joshua stepped backward, his eyes flashing larger.

"That's blackmail," he said, not unpleasantly.

"No," she said. "We agreed on every single term here. You're the one telling me today you don't sign contracts on principle."

"I said I didn't like to sign contracts. I didn't say I *never* sign them."

Josie handed them back to him. "It's up to you. I'd love to go with you. You're my first choice."

She looked out the window and counted. She needed to stay quiet. If he did not sign, she would have to admit to Phillip Giberson, to Esther, to Henry, she had lied. She knew the premiere was the hottest event in town on Friday, but Joshua might sacrifice it to keep his independence. If anything was consistent about Joshua, it was his unpredictability.

176

"What's the deal, Josie?" Joshua asked. "What's the hurry?"

Josie deliberated quickly whether she should tell Joshua that Henry had become firmly attached to his project.

"There is no hurry," Josie lied, deciding not to give Joshua any additional ammunition for not signing. "We either have a deal, or we don't."

She put the tickets back inside the envelope. She waited. Joshua's face was clenched; she wondered if this would work.

"You got me, Josie." Joshua walked toward Josie and grabbed the pen from her hand. He scribbled his signature four times, on four different contracts. He handed her back the documents, and as Josie took them, she felt appeased, a storming ocean gone placid.

"Thank you," she said honestly, with the assurance of someone who liked to be kind when events fell into place.

It suddenly dawned on her that Henry could announce to the press his involvement with her film today, tonight, or at the premiere. All the major outlets would be there, including *Access Hollywood* and Eonline and *Entertainment Tonight* and all the magazines and news-papers . . . did she have a picture?

"Josie?" Josie snapped out of her fantasy.

"Thanks for inviting me," Joshua said.

"Thanks for doing business with me," she replied.

"No problem," he said.

He ambled to the door, more student than writer. He opened the door and was almost through when he spun around and headed back inside.

"I forgot—"

"What?"

"Don't I get a copy?" Joshua asked, pointing to the contracts Josie still held to her chest.

"Oh, of course, of course you do," Josie replied, taking one and handing it back to him. "There it is."

Joshua removed the backpack from his shoulder and unzipped

the largest compartment, whereupon he shoved the papers in, wrinkling all of them. "Thanks, Josie, thanks for coming through for me. Aren't you proud to be going to a Henry Antonelli movie with the writer of the *next* Henry Antonelli movie? Someone with a big, lucrative career ahead of him?"

"How do you know that?" Josie was shocked.

"Know what?" Joshua asked. "Why else would you want me to sign the contracts so much? You've got to want Henry to be attached, right?" Joshua looked at her closely. Josie determined he didn't know Henry was already attached, just that she wanted him to be.

"Right," said Josie. "Exactly right."

Their eyes met, and for a moment, Josie thought he was going to confront her. Instead he said "catch you later" and strolled out of the office, backpack slung on one shoulder as he cocked his head about a quarter of an inch as he left the room.

Josie ran to the door behind Joshua and closed it. She strode back to her desk and picked up the signed documents. She looked for his signature, and as she saw that it was full and florid and clearly said "Joshua King," she felt a relief so strong she thought it would sweep her up like the tornado in *The Wizard of Oz*.

She paged an assistant named Anna on the intercom. "Get Phillip Giberson for me," she barked.

She secretly picked up the handset, glowing when she heard Anna say to Phillip's assistant, "Josephine O'Leary for Phillip?" She held her breath.

"One moment for Phillip Giberson," said the assistant.

Josie held her tongue.

"Phillip Giberson here."

"One moment for Josephine O'Leary," said Anna.

She felt it, a shiver on her neck as the Invisible Hand lifted her up and placed her on a pedestal.

"Hello, Phillip," she said as she inwardly cartwheeled and somersaulted and backflipped. For not only did she have signed documents and the option agreement in hand, not only did she have a date for the premiere, not only did she have a movie *with Henry Antonelli*, but two seconds ago, she had bested Phillip Giberson in Hollywood Telephone by getting on the line *last*.

Chapter Twenty

The premiere for *The Last Counselor* was held at Grauman's Chinese Theater on Hollywood and Highland Avenue in Old Hollywood. Spotlights splashed the façade, blending with the suffused light of the ninety-foot-high jade-green bronze roof. Marked by spectacular coral-red columns, emblazoned by stone-carved Fu Dogs that emphatically deterred evil spirits (or, since so many movies premiered here, evil film critics), the Chinese Theater had been one of Hollywood's majestic landmarks since 1927. It would have been lauded for the architecture alone, even if actress Norma Talmadge had not unwittingly (or not) stepped in the cement outside the theater leaving her footprint preserved forever, triggering a parade of cement-etched foot- and handprints of the country's most famous stars.

For Paulette Giberson, formerly of Wilmington, Delaware, then of New York, Paris, London, Warsaw, Vienna, Leningrad, Cairo, Beirut, Belfast, Dar es Salaam, Accra, Madrid, the Seychelles, and Santiago, the entire event was ponderous. She had been at the Ivy in Beverly Hills, on North Robertson Boulevard, for an hour suffering the sweet glances of the waitresses, as she waited for Henry Antonelli and his wife, Cecilia Rosenberg. They had never come, and it wasn't until she called her hotel that she received the message from Henry saying he had been waiting at the Ivy in Santa Monica but was going to have to leave to make it to the premiere on time. His message relayed the hope that he would see her at the premiere, and the information that she had a reserved ticket for the VIP section.

She remembered he had always been a flake.

In another limousine paid for by Mike's money, Josie and Joshua waited to step out of their car until Josie's friend Catherine, the publicist, gave the okay. Joshua had shown up in Hollywood casual, with a blue long-sleeved shirt that matched his eyes, and cargo pants, and Josie remembered, suddenly, how attractive a man he was, and how long it had been since she had slept with anyone.

"I hate these things," said Joshua. "I really do."

"I'm not surprised," Josie answered. "I do too. We have to go, you know. Perils of the business."

Joshua nodded as he checked his hair in the mirror. Outside, Catherine gave them the signal, and the chauffeur opened the door, and Josie extended one of her tan, hairless legs. She felt Joshua's hand on her back and quietly, ecstatically, shuddered.

At the same time, Carla was discussing her evening with her nephew, Christopher.

"What do you think?" she asked, turning to him with a big smile.

"Of what?"

"Of this lipstick." She had put on a bright red color that she thought illuminated her face.

"You look like a clown." She looked back at the mirror. He was right. She took it off with a tissue.

"What about the hair?"

Christopher looked closer. "Hmm . . . ," he said, examining her. "I think you should let it grow long."

"Long. Okay." Carla took a step back. "Is anything good?"

"You're beautiful," he said honestly. "And I like your shoes."

"Come here, you charmer," Carla said, pulling Christopher to her in an embrace. He wriggled away just as the doorbell rang. She was instantly nervous. When she opened the door, David Stegner was standing under the porch light, carrying a bunch of fresh lilacs.

"I know him," said Christopher.

"I'm your father's friend," said David.

"I know," Christopher said, extending a small-boned arm. He shook David's hand.

"Well, my goodness, Master Giberson. A good evening to you too, kind sir."

Christopher looked back at his mother with a bewildered expression. Samantha motioned for Christopher to turn back around.

"What grade are you in now, Christopher?" David enunciated every syllable, as if the boy didn't speak English.

"Third."

"Third? And what is your favorite class?"

"Recess. And science."

David beamed approvingly. "Well, provided you are applying yourself, it's a good thing you're enjoying recess. At least you're not watching television."

At this, even Carla turned back to look at Samantha, who shrugged.

"He loves math and science. And maps. Our own Magellan, Phillip always says." Samantha turned toward her son. "Chris, David works with scientists all the time, at an energy plant."

Christopher practiced opening his eyes bigger, and then smaller. He wanted to show his friends at school how he could stretch his eyelids almost out of their sockets.

"What if I take you down to the plant one day, Master Giberson?" asked David.

"Okay," the boy said.

"Maybe you can help him with his energy report?" Samantha asked. "Third grade stuff, but you could be his expert opinion."

"Could you do that?" Christopher's eyes had shot up, knowing already, in his third grade mind, that if he did well on his report he could get the new Sony PlayStation.

"I could," David replied, "and I shall." He looked over at Carla. "Are we off?"

"Are you sure you don't want to come with us?" asked Samantha. "Phillip will be home in a second."

"We'll meet you there," said David. "I need some time to get reacquainted with Carla Trousse. I can barely recognize her."

He looked into her eyes, and Carla felt ready to take on the world.

"Let's go then. See you there, Samantha," Carla said.

David opened the door for her, and waited for her to put on her seat belt before he moved. She was tense in the car, suddenly drained of conversation. He was different from how she remembered him, and she was shocked to see that his nose was shunted to the side and his tiny, pebble-sized eyes seemed even smaller underneath an impressive cliff of brow.

"Cars aren't very important to you, are they?" asked Carla, as she looked at the chipped gray paint of his Honda.

"Think how much better the world would be if everyone were forced to use bicycles. They'd be in better shape, there'd be less pollution, the whole world would be better."

"But you can't really bicycle from Santa Monica to Old Hollywood," Carla said.

"Well, you could, but it would cramp the dating situations, that's for sure." David grinned, which made her take the fingernail she was biting away from her mouth.

"Ready?" David asked.

"Ready," said Carla.

David pulled away from the curb.

At that moment, Henry was preparing to step out of his limo. Cecilia, Esther, and Esther's husband, Aram, were waiting for him to leave first. Cecilia looked gorgeous, and Henry was happy that the restlessness that had plagued him earlier in the summer had vanished. Now he was confident again. He placed his foot on the curb. A cheer erupted. He had done this many times, but each time he walked through the press to get into a theater, he was infused with delight and fear.

"Everyone ready?" he asked. They nodded. "All right, then," Henry said, fully emerging from the car.

"Showtime," he said, as the lights hit.

Chapter Twenty-One

"I loved it," said Carla. "I really did."

The crowd outside the theater moved in a rumbling, boisterous throng to the afterparty—a football-stadium-sized room, where people spilled from every conceivable crevice and black-tie suited waiters served drinks and food.

By the closing credits, Carla had been swept away by the charm of the story, about an old lawyer trying his last case before his retirement. "Understated, dramatic, a love story—I didn't think Henry did these kinds of movies."

"What kind of movies did you think he did?" asked Paulette.

"Action, rock 'em, sock 'em, you know."

"No, I don't."

Carla locked eyes with Paulette and for a moment considered challenging her. But instead, Carla leaned in and kissed Paulette on the cheek. "One day I'll tell you how thankful I am." She spun around. "But not now."

David was standing awkwardly in the center of the room. She looked at him amid the crowd and was embarrassed to see his discomfort. She sensed a churning ego within David, mostly because of the way he yelled at other drivers when they passed him on the freeway or drove too close to his car. "I'll show you, buster," he had said at least twice. Yet he had insisted on opening all the doors for her, and even complimented her that she wasn't too much of a feminist to disdain good old-fashioned chivalry. She had beamed.

She walked up to David. "How are you doing?"

"Fine," he said, straightening. "Your aunt is a tough nut."

"Tell me about it," Carla said.

"Do you want a drink?"

"I'd love a drink."

David flagged down a waiter carrying champagne.

"Have you gone over to the dark side yet?" Carla asked.

"The dark side?"

"Drinking? Remember last time you told me you had never been drunk."

"Still haven't. And never inhaled either."

"The schoolboy."

David patted his stomach. "The machine."

Carla turned around. She saw everyone: the elaborately costumed, the waitresses, the VIP section, the business-suited, the baseball-hatted, the casual sandal-wearers, and the perpetually tanned. She felt the warmth of a crowd proud of themselves, proud that for the next week, they had bragging rights.

She finished her first glass of champagne and signaled for the next. She felt like a woman who had been cooped up inside a house for twenty years. She was going to take full advantage of this party.

On the other side of the room, Esther walked toward Josie with Phillip.

"Josie, there's someone you should meet." Esther approached her, dragging a man with a broad fair-skinned face, a balding pate, and big hazel eyes looking through thin gold eyeglasses. He wore khakis and a button-down oxford shirt, but he did not exude the jittery nerves of many of the people in the room. He looked both smart and confident. Josie extended her hand to the man.

"Phillip Giberson," he said.

"Josephine O'Leary," she said, beaming. "Did you get the papers?"

"I did," he said. "Late this afternoon."

"Assistants," Josie said wearily, as if stories of their competence were a universal falsehood.

"Who are you talking about?" asked Esther. Josie had forgotten she was there.

"No, no one," Josie said, backpedaling. "I love my assistant."

"Great to meet you," Phillip said. "We'll have a chance to talk about business later." He smiled at Josie and left for another part of the room.

Joshua tapped Esther on the shoulder. "Mrs. Rabinowitz?"

"Yes."

"Maybe Josie's told you about me? I'm Joshua King."

"Joshua!" Esther brightened considerably. "What a pleasure. Call me Esther. Josie has definitely talked about you—we're so thrilled we're going to be working with you! Very impressive script."

Joshua scratched his head and Josie saw that he held her world in his hand, a simple toss to Esther could finish her off.

"Thanks," Joshua said to Esther. "Glad you think so. We'll be in touch." When he turned away, he pinched the upper flesh of Josie's arm.

"Ow!" blared Josie when Joshua had pulled her away. "Stop doing that."

"What was she talking about, Josie? And tell me the truth."

"I was going to tell you," said Josie. "Henry said today he wanted to play the lead."

Joshua said nothing for a long moment. Then his face broke into an impressed smile. "You're a piece of work, Josie. Don't let anyone tell you different. You're a piece of work."

"I assume that's a compliment, so thank you," she answered. Joshua did not reply. "What?" asked Josie. "Don't be mad. You've got Henry Antonelli *in your movie.*"

"What do you get?"

"What do you mean, what do I get? I get what I deserve."

"And what's that?"

"Same old, same old. Credit and money."

"What credit? And how much money?"

"Producing credit, of course. And the money isn't your business."

"No? There's no movie without my material."

"Joshua, handsome?" Josie placed her hand on his elbow and looked up into his eyes. "Can we not talk about this now? We should be celebrating."

Josie could not see his face.

"Don't be like that," Josie admonished.

"I'm fine," Joshua said, looking down at her. "Don't worry, luscious. I'm fine."

"Good," said Josie, as she watched Juliet Eckhardt, the woman who hadn't invited her to her birthday party, cross the room.

"Josie!" gushed Juliet. "It's been so long!"

On the other side of the room, Henry, Cecilia, and Paulette had finally managed to move to a table in the VIP section. Paulette, her cashmere scarf around her neck, embraced Henry.

"You look superb, Henry, you really do."

"Thank you, Paulette."

"You're quite the celebrity, aren't you? A far cry from our galloping days."

"I still get out there from time to time."

"When could you? This lifestyle seems to be pervasive." Cecilia exchanged a look with Henry, as Paulette continued. "One gets used to all things, of course. But I can't help but think that all this money could be better spent."

"No doubt about it," said Henry. "It could."

"Well," Paulette opened up her purse. "There's something I want to tell you—"

"Henry Antonelli!" said a man's voice. A spotlight swung to his seat. The crowd burst into applause. Henry stood. "I have to answer a few more questions." Henry reached over to touch Cecilia's shoulder. "Later, okay Paulette?" Henry left before Paulette had a chance to respond.

Meanwhile, Carla had finished her fourth glass of champagne. David was leaning against the bar, swatting cigarette smoke from his eyes.

"You're different," David said, looking at Carla flitter around him. "I don't remember that you drank." He sounded unduly grim. Carla did not remember this quality.

"I don't. Just for tonight. For my Hollywood premiere . . ."

"Do as you see fit," answered David.

"Are you having a good time?" asked Carla.

David looked contemptuously at the crowd.

"C'mon, it's a movie. You're not enjoying this?" Carla looked at David with genuine surprise, not believing that anyone would not enjoy the spectacle of a Hollywood movie opening.

"No," David said. "Several elements to this evening trouble me. I'd be lying if I said they didn't."

Carla, who had stepped closer to listen to David amid the noise of the crowd, now took a full step backward. "What?" She was puzzled.

"You heard me," he said.

"But it's just a movie," Carla replied. "How hard is it to have a good time?"

"Maybe I don't think like you," he replied. Inwardly, David Stegner was furious with himself. He had gone on this date with Carla Trousse hoping to find a woman as mature and sophisticated as himself. Eve Marvell, his erstwhile, insipid ex-girlfriend, had broken up with him two weeks ago. Carla's phone call had arrived just when he was ridding himself of all of Eve's appurtenances. He had had high hopes for tonight, all of which were crashing as he watched this woman dazzled by a group of idiots.

"I'll be here watching," David said.

David's expression was unreadable to Carla; it seemed a smile but it could also have been a grimace. Carla flitted around him, and David's eyes flashed to either side. "Are you really upset?" said Carla. "What did you think this was going to be? Wait—I know that person." Carla had spotted someone near the bar. "I'll be right back."

David shrugged. "Do what you want," he answered.

Carla charged up to her NYU friend, Jimmy Stigwood, a medium-sized man with a tweed jacket and small shoulders. His hair was the color of a ripe beefsteak tomato. "Jimmy!" she exclaimed. "It's Carla. Carla Trousse."

The man raised his eyebrows. "It's James now, James Stigwood." He examined Carla. "I almost didn't recognize you, Carla." He lowered his voice. "I don't call myself Jimmy anymore."

"Before I thought you were going to say James, James Bond."

"Haven't heard that before," Jimmy said. "Ever."

"Hey—I live here now. Why didn't you call me back?"

"You know," Jimmy answered, as he looked over Carla's right shoulder. "Don't take this the wrong way but—" he looked over her left shoulder. "I have to go talk to that bald guy over there. Good to see you." Jimmy walked away.

"But—" Carla spoke to the air. She twirled around, curious. It was considerably better to be snubbed when she was partly inebriated.

She strutted back to the table where Paulette sat by herself.

"So," Carla began. "Paulette."

"Hello, Carla."

"Okay. Go. Shoot. I'm here before you with all of my inimitable intransigence. What do you want to tell me?"

"Now's not the time, Carla. Tomorrow."

"No, I think now's a good time. Don't you think? I mean, you and I aren't very close anyway, so we shouldn't pretend. And just name me a better time than this. Name one!"

"Tomorrow, Carla."

"No, Paulette," Carla matched the tone of Paulette's voice with her own. "Now. I've waited so long. What could it be?"

"You're drunk."

"No, I've been drinking. There's a difference. I'll tell you when I'm drunk."

"That isn't funny."

"It is to me."

"Carla, I suggest you find yourself someone to serve you a cup of coffee."

"Paulette, please," said Carla, raising her voice. "Would you just do one thing for me, one thing in your whole life? Could you just once, right now, do something I asked you to do just because I asked you? I want to know what you wanted to talk to me about. Tell me!"

Paulette sat, impassive.

"Tell me!" Carla was now shouting.

"Fine," Paulette's eyes flashed. She spoke in even, cutting words. "I am your mother, Carla. Henry Antonelli is your biological father." Carla stared at Paulette. "I repeat, I am your mother. Henry Antonelli is your father. Candace is your aunt. I was not prepared to raise a child when I became pregnant and Candace and I both agreed this was the proper way to proceed. Candace couldn't have children of her own. That's what I wanted to tell you."

"Ha!" Carla laughed, and then shook her head a little, tilting it to the right, and left, and back and forth. She turned back to the crowd, spotting David alone at a table, unsmiling.

"Did you hear me?" Paulette spoke crisply, as if the words sliced her tongue.

"What is the matter with you, anyway?" Carla stared at Paulette. "Really? How did you come up with a story like that?"

"It isn't a story. It's the truth."

"Paulette, everything is going right for me now. Why do you want to ruin it?"

"I resent that. I'm not ruining anything. I'm telling you the truth so you can stop griping about how life's mistreated you."

"Right, Henry Antonelli's my father."

"Yes," said Paulette. "He is."

Since neither Paulette nor Carla were involved in the true Hollywood network of publicists and reporters and columnists, they had not recognized Nell McKnight, friend of Josie O'Leary's and roving entertainment reporter, standing behind them, listening to every word.

She took notes, and then rushed over to Josie.

"Josie," whispered Nell. "Boy, are you going to want to hear this."

Josie whipped around to see her thermometer-thin friend Nell leaning into her ear. "Did you find out already?" Josie thought that Nell must have gleaned information from someone at NJTF that Henry had agreed to star in her film.

"Find out what?"

"You tell me."

"That woman over there, the chubby one with the red glasses? She's Henry's daughter."

Josie peered across the room. Nell pointed toward a woman with dark brown hair and red glasses, wearing a royal blue button-down shirt with a bright orange skirt.

"You're slipping, Nell."

"I heard it." Nell shook her head. "I don't know. My gut says it's true."

"Did you hear it from Henry directly?"

"Nope, from that woman talking to our fashion victim."

"Oh come on, Nell. You're better than this. Do you eavesdrop on my conversations too?"

"Of course. You can doubt me, Josie, but I'm going to call some sources. That woman spoke very clearly and I wrote it all down. If it's true, I'm going huge with it. Don't forget I gave you the heads-up."

Nell rushed off, her cell phone pressed against her skull. Josie looked at the chubby woman again. She was dressed like a court jester without the funny shoes, and Josie turned away.

But as she crossed to the anteroom of the party, Nell collided with Henry Antonelli. She would have preferred to wait for confirmation, but she had to seize the chance before her.

"Henry," Nell said, as Henry apologized for walking into her. "I've just heard a bombshell."

Henry shook his head. "I've finished my interviews for tonight. You can schedule something with my publicist."

"Do you have a daughter?"

"What?" Henry grew annoyed. "No."

"Then who's that?" Nell pointed to Carla.

"I have no idea."

"Really? Because the woman next to her just told her that you're her father."

Henry squinted his eyes to focus in on the table where Nell was pointing. A woman with red glasses was talking to Paulette.

Paulette.

"Excuse me, will you?" Henry's facial expression was unchanged, but Nell sensed opportunity. She found Josie at the bar.

"Watch, Josie, watch. Look at Henry right now. He's talking to that woman. I think it may be true."

"It can't be—" Josie was now staring at the table. Henry was huddled over between the two women, and when he rose again to his full height, she saw that he looked perturbed.

"I'm going to get this confirmed, but be warned. This is going to be huge."

Nell ran away from Josie, whose eyes had not left the sight of Henry, Paulette, and Carla thirty feet away. "I get it," said Josie, to no one in particular. She began to move through the crowd to get closer.

"This is ridiculous," said Carla.

"What is ridiculous is this forum," Paulette replied. "I had nothing to do with that. It's all your own choosing."

"Are you serious, Paulette? Forty-one years ago? You're telling me now? Now?" Henry raised his voice enough that other people began to look over, and when they saw he was agitated, they remained looking.

Josie had edged closer.

"We need to leave," said Henry. "We need to discuss this. Cecilia. Come on," he ordered. Paulette and Carla stood behind him. Carla held on to the back of a chair. She looked around for David but could not find him. Phillip was not visible either. She found herself focusing on details like the weave of thread on the tablecloth, the flower in the hair of the ingénue. Keeping her eyes focused on a door in the distance, she followed Paulette, who followed Henry and Cecilia. Like children behind the pied piper, they walked fast behind their leader, Henry.

Carla willed her eyes to remain steadfastly on the red EXIT sign in the corner of the room. She walked nervously behind the others but tripped when they were only a couple of feet away. Her knees buckled, and she fell to the floor.

Skinny arms pulled her up again, but Carla could not see who was helping her because blonde hair was in her face. When Carla was standing again, the woman pushed her hair out of her eyes. It was the awful woman from the Ivy, Nadine's old boss.

"I'm Josie," she said. "Is it true?"

Carla stared her in the eye, drunkenness gone, meanness in its place.

"We've met," she snapped. "Get out of my way."

Part Three

Chapter Twenty-Two

Looking in the mirror in her room at Phillip's, Carla examined her face just as she had in New York. The flushed tone of her skin that had emboldened her during her first six weeks in California had begun to fade during the three weeks since she had quarantined herself in her room; her East Coast paleness had returned and she felt strangely comforted.

The mirror in her California room was heavy and horizontally arrayed; Carla stepped back for a second but still could see only from her waist to her head, like a magician's assistant, sawed in half. Her hair was still wet, from the shower. She stepped back to the mirror and picked up a comb. When it did not go smoothly through the tangled mass, she yanked at it, harder and harder, until she tore the snarled clump from her head. She looked at it, the matted knot of hair, strangely pleased. She didn't look at herself again in the mirror. Instead, she threw the knot into the corner and pulled on sweatpants and an extra large T-shirt, sat back down on her bed, and began to eat Oreos, one after another, until the entire sleeve was gone.

"Carla?" asked Christopher through the closed door. "Carla?"

"Code word," she answered.

"Bilbo." Carla was going to force-feed *The Hobbit* to Christopher whether he liked it or not.

"Enter," she said.

Christopher walked in, carrying a paper bag.

"Did you bring the stuff?" she asked.

He nodded. She took the bag and removed the pint of Ben & Jerry's Vanilla Heath Bar Crunch.

"And?" she waited.

He took out a spoon from his pants pocket. "Mom said to give you this," he said. He handed her a sheet of paper.

Calls

1. The *Times* (LA & N.Y.), the AP, the *Sun* (UK), the *Guardian* (UK), all the Delaware papers

2. The TV hostesses keep calling—even a message from Oprah (which I saved)

3. James Stigwood (that asshole)

4. Clive from New York???

5. Gerry Simpson, says he works with you

6. Henry, for the seven hundredth time.

We miss you.
Love, Samantha

Carla crumpled up the paper. "Time for *SpongeBob*," she said.

"I can't," said Christopher. "I have piano lessons."

"Well, come back when it's on later," she said.

"Tennis," he said. "And then I have a sleepover at Danny's."

"Fine," said Carla. "Abandon me."

"What?"

"Nothing," she said. "Go away."

Christopher didn't move.

"Go away," she repeated.

"I'm coming back," he said. "Maybe we can watch *SpongeBob* tomorrow."

"Maybe," she said. "Hey, wait a second. What do you think of my hair?" She pulled up the thick patch of hair. "I ripped it out."

Christopher shrugged. "Why'd you do that?"

"Felt like it," she said.

"Mom could have helped."

"I don't want any help."

He shrugged. "All right," he said. "Bye." He left the room.

"Hey—wait!" Carla called after him. Christopher popped his head back in.

"You know I love you," Carla said.

"Yeah."

"I'm just—I'm kinda playing hide-and-seek with the world right now, and it makes me grumpy."

"I know. It's okay."

"Have I been that bad?"

Christopher shrugged. "Yeah."

"Want some ice cream?" she pushed the pint toward him. "I won't tell your mom."

He smiled widely, as he took the spoon from her and dug into the carton.

"You're my protector?" Carla asked him. He nodded happily, still swallowing. "All right. Let me wallow, go to your piano lesson."

"Mom said you'll be normal soon. Don't worry."

Christopher spoke with the certainty of the innocent. Carla felt her heart expand, as she allowed his words to comfort her.

"Thanks, sweetheart," she said, as he handed her back the pint and left the room.

Alone again, Carla spun through the channels. She wouldn't watch any news programs, refused to read any newspapers or magazines.

From her window, she watched the clouds build and dissipate; she saw the glorious skies of summer and the profuse flowers that spread colored swaths around every household. But she didn't go outside. She was too angry and too helpless. Christopher was her one respite. She still did not know what to do.

Of course, she blamed everything on Paulette. Her mother. Her *real* mother. Candace, Carla's "former" mother (what would she call herself now?), had called Carla after the revelation.

"Well, now you know," she had said. "Good."

"Mother—I mean Candace—you can't think—" Carla had stammered.

"Oh, Carla, please do not be so dramatic," Candace said, through the scratchy phone lines stretching over the oceans. "Does it really even matter? Paulette and I are sisters. Are we that different?"

Carla hung up the phone staggered at Candace's rightousness, at her inability to admit she was wrong.

Paulette, on the other hand, dealt only in the big-ticket items, the explosive revelations and the page one headlines.

"There's nothing more I need to say," Paulette had told Carla, Henry, Phillip, and Cecilia immediately after the premiere. "I thought you two should know about each other. It isn't life-changing—you are what you make of yourself, Carla, not who your parents are. I thought this information would help get you out of your lifelong devotion to self-indulgence. I do not need to apologize for your upbringing. You were safe, healthy, and cared for."

"What about me?" snapped Henry, irate. "Did you think once you could have told me?"

"No," Paulette had answered. "Not even once. You were twenty-one. We were dating. It had nothing to do with you."

Henry fumed, Cecilia had put her hands in her hair, Phillip had jumped up from his seat.

"Mother, do you realize what you've done?"

"What do you mean?"

"The press? Do you understand Henry's stature?"

Paulette had looked at Phillip with defiance. "You, Phillip, can choose to let this business rule your life. I, however, refuse to pay any attention to the lowest common denominator of our country, who would prefer to ogle *actors* than concentrate on the poverty and diseases that are annihilating entire countries. I thought I would be helping Carla, and, I may point out, it was Carla who insisted I give her the information at the premiere. That was not my choice."

Carla had bit her nails, one after the other, cuticle, nail bed, skin around the soft flesh of the tips. They were all in the living room at Phillip's house, limousines idling outside. Carla had taken in the information imparted by Paulette as one would hear the news about the famine in Ethiopia. She could and would dwell on it at some point in her future, but right now she thought instead of David Stegner who had abruptly left her side when she became the target of the paparazzi.

"Carla," said Henry. "What do you want to do?"

Carla turned toward him. "Do you remember when we spoke?"

"What?"

"At the Ivy. I went up to you and said I knew Paulette."

"Right," he said, remembering. "Right. That's a hell of a coincidence." He paused. "Was I civil?"

"Yes," said Carla. "Very."

"Are we through?" asked Paulette, looking impatiently at her watch.

"Through? No, we're not through," said Henry. "Carla hasn't answered my question. Her life does change now, whether you want to recognize it or not. I'm not a private person. And now, courtesy of your outburst, the entire press knows."

"They'll forget about it in a week," Paulette said.

"Not quite," said Samantha.

"I think I'm going to call my friend LK," said Phillip. "She's a great publicist—she'll know how to proceed—"

"I could put in a call too," said Henry.

"What?" Carla interjected. "Publicists?"

"Unless some old movie star dies, or there's a terrorist attack, or a serial killer shows up, you're the news," said Phillip. "It's just a fact."

"That just proves my point," said Paulette. "People are stupid. You don't have to stoop to that level, Carla."

"Carla," said Cecilia, who had been quiet. "What is it you want? This is going to affect you most of all."

Carla closed her eyes. She wanted to go to the Glomming Company and read her scripts and talk to Nadine. She wanted to go on a real date with David Stegner—where he would be relaxed and charming. She hated the thought that she might have wasted all these years—positive that the memory she held of David was valid, that he was in fact like a sexy Einstein, rather than the rigid Mussolini he seemed at the premiere. She hoped she was wrong.

"I don't know," Carla had said. "I'm going to sleep."

She left the living room, walking up the stairs to her room. She pulled down the shades, locked the door, and lay down on her bed. She had been awake all night, trying to remember John Trousse, the man who had died when Carla was three. When she was a child, Candace had told her she was lucky to have even one parent, as there were so many unloved orphans in the world. All the while, Candace knew about Henry. It was almost unfathomable to Carla, except that it was true.

By Monday morning, Carla had convinced herself that she was capable of resuming her life. She showered and came downstairs as was her habit, but Samantha had ushered her straight into the basement, where there were no windows.

"They're on the front lawn. And in the back. Maybe you should stay home today."

"No," asserted Carla. "No way. I want to go to work."

Phillip clamored down the stairs, "Really, Carla, I think maybe you should stay."

Carla looked at him pleadingly. "Please," she said. "Please. I need to do something normal."

Phillip acquiesced, but as soon as she walked outside, the reporters had swarmed, and she got into the car gasping.

"We can turn around and go back," Phillip told her. "I've called a security service." He drove slowly down the street. "You know—don't take this the wrong way, Carla, promise me that—but Henry says you can go and live with him; it may be more private."

"Do you want me to go?" Carla knew she sounded hurt.

"No, no," insisted Phillip. "You can stay with us as long as you want. As long as you want. I just—I just hate to see all these people around. Henry probably has a locked gate. You wouldn't have to deal with all of this."

Carla turned her face out to the freeway. They were heading east on the 10. "I'll be fine. Please let me stay."

"Of course," Phillip answered. "Anything you want. But you will have to talk to him sometime," Phillip added. "Not today, not tomorrow, but—"

"I understand," said Carla.

"Okay then," answered Phillip, driving through the gates to Studio X, where both Phillip and the Glomming Company had their offices.

When Carla stepped through the doors of the Glomming Company, Magda rushed to embrace her.

"Oh, Carla!" Magda exclaimed in her baritone voice.

"What are you doing?" Carla pulled out of Magda's arms.

"Congratulations!" said Magda.

"Excuse me?"

"For being Henry Antonelli's daughter! You're so lucky!" Carla stared. "You can be in his movies now, I bet. I bet a million dollars."

Rilke, the girl from Baltimore, had appeared in one of the archways. "It's all so droll," she remarked.

"It's many things," Carla said, "but I don't know if droll is one of them."

"You know. Predictable."

"My being Henry's daughter is predictable?" Carla said.

"No, just that you of all people turn out to be famous."

Carla blanched.

"Don't get upset," Rilke continued. "It's just that you're famous now and didn't have to do anything. It's kind of unfair." Rilke pursed her lips as she walked by Carla. "The rest of us work so hard and you—"

"What's that?" Gerry Simpson barged into the lobby. "Carla. Glad you're here. Good. A real trouper." He put his hand on Carla's back, pushing her toward his office. "Let's have a seat, okay? We have to keep talking, keep communicating, that's the best thing."

"I just want to go to my desk—"

"Sure, sure thing. But let's talk first." Gerry looked back at Magda. "Hold my calls."

He ushered Carla to the purple armchair in front of his desk. "I've been thinking all night. We can spin this the right way, I know it. I've been on the phone with some reporter friends of mine—I really think *The Reporter* is the way to go, *Variety* is so, well, obvious, and I've promised I've got the exclusive. So what I'm thinking is that we leak that you're a real development person here, give you Nadine's title probably, and then get Henry to issue some kind of quote talking about how glad he is to have you as a daughter. I told Roland that Henry and Kirk Gordon would get that film about the nomads green-lit in a heartbeat. In a heartbeat."

Carla listened to Gerry as she looked around the room. There was a picture of his wife and two children, all of them similarly skinny, similarly curly-haired. There were also photographs of Gerry with all kinds of celebrities. Gerry walked over to the mantel.

"We can set you up with some trend-makers. And we've got to get you a trainer; don't take this the wrong way, but maybe you should think about dropping some poundage. We should come up with some kind of press release." Gerry spoke without stopping, braying his information loudly, aggressively. Carla stood up.

"What are you doing?" Gerry asked.

"Going to my desk."

"Come on, Carla. Be serious. You're not working at that cubicle anymore. That's for *D-girls*, not you."

"Are you firing me?"

"That's funny. You're of some use to us now! Why would I fire you?"

"Now?" Carla walked to the door. "What was I before?"

"You were in *development*," sneered Gerry. "This is the big leagues."

When she got back to her cubicle, Carla was stunned to find flower arrangements covering every available space. She picked up some of the cards: *From your friends at X*, said one, and *Please call, I can help. Jimmy Stigwood.*

"Wow," said Nadine, from behind her. Carla turned. "You've got a lot on your plate."

"This is crazy," Carla said.

"This is Hollywood," answered Nadine. "What are you doing here?"

"I wanted to go to work."

"Well, you should want to get right back home. Your work here is effectively done." Nadine picked up an errant tulip from one of the arrangements. "Did Gerry try to sign you?"

"Sign me? For what?"

"He's going to want to handle your publicity, hand it off to one of his friends, at least until you're not famous anymore."

"I'm not famous."

"Carla, I'm not joking here. Wake up! Your father is Henry Antonelli. You're not normal anymore."

"I am exactly the same," Carla said stubbornly. She crossed her arms in front of her chest. "I just want to do my job and go home. That's what I want to do."

"I'm sorry," Nadine responded. "But that's impossible. It isn't up to you right now. It'll go away and no one will care. Then you can do what you want. But right now—forget it."

Carla blinked. She felt tears behind her eyes and she was determined not to let anyone, even Nadine, see her cry.

"C'mon," said Nadine. "Let's go into my office."

Carla followed. Rilke, Magda, and Gerry were standing in the corner of one of the empty cubicles, ostensibly talking about a script. Carla felt their gaze as obviously as if their faces were hovering in front of her nose. She closed her eyes again, angry that she could not control her trembling.

Nadine shut the door behind them. "Carla, I'm sorry. Really. But—"

"But what?" snapped Carla. "But what?"

"But it may not be all bad."

"All bad? All bad?" Carla couldn't stop herself, she started to cry. She held herself tightly. "Just have them leave me alone."

"They won't." Nadine handed Carla a Kleenex. "To them, you're the luckiest person in the world. Now everyone's just waiting for you to make your monetary demands."

"They think I'm going to ask Henry for money?" Carla asked, incredulous.

"Uh, yeah," answered Nadine. "And some people even think that you may have engineered this by yourself to get some attention."

"That's the most ridiculous thing I've ever heard." Carla stopped crying. "It's just insane. Who would do that? Who would willingly bring on this kind of attention?"

"Happens every day out here," said Nadine. "Everyone wants to be famous. But people really are going to think this is about money. You know that, right? What are you going to do?"

"What am I going to do?" Carla repeated. "If that isn't the question of the hour, I don't know. What does one do when this happens? Is there a precedent?"

"What does Henry say?"

"Henry? I don't know. I haven't talked to him."

"Has he called?" Carla nodded. "Then how come you haven't spoken to him?"

"The weekend was too fraught," said Carla. "And today Paulette left."

"Paulette left?"

"Yes," said Carla.

"She left you?" Nadine's face grew concerned. "She really left?"

"Yes."

"She couldn't wait to see how things went for you?"

"She said that while she could wait, the people of Indonesia couldn't."

"Uh-huh," stammered Nadine. "Right." The internal intercom clicked. Nadine picked up the receiver. "Hello?" And then, "Okay, I'll tell her." She hung up.

"Roland wants to see you," said Nadine. "Immediately."

"He's never even spoken to me before," Carla said.

"I bet the idea of Kirk Gordon working with Henry has got him foaming at the mouth."

"Why does everyone think I can tell Henry what to do?" asked Carla.

"Because it's all about access," Nadine shook her head. "You've got it in the palm of your hand. Access. You can do anything in this town because of him."

"That's ridiculous. I barely know Henry."

"You're his daughter."

"Words. Semantics. Biology. I don't know him at all."

"Carla—"

"What?"

"It's up to you what you do."

"Yeah."

"This will blow over."

"Right."

"But people out here would kill for this kind of relationship with a movie star. Other people will think you can tell Henry what to do, that you have his ear. And the truth is, you may even have it—who knows? You could become close with him. You won't ever have to do a coverage again."

"That's just it, Nadine," said Carla. "It may sound bizarre, but I like writing coverage."

After Carla left, Nadine called Ernie to give him an update. "She wants to write coverages, still! But what do you think, could she maybe get me a job at NJTF?"

Carla's meeting with Roland was as brief as she could make it. She left, telling him she needed some time to think everything through.

Outside the Glomming Company, she was forced to step around an idling golf cart.

"Miss Trousse?" said the driver from underneath the vinyl top. He was a kid of about twenty-five, with blond hair greased upward and a red collared shirt.

"Yes?" she had said.

"I'm here for you," he said. "I heard you were here, and figured you probably needed a ride to your car. I'm Damien. I love Henry Antonelli. He's the bomb, like, just the bomb."

"Leave me alone," she had said, storming away. She put on sunglasses and stomped over to Phillip's office, on the third floor of one of the older studio buildings. She remembered what it was like to climb the floors to her old New York apartment. It was a momentary infusion of confidence.

But at Phillip's, she had wilted again. In the anteroom, before she was led into Phillip's office, it had been the same thing. A furor of whispers and nudges, a welter of "How are you doing?" and "What shocking news!" and "What are you going to do?" She felt weak and agitated. Phillip had driven her home in silence, and this time, when she emerged from the car, she had barreled through the reporters with her elbows outstretched.

But when she saw who was waiting on the front doorstep, she stopped.

"Carla!" said the reporter, a small wire-bound notebook in his hand, a grim expression on his face. "I know you're probably overwhelmed, the last thing you want to do is talk to a reporter, but since we're old friends, I thought maybe I'd be the one you'd speak with. Obviously the stories will be written—you should have someone on your side."

Carla stared at Jimmy Stigwood, in his pressed gray trousers and Gucci loafers, his white collared shirt and bright red hair, and thought, *he looks so much like Howdy Doody.*

Carla looked over Jimmy's shoulder, just as he had done at the premiere. She felt her anger intensify—with no sleep and no outlet for her new status, she felt combustible.

"You will *never* interview me," she yelled at Jimmy. "Do you think I've forgotten how you treated me?"

"That's old news, Carla. You won't get anywhere if you hold grudges. Carla, listen. You need me. Not the other way around. I'm going to write the profile no matter what."

"I wouldn't expect anything different," Carla railed at him. "You shallow piece of—you know, don't take this the wrong way, *James,* but I have to go inside now. I don't need you."

She walked by him and inside the front door, which she slammed as hard as she could.

She felt momentarily purged, but only until she read Jimmy's profile of her in a respected literary weekly. It was the beginning of Carla's learning curve about the media. Jimmy's story turned out to be the most vicious profile possible, damning with faint praise, magnanimous about her "controlling" personality, and scornful of her literary pretensions.

Even Carla disliked Carla when she read Jimmy's portrait of her.

Since then she had stayed inside her room. Eating. Watching television. Reading novels, classics and contemporary fiction, like E. R. Robin's newest novel, *Secrets My Friends Have Told Me.* She had picked up a pen and tried to write in a journal, but it didn't help. Her creative writing hit a roadblock too; she could not get herself to turn on the computer.

Every day she reread Jimmy's article. The one indisputable truth contained in it was his contention that she was in the news by virtue of a long-ago sexual encounter, a consequence of a coupling that may have been loving, but which was also essentially forgettable. Paulette had gone on to save the world. Henry's achievements were well documented. Carla, on the other hand, had lived miserably in New York City until a caved-in roof pushed her to this coast, where she had begun to assume a viable life, until this.

She knew she was bitter, but not because of the revelation. She was bitter because she now realized that one of the reasons L.A. had been so invigorating for her was because she had figured out a way to be productive. Now anything she did would be attributed to Henry's fame.

She didn't hold this against Henry. Henry was a cipher to her, and she was not sure she would be capable of—or that she would want—any kind of relationship with him. She was fine without one, right?

Wrong?

Suddenly, she felt as if she wanted to rip off her skin and change, fundamentally, from toe to head, from finger to finger. She needed to be tougher, to be more confident, to acquire, somehow, a killer instinct, like that reporter Nell, like that virago Josie. Up to now, Carla had shied away from these women, certain that she was, at least ethically, better than they were.

But here she was, forty-one years old, and unprepared for anything, let alone forging a relationship with a newfound father *and* establishing a career path at the same time.

And then she had an idea. She sat up in the bed. She looked out the window. The idea was taking shape—a flutter springing into the wings of a bird, flapping in her mind until she had enough courage to open her mouth and let the idea become reality.

"Aunt Carla?" Christopher pushed open the door again.

"I thought you left," she said.

"If you want me to stay with you I will," he said.

"Thanks, sweetheart," she said. "Come over here." Christopher walked over and she hugged him. "Now go play the piano. Make your mother happy."

"She wants you to come downstairs."

Carla looked at the television, at the Ben & Jerry's, at the open novel. She turned back to her nephew, waiting for a response.

"Okay," she said. "I'll come."

Christopher closed the door. "Mommy!" she heard him yell, and was grateful for the unconditional, nonjudgmental love of an eight-year-old boy. "She's getting up."

Chapter Twenty-Three

Josie sat in a beanbag chair at NJTF, examining the contracts she had just received from Studio X.

A. PICTURE:
   THE BEAR THAT SAVED CHRISTMAS

B. PRODUCERS:
   HENRY ANTONELLI, ESTHER RODRIGUEZ RABI-NOWITZ, and JOSEPHINE O'LEARY. (Antonelli, Rodriguez Rabinowitz, and O'Leary are individually and collectively referred to herein as "Producer.")

C. COMPENSATION:
   Fixed compensation: $1,000,000 to be split 50/50 between Antonelli/Rodriguez Rabinowitz on one hand, and O'Leary on the other.

D. CREDIT
   Studio may designate three individuals who shall receive "Produced by" credits on screen, in main titles, if any. Antonelli and Rodriguez Rabinowitz must get two of the three producer

credits, with Antonelli and Rodriguez Rabinowitz in 1st and 2nd order in the billing block.

Five hundred thousand dollars. *Five hundred thousand dollars.* She was giddy. She picked up the telephone.

Her instinct was to call Mike. Josie replaced the receiver. She sat back in the beanbag chair, one of several Esther had strewn around the office, and looked again at the documents. As she reread the CREDIT section, she stopped. This time she dialed a number vehemently, as if punching the numbers.

"Seth Levin, now," she barked.

"Hi, Josie," said his assistant, unperturbed by her tone. "I'll see if I can get him."

Josie checked her watch. If Seth kept her waiting more than two minutes, she would hang up.

"Hey," said Seth.

"Listen. I'm looking at the documents now for *The Bear*, and I see that my credit isn't assured."

"Josie—"

"I want *second* position on the credits. Second. I go before Esther; I found the script."

"Actually, Josie, *I* found the script. And no, even if you're foolish enough to want to ruin your career, I'm not going to go back to them about position on credits when you're lucky you're even getting one. Henry and Esther are a team, and it's because of them this movie's getting made."

"If it gets made."

"Exactly."

"Wait—" She pictured Tess Johnson calling her, informing her the project was now in turnaround. "I wasn't being serious. Do you know something? Is the studio not going to do the movie?"

"Don't be so paranoid," Seth said. "Henry's got some other things on his mind right now."

"It's been four weeks since the premiere."

"What is four weeks when you find out you have a forty-one-year-old daughter? He's probably a little distracted."

"What does that mean?" Josie's voice tightened.

"Nothing. Listen, the contracts are fine. You're lucky. You've done nothing and you're getting half a million bucks. I think you should pass some of that my way."

"I do. Five percent."

"Don't be a pain, Josie," Seth said. "I say this as your lawyer, who wants you to make lots of movies. Don't alienate good people. I've gotta take this call."

Seth hung up the phone without saying good-bye, leaving Josie back on the beanbag chair, her anger now suffused with irritation at her lawyer. *Don't alienate good people?* Why was her lawyer allowing her to get screwed?

"Josie," beeped an assistant's voice over the intercom. "Esther wants you."

Ever since the premiere of *The Last Counselor*, Esther had avoided Josie. The fact that she had received the contracts today had given Josie reason to think that Esther was no longer jealous of her. Perhaps this was the reason for the sudden meeting too. Josie walked into Esther's office.

"I want to schedule a notes meeting with Joshua King," said Esther. "For next week. Please arrange it."

"What?" asked Josie.

"His agreement is nearly done, and I want to get moving on this project. I think it needs a comprehensive rewrite, and he should get started. Do you have your notes?"

"Yes," Josie lied. "I just have to edit them."

"Good. Tell me after you've set it up."

"Will Henry be there?"

"Yes," said Esther.

Esther's office—a former library with a fireplace carved deep into a wooden beam, and books lying everywhere—was the most cluttered place in the building.

"Esther." Josie wanted to confront Esther about her position on the credits. She deserved second position, not Esther.

"What?"

"I think—" Josie was ready to argue, but Esther's countenance looked so forbidding that Josie decided to wait. Something was clearly on Esther's mind.

"Nothing. I'll tell you when the meeting's set up."

"Thanks. Bye, Josie." Esther looked down at her desk.

Josie left Esther's office and flung herself onto the soft couch in the first-floor living room. Heather Kavakos was on the telephone to her right. She motioned for Josie to wait a minute until she finished the call.

"Kiss kiss," said Heather to the receiver. "Love you!" She hung up. "He can be such an idiot," she murmured.

"Who?"

"Andreas." Andreas was Heather's Danish fiancé. "Listen, honey," Heather said to Josie. "Did you know that your friend Joshua just signed with Shep Adams?"

Josie's stomach, which had only just begun to settle after her conversation with Seth, grew agitated; she found herself holding her breath. "Shep?" Josie stalled. "Well, he had told me he was friendly with Shep and that Shep desperately wanted to sign him, but I didn't know . . ." Josie's voice trailed as she felt herself grow angry and nervous about Joshua's treachery. Everyone knew that you told your producer when you signed with an agent. And Josie was Joshua's producer, because she was the person who got the project set up.

"You didn't know, did you?"

"I didn't know *for sure*." Josie wanted to call Joshua immediately, but she didn't want to show Heather how disturbed she was. Agents could mess a deal up, even a deal as good as the one she had with Henry. And an agent like Shep—notoriously duplicitous and aggressively stupid—was exceedingly dangerous. God knows what demands he would make on behalf of Joshua. Josie forced herself to smile warmly at Heather, as if the appearance of bonded teeth would cover the fact of Josie's discomfort. Shep could ruin everything.

Heather extended both of her legs out in front of her. "What do you think?" She gestured to the tan.

"Great. Natural?"

"No," Heather grinned. "Tanning booth." Heather stood. "If I were you, honey, I'd call Shep Adams immediately. Start the lines of communication. Nothing bad is going to happen, for sure, but you know, I wouldn't trust him with my worst enemy."

Later, after she had left Joshua five messages and had called three different people to get assessments of Shep Adams, Josie decided to take a page from Joshua's book and confront him directly.

Luckily, she knew exactly where he would be. Armond Fellman had a weekly soiree at his house in the Hollywood Hills. Joshua was a regular. It was unseemly for her to have to track him down, but on the other hand, Josie hadn't been out socializing for a long while. Armond had earned a boatload of money when he had produced the unlikely independent film hit of three years ago; he parlayed it into an overhead deal with a studio that paid him about half a million dollars a year. Josie knew from Joshua that Armond didn't even have an office, really—he just kept the money himself and every once in a while submitted a script from one of his friends to the studio. He had bought this house from an old movie actor who had recently been diagnosed with Alzheimer's. Armond's parties were something of a Hollywood scene—it would do her good to dress up, to feel sexy. She was a beautiful, unattached woman in the city with the most attractive men and women in the world. It was about time she put herself first.

There were eight cars parked haphazardly in Armond Fellman's driveway. He lived in one of those tiny streets in the canyon where the houses, nearly on top of one another, tower over the drivers and appear precarious enough to be a metaphor for the entire city of Los Angeles, built on the precious truths and lies of its most creative denizens, all of which could come tumbling down at a sudden unleashing of nature's (or, in the metaphoric sense, the market's) whim.

The door was open, music was loud. People Josie did not know moved in front of her, all of them young, dressed in bright colors and flashing bright smiles. A man with curly dark hair stopped her when she walked in. "Do I know you? Could I?" Josie rolled her eyes and walked past him.

She spotted Joshua immediately, on a couch next to a gorgeous African-American woman. She strode over to them and stood in front of the couple on the couch.

"Josie! What a great surprise!"

Josie smirked at the woman. The woman glanced at Josie, taking in her outfit, her hair, and her shoes, and then, seemingly deciding that she wasn't worth even this bit of attention, put her hand on Joshua's knee.

"This is Karen," Joshua said.

"Don't tell me," said Josie. "You're an actress."

"Actually, I'm a rocket scientist," she said. Joshua caught Josie's eyes and grinned.

"She's telling the truth," he said. "She's just back from Barcelona where she was working on a wide-ass telescope. I don't know what she says half the time, but it sounds very intelligent."

Karen pressed Joshua's knee with her long fingernails. "Don't tell me," she said, looking at Josie, "you work in this business."

"She's the one I mentioned," said Joshua. "She's the one I'm working with on *The Bear.*"

Karen's face softened. "You work with Henry Antonelli?"

"Yes."

"Lucky. And to work with Joshua too," she dragged a finger down Joshua's cheek. He looked up at Josie with a bemused expression.

"I'm just a regular good luck magnet," Josie said. She smiled sweetly at Karen. "Karen, would you mind terribly if I talked to Joshua by myself for a minute?"

Karen looked at Joshua, who shrugged. "Fine with me," she said.

Karen stood, straightening her blue macramé dress.

"She could be a model," said Josie.

"She was," said Joshua. "But I really do think she's the only rocket scientist in the world who looks like that."

He turned to her and looked appraisingly. "And I think you're the only producer in this city who looks like that." He looked at her blonde hair. "That sun must be pretty strong in Beverly Hills. You're getting blonder all the time."

"We all are," said Josie. "There isn't one natural blonde in this room." She took the space vacated by Karen. "In fact, there isn't one natural person in this entire town," she said, as she watched a woman with fake breasts, a nose job, and yellow hair, wearing a white oxford shirt, tied at the waist, walk by her.

"Nature's overrated," said Joshua.

"Why are you not calling me? What are you doing with Shep Adams?" Josie demanded.

"Shep who?" Joshua joked. "What are you talking about?"

"Don't play around with me," said Josie. "I'm not buying it. Did you sign with Shep?"

"He's a friend," Joshua said.

"Since when?"

"Since I moved here."

"That was three months ago. You make friends fast."

"One of my better qualities. Are you saying I can't sign with an agent?"

"No," said Josie, alert to the change in his voice. "No," she continued. "Of course you can have an agent. But Shep Adams? He's not worthy of you."

"I know," Joshua said simply. "But he'll do for now. I was just in over my head, and Shep said he'd help out. He thinks I'm very talented."

"I think you're very talented too," Josie said. "And you should have an agent, absolutely." She knew she was venturing into the territory of appeasement, and she had to be careful. "But sometimes agents like to get involved just so they can say they've done a good job."

"What are you saying, Josie?"

"Just that Shep may go to the studio and screw things up. For you," she flicked her eyes up to meet his. "And me."

"That's what you're scared of? That I can't control my agent?"

"No . . . it's just—I've seen—listen. I don't like Shep, he doesn't like me, and to be perfectly honest, I think he'll try to get me off the project." She stopped. "Not that he could, of course."

"Are you kidding? Do you think I'd do that to you? What kind of a person do you think I am?" Joshua shook his head, and Josie felt relief wash over her. He reached out and touched her arm with his hand. "Don't worry."

"So Shep will leave this alone?"

Joshua nodded. "Yes. He will." Joshua shifted in the couch, moving slightly closer to Josie. "What's the status of it at Studio X?"

"Esther wants a meeting next week. Henry will be there, and the executive at the studio, Tess Johnson. You'll get notes for the script—for the rewrite."

"Tess? I know Tess." Joshua looked around the room, using his hand to cut away the smoke from his face. "Cool. I'll rewrite it. Cool." He brought his arm up to the back of the couch. "What's the deal with the daughter?"

"The daughter?"

"Henry's daughter, the fat chick."

"Haven't heard a word."

"She probably just wants his money."

"Yeah . . ." Josie wanted to get Joshua to promise not to cause any problems for her, and for a brief second, she realized she was a producer now, since a real producer was attuned (according to Seth) to any potential disaster, real or imagined. "So . . ."

"You know, it feels like it's happening the way it should happen,"

Joshua said. "I'm just lucky that you even gave it to him. I know that."

A woman with glitter on her eyelids walked over to Joshua. "Hey, handsome," she said. She put out her hand. Joshua kissed it. She winked at Josie, and walked over to a man waiting for her by the fireplace.

"What kind of place is this?" Josie asked. The fireplace was electric, and the wallpaper was composed of pages of comic books. There were two dogs, a shaggy, chocolate-colored mutt and a small ratlike white dog she instantly took a dislike to. The men wore shirts open to the third button, exposing chest hair, and most had hair shorn in a circle around their scalps.

"I'm glad you're here," he said. She turned to him, and Joshua pulled his arm from her shoulder and put it on his knee. He hoisted himself up. "Come on," he said. He stood first, and she followed. Some of the rooms in Armond's home were broken up in curved lines, so that spaces like the kitchen and the dining room were almost complete circles, while others, such as the one Joshua and Josie were approaching, were enclosed by straight, cutting walls.

"Look at this," he said, and pulled her into a room that was cut in the shape of a triangle. "Feel the wallpaper." Josie pressed her fingers against it—it was soft, like the seat of a car. "Do you like it?"

Josie took in the purple embossed texture of the fabric. "What is it?"

"Don't have a clue," said Joshua. "This is where I was staying when I first got here." African sculptures and candles and the movie poster from *Spider-Man* lay about in various states of assembly. Joshua lit a candle.

"What's this?" asked Josie.

"The seduction scene," he said.

Josie wavered. She was not sure she wanted to get into a physical relationship with Joshua.

"I'm not in the mood for seduction," she said.

Joshua didn't answer. He went over to the stereo system and put on a CD of African music. It was in French, and Joshua began dancing around the room.

"Now what are you doing?"

"I tried seduction, now I'm dancing," he answered. "Come on," he said, pulling her to him.

"I can't dance," Josie said, but she laughed. She let him pull her close to him and was surprised at the rush of blood she felt throughout her body.

"See, you can," he said.

"You're still seducing," she said.

"You think what you want. I'm dancing."

The door opened and the curly-haired man who'd greeted Josie at the door stepped in. "I knew it," he said.

"Armond!" Joshua exclaimed. "Pal. This is Josephine."

"Jos-a-fiend!" Armond exclaimed.

"The one I told you about?" Joshua said.

"I know all about sweet Josephine," Armond said. "Sorry for the interruption." He closed the door.

Josie moved to sit by the window. Outside it was dark, and she imagined she could see the outline of the yucca trees from Armond's backyard.

"What is it?" asked Joshua. He sat down next to her. She felt power fill her veins; he was looking at her tenderly. She was attracted to him—she always had been. But now the idea that Joshua would be disloyal to her evaporated. He was exactly like her; he was ambitious, which was not the same as saying he was incapable of sustaining feelings for someone important to him.

"I just get so anxious about everything," she said.

"I know," Joshua said. He touched her hair. "I like your hair."

"Thanks," she whispered. "But Josh—"

"What is it, baby?" He pulled at her hair, turned her close to him.

It had been so long since anyone had touched her. "I just get so worried . . ."

"Nothing's wrong, Josie. Relax." He wrapped his arms around her, clenching her waist. "Sssh," he whispered.

Josie knew he was going to say he had been thinking about her for so long.

"I think about you all the time," Joshua said into her ear, "every hour, every day." He ran his hands over her body, over her tanned and toned and perfect body.

"Josh—maybe you could—"

"Could what, baby?" he said, kissing her neck, her shoulder, pushing down her shirt.

"Could—" Josie thought of all the ways she could ask him to dump Shep without being specific. "Could—"

"Could what?" Joshua repeated as he kissed her, and then picked her up, carrying her to the bed. He unbuttoned her shirt. He lifted a sheet and placed the two of them under it. Somehow, in the last two seconds, his shirt had come off.

"Could you just tell Shep—"

Joshua stopped, and looked at her. He was gorgeous in this dusky light, his smile as sincere and wide as the California sun. "If Shep causes any problems, I'll talk to him, Josie. I will. But do you think you could concentrate on me for a second?" He ran his hand over her stomach. "I mean, do you really want to stop now?" He kissed her again, lying on top of her. "At this second? To do business?"

Josie considered his questions as Joshua kissed her stomach. She knew what would happen. They'd flitter and press their hands over each other's bodies as if each caress meant something simple but profound.

And maybe it would.

Joshua touched her hair again. He turned her to him. "Are you okay with this?" he whispered. "I've been wanting to do this ever since we met."

"Me too," said Josie just as gently. "Me too."

Chapter Twenty-Four

"Will you give me a job?"

Henry's black Mercedes ML 55 AMG was parked in a VIP space at the Getty Center, the extraordinary Richard Meier–designed museum set high in the Santa Monica Mountains. Henry was a trustee and had access to the buildings that were not part of public consumption. Carla, his daughter, sat in the passenger seat.

"Will you give me a job?" she repeated.

Carla had chosen the museum as their meeting space when she had called him out of the blue, after four weeks of not returning any of Henry's calls.

"I have a favor to ask you," she had told him on the phone.

"Sure," Henry said.

"But I'm going—I want—what about if we meet in person?"

"I'm—" Henry was startled. "Okay. Fine. I know this is odd, Carla, it's odd for me too—"

"The Getty Center."

"The Getty Center what?"

"That's where we can meet. I can take the bus."

"I can pick you up. Or send a car."

"No," Carla said instantly. "I'll just meet you there."

And now she sat next to him, wearing clothes that did not fit her correctly, prettier than he remembered.

"Okay," he said. She had not wanted to go into the museum. She was jittery, he saw, biting her fingernails, shifting in the seat. He too was nervous, which he had not expected. He and Cecilia had rehearsed this meeting, anticipating the requests of a person who had just found out her father was a multimillionaire.

"Maybe she wants the house in Telluride?"

"Maybe the one in Italy?"

"We don't have a house in Italy."

"I know."

"Maybe she doesn't want money. Maybe she wants to be in a movie?"

"Phillip says she has no interest being on that side of the camera. He says she's smart, she's quick, and she's upset."

"Wouldn't you be?" asked Cecilia.

"Yes," said Henry.

So Henry had departed his home in Malibu with hopes of forging some kind of initial bond with Carla, something that could expand into a more significant relationship in the future.

He had not expected that she would want a job.

"You already work in the business, right?" Henry asked.

"For Roland Starr. At TGC."

"Right."

"It's okay," offered Carla.

"He used to sell ties at Barneys."

"Who?"

"Roland Starr, formerly Ralph Sitkowsky from Roslyn. Hooked up with Kirk, the rest was history."

"You're kidding." Carla stared at Henry from across the car. She looked in his eyes, and now knew where her own blue eyes had originated. Neither Candace nor John Trousse had blue eyes. People had assumed that Carla's eyes evolved from some latent recessive gene, surfacing years later from the forgotten past.

228

So forgotten that no less than the *New York Times* commented on the "startling blue eyes" of Henry Antonelli in every single article. Carla was happy she had Henry's eyes—and thought how much better her life would have been if she had also inherited his instincts, and his charm.

"I can tell you stories. I've been here for a long time."

She sank deeper into her denim jacket. Her hair covered her face, but he could see from the way she moved her hands, clenched, unclenched, that she was still nervous.

"You're really Italian?" she asked.

"Yep."

"Mafia?"

Henry chuckled. "No Mafia to speak of. My uncle was a judge, though, and put a lot of bad guys in jail, Italian and otherwise, if that helps."

"Oh," Carla answered. She pushed her hair from her eyes. "So I'm Italian."

"Yep."

For a long moment, neither of them said anything. "Of course you can have a job," Henry finally said.

"At NJTF," said Carla.

"At NJTF," agreed Henry.

"Thanks."

"No problem. That one's easy."

Carla shook her hair back, away from her face. "Something else," she said.

"All right," Henry swallowed emphatically. He cast his eyes about his car. Was she going to ask for money? For something—

"I want to work with Josie O'Leary," Carla said. Henry snapped his head toward her.

"What?"

"I want to work with Josie O'Leary. I want her to be my mentor."

"Josie O'Leary," repeated Henry, chuckling. "You know her?"

"We've met," answered Carla.

"You're very different from each other," Henry commented, remembering the first time he had met Josie at Wallace's.

"Exactly," Carla said quickly. "That's exactly the point."

Carla had decided she was fundamentally unprepared for her new life. She was not brazen enough, she was not charming enough, she was not manipulative enough, she was not shrewd enough. She didn't know how to protect herself against the Jimmy Stigwoods or the Gerry Simpsons, and she still could not decipher the language of the heavy hitters in Hollywood.

Josie O'Leary seemed to be the perfect person to emulate. Nadine had told her she'd been working for NJTF for about a month and had already found some hot script that was fast-tracked at the studio. Carla's encounter with her at the Ivy had made a deep impression: She still had no idea how to respond when someone was so rude without cause.

What had proven to be the final catalyst, though, was the gentle, placating tone in Josie's voice when she helped her up at the premiere. Josie appeared never to have considered that Carla might remember her earlier slight. This was a character trait that inspired something close to awe in Carla. Out here, people didn't just seize the day, they seized the second.

"Fine with me," said Henry. "And it'll be fine for Josie too."

"Well, that's probably not true," remarked Carla. She smiled. "I don't think it will be fine for Josie, but because of you, she'll have to pretend."

"You're going to do well out here," he replied. "If you stay."

Carla had contemplated moving back to New York ever since the Stigwood article had run, but something made her resist the urge.

"I'm staying," she said. "For now." A concerned expression crossed her face. "Aren't you going to ask me what I'll do?"

"Do? Where?"

"At your company. If I weren't your—if I weren't your, relative, you'd want to know what I do."

"From what I understand, you're very smart. My mother's very proud of you. Amassing degrees that I never bothered to get."

Carla had not fully considered that accepting Henry as her father meant an entire host of ancillary relatives, like this mother—*her grandmother?*—he just mentioned.

"It's debatable. I haven't exactly saved the world during my forty-one years on this earth. Haven't you read that article about me by Jimmy Stigwood?"

"Yeah, but I don't believe what I read. What do you like to do?"

"Like?" Carla smiled. "I *liked* being mean and critical about everyone who didn't help me out."

"I call those people movie critics."

"I love reading scripts. I like to write. That's what I want to do for you—what I did at TGC."

"What happened over there?"

"You mean when they read the news about me? Roland said that the synergy of you and Kirk Gordon would be like the supernovas colliding."

"He said that?"

"Close enough. I lost track after he said 'galaxically.'" Carla paused. "But then I think he fired me."

"You think? Or he did?"

"Actually I don't know if he fired me, exactly. But apparently I'm not fit to write coverages anymore, because of you. I think he'd let me run the company, despite the fact that *I know absolutely nothing about producing movies.* That, it seems, is irrelevant. The implication is that my use to him has grown exponentially because I can call you on the telephone, but my worth to him as someone who can critically analyze screenplays and tell him which movie to make is meaningless." She paused. "Ironic."

"There's room for both. Relationships and appreciating material."

"I think you're giving them too much credit."

"Well, I know you'll like Esther, you'll see. She runs my company. A superstar."

"Is she anything like Josie?"

Henry shook his head. "Nope. As far away from Josie as can be. She'd be horrified if anyone thought they were similar." He drummed his fingertips on the steering wheel. "Actually, you two may be kind of alike. She reads all the time."

"I want to work with Josie." Carla wanted to be certain there was no miscommunication.

"Okay."

They sat in silence on the hilltop. The museum beckoned to them—the undulating walls, the glass windows, the sunlight hinting at the treasures inside. Carla resisted the pull of the museum; this was the first time she had actually talked to Henry. He was calmer than she had expected. Normal.

"Do you like to act?"

Henry had been allowing himself to fantasize about growing up with a child, with a little girl.

"What's that?"

"Acting. Do you like to act?"

"Yes," he said immediately. "I do. I like it and I'm good at it."

Carla heard his absolute control of the words *I'm good at it*. "You always knew that?"

"Yes."

"Is that all you do?"

"What do you mean?"

"Like, do you just act? Or do you direct? Or whatever else there is to do? You're rich, right?"

"Yes. Very rich." Henry shrugged. "I do like to direct. And what I've really enjoyed is producing films."

"That you're in?"

"Not necessarily, although in the beginning I always had to be in them. But I started a company and it's gone well, knock wood." Henry rapped his knuckles against the dashboard. "It's a blessing to have found one's place in life. Not that there weren't others that would have made me happy. But this one was good for me . . . and I hope me for it . . . that is, I hope I've had an impact. What—you're probably sick of this, but besides working at NJTF, what is it you want?"

"Want?"

"Worldview, overall. What you want."

"I don't know." Her lips pressed together; she was irritated. "I don't know I don't know I don't know. Is there a primer somewhere?"

"Primer for what?"

"For when you find the father you weren't looking for at forty-one."

"I wasn't talking about that, necessarily, but I suppose there is a primer. I think you're supposed to demand money from me."

Carla turned toward the window. "Don't think I don't know you're charming me. You're an actor. It's what you do. You act. You pretend you're charming to get me to do what you want me to do."

"I don't know what I want you to do."

"Really?" Her voice softened.

"Yes. Really."

"Why didn't you have kids?"

"Who the hell knows. Bad luck. I wanted a child. So did Cecilia. Cecilia couldn't conceive. We're both busy, my career isn't one for kids, so we made a decision, no kids, and convinced ourselves it was for the best."

"And now I'm here."

"Right."

"You've messed up my life," said Carla. "I won't belabor this, but I was doing pretty well here in Los Angeles. Not by your standards, but I was . . . doing well."

"Can't be that bad. You've only known about me for five weeks."

"Wrong. I've known about you my whole life, just like the rest of America."

Henry pulled an old valet coupon from the rearview mirror. After a long moment, he spoke.

"Here's my side, Carla. I've got money and fame and all the stuff you know about. You can do what you want with any of it. No strings.

I'm too old to care, and I don't—it's just the way it is for me. Cecilia agrees. You want money, fine. You want the perks of fame—a private museum tour, Oscar parties, I don't know, a home in Ibiza—fine. But I want something more."

"I've never been to Ibiza."

"You get my point."

"You want a *relationship*."

"Yes."

"This is complicated."

"Yeah," Henry shifted in his seat. He was beginning to sweat from the heat. "You know, it doesn't have to be so fraught. Some women would be happy to be my daughter."

"The mercenaries, yes. You've already said so."

"I am very rich."

"I've always wanted to be a trust fund baby."

Their tone was amused, polite, but Henry wanted more. He wanted to say something else to Carla, something suitably profound. Too many years reading other people's scripted words for the most intense of situations (imminent world destruction by an asteroid; a combustible submarine; evil Nazis/Mobsters/Russians/Arabs) had led his subconscious to believe there was always a way, visual and verbal, to make the exact right point.

Right now he could come up with nothing. Instead, he visualized Josie O'Leary, and laughed.

"What?" asked Carla.

"Just thinking about you and Josie," he said.

"What's so funny?"

"Like I said, you're just different. But—this may be none of my business—but I think I see where you're going. There is a specific animal in Hollywood, and Josie's one of them. Frankly, they've always been a fascination for me too."

"I hardly think it's the same thing," Carla retorted, thinking about Josie's perfect body and its effect on men.

Henry felt as if Carla had nailed him on his once-lascivious feelings toward Josie, so he kept quiet. Carla too didn't say another word as Henry pulled out of the Getty Museum and headed toward the freeway.

"I'll drop you?" he asked. He hoped she wouldn't insist on taking the bus back to Santa Monica. She was prickly, this woman, *his daughter*, but Phillip had been right. There was something more to her, something he wanted to divine.

"Sure," said Carla. "That would be great." She didn't smile at him, sensing it would taint a genuine, serious moment. Besides the true challenges that lay ahead for both of them, there were all kinds of opportunities to lapse into intolerably sentimental moments that were fundamentally false. Carla knew she had to change herself before she'd be ready for whatever relationship she and Henry would share. Before that, it was all baby steps.

Chapter Twenty-Five

It was about eleven in the morning, and the relaxed atmosphere of NJTF belied its mellow productivity: Danny Cohen was charming an executive on the telephone. Heather was painting her nails as she turned pages on a script. Esther was editing pages of her newest manuscript. Josie was nowhere in sight.

Carla Trousse had walked from Phillip's house in Santa Monica to the offices of NJTF. She had deliberately dressed down for her first day, unsure of what Henry had told Esther about her arrival.

The door was unlocked. She walked inside and immediately saw Esther's Rules of the Office on the front wall. A young woman was sitting on a couch reading a script.

"Can I help you?"

"Yes," said Carla. "I'm here to see Esther." The girl squinted her eyes.

"Oh, you're—"

"Yes."

"Come with me." The girl ushered Carla down a hall, to a room at the end of the building. "Here it is."

"I've got it," said Carla, her voice steady despite a growing nervousness.

"Terrific," said the girl. "See you."

In the minute before she knocked, she examined the office environs. More like a home where there was no television set, the office was quiet except for a strain of classical music escaping from the bottom of Esther's door.

She knocked. "Yes, come in," Esther called. Carla pushed open the door. "Hello?"

Esther raised her head. "Carla," she said, smiling warmly as she put on her glasses. "Carla. Hello. Henry said you'd be here today."

Esther stacked her manuscript pages together out of habit before she rose to greet Carla. Henry had told her last night about Carla's request, and Esther had been waiting for her, intrigued.

"Hi." Carla sat in the chair opposite Esther. "Nice place."

"Thanks."

Carla wore a red sweater with dark blue jeans, and red glasses perched on her nose. She looked different from the photographs, more appealing.

"I worked at the Glomming Company before."

"I know."

"Much different atmosphere. Much different."

"Good to know," Esther smiled.

"Have you ever worked anyplace else?" Carla asked. Esther shook her head. "I didn't know—when I was in New York, I never realized—well, rather—I never believed I could be a part of the world that actually makes movies, puts on television shows. I assumed it was a different planet, where people like Spielberg and Tom Hanks lived and worked while the rest of us toiled in vain."

Carla kept swerving her head, absorbing Esther's clutter. "Lots of books," she said.

Esther nodded. "You're a literature major, right?"

"I was."

"Ph.D.?"

"No," Carla's lips wrinkled. "No. Haven't finished my dissertation yet. I'm not sure if I ever will." She paused. "Now."

"Still, very impressive," murmured Esther. She wanted to tread lightly here, with this woman. Since the revelation that Henry had a daughter, a forty-one-year-old, intellectual daughter who had recently begun writing coverage for TGC, Esther had been concerned about NJTF. Change always disturbed Esther, even when she knew it wasn't, necessarily, bringing with it any dire circumstances.

Esther had read what she could about Carla's background, especially James Stigwood's mean-spirited item, and she had spoken at length with Phillip, Carla's cousin—brother? Still, she did not have a handle on the woman's desires. Phillip had said she was morphing into someone different from the woman he had known all his life, and he was crossing his fingers. So far, so good.

"I want to work here," announced Carla. "Did Henry tell you?"

"Yes," said Esther. "He did." She remembered the golden rule of successful businesspeople. *Keep your mouth shut.* Esther had no problem with Carla working at NJTF—but she did wonder why she wanted to work with Josie.

"I'm good at coverage," Carla said. "You'll see."

"You don't have to sell yourself to me."

"I wish I did."

"Really? Why?"

Carla stared at Esther. She expected Esther to be more intuitive. "I don't like handouts—I mean, that sounds ridiculous, right, coming from me?—but I don't have a job at TGC anymore, and I want to keep doing what I was doing. This is an unusual situation, obviously, but I really think I can be—I'm good at—I can cover scripts. Honestly. Not just because of Henry."

"Of course," Esther recognized the difficulty Carla had with expressing her merit. She was selling herself for a job she already had by virtue of nepotism. Esther found this endearing.

"But why do you want to work with Josie?" Esther saw no reason to beat around the bush with Carla. "Why her?"

"She's a nightmare, right?"

Esther tried not to smile. "No comment."

"This is bizarre, I know, but I'm—I think I could learn from her."

"Surely—" Esther was ready to tell Carla that under no uncertain terms should she learn *anything* from Josie. That Josie embodied Evil Hollywood; that she was one of the barracudas. "Josie's not exactly the best role model for—"

"Henry said it would be okay." Carla dropped Henry's name as a warning. She did not want Esther to get in the way of her wishes.

"It is," said Esther. "It is okay."

"Is Josie here?"

"I don't know. Let's see."

Esther escorted Carla to the downstairs bedroom where Josie had fashioned her office.

"She's not in yet, I guess," Esther said, as she opened the door to Josie's space. It was empty.

"I'll wait."

"Do you want to meet anyone else?"

"No," she said softly. "I'll just sit here." Carla had already stepped inside Josie's room. It was spotlessly clean, with no mark of Josie's personality anywhere, except for a signed photograph of her and George Clooney.

"Do you want to read anything?" asked Esther.

"I have a book," Carla said, pulling a novel out of her bag. It was *Secrets My Friends Have Told Me*.

Esther took a step backward, looking startled.

"What? Have you read it?" asked Carla.

"Uh, yes," Esther stammered. "I have."

"I love it," said Carla. "I've read everything of hers." She grinned. "Or his. But I'm pretty sure it's a she."

"Me too," said Esther. She always felt uneasy when she saw someone reading her books.

"I'm okay," said Carla.

"All right," said Esther. "If you need me, I'll be down there." She motioned to her office. Carla looked through the archway into the wide-windowed space, where the sun cast golden light onto the couches, the other people.

Then Carla turned back to Josie's area. Flowers were arranged perfectly, and her Apple PowerBook G4 was shut tight. Except for two black fountain pens, a set of cards with Josie's name etched on them, and George, there was no evidence that anyone worked in this space at all.

She sat down in a deep-banked armchair. She held her novel in her hand, but then she saw scripts stacked on the coffee table and reached over to pick one up. *The Bear That Saved Christmas*, by Joshua King. Property of NJTF. Carla looked at her watch. It was eleven-thirty in the morning. She turned over the first page. She would read until Josie arrived.

At that moment, Josie O'Leary was finishing her shower at her apartment. She had left Armond's at around eight o'clock. Joshua was still sleeping, and Josie had allowed herself to stay wrapped in his arms for a full ten minutes longer than she had expected. She reveled being held by Joshua—she loved how strong his arms felt, how protected she was, how he slept with his head right near her ear. It was also wonderful to feel settled, that her relationship with Joshua was organic, that everything was—as Joshua had said—happening the way it was supposed to happen.

Without the anxiety about Shep Adams and with the knowledge that the studio was moving ahead with *The Bear*—and with the all-important contract stating $500,000 as compensation—Josie moved about with bravado, with a brimming ebullience.

Henry Antonelli had begun all of this with that note under her windshield wiper. Or maybe Joshua had, writing the script long ago in Miami. Or perhaps it was the ghosts of all the studio chiefs, benevolently pushing apart the gray clouds of the business that stymied everyone else so that she, Josie O'Leary, could breeze through.

She began casting *The Bear* in her mind. Henry would be the Wall

Street guy; perhaps they could convince Warren Beatty to do a cameo. And the female lead had to be J. Lo . . . or else Renée Zellweger.

She didn't arrive at NJTF until noon. She had driven with the roof of her Saab convertible up, abiding by the directive of her dermatologist to keep the sun's rays from battering her scalp. But she still felt like one of those California girls from the Beach Boys songs.

She pulled into the parking lot, locked her car, and walked sprightly to the door of NJTF. She said hello to the girls sitting in the living room. She had one hand inside her bag to make sure she did not forget her cell phone and the other near her eyes, about to remove her sunglasses. She pushed open the door to her office with her foot.

"Hi," said someone. Josie dropped her sunglasses.

"What—" She saw who spoke. It was Carla Trousse, Henry's daughter, sitting on the armchair against the wall. She held a script in her lap, and looked remarkably composed.

Carla had heard Josie enter the office building and had forced herself to stay seated in the chair. She had prepared for this meeting all night, remembering in great detail her previous encounters—she would call them collisions—with Josie.

"You probably remember me," opened Carla, in a pleasant tone. "Carla Trousse."

"I do," said Josie, immediately configuring her face to an amiable expression as her mind raced with questions. "I certainly do."

Chapter Twenty-Six

"So this is a surprise," Josie said, still framed in the doorway. She extended her hand. "Welcome."

"Thanks."

Carla didn't rise from her chair. Josie bent down, retrieved her sunglasses, and then walked slowly to her desk. She saw that her framed picture with George Clooney had been pushed askew, and she righted it before she walked to the chair behind her writing table and sat down.

"Well," said Josie graciously, "what can I do for you?" She opened a drawer and pulled out a small jar of dried figs. "Fig?"

"No," Carla shook her head. "The long and short of it is, I suppose, that I've asked to work here, and with you."

"You—excuse me?"

"For the past weeks, everyone has asked me what I want to do. I've thought about it a lot, and I decided that I wanted to work here." She paused. "Nadine Dillenberger told me long ago—I think you were there—that NJTF was a fabulous place to work."

Carla watched to see if Josie would reveal any memory of that evening at the Ivy. But Josie's face was carved into a smile.

"It is," Josie said. "It is fabulous. Everyone's so terrific here, and so smart. And there's Henry, of course. I mean, he's the reason we exist, right? No Henry, no—I don't mean to be disrespectful of Esther, she's fabulous too—but this town survives on talent, right?"

"We agree," said Carla. "I have a lot to learn, but we agree on that."

"Well then," Josie tapped her fingernail on the table.

"Yes."

"So you're going to work here. I suppose you got the job, right?" chortled Josie.

"Yes," Carla smiled back at her. "No surprise there. Henry seems determined to have a relationship with me." Josie raised her eyebrows, and Carla was pleased that her name-dropping had its intended effect. "Obviously, my life's changed, and I need to change too. So I told Henry I wanted to work here, and with you."

"Right."

"Right."

"Why me?"

"Honestly?"

"Yes," Josie beamed. "I mean, I am flattered. But curious."

Carla waited to deliver the sentence she had practiced that morning in her bedroom. "Because you are, more or less, the worst person I've met in L.A."

Josie's smile intensified. "Me?"

"Yes. Granted I haven't met many people yet, so maybe there are people even more awful than you." Carla smiled brightly back at Josie.

"What constitutes 'awful'?" Josie remained composed. The situation was ridiculous.

"Do you remember the first time we met? At the Ivy?"

Josie shook her head. "You have me confused with someone else."

"No," said Carla. "I was with Nadine Dillenberger. You were meeting Henry for dinner."

Suddenly, a swath of red flashed through Josie's mind—she looked at Carla's crimson glasses and remembered them. "I think you're mistaken," Josie persisted.

"I'm not. But see, you're proving my point. You do remember me, yet you're lying—effortlessly—and it's impressive to me. You snubbed me—you purposely ignored me—and while you didn't say this part, I'm assuming you determined that a fat, ungainly, ill-dressed person like myself would be of no worth to you." Carla raised her eyes to meet Josie's. "How close am I?"

"Way off." Josie considered this fat, ungainly, ill-dressed person in front of her. "But this is a town where the imagination flourishes."

"And now you have to deal with me because I'm Henry's daughter, and you want to keep your job." She motioned to the screenplay of *The Bear*. "And this movie."

"What about that movie?"

"What?"

"You just implied that I want to 'keep this movie.' That isn't in doubt."

"Oh."

"It isn't."

"Right."

"Well," Josie placed both hands on her desk. "This is a bit of a surprise. I'm sad you have such a low opinion of me."

"Actually, I'm kind of awestruck."

"Really?"

"You seem to do things that, that confound me. I'm not usually like this, but extraordinary circumstances require extraordinary behavior," said Carla. "I want to study you—I want to be able to replicate your behavior."

"Why?"

"So I can survive out here."

"You don't need me. You have Henry."

"True. But I'll be even better if I acquire some of your—your strengths."

"Fine," said Josie. Irritation grew; she snapped off a daisy from the arrangement in the corner of her table. "What's on the agenda?"

"You tell me," said Carla. "You're my teacher."

Josie and Carla stared at each other, amassing information on both sides for future battles.

Josie on Carla: *ugly clothes, ugly glasses, ugly legs, ugly ugly ugly.*

Carla on Josie: *fake nose, fake lips, fake hair, fake fake fake.*

"Well," said Josie.

"Well," said Carla.

"Do you have any questions?" Josie asked.

"Not yet," said Carla. "I'm just watching."

"Well, then," said Josie. "Well."

She had no idea what Carla wanted of her. If someone had asked, she would say that Carla's best chance at being like Josie was reincarnation.

The phone rang on Josie's desk. She picked up the receiver and placed it against her ear. "No. I'll call back." She returned the receiver to its place. "I have headphones somewhere."

"Like Ernestine?"

"Who?"

"Never mind."

The phone rang once more. Josie again said she would return the call. When she looked back at Carla, she smiled her square-shaped grin and said pleasantly, "Writers. They should learn that if you don't call them, you don't want to."

"Right," said Carla. "Why are they calling?"

"To follow up on material they've submitted."

"Did you read it?"

"No."

"Why don't you tell them that?"

"I suppose I could. But it isn't their business. If a writer submits a script of their own accord, I'm under no time restriction to read it."

"Could I?"

"Could you what?"

"Could I read it?"

Josie's head shook slightly, a shrug of disbelief. "You could, but why would you?"

Carla replicated Josie's shrug. "Because I like to read."

"Well," she beamed. "You can certainly do that."

When the phone rang again, Carla heard Josie say for the third time she would call the person back.

"Another writer?" Josie nodded. "Then why not talk to them?"

"Aha! I do have something to teach you." Josie sat back, and her smile softened around the edges. "In Hollywood, the telephone itself is a weapon. I am under no obligation to return a call just because someone made it. Think about it—just because a Jehovah's Witness stops by your house doesn't mean you have to convert. Does it?"

Carla didn't respond.

"Have you ever considered LASIK surgery?" Josie asked. It was the nicest thing she could say to her, under the circumstances.

"I have thought about it," said Carla. "But eyes—only have two, right? Remember the Earl of Gloucester, and Regan plucking out his eyes, 'out vile jelly' and all?"

Josie looked at her blankly.

"From *King Lear*?" she said weakly.

"Right," she said, smiling again. "I read it so long ago. Look if you ever change your mind, I have the name of a good ophthalmologist," said Josie. "It really isn't that frightening an operation. Heather, in our office, had it done last year. She's even thinking of changing her color to violet—apparently they can do that now."

"Soon you'll be able to go in like me, go out like Julia Roberts."

"I doubt that," said Josie. "I sincerely doubt that." Carla recoiled. "I mean, who would want to look like her anyway? She's getting old."

"Aren't we all," said Carla.

"Yes, we are," agreed Josie. "So . . ."

"So call someone, do something," said Carla.

"It doesn't work like that," she answered. "Our business is different."

The truth was that Josie did not like to talk to people on the phone with others in the room, but she certainly couldn't ask Carla to leave.

"Sure it does," said Carla. "All businesses are similar, I think. I've worked in a lot of them. A lot." She paused. "One person calls, the other answers, business gets done."

"What kind of business?"

"Nothing as important as what you do—I mean, I reviewed books once, for this Manhattan literary journal. I had to talk to some writers, and some publishing houses—"

"Wait—" Josie sat up. "Maybe one of those books could work. We're always looking for material. Maybe there's something you read that nobody picked up—that no one out here heard about? That's how you'll get ahead here, Carla, with your book connections." Then Josie abruptly tapped her head. "My mistake. As if you needed to 'get ahead' here. Henry Antonelli's daughter."

"Right," said Carla. "You don't have a choice, do you?"

"Choice about what?"

"You have to deal with me, right?"

"No, I have a choice, of course I have a choice," Josie said, thinking *No, you fat cow, I do not have a choice. I want my movie made so I'm stuck with you and your sadistic little game.* Josie gripped her hands together.

"What I really care about is what it means to be a producer," said Carla. "What is it? Exactly? What is it you do?"

"Do?" Josie repeated. What she wanted to *do* was tell Carla she was a sad woman who had done nothing worthwhile in forty years and that she, Josie, was only persisting in speaking to her because she needed Henry for her movie.

"Listen, why don't you tell me what you want to do. You could still write coverages."

"Do you do them?"

"No."

"Then neither will I."

Another impasse spread out across the cozy room.

"Carla," Josie felt her patience stretch. "This business—here's a bit of wisdom. I've done this for years now. This business runs on relationships. You—you have the best one in the world with your father—do you call him Dad? I was wondering, anyway, I can't just sit here and call someone up. I mean, I can, I can call an agent—"

"So call."

"Let me finish. I can call an agent and ask for material, which someone here can read, or I can call a manager and set up meetings, but none of that happens without a plan. You—you don't need to do any of that."

"I know that part already. But I want to know about you. What's your plan?"

"My plan—it's more complicated than that. And everyone does it differently. But here's the thing. What we do here is all for Henry."

"He's not in all the movies, is he?"

"Well, no, but without him, we're nothing. Even Esther, no matter what she thinks."

"You don't like Esther?"

"I didn't say that."

"Tell me about *The Bear*," Carla asked. "I've been reading it."

"*The Bear,*" Josie's face brightened. "It's fabulous, don't you think?"

"I'm not finished."

"That's what you should do. Finish the script. It's being greenlit, you know."

"By Studio X?"

"Yes. We're having our first notes meeting next week with Joshua."

"Joshua?"

"The writer. Joshua King."

"Right."

Josie waited for Carla to resume reading.

"Don't you want to finish it?" asked Josie.

"No," said Carla. "I told you, I want to watch you work."

"Fine," said Josie. "No problem." She went through her Rolodex of people to call, as a way to stall. "What I'm going to do, though, is reread *The Bear* myself. I need to compile notes."

"Notes for—"

"To make it better. To give to the writer. Although I think it's pretty good, don't you?"

"Haven't finished. But if it gets made—"

"When it gets made—"

"What's your job?"

"I'm a producer, carved in stone."

"But what do you do?"

"It's always different, but in this case, I found the script, gave it to the right people, and dealt with the writer."

Carla nodded, impassive.

"Are you going to sit there looking at me?" Josie asked, annoyed. She felt suddenly as if she were a babysitter. "I'm going to read now."

"Me too," said Carla, as she returned to the script. Josie couldn't see it, but Carla grinned widely behind her drape of hair. She had worried about this initial conversation, and now felt triumphant.

"I'm going to the bathroom," Josie said.

"Okay," Carla murmured, still grinning.

In the hallway, Josie stopped, leaning against the wall. Danny Cohen sped by.

"How goes it with the heir apparent?"

"How did you know?"

"Word travels fast."

"Wonderful."

"Yeah, right. You may fool many people, Josie sweetheart, but you don't fool me. Not for a moment."

"Don't tell anyone," Josie whispered, looking around for other colleagues, "but I think she's a little, like, mental, cuckoo." Josie twirled her index finger in a circle around her temple.

"Be patient. You get a good thing like that, you can't throw it away. You gotta wise up, Josie."

"I know."

"She's probably not so bad, anyway. Think of what's happened to her. I wouldn't wish that on my worst enemy."

"Right, it's so terrible to be Henry's daughter. Just a tragedy. Forget it, Danny, you don't understand."

"You'd be surprised," Danny said. "I'm smarter than I look."

He patted her on her shoulder as he raced by, always moving, always speeding by, the best salesman in town. Josie stood in the hallway, unwilling to reenter her office. Carla Trousse wanted to be like her, the worst woman in L.A. *Okay, then,* Josie thought. She'd show Carla awful—she would teach Carla everything she knew, and then wait for her to run out of town and live off of Henry's money. Carla didn't have the stomach for this business; Josie knew that for a fact.

Chapter Twenty-Seven

The notes meeting had gotten off to a bad start.

"I get it, I get it," Joshua King said, his Florida Marlins baseball cap turned backward on his head. "But like I'm saying, I think the third act kinda works."

Esther and Tess Johnson, the studio executive, sitting next to each other, exchanged a long glance. Carla sat to one side, scribbling on a notepad but saying nothing. Henry tapped his pen on the table. Josie felt compelled to intervene.

"Of course it kind of works, Josh," she said, "but what Esther is saying is she wants it to work more, right, Esther?"

"Yes, thank you, Josie," Esther echoed, only a touch sarcastically. "I want it to work *more*."

"No problem," said Joshua.

"Do you think you may want to write something down?" asked Tess.

Joshua tapped his forehead. "Don't worry about a thing. I've got it all right here." He locked eyes with Esther. "But there's something else I wanted to talk to you all about. I don't know if Shep called you, but I've got a pitch for you—it'll only take a second."

"We're talking about *The Bear*," said Henry.

"Like I said," Joshua continued. "It'll only take a second."

"I'll hear the pitch later, Josh," said Josie, cajolingly. "Now maybe Tess and Esther can continue with their comments."

"I'm about through," said Esther in disgust. Her gut instinct on Joshua King had been decidedly negative. He had not opened his notebook since he sat down. She could be wrong, but she doubted that Joshua would spend more than two hours on the "rewrite." A sense of entitlement seeped from him, and Esther had to keep herself from pulling off his cap and smacking him with it.

"Okay, then," said Joshua, pushing back his chair, "I guess we're—"

"I've got a comment." The people at the table turned to look at Carla, who up to now had remained silent. She had begun to look more presentable in the week since she'd started working at NJTF—Josie attributed it to her own impeccable fashion sense.

"What's that?" asked Josie.

"There needs to be a tangible explanation of how the protagonist is able to save Christmas," Carla stated. As she spoke, her voice grew stronger. She had planned this moment ever since she had been invited by Esther to join the notes meeting. "I mean, essentially we're talking about the story of Adam in the Garden of Good and Evil. You've set it all up really well. The lead guy, Carrington Clark III, has all the money for the kids' toys in safe government bonds. But he feels he has a sure thing in the stock market. He could make millions, trillions for toys, and of course, some left over for him. What's a Master of the Universe supposed to do?" Carla looked around the table. Everyone was listening. "Naturally, he puts all the money in the stock market—the same exact paradigm as Adam biting into the apple. And then what? He loses everything.

"You have all the elements. There's the guy, against all odds, finding his soul at the same time he gets the Santa Claus franchise back on track. But you need a specific. *How* does he do it?"

Joshua stared at her blankly. "It's there, right?"

"No," Carla spoke resolutely. "Sorry. There is no third act, just the intimation of one."

Henry and Esther exchanged glances, both of them surprised and impressed.

"She doesn't mean no, like absolutely no, do you, Carla?" asked Josie. Was Carla trying to sabotage her?

"I do, actually."

"Well, then," said Josie. "Maybe the studio can shed some light on this."

Tess Johnson had been watching Joshua King for the last twenty minutes, remembering the time they had slept together two months ago. He had not been quite as dashing as he had thought, but she had—briefly—enjoyed herself.

"Carla's absolutely on point."

Joshua locked eyes with Tess. "I knew you'd say that."

Tess stared back at him. "Did you?"

Josie felt uncomfortable. Joshua had said he knew Tess, but how? How exactly? Josie had seen him only one time since Armond's—Joshua had said he was busy working on the new pitch he wanted to sell to NJTF during this notes meeting. He would be furious that she had not engineered a better opening for him to sell his new story. But he should be smarter than that—didn't he see that the room was turning against him?

"Joshua," began Josie. "I think what we'll do is type up the composite notes from this meeting and send them off to you. You should pay attention to the third act. Then we can get the script back in, say—"

"The contract says four weeks," said Esther.

"Four weeks then," said Josie.

"I can do it in two," Joshua replied. "Don't worry. Good point, Carla. I see exactly what you mean." And then he winked at her.

Carla closed her notebook. *What a jerk.*

Josie looked across the room. *What a flirt.*

Esther picked up her things. *What a brat.*

Tess smiled. *I'm going to have him fired.*

"Thanks for coming, Joshua," said Henry. "Looking forward to seeing what you come up with."

"Third act," said Joshua. "I heard you. Like I said, I've got it figured out." He hesitated. "Are you sure you don't have time for my pitch?"

"No," said Henry firmly. "I don't."

"I'll walk him out," said Josie, as she pushed Joshua toward the door. As they walked down the stairs, Josie whispered angrily to him.

"Were you trying to get everyone to hate you in there? Or just me?"

"It wasn't that bad."

"Esther looked like she was going to throw something at you."

"I won't have a development executive ruin my script."

"What?"

"C'mon, Josie, you know how it works better than I do. Everyone just yammers about their points so they can put their imprint on the script. You and I both know the script's fine the way it is. Yet we'll all spend hours at these stupid meetings to get everyone's rocks off. It's dumb." Joshua ran down the last three steps.

"You're not going to change anything?"

"I'll change some things, just so everyone earns their paycheck." Joshua pulled Josie outside. "Come with me for a second."

Josie followed him outdoors. "What?" She smiled prematurely, expecting him to kiss her.

"Josie," Joshua said. "Listen. You can't let me down like that."

"Excuse me?"

"I said I wanted to pitch today."

"Are you—what?"

"I was all ready for my second story."

"But—"

"Josie, are you on my side or not?"

"Of course—"

"Then next time I expect you to do what you said you were going to do. Okay?" Joshua had grabbed both of her shoulders. He leaned in and kissed her quickly on the lips.

Josie's face flamed. "I'm the reason you even have a career."

Joshua walked out onto the sidewalk. "I think you have that backward, darling," he said, as he stepped away.

"Wow," said Carla, who was standing behind Josie on the doorstep. "What's that about?"

"Nothing," snapped Josie. "Were you eavesdropping?"

"What? Nope," Carla said. "Just going to get some coffee. Want some?"

"No," Josie said. "Thanks." She spun around and stormed back inside NJTF, unable to pretend she wasn't angry.

Outside Carla walked to her car. She had, of course, eavesdropped; she had eavesdropped all the way down the stairs, out the door, and onto the street. She was learning from Josie directly—but she had also learned that indirect ways of absorbing information could be equally important.

Now she had confirmed her suspicion that Joshua and Josie were involved with each other. Now she knew for sure that Joshua was a hack, albeit a hack with charisma. And now she knew that she could fix the script *The Bear* herself, rewriting without any fear that the work would be for naught. She would begin tonight, after she and Phillip and Samantha and Christopher had dinner with Henry and Cecilia. It would be her secret, until the time was right. For of all the lessons Carla was learning, the most important one was knowing when to keep your mouth shut.

Chapter Twenty-Eight

For the next two weeks, Carla worked two jobs—at NJTF by day, and rewriting *The Bear* by night. She told no one what she was doing.

The night after the meeting with Joshua, Carla sat at a small child's desk in the corner of her room and worked until two in the morning. Since then she had been diligent, in a way that surprised her. Even when she had been a student, she had been unable to summon up the stamina to stay awake. Now she found it hard to go to sleep, as so many ideas kept propelling her out of bed and back to the laptop.

It wasn't easy. The script had an original voice, which Carla did not want to dilute. There was also a set of laws governing screenplays that she had to teach herself. Some she acquired just by reading other screenplays, but she also pored through all the available screenwriting manuals in the NJTF library. The ideas flowed, and she was happy she didn't have to suffocate them. It wasn't that Henry or NJTF had given her validation. It was that she liked what she was doing. She didn't know what to expect when she finished the script—she supposed she would give it to Henry and Esther to see if it was any good—but for right now, it was invigorating just to be focused on something outside of herself and her new identity.

Josie, of all people, guessed that Carla was working on something.

"Come on, tell me," Josie coaxed. "I know you."

"I don't think so," Carla retorted.

"You've got these big circles under your eyes, you're reading screenplay manuals. You're either writing, or you're sleeping with a writer."

"The latter. Aren't I lucky."

"You have three academic degrees, Carla. You should be writing. I know I'm 'the worst person you've met in L.A.,' but am I worth it? You could be finishing the great American novel instead of dealing with me."

"I'll risk it," said Carla. "I told you, I need to know the underbelly of this business."

"You're not learning a thing if you haven't figured out it isn't called the 'underbelly.' It's called reality."

Carla was tempted to tell Josie about her rewrite, aware that the Carla of days past would have already told Josie every detail. But Carla had grown to appreciate the value of keeping a secret, especially if it was one about herself. Additionally, Josie was presumably still close to Joshua, and would undoubtedly tell him.

"Hey," Josie said. "Want to come to a party with me tonight?"

Carla stared at her. Josie had never invited her anywhere after business hours.

"Me?"

"Yes. Who else is in the room?"

"To what?"

"It's a book party for that writer you like. E. R. Robin. At the Mondrian."

"But no one's ever seen her."

"That's why they have these parties. She's kind of a cult writer, right?"

"You don't know anything about E. R. Robin, do you?"

"No—no more than what I read in the *L.A. Times*, anyway."

"Why does anyone go?"

"Because it's a party. And they're always hoping Robin will show up. It's a very hot invite. The whole place will be filled with people who thrive on being able to show they're a VIP and intellectual at the same time," Josie paused. "Kind of like you."

"That's the nicest thing you've ever said to me," said Carla. "I'll think about it."

"Don't think too long," Josie warned, "this is a coveted invitation."

"I'm just listening to your rule: 'Don't ever act like you're eager to go somewhere. People will think you're a loser.'"

"I said that?" Josie asked. "Sometimes I surprise myself."

"Here," Carla opened her bag. She pulled out *Secrets My Friends Have Told Me*. "Read this."

"Gosh, Carla, I can't. See, some of us have work to do—"

"Try it, Josie," Carla said. "I'll go with you to your party if you promise to read at least one chapter." Carla placed the book on Josie's desk, and walked out of Josie's office.

"It isn't like I'm desperate for you to come," Josie yelled after her.

She sank into her armchair, still holding the novel, and turned over the first page. She didn't have anything pressing to do this morning. It couldn't hurt to read one chapter. Josie would like to see for herself if E. R. Robin merited all this attention.

Six hours later, Josie was still sitting in the armchair. She hadn't felt this satisfied by a book since she read Edith Wharton's *Custom of the Country* back in college. She even missed a call from Joshua, who left a message on her voicemail telling her that he would be working all night so he could finish the rewrite by Friday. By the time Carla arrived to tell her they needed to leave for the party, she was three-quarters of the way finished.

"Good book," said Josie, putting down the novel.

They parked their car with the valet at the Mondrian, a rectangular white building that looked like a standing ice block on Sunset Boulevard. Carla gave her name to the hipster doorman, who crossed it off the list and then pointed her toward the SkyBar to her right. She found herself strutting through the glass doors; inclusion to exclusive events did breed confidence. She and Josie walked out onto the pool area, attempting to spot people they knew.

The first person they recognized at the party was Esther.

"Of all people," Carla said.

"I never expected to find you here," Josie said to her boss. Esther was standing in front of a giant clay pot that held one of the SkyBar's massive palm trees. She looked even smaller than usual, Hollywood's own Thumbelina.

"Sometimes I make it out of the house," Esther replied. "Although not often." She turned to Josie. "I didn't know you read Robin."

"I didn't, until today," Josie said.

"I'm surprised," said Esther.

"I do know how to read," growled Josie.

Esther burst into laughter, and after a moment, Carla couldn't help herself and joined in.

"I don't know what is so funny."

"Sorry, Josie. It's me. I've been laughing at things all night. Here—Josie, Carla, meet Lee," said Esther. "She's an old friend. And E. R. Robin's agent."

"So you've met her in person—" said Carla.

"Lee!" Two of Hollywood's most successful literary agents walked toward them. Josie didn't know their names, but she knew they were famed for selling even the most arcane novels to studios for millions.

"C'mon, Lee, no one would treat the book better," the first agent cajoled. "We'll get it to Rudin, we'll get it to people who will treat him better than J. K. Rowling!"

"I still think it's a her," said the other agent, the one wearing the horn-rimmed glasses.

"Can't you at least tell us that much?" asked the first agent.

"Sorry," said Lee. "I can't reveal my sources. I wish I could." Lee glanced at Esther. "Just think of my commission!" Lee turned back to the agents. "Do you know Esther?"

"Sure thing," said the one without the glasses. "How's Henry doing? Can't you get him to sign with us?"

Josie pulled Carla over to her side. She had a margarita in her hand. "Books don't make any money," she declared, as she pointed out the people she thought were important—Eddie Cleveland and Gordon Kelly, the talent agents; the ingénue from the new Aronofsky movie; Marcus Hernandez, and the actor-writer-director-producer who was going for broke in his epic picture about Easter Island.

"I can't believe she's not here. If I ever wrote a book, I'd be front and center at all the book parties," said Carla.

"If you ever wrote a book, I'd be at the door, making sure you didn't invite all the indigent people in the city."

"Maybe it would be a book about indigent people."

"Then we'd have them come just so pictures could be taken and we privileged people could gawk. Don't blame me. I don't make the rules."

"Josie?" Carla pulled at Josie's elbow. "Hey, is that Joshua?"

Josie turned to where Carla was pointing. There, in the same T-shirt, the same khaki shorts, towered Joshua, the peanut-headed behemoth. But it was the person next to him that caused her to close her eyes and open them again, sure she had been mistaken.

Priscilla Pickering. The woman who had fired her.

Josie felt her stomach clench, jealousy and fury mixing together. The message had been as clear as if he had been speaking to her directly: I'm going to be home working.

"Do you know her?" asked Carla.

"Yes," said Josie. "We've met." Josie stared across the room at the two of them. Joshua was *writing*, he had said. He was *busy*. That—

"He is such a—" Josie stopped, looking at Carla, who seemed to be waiting for Josie to react. Josie didn't want Carla to know she was upset. She smiled brightly. "He better have finished that rewrite . . ."

"You don't have to pretend," said Carla. She knew Josie was prideful, but she had also seen Joshua kiss her on the steps of NJTF. Josie had to be affected by the fact that Joshua was here with another woman.

263

"What are you talking about?"

"I'm not trying—c'mon, Josie. Don't be like that. Just—"

"What? Tell the truth like you?" Josie's eyes flared. She finished her drink and promptly grabbed a glass of champagne off of the tray of a roaming waiter. "Leave me alone."

"Fine," Carla told Josie. "But you're the one who brought me here. And I think it's ridiculous that an adult woman can't be honest about—"

"Carla?" Carla looked behind her. Nadine Dillenberger stood there with a delighted expression on her face. "And Josie too. Wow!" Nadine nodded approvingly at the two of them. "I would have lost a big bet on this."

"She works for—I mean, with, she works with me," said Josie.

"I know all about it," said Nadine. "Nice of you to call," she told Carla.

"I meant to—it's been really busy. Really busy. You can't imagine—"

"I'm sure. If there's one thing I'm sure of, I can't imagine."

"How's TGC?"

"Same old, same old. Roland's a joke, and Gerry's a prick. They're still irate over *The Last Counselor.* I guess Esther and Henry got it away from them, and now it's made like a hundred million for you guys. You should hear what he says about Henry and Esther. No love lost there, that's for sure."

"How do you two know each other?" asked Josie.

"Nadine was my assistant in New York," said Carla. "And then I was hers in L.A."

"Nadine was *my* assistant in L.A.," exclaimed Josie.

"That makes it your turn, Josie," announced Nadine. "You have to be my assistant at TGC!"

"Could happen," said Josie. "I'm hanging by a thread at NJTF. I don't know why Esther hates me so much."

"She doesn't hate you," Carla responded.

"Right." Josie spoke to Nadine. "The two of them," she pointed to

Carla, and then to Esther across the room, "couldn't control themselves when they heard I'd read one of E. R. Robin's books."

"You did?" Nadine's eyes grew wide.

"What is the matter with all of you?" Josie yelled. "I went to law school, I read."

"All right," said Nadine. "That's cool. I've never read E. R. Robin's stuff. Don't worry."

"I'm not worrying. Jesus. Listen, I'll be right back."

"Where are you going?" asked Carla.

"I'm a big girl," Josie answered. Dramatically, she downed her champagne and left.

"She's unbelievable," Carla said to Nadine. "That guy over there, the tall one, wrote *The Bear*. I happen to know they've had a little tête-à-tête."

Nadine looked across the room. "He's with Priscilla?"

"You know her?"

"I worked with Josie, remember? Priscilla was her boss. She despises her. For a big city, this is one small town." Nadine examined Carla closely.

"What?" asked Carla. "What is it?"

"Just glad you got rid of that orange sweater."

A waiter bearing a tray of champagne came by, and the women each picked up a glass. "This party is silly," said Carla.

"This is the beauty of this town," answered Nadine. "It's probably better that E. R. doesn't come."

The sound of glasses clattering on concrete filled the air. Carla and Nadine turned to see a waiter standing apoplectically by Josie, who was ignoring him as she stood in front of Joshua. Carla could see her from afar, her Burberry miniskirt twitching slightly with every movement. Because the crowd had suddenly gone silent, everyone heard Josie's last words, ". . . you lying, no-talent son of a bitch!"

"Oh my," said Carla.

"Better go get your boss," suggested Nadine, "before security does."

Carla walked toward Josie. She saw Joshua take Priscilla's arm and walk off the patio, toward the ultra-chic fusion restaurant, Asia de Cuba. Josie stood watching them leave.

"Uh, Josie?"

"Let's get out of here," she said, not even turning to look at Carla.

"Good idea," Carla answered, as they left.

The valet retrieved Josie's car, but Carla stepped over to the driver's side. "Get in," she ordered Josie. "I'll drive you home."

"How will you get back?"

"I'll call a taxi. I'm Henry's daughter, remember? I can even call a limo."

"You are the luckiest person I know," said Josie. She latched on her seat belt, as Carla screeched out of the Mondrian driveway. She was unaccustomed to the quirks of a manual transmission car.

"Even drunk, I could drive this car better than you," said Josie.

"We're not going to find out," Carla replied. "Where to?"

Josie gave Carla the address of her apartment. It was off Burton Way, in the flats of Beverly Hills.

"So what happened back there?"

Josie had opened the window to her car. "It's weird to be in the passenger side of your own car. Know what I mean? I remember the first time I bought a car—well, Mike bought it for me. But I remember—"

"Who's Mike?"

"What?"

"Who's Mike?"

"Turn there," Josie ordered. "That's my place." She pointed to an apartment building with a white stucco façade. Carla pulled the car into the underground driveway.

"I guess you'll have to come in," Josie said. "To call the car service."

"Don't bother," Carla said curtly. "I can call from out here."

"Someone's sensitive. I'm kidding."

Carla pulled her cell phone out of her purse. It was a present from Phillip, but as she flipped open the receiver, she realized she had not turned on the service yet. She flipped it shut again and looked back at Josie. "Okay. I'm coming."

Josie's apartment was decorated as immaculately as a bedroom depicted in *Elle Décor*. This was because it had first been depicted in *Elle Décor*, and Josie had copied it, piece by piece, so perfectly that she had framed the original article to show people her inspiration.

Carla called the car service as soon as she stepped inside.

"Want a drink?" Josie asked.

"Just water."

Josie returned with two glasses, each with a slice of lemon floating in the water. "Joshua King should not be trusted. Remember that."

Carla drank from her glass as she waited for Josie to continue.

"Who's Mike?" Carla repeated.

Josie looked sullenly at Carla. For the first time since they had met, Josie appeared to Carla to be haggard, unattractive. She put her head down, still silent.

"Listen, Josie, I'm a lot older than you. I know it's none of my business, but—"

"No sermons, Carla. I told you."

"It's called empathy."

"No, it's called patronizing. I don't need that, Carla. I really don't. Some of us don't have fairy godfathers handed down to us—oops, there's my dad, a world-famous movie star!—we can't go around emoting every place we go. We have to work."

"Well, yes, work. You do work. Working all the time, Josie is. Let's see. Check *Variety* to see whose name is printed. Read *Vanity Fair* and get angry you're not in there. Look at e-mails to be sure no one's doing any better than you. All this and staying paranoid that everyone's out to get you. That is a job. Amazing you can do anything else."

Josie put her head on the table. "Caught me. You are a regular Sherlock Holmes."

"It just seems to me that there's got to be a way that you don't have to be so nervous—anxious—all the time."

Josie rolled her head up to meet Carla's gaze. "I am not nervous all the time. I am aware that I'm playing in a game, Carla, just like you, just like everyone, whether you want to recognize it or not. There are greedy bastards out here, everywhere, even your saintly Henry, even Esther the Magnificent. You cannot let your guard down. I know you wanted to work with me as some kind of sociological experiment, but I've been really trying to show you something, because I can see how clueless you are. What? Don't look at me like that all the time. The cream will rise to the top. Good people always win. News flash, Carla, they don't. Henry's done okay because he's lucky. But there are a million people in this town who would tear him apart. People are cheap, people are panicked, people are desperate, and people want to make money. Lots of money. I want to make money. And I want my name in big letters. And that's why Joshua King is such a major, major, major bastard."

The air-conditioning in Josie's apartment spread an air that was so thick with coolants that Carla felt it could be noxious.

"Well?" Josie challenged Carla. "Are you sick of your experiment yet?"

There could be no advantage to provoking Josie further. Carla didn't answer her.

"Talk to me!"

"You don't have to convince me," offered Carla. "I already knew Joshua King was a bastard."

"How?"

"Simple," Carla said, as she looked out the front window. The car service had arrived. "He wore high-top sneakers."

"You wear high-top sneakers."

"Yeah, but I'm not a twenty-five-year-old guy. The backward baseball cap is just like a double penalty. The guy has bastard written all over him."

Carla reached Josie's door. "Sorry about tonight, Josie."

Josie had not moved from the living room couch. "It's okay," she said softly. "I made a mistake tonight. It happens. Usually I know how to hold my temper. I know how the game works."

"See you tomorrow?"

"Yeah," Josie said.

Seeing her on the couch, surrounded by perfectly placed throw pillows and a thick chenille blanket, Carla had a sudden vision of Josie as an old woman, skinny with too many face-lifts, and alone.

"See you tomorrow," Josie murmured once more as she heard Carla depart, laying her head on the back of the cushion and closing her eyes.

Chapter Twenty-Nine

Josie awoke at five the next morning and immediately went outside and ran for an hour and a half, charging up Doheny to Sunset, and then over to Runyon Canyon. She pushed herself hard, sprinting up the curving trail, ignoring the steep inclines, rushing by women in tank shirts walking their dogs. She needed to inject adrenaline into her world; she had to compel the Invisible Hand to come back into her life and pay her some attention.

When she returned to her apartment building, Casey Cortellessa was leaving.

"Casey!" Josie said. "Casey! How are you? I've been thinking about you." Josie wasn't lying. All night she had wanted to talk to Casey about what happened between her and Joshua.

Casey put her hand up to her forehead, to shade the morning sun from her eyes. She squinted. When she saw it was Josie, she shook her head, amused.

"What?" Josie asked.

Casey pulled her bag up to her shoulder and walked directly by her, not saying a word.

"What?!" Josie yelled. "What is so hard about talking to me?"

By this time, Casey was in the parking garage. The benefit of the run was lost—Josie was irritated, yet again.

Inside her apartment she called Rebecca.

"Just wondering. When was Roman's party again?"

"Saturday. Are you coming?"

"I don't know, I have a ton of work, but I thought—"

"Mike will be there. With his girlfriend."

"Girlfriend? 'Someone special' has become his girlfriend?"

"Yes. Eve Something. She's a production designer," Rebecca answered. "Works on all kinds of big movies, apparently."

From there, Josie had to abide a ten-minute conversation on the wonders of Eve, how kind she was, how lovely she was, how happy she and Mike were.

"You're okay with that, right, Josie?" asked Rebecca.

"Sure thing," said Josie. She kept herself from reminding Rebecca that she had been the one who had left Mike, not the other way around.

"Hey," Rebecca added, "do you have any interest in coming skiing with us?"

"When?"

"In February. We're planning the trip now."

"Maybe," said Josie.

"You'll never come," said Rebecca, "but don't say I didn't ask."

Josie had finished the phone call gracefully, but after she hung up, she had the unfamiliar sensation of feeling she was about to cry.

Josie knew that everyone hit a dry spell—that Joshua's antics were not unprecedented, and that she shouldn't even be surprised. Moreover, she had never really been interested in him anyway. She had been alone for a long time, so naturally she had succumbed to his overtures. Any woman would have.

Mike having a girlfriend, a "great" girlfriend who was so "wonder-ful" and so "kind," was more troubling; she had not expected him to rebound so quickly.

It was time for her last resort. She did the one thing she always did when no one else could make her feel better. She called her father.

"Daddy?" Josie cried.

"Don't worry, Princess," Dr. Paul Hibberd said, right on cue. "You're doing everything exactly right. Don't worry about a thing."

But later, driving to work, Josie was still agitated, not at all placated by her father. Too many of the plates that held Josie's life together were moving. She felt untethered, almost out of control.

In Santa Monica, Carla was running late—or at least late for her own self-imposed arrival time for work. No one cared when Carla arrived; no one cared when anyone arrived. It was Esther's policy. But Carla liked to be there by ten o'clock. But today when she got there, NJTF seemed empty.

"Hello?"

"Yo, Carla!" yelled Danny Cohen. "Upstairs. Your dad's here. Staff meeting."

"Now?"

"It just started."

Carla ran up the stone steps and rushed into the converted dining hall. Everyone was already seated, including Josie, who barely looked up when Carla entered the room. Carla slid into the seat next to her. Henry was standing at the head of the table.

"Morning, Carla," Henry said. "Don't worry. I'll keep this short," Henry began, both arms outstretched, knuckles grazing the tabletop. Esther sat to his right, and in front of him were the rest of his employees, fidgeting and anxious. "I've made a decision," Henry said. "It may come as a shock, but I promise I've spent a lot of time thinking about this." He looked around the room. "Here's the thing. I'm pulling out for a while."

There was a perceptible movement in the air—a vibe emanating from his staff as clearly as if Henry had plucked a string that was connected to each of them. Danny Cohen shifted in his seat; Josie, seemingly in a trance, held her chin in her right hand.

"Esther will continue to run the company and will keep me up to date. But my day-to-day function will stop, effective immediately."

Everyone sat up now, elbows on the table, brows fixed, and eyes glancing around for some kind of translation.

"What are we talking about here?" Danny Cohen hit his forehead with a broad hand. "I mean, Henry, come on, talk to me, we've got sixteen projects going on, I'm working my ass off, I've got the studio coming down on me hard, and I've virtually guaranteed you're gonna do that prison drama."

"They'll understand," Henry answered.

"I mean—this is for good, like—you're not—okay, okay okay," Danny continued. "I mean, you can do what you want, obviously, *obviously*, but this is just a wrench in things."

"Are you sure the studio will keep funding us?" asked Heather. "Or do we have to get another job?" Heather spoke calmly—assured, certainly, by the security of the almost limitless wealth that enclosed her in the trust accounts established by her father.

"Of course," said Henry. "I'm just leaving for a while, I'm not shutting us down."

That morning, when Henry had told Esther about his decision, she had felt as if the firm ground she had been standing on was really a magic carpet that could fly away at any moment. Just as quickly, she remembered that Henry had never before taken a sabbatical, and that if anyone deserved it, it was he. What she had always liked about Henry was his decency, and his ability to separate the worlds of fiction and personal reality. He was an artist, not a poser, and it was because of this that he was a good person and a successful one. He had had a major revelation dumped on him. Of course he should take the time to figure it out.

"What about *The Bear*?" Esther looked up to see who was speaking.

"What's that?" Henry turned his head.

"What about *The Bear That Saved Christmas*?" Josie spoke calmly, but her fingers squeezed the pen she was holding so tightly it looked as if she were trying to wring the ink from it by force.

"Like I said, I'm out of it for a while," said Henry pleasantly. "I'm looking forward to taking a good, long vaca—"

"That's a cop-out," Josie announced. "A cop-out."

"What?" Henry asked. Everyone in the room turned to stare at Josie. None of them had ever seen any kind of confrontation with Henry Antonelli before.

"Josie," whispered Carla, "maybe you should—"

"I just think that the writer has been working on this project diligently," Josie cut Carla off fiercely, "and it isn't fair to kick his legs out from under him."

"The writer? Joshua King? That's good, Josie, that's funny," laughed Danny. "No writer worth anything expects that his project's gonna happen. And if he does, he's a stone-cold moron." Danny paused. "And Joshua King has *not* been working on this project 'diligently'—unless you say that partying up in Laurel Canyon every weekend is 'diligent.' I'm not accusing anyone, but I didn't see any writing going on."

"You're not funny," snapped Josie. She knew she was pushing the limits here, but Henry had taken her completely off guard and something snapped. "Why can't this sabbatical happen after *The Bear?*"

"Well, if that's gonna happen, then after my movie too," rejoined Danny.

"Josie," Carla looked at her questioningly. "Do you know what you're saying?"

"I'm sorry, everybody. This is how it is for the time being. It doesn't affect your work. Find good movies, get them made," offered Henry.

"That's what we have done." Josie spoke loudly, ignoring Carla. "We all know what this is about. You have a daughter. We all know this now. Lots of actors have children—most of them. They don't stop working."

"This is *not* because of me!" Carla exclaimed.

"Of course it is," said Josie.

"You are completely out of line," Henry barked at Josie. "I don't owe you any explanation at all. Carla, yes—Esther, yes—but you, I don't owe anything." Henry breathed deeply, attempting to maintain his composure.

Josie inclined her head. She knew she had gone too far.

"I'm sorry," said Josie. "I kind of—I wasn't thinking."

"Esther," Henry said, ignoring Josie. "Do we own the script?"

"The studio does," she said. "We're producing it."

"Have we paid Josie?"

"Her payments are up to date."

"Josie," Henry spoke slowly. "I've never fired anyone here. We haven't had to." He looked quickly at Esther, who nodded back at him. "If you want to leave, here's your chance. If you want to stay, I suggest you keep your mouth shut. We all have enough to deal with every day; we don't need—I don't need—your self-righteous bullshit just now."

Josie stared at the table.

"Do you understand?" asked Henry.

"Yes," said Josie.

"Good." Henry looked back around the table. He took a moment to recompose himself. He was never again going to be charmed by a woman like Josie O'Leary.

"I'll be in touch." He started to stride out of the room. "Carla?"

Carla jerked her head up.

"Can I see you for a minute?"

Carla gathered her things and stood. She was conscious that everyone was already focusing on her because of Josie's outburst, and as she walked out the door, she was sure she felt daggers in her back.

Henry was waiting for her outside.

"That was a bit of a surprise," said Carla.

"I didn't want to tell you—thought it would put you in a strange position. But listen. I don't want you to feel obligated."

"Obligated? I don't feel—"

276

"You can keep working here. Or not. They're right that I want to—my plans are more family-oriented than ever before. But you don't have to change your life. Not again."

Carla crossed her arms against her chest, processing the events of the previous minutes. "You did this because of me?"

"Not only. I'm going to take a vacation. Spend time with Cecilia, my mother. And yes, hopefully, you."

"Listen. I want—I think Josie should—"

"The only reason I didn't fire her then and there was because of you."

"You do what you want," Carla said. "But there's no need to get rid of Josie. She's good at—I mean, she does rely on this job. She just wants her movie made. And I think—I know she's having a rough day."

Henry had leaned against the wall, raising his eyebrows so high they extended over the top of his reading glasses.

"She's no different from most people out here," Carla continued. "And she's just—I'm learning all the time, that's all, whether she knows it or not."

"All right."

"Listen, Henry, you don't have to treat me with kid gloves, you know. In fact, I'd rather you didn't."

"Yeah," he said. "I get it."

"I'm not mad—I just want to be fair. To everyone else."

"I get it," he repeated, kindly.

They looked at each other, and for the first time since they had met, Carla sensed that Henry was about to hug her. Instinctively, she stepped away from him. She was not ready for that level of familiarity. Right now he had gone from stranger to boss. It would still take time for him to become a father.

"Hello?" Someone had come into the building and was calling from downstairs.

Henry walked to the top of the stairs to see who it was.

"Yes?"

"Hey, Henry. It's me, Joshua."

Henry looked at Carla, who rushed immediately to the stairs. "Let's keep him away from Josie, okay?"

"Josie?"

"Long story."

Carla ran down the steps. Joshua waited for her at the bottom. "Well, Miss Trousse, how are you today?"

"Come outside," Carla ordered. She walked to the front door and pushed it open. Sunlight burned her eyes. When she opened them again, she had to squint to see Joshua. "What do you want?"

"So Josie told you?"

Carla didn't answer him. She suddenly felt as if her time with Josie had taught her nothing at all—that she was as unprepared to deal with someone as cagey as Joshua as before.

"What is it?"

Joshua handed her a 10 x 12 envelope. "Here it is. A day early."

"The rewrite?"

"Yes indeed."

"Great," said Carla. "Thanks."

"Hey, is Josie around?"

Carla looked at him incredulously. "Yes."

Joshua walked toward the door. "I just want to explain—"

"Get away from that door."

"What?"

"If you go in that door, I'll—I'll make sure you don't work for us again."

A mean smile crept across Joshua's face. He began to laugh. "Threatening now? How quickly we turn."

"I'm not threatening. I'm appealing to your—just don't go in, Joshua. Why?"

"Josie's tough, Carla. I'm not worried about her."

"No," Carla said again, walking up the steps to the door. "You can't come in." She clutched the envelope to her chest. "I'll make sure everyone gets a copy."

"You can't keep me from going in there."

Joshua turned his cap around to shield his eyes from the sun. He looked younger this way, more malleable.

"I can," said Carla.

Joshua stared at Carla, his eyes tracing her from head to toe. "Okay then," he said. "All's fair in love and war, right? Catch 'ya later, Miss Trousse." Joshua turned his back to her and sauntered down the sidewalk.

Carla waited on the front step until she saw him reach the parking garage. Then she turned and went back inside, walking straight into one of the spare reading rooms and shutting the door. She was going to give everyone a copy of Joshua's script, for sure. But first she was going to read it herself.

Chapter Thirty

After Henry and Carla left the room, Esther issued her own statement about the change in the company.

"I see this time as an opportunity. We can prove to everyone once and for all that we are not a vanity company, that we can develop and produce projects that have no role for Henry Antonelli. We've done it before, and now we'll do more of them, for every medium.

"We need to handle the news of Henry's sabbatical with care— Henry is meeting with his publicist this week to figure out the details. In the meantime, please keep it quiet. Like many people, studios are reflexive; they may hear Henry's out and put our projects in turn-around. That doesn't help any of us.

"Any questions?"

Josie slumped in her chair; she wondered if she was going to be fired.

"Last time. Any questions?"

No one spoke.

"I'll be in my office all day if any of you want to talk about this," Esther said, leaving. Josie didn't move until Esther was gone. She knew that while most people in Hollywood would attribute Josie's attack on Henry as a misstep, Esther would consider it an egregious breach of conduct. But was it so bad? Wasn't she entitled to fight for her movie? Isn't that what producers did?

She walked downstairs, hoping to find Carla. She wanted someone to tell her that what she had done was forgivable, someone to assure her that her job was safe. But Carla was not around. Josie went into her office and shut the door. She picked up *The Bear*. No Henry. Esther was right. No movie star meant that the studio would probably let the project lapse. All that money, gone, because Henry Antonelli wanted to spend time with Carla Trousse. It was almost funny.

She left her office and walked to the kitchen. She was almost inside when she heard Esther on the telephone in the adjacent room.

"Listen, Tess, I think that's an overstatement. Josie assures me the script will be fine. Really. Henry and I expect it any day. We can talk about the credits then. What? No, Josie's ultimately harmless. She won't do anything drastic."

Josie spun around and hurried back to her office. Tess and Esther were demoting her—they were trying to reduce her credit, push her off the movie. She would not let this happen. This was her project; she would—

Suddenly she remembered what Nadine had said at the Mondrian. *Roland's a joke, and Gerry's a prick. They're still irate over* The Last Counselor . . .

TGC's business partner was Kirk Gordon. *He* was perfect for the lead in the movie; he was possibly even more suitable than Henry.

Immediately, she pulled out her cell phone. "Hello?" Josie whispered. "Hello. I need to talk to Roland Starr. This is Josie O'Leary, from NJTF . . ."

Two hours later, Josie was pushing through the glass doors of TGC on Pico Boulevard. Already she was breathing better. This was a normal office. This one wasn't trying to be some kind of über-writers' commune. This was an office composed of professionals.

"Hey Josie," greeted Gerry Simpson, "good to see you. Thanks for calling."

Josie's eyes darted around the office, looking for Nadine Dillenberger. She had warned Roland about Nadine's ties to NJTF when they had spoken. He had assured her that they would handle Nadine.

So far, so good. Nadine was nowhere in sight.

Gerry ushered Josie into TGC's conference room, a large, aqua blue painted space with a black onyx table, shaped in a narrow oval. High-tech equipment was everywhere, and an original Georgia O'Keefe painting hung splendidly on the wall. The next minute, Roland burst through the door in two great steps. He opened his arms wide. "Josie." He spoke in masculine, paternal tones, and Josie felt succored, pro-tected.

"Josie," he said again. "You have come to the right place."

"We are so excited—" said Gerry.

"You have no idea, our plans for this project are skyrocketing, they are—" cut in Roland. "We care about story first. First and foremost. A creative community, we want that to thrive here, and we can only do that with exceptional projects. Like this one."

"Do you think you can get Vin Diesel to play the second lead?" queried Gerry.

"I remember first hearing about you," continued Roland. "I was watching. I knew what you were doing over there. I said to Gerry, I'm going to be working for her someday."

Josie nodded, and waited for one of them to ask for the script. She had it stuffed inside her purse.

"Maybe Catherine Zeta-Jones will be the female lead. There is a female lead, right? These days, we need a chick, a love interest. Can't get around it. Maybe there's someone cheaper. I've got to think."

"Story and development and production and publicity and market-ing—we do it all here," jumped in Roland. "You know that. Kirk is just thrilled. Overjoyed. Elatious. We haven't told him yet, of course, but he's going to be. A blockbuster movie."

"A blockbuster movie," echoed Gerry. "Terrific job, Josie. Thanks again."

"Now what do you want?" asked Roland. He put the flat of his palm against her back. "What can we do for you? Is there anything we can do to make you comfortable?"

"A glass of water?"

"A glass of water! Ha!" Gerry exclaimed. "He meant if *you* were comfortable, overall, with us. We're a service organization. We're not going to be one of those places where you sit around, holding a dick in your hand. Here, we do things."

Josie stared at him, dumbfounded.

"We just want you to feel good, Josie. If you don't, we have an unhappy person, and that's just not going to work for any of us."

"Well," Josie began, "I thought you might want—"

"Billing above the title?"

"No," answered Josie. "I was talking about the story . . ."

"The story, the story," said Roland. "Exactly. It's wonderful. You said Henry loved the script?"

"Yes," she said. "Absolutely."

"You're not lying are you, you're telling the truth?"

"Of course."

"So what's the problem?" Gerry asked. "Why is it suddenly available?"

The two men released Josie from their verbal grasp.

"The script's available because—well, it isn't yet, but it will be because—and please, I'm a little hesitant to reveal this, but . . ." Josie stopped. Roland returned his hand to her back.

"You can trust us, Josie."

"Not a word will leave this office," said Gerry.

Josie paused, realizing she was about to reveal information upon which all of Hollywood would pounce. "Henry's leaving NJTF. He's pulling from the film."

Roland leaped back into his seat. Gerry shook his head admiringly.

"You've got balls, Josie. You've got big ones." He turned to Roland. "This is fucking great. Fucking over-the-top great."

"Henry's leaving?" Roland repeated. "And why?"

"Because of his daughter," said Josie. "His daughter surfaced—"

"We know, we know," said Gerry. "She worked here."

"She worked here?"

"Didn't you know?" They stared at her.

"Oh I knew," Josie said. "I just forgot, in all the—the frenzy of activity. After Henry made his decision—and who can blame him? He wants to have a relationship with his daughter, after all—I got the idea that you all might, you might have room for this kind of project."

"Josie," said Roland. "You are one smart woman. You are a credit to all womankind everywhere."

"Thank you," she said. "That's very kind of you."

"Kind?" said Roland. "You're giving us the opportunity to produce a high-grade movie with premium stars that's sure to have an impact on the young audience."

He stopped, and exchanged a glance with Gerry.

"Yes," Gerry took over for Roland. "Could you tell us—in broad strokes—what the story's about?"

Josie reached into her bag and pulled out the script. "I'll give you an outline, but here's the script."

Gerry took it from her hand. He pressed the buzzer on the intercom. "Laura? Can you come in here, please?"

Gerry looked back at Josie. "We'll have coverage on this in an hour. Two, tops. But Henry and Esther thought this was good, right?"

"They did."

Laura knocked on the door. She came into the office, and Gerry handed her the script.

"Make a bunch of copies, okay?"

"Please—" Josie interjected. "It cannot get out that it's over here. No one knows yet about Henry."

"Sorry," Gerry said. "Make two copies and leave them, and the original, on my desk."

"Okay," Laura said, and left the room.

"Now, Josie," Roland said. "Tell us about yourself. How were you treated at NJTF? Are there any other projects over there worth talking about?"

As Josie settled back into her leather chair, Laura, the assistant, was outside in the D-Girl area, handing the script to Nadine Dillenberger, who was squatting in the back of the cubicle outside of the conference room, hiding from Josie.

"'No one knows yet about Henry,'" Nadine repeated. "You're sure that's exactly what she said?"

Laura nodded. "Yes. And she also said that it cannot get out that the script is over here."

Nadine examined the script in her hands. *The Bear That Saved Christmas* by Joshua King. Property of NJTF Films.

"Just when you think you couldn't be surprised," said Nadine. "Thanks, Laura. I'll remember this."

She stood up, shook out her legs, and dashed into her own office. She pulled out her cell phone and dialed a number.

"Hi. It's Nadine, for Carla. No problem. I'll hold."

Chapter Thirty-One

Carla had already finished reading Joshua's rewrite when Nadine called. He had changed approximately six words, including the word "the" on page forty-seven. Before the call, Carla had expected that the crowning moment to her day would be the recognition that she had rewritten *The Bear* better than Joshua. But now, everything was different.

It was a day of reckoning. Carla now had information. Josie was trying to sell the script out from under NJTF. Carla had learned well. *Information is power.*

"What are you going to do?" asked Nadine. "What do you want me to do?"

"Nothing," Carla answered. "Nothing, for now."

Carla was going to be the *controller* of information. She had listened for weeks; she had abided the idiocy of TGC, the nastiness of Gerry, the machinations of Josie. There was the creative side—her writing at home—and there was this more intriguing, more visceral side. She loved to write, but it was a solitary, lonely experience. To be in the thick of the industry—to be the holder of information that she could either disseminate nobly or toss about recklessly—was enthralling. Carla had not realized she had been waiting for her chance to display her new set of skills.

"Hey, Cinderella," said Danny Cohen. Carla didn't move, unsure if Danny was speaking to her. "Yeah, you."

"Hardly Cinderella."

"I don't know about that. Henry's at least one of the kings of this sordid kingdom. That makes you the princess."

"You may appreciate this—and I don't say this lightly, but I've never been called a princess before."

"Well, get used to it. Whether Henry's here or not, you're still his relative. Enjoy it."

Carla murmured, "I am," as Danny rushed by her, but he didn't hear her. "I am," she repeated, to herself.

When Josie returned an hour later, Carla was still in the living room opposite the entryway. Josie wore her sunglasses inside, and Carla waited for Josie to speak.

"What?" Josie glared.

"Nothing."

"Anything happen when I was away?"

"Nope. Anything happen to you?"

"No. Just went to have a coffee to clear my head."

"I went to get some too. That Starbucks on Montana? Is that where you were?"

"No." Carla was playing one of her petty games that she didn't admit she played, and Josie was too exasperated to deal with her. She didn't need Henry Antonelli anymore; she was back in control.

Josie walked into her office. She had just removed her sunglasses and sat behind her desk when the door opened. Carla walked inside and sat in the armchair.

"What do you want?" Josie spat out. "I'm not in a good mood today, maybe you've noticed."

"Sorry."

"Just say what you want to say and leave me alone."

"What do you want to say?"

"What do *I* want to say?" Josie felt her mind turning black, filling with the smog that almost always had a disastrous effect. She needed to remain calm—she should not alienate Carla Trousse.

"Carla," Josie began anew. "You were with me last night. You know what happened. I admit it. Being publicly humiliated by Joshua King was not any fun. I'm ashamed at how I behaved. I'm ashamed of how I behaved this morning. All in all, I'd like to sit quietly in my office until it's time to go home."

"Well, here," Carla stood, walking to Josie's desk. She handed her Joshua's revised script.

"When did this come?"

"This morning. When you went for coffee."

"Any good?"

"Well . . . you should read it yourself."

"All right then," said Josie. Carla walked to the doorway.

"Hey, Josie?"

"Yes?"

"I'm having drinks with Nadine tonight," Carla bluffed. "Want to join us?" Carla watched Josie's face to see if there was any flicker of anxiety when Nadine's name was spoken. But Josie was a pro—she betrayed nothing, and instead put her hand to her mouth and yawned dramatically.

"I'd love to, you know that, but I can't. I just can't. Me and the bed tonight, and maybe by tomorrow I'll be my normal lovely self." She picked up Joshua's script. "I hope this is good. You have no idea. I'm almost scared to read it."

"Don't worry," said Carla. "It's just a movie."

Carla walked home to Phillip's along the beach, as she used to do in the mornings when she first arrived in California. The cement path along the shoreline was filled with in-line skaters and joggers, more crowded than she remembered it in the mornings. Up above, on the pier, fishermen hung their invisible lines, waiting for some attention from the fish. Carla read while she walked, an old habit she had perfected in New York, avoiding the footsteps and hand-holders with aplomb. She was rereading her own draft of *The Bear*, and comparing it in her mind to Joshua's.

When she finally reached Phillip's, she saw a Toyota Corolla parked in the driveway.

"Hi—" she said, entering.

In the living room, Christopher was playing Scrabble with Henry and Cecilia.

"It is not a word," Cecilia was telling him. "It's a name. I know it's in *Lord of the Rings*. But it isn't a word."

"Yes it is," said Christopher stubbornly. "Hey, Carla—where were you? We've been waiting."

"I walked back," she said. "Waiting for what?"

Christopher exchanged glances with Henry and Cecilia. "It's a surprise."

"I don't want any more surprises. There's been enough today, right?" Carla eyed Henry.

"This one—"

"It's for you! It's your birthday!"

"My birthday is next week."

"But Henry and Cecilia have to go to—where are you going again?"

"Massachusetts."

"Massachusetts. So Mom made you a cake. Peanut butter chocolate."

"You arranged this?" she asked Henry.

"We did," he replied, including Cecilia in the response. "After we realized we wouldn't be around for the actual day. We're heading to the Vineyard on Monday."

"Monday?"

"Yeah," Henry said.

"All right then," said Carla. "Hey, Christopher!" She turned to her nephew. "If it's my birthday, where's my present?"

"I dunno," he replied.

"Right here," said Phillip, entering the room. He handed her a small box with a red bow. "This is from all of us."

"What—?" Carla sat down.

"Speechless," said Samantha. "I never thought I'd see the day."

Carla unwrapped the box. Inside was a key ring, with two gold-plated keys. "I don't get it."

"There's an apartment down the street."

Carla studied their expressions—all of them gleeful, expectant. "An apartment . . ."

"Mom found you your own place! It's only a block away. Don't worry," Christopher assured her. "She put in a bed for me. And a PlayStation."

"You didn't buy this—"

"No," said Phillip. "It's a rental. If you like it, *you* can buy it."

"What did you have to do with this?" Carla asked Henry.

"Not much, truthfully," Henry said. "I just contributed some—well—some family stuff. Photographs, things like that. You'll see."

"We heard the story about the collapsed roof," said Cecilia. "This place has sturdy beams, we checked."

"You're not allowed to say no," said Phillip. "We're throwing you out."

Carla, stunned, looked around the room. "I don't know what—I mean—this is just surprising. Very . . . Thank you. Thank you very much. I accept." She turned behind her and picked up the script she had placed on the hall table.

"I have a present for you," she said to Henry, handing him the screen-play. Henry looked at it, examining the title page. Phillip grabbed it.

"So this is what you've been doing," he said, showing the screenplay to Samantha.

"I knew I'd never get away from it," Henry said, but he grinned. "This script will haunt me till I die."

"No it won't," Carla replied. "It'll be made before then. I'm sure of it."

Chapter Thirty-Two

Josie couldn't sleep.

She had spent the entire night awake, looking at the digital display of her clock, watching the time pass, staring at nothing, willing her thoughts to stop.

She thought she might be having a breakdown. She had no idea what "having a breakdown" actually meant—did one have to have a seizure, froth at the mouth, flap one's tongue around? Or was it just a racing heartbeat and sickened stomach?

Joshua had not changed one word of his original script. Carla must have known it when she handed it to her. She told herself it was permissible to have gone to TGC, because the project would assuredly go into turnaround now, without Henry, and with an abysmal rewrite. Joshua had alienated himself completely from NJTF and Studio X— you didn't have to be a genius to see his effect on Esther and Tess. At TGC, Josie could start anew with the project. She could find a writer herself; she could maybe attach a director who would also attempt a rewrite.

She considered the aftermath of NJTF and Studio X discovering her breach of confidence. It was all in a day's work in Hollywood, Josie knew that, but she also knew that as soon as it was public knowledge, she would have burned the proverbial bridges to the ground.

She sat up, her back against the cushioned wall she had installed just as her interior designer had advised. She knew, she fully expected, that her confidence and optimism would return—that she would be able to allocate her feelings of anxiety to specific compartments so that she could again delight in the vigor of the game. She just couldn't do it right now.

She needed to talk to someone.

But her father and Rebecca were asleep.

She felt like talking to Mike. For a moment, she allowed herself to remember him. He had not wanted to move to Hollywood; he was happy in San Francisco. She had insisted, and he had agreed. It was all a long time ago—she felt like the girl she saw in her mind was some-one she used to know, a friend from college, an unformed, soft bubble of impulses.

She had a glimpse of Mike holding her hand, and a memory of a deep swelling in her lungs, as if she would drown if she didn't tell him she loved him.

She shook the memory from her head. This would not help her at all. She needed to toughen up, not fall apart because of a marriage she had willfully, willingly abandoned.

But had she made a mistake?

She did not know what was happening. There had never been a time in her life when she was so fraught, when she had questioned every move. This was unbecoming.

We're not going to be one of those places where you sit around, holding a dick in your hand. Had Gerry really said that to her? Did she really want to partner with people who spoke like that?

Yes. She kept reminding herself to keep her eye on the ball. She needed to get the movie made. That was what she had been working toward, right? All this time? She was just going through a phase. Who was she to question how Gerry Simpson spoke?

She leaned over her bed and picked up the phone. She felt her heart race, and she knew even as she was dialing that she was losing to whatever demon was inside of her, pushing her to examine the most effortless of her beliefs.

"Carla?" Josie whispered. "I need to talk to you."

Chapter Thirty-Three

Carla looked at herself in the mirror and considered changing. She wore gray sweatpants, L.L. Bean slippers, her glasses, and a T-shirt with a picture of Gumby on the front. Her computer was on, and she had been puzzling over the correct use of the word *velleity*. Was it too much, too pretentious to put it in her new screenplay?

Carla crossed it out as she heard Josie drive up outside. She had sounded frantic. Carla had told her to be quiet when she arrived.

It was no surprise, though, when Josie not only rang the doorbell but also set off the house alarm system.

"What the hell's the matter with her?" asked Phillip, glowering at Carla.

"It's just how she is," Carla explained. "I did ask her to be quiet."

"I can hear you," said Josie, from the kitchen. "I said I was sorry. What else do you want?"

When Josie called, Carla had been sound asleep. Before she had gone to bed, she had written out her plan for handling Josie. It had boiled down to two choices:

1. Josie had to call up TGC and take the project back; or

2. Josie had to tell Esther and Henry what she had done.

But then Josie had called, gasping, seemingly desperate. Carla was not accustomed to female friends; when the phone had rung, with Josie ranting in her ear, she had the vague sensation that there was some magic phrase she could use to make her shut up.

Instead, Josie had rambled on about her father and Joshua, and Carla had told her to come over.

She guessed that Josie knew now that Nadine had told her everything, and that Josie was coming over to beg forgiveness.

But when Carla and Josie finally settled into Phillip's study, enclosed by a grand bay window that looked out—in the daytime—on Samantha's garden, Josie's first words surprised her.

"Mike's my estranged husband."

"What?"

"Mike O'Leary. Former frat boy, investment banker, cancer victim, all-around great guy. My estranged husband."

Carla listened.

"He has a girlfriend. A 'wonderful' girlfriend. A 'wonderful, stupendous, beautiful' girlfriend. My best friend told me about her this morning."

Carla leaned back in her chair, attempting to hide her surprise. Josie, it seemed, had not come over because of *The Bear*. She had come over because she was lonely.

"I left him when he had cancer. I came home—the day I read Joshua's script, the very same day, and he was there, and I let him leave. He had *cancer*. And I miss him, but—but I don't regret it. I don't. It was the right thing to do, you don't have to believe me, but it was." She caught Carla staring at her. "You're just going to look at me?"

"I, well, what did you—did you really?" Carla stammered. "You left him?"

"I sincerely hope you write better than you talk, because right now you're not making sense."

"I'm surprised. This is surprising."

"I don't know why I'm telling you all of this. I remember. You asked about Mike. That's my Mike story. Married four years ago. Will be divorced by January." She paused, turning to Carla. "Are you dating anyone?"

"Me? No."

"Why not?"

"If I knew that, I'd—the last guy I dated—anyway, it's the same boring story. Bad men. I've stopped worrying about it. I tell myself that just like everyone, I have strengths and weaknesses. Men are my weakness. Now I try to concentrate on the strengths."

"Like?"

"Like, I don't know. I'm still figuring it out."

"So you're single."

"As a dollar bill."

Carla sipped from a mug of tea. Josie rubbed her eyes.

"I can't believe I called you. This was really good of you, Carla. I owe you."

Josie stood up and lifted her arms high, raising her T-shirt, and stretching her thin, tan stomach.

"I better get going," she said.

"You can't go," Carla said. "Not yet." She blurted out the words before she had time to consider them, but she couldn't let Josie leave. They hadn't even begun discussing the most important issue.

"Why can't I go?"

"Because—" Carla groped for words. "Because we're not finished."

Josie sat back down. She stared coolly at Carla. "I'm not teaching you anything tonight, Carla. I'll see you at work on Monday."

A ripple of heat coursed through Carla's body; her neck grew warm, and she felt her cheeks reddening. She stood, absently, walking over to the fake fireplace, dragging her finger across the mantel.

"You came over here to talk to me about men? About relationships?"

"No, not exactly. I just—"

"You—I know what you did."

299

"What I did?"

"What you did today."

"Today. When I lost my temper with Henry?"

"No, not that. I talked to Nadine, Josie. I know everything." Carla paused. "I know those guys—what's the matter with you?"

"It's none of your business."

"It is my business. It's exactly that."

"This isn't black and white. Tess was trying to blackball me, I know it. I heard Esther talking to her. I need to protect my project."

"With The Glomming Company?"

"They like it."

"They don't know how to read."

"Carla, you can afford to be righteous. You're Henry's daughter. The rest of us have to scramble around, do anything we can to get our movies made."

Carla shook her head. "That's not true. That is just not true."

"You're wrong."

Josie stood up too, and moved with grace and confidence to take up a position behind an armchair. "You don't understand how it works, Carla." She picked up her bag. "I'm leaving."

"You have to tell Esther what you've done on Monday, or I will."

"I'm going to kill Nadine."

"That's what you care about?"

"I don't care, what about that? I don't care if you tell Esther."

"Okay, but what if I tell Henry?" Carla saw the effect of Henry's name on Josie's face. She didn't even care about the principle of her argument anymore—it had boiled down to Josie admitting she was wrong and Carla was right.

"Henry. You do what I say, or I tell Henry."

Josie's face hardened. "You don't understand anything, Carla. You think you do, but you're wrong. You hate ambitious women, you hate it that I'm pretty, you hate me because your one feat in life is going to be that you're a famous man's daughter."

"What I hate is that you're smart and you're missing something so obvious. You want money, you want your name big on the screen? You want to be a big Hollywood monster? Here's what you can't figure out. The most successful people, monsters and otherwise, value material. They read books and scripts and care about what they do. The other people ultimately don't matter. That's what's sad, Josie. That's going to be you."

"As usual, you're missing the point."

"See if those guys even read the script. Just ask them. And then tell me what you're going to do."

Carla and Josie stood opposite each other.

"Thanks for the tea," Josie said, and she left.

Chapter Thirty-Four

Carla expected to be overwrought about her Monday deadline with Josie, but she found herself easily distracted. On Saturday, she and Samantha had gone for a "day of indulgence," and on Saturday night, she had agreed to go with Danny Cohen and some of his friends to the movies. It was surprising, but it turned out to be an easy evening for everyone—pleasant, humorous, and ultimately forgettable. On Sunday morning, she saw her new apartment for the very first time. And on Sunday night, Henry and Cecilia had invited Carla and the Gibersons over for their last evening in California. Antoinetta had taught Carla how to make sausage-and-pepper sandwiches: *"Flatten the sausage between wax paper, fry it with a little olive oil, cut the peppers in strips, and then put it all together."* Henry had eaten two and a half sandwiches himself. Later, Christopher fell asleep on Henry's sofa and Antoinetta retired to her room. The rest of the family convened outside on Henry's terrace, surrounded by a container garden of white roses and red hollyhocks and looking out onto the dark Pacific.

"Did you ever hear from him?" asked Cecilia. Cecilia had asked Carla about her past relationships. Carla had told her about David Stegner. Since the premiere she had left him three messages. He never called her back.

"Nope," Carla said.

"I did," said Samantha.

"What?"

"I've heard from him. By email."

"Now don't start," warned Phillip. "Another David-bashing session."

"Who's David?" asked Henry.

Phillip looked at Carla. She looked at the floor, amused. "He was my soul mate," she said. "Or so I thought. What did he say?"

"Remember when he said he'd help Christopher with his summer energy project?" Samantha queried.

"Yes."

"Well, I e-mailed him the questions. Really difficult." Samantha shook her head. "The questions were, I'm not kidding, who discovered electricity, what is the word for energy burned in our bodies—which is *calorie* for anyone who doesn't know—and how does evaporation work. This is a guy who works for the *energy* commission."

"He wrote me back an e-mail that said these questions were entirely too time-consuming and suggested I check on the Web under the California Energy Commission's website."

"No way," Carla said.

"What do you do with someone jealous of an eight-year-old?" remarked Phillip. "Nothing. You leave them alone."

"You just weren't ready for a relationship," offered Cecilia.

"Jane Austen never married, you know," Carla said.

"She died when she was forty," said Phillip.

"Gloria Steinem was sixty when she got married," offered Henry. He put both hands behind his head and leaned back in his chair. "So, Carla. Did you learn what you had to learn with Josie?"

"The woman who came over the other night? What could you possible learn from her?" asked Samantha.

"Knowing about people like Josie was the goal," Carla answered. "I had to learn that if I was going to stay here. Which I guess I am, now that I have the keys," Carla waved them. "I have to admit, I'm enjoying the leveling power of your fame," she said, looking directly at Henry.

"I'm glad you are," said Henry. "Someone should."

When Carla left, she leaned in and hugged both Henry and Cecilia good-bye. Phillip noticed, but Carla shot him such a warning look that no one said a word about it on the way back to Santa Monica.

Later, Henry went for a walk alone on the beach. He looked out at the Pacific, remembering long-ago nights with Paulette, a young girl with remarkable poise and a determination that had both attracted and repelled.

Carla looked nothing like Paulette. She had his eyes, and if he were to look more closely at his family tree, he was fairly certain she was a dead ringer for his aunt Frances, a tough, smart, loving woman who had died recently after an excruciating illness.

There was hope for Carla, he felt. And he was more optimistic about the new reconfiguration of his family than he had ever been. He stared at the black night, the stars, and the splash of the ocean. A sadness gripped him, as he felt the brunt of mortality, realizing not only that he would not have much time on this earth to spend with his only child but also the likely event that he would have no grandchildren. He had ceased to think about this before Carla, but now, given her age, he recognized it had been an ambiguous hope.

But he had a new family, with Phillip and Samantha as well, and with luck he could inveigle his way into Christopher's life. It was different, he thought, having your own child. Not better, not worse, but assuredly, remarkably different. He had only himself to blame if he failed to see the complexities of his daughter during the time they both had left. Take that, *People* magazine. He could be one of the biggest movie stars in the world, and he still couldn't have a happy family unless he made the effort.

He would start by reading Carla's script. If she was any good, he could set her up for life.

Chapter Thirty-Five

Josie had arranged for an eight o'clock meeting with the Glomming Company. She had thought about it all weekend. Carla's righteousness infuriated her. She was going to do what she wanted—what she thought was best, not what Carla demanded.

But before she did anything else, she had to make her agreement with TGC.

The three of them—Josie, Roland and Gerry—met at the Chateau Marmont for breakfast.

"I want to be clear about the terms of the contract."

Gerry and Roland exchanged a glance.

"I think we should wait," Gerry said. "Why—"

"Because I want it this way," Josie interjected.

"This seems to be a comfort zone question," Roland ventured. "What can we do to make you more comfortable?"

"You can sign this document that says that no matter what I receive the following: five hundred thousand dollars and first-position producing credit in all main titles and paid advertisements, in the largest font possible."

Roland and Gerry both reclined in their chairs. Gerry was uncharacteristically quiet. Roland drank from his green tea for a long, slurping moment.

"Josie," he said. "Josie Josie Josie." He sipped again. "Let's talk about the underlying issues here."

"No," she said. "Here's a pen."

"I'm sure you'll understand. Listen to me. I remember what it was like, coming to Los Angeles, fearful of everyone. You don't have to be like that with us."

Gerry was looking down at his espresso cup.

"We're different from the other places. We listen. We—"

"With all due respect, I'll listen to everything once you sign this and I know you're negotiating in good faith."

"Are you accusing us of doing otherwise?" Roland warned.

"No accusations, just a request. This is a straightforward document. Once you two sign, we can talk about anything you want."

"Why are we talking about credit? Why aren't we talking about the movie?" asked Roland. "The public doesn't care about the credits. They care if they're entertained, if they're enlightened, if they're happy."

There was a long silence.

"Okay. Let's talk about the movie. Have you read the script?" Josie asked.

Roland looked at Gerry. "I'm going to this weekend."

"Me too," said Gerry. "I've just been so freaking busy. You know how it is."

Josie blinked. Then she looked back down at the document she held on her lap.

"I don't understand your hesitation," Josie resumed. "I told you the terms when I came by last week."

Roland folded his napkin neatly on his lap. He moved his tie around, fiddling with the knot.

"Oh, Josie," he said. He turned to Gerry. "Okay. You can tell her." He sat back in the chair.

Gerry looked at the piece of paper and then replaced it on the table. "Josie, you are fucking nuts if you think we're agreeing to this piece of shit letter."

He turned to Roland. "Am I right, or am I right?"

Roland nodded.

"First-position credit? The biggest font? Pardon my French, but no fucking way. No fucking way. You'll be lucky to be in the roll-up credits at the back. Assistant, associate, who the fuck cares. You are playing with the big boys now, Josie. Don't fuck around."

Gerry had to take off his glasses, because of the fog amassing on his lenses. Roland smiled.

"Now, Josie, Gerry's always a bit aggressive, but you get the point, right? Now why don't you leave the negotiating to us, and we promise we'll give you the very best credit and compensation package someone of your stature deserves."

As he spoke, Josie closed her eyes. She wished she were surprised, but she wasn't. All her fears were realized; this company would screw her—everyone wanted to screw her. It was the way of the business.

She allowed the napkin to fall to the carpet when she stood, and she walked out.

Josie drove fast to Santa Monica, swirling around cars and racing through amber lights. She didn't focus on any of the thoughts rumbling in her mind. She just made it her goal to get to NJTF as fast as she could.

She burst into her office. "Carla—" She stopped, and saw that it was empty. Suddenly, Josie felt faint. Her knees gave, and she fell into the chair, covering her head.

"Josie?" Carla stood in the doorway. "I thought I heard you. Listen—"

"You win," Josie kept her eyes closed. "You win."

"Are you okay?" Carla walked over to her.

"Just a moment, just for a second," Josie murmured. "I think I drove too fast."

"A panic attack over driving too fast?"

"This isn't a panic attack."

Carla stood by the chair. "Listen, Josie, I need to tell you—"

"You were right. I just listened to them today, and I thought, Jesus, Josephine, what is this about? And then I keep thinking, I must be weak. All this time I thought I was tough. But nope. I'm just weak. I don't care. I really don't."

"But Josie, listen—"

"They never read the script," Josie said, as she closed her eyes tight.

"Everything okay?" A man's voice spoke to them from the archway. Carla turned. Josie opened her eyes. It was Henry.

"What are you doing here?" asked Josie.

"I'm staying," Henry said. "I'm doing *The Bear*."

"But I thought—aren't you going on vacation?" asked Josie.

"Martha's Vineyard isn't going anywhere," Henry said.

"I don't understand," said Josie. "I have no idea what anyone is talking about. Joshua didn't listen to any notes. He didn't rewrite a thing."

"You're right, Joshua didn't do anything," said Henry. "But Carla's rewrite was great."

"Carla?" Josie turned to her. But before Carla could answer, Esther arrived in the room.

"So I guess you've all heard? It's official. I just talked to Tess. The movie's a go. Congratulations, Josie. And Carla."

"But—" Josie looked at Carla questioningly.

"I've got it all under control," Carla said. "That's the difference between you and me. You go and make yourself sick thinking everything's about you, and I'm the one stuck here doing all the work."

Josie opened her mouth to protest, but then decided better of it. "Whatever you say, Carla," she said. "Whatever you say."

Chapter Thirty-Six

The announcement that Studio X had greenlit *The Bear* for immediate production was in *Variety* on Tuesday morning, the lead article blaring: HENRY SAVES CHRISTMAS, *Antonelli Project Fasttracked For December Release.*

Tess Johnson was quoted as saying that Henry Antonelli was the only person who could adequately capture the complexities of Carrington Clark III, the marvelous lead character in Joshua King's original screenplay.

Esther Rodriguez Rabinowitz was cited in the same article as saying that the project has been a passion of the company's ever since it was first brought in by Josie O'Leary, creative executive.

Josie O'Leary saw her name for the first time ever in *Variety*, and read with an amused smile Esther's confirmation that she was responsible for finding the project.

Carla Trousse, whom everyone at NJTF and Studio X knew had rewritten the script, was given a blind script deal for her next screenplay. She called it *Clive.*

A few weeks after the news broke, Josie drove Carla to her LASIK surgery. Carla had already downed two Xanaxes by the time Josie walked through her front door. When Dr. Richard Reynolds escorted Carla to the operating table, she was having difficulty keeping her eyes open.

"She's terrified," said Josie to the doctor.

"I know. They all are. Nothing to worry about."

In the operating room, Carla lay with her eyelids taped open and the laser positioned directly above her eye.

"We're going to do one eye at a time, and I'll explain every bit of the way," Dr. Reynolds told Carla, who was staring myopically toward the bright speck of light that was splashing out in multiple points from the base of the laser.

"I'm going to be sick," said Josie, watching from the side. Dr. Reynolds sliced open Carla's cornea.

"But I don't feel a thing—" Carla said.

"Just stare at the light, please. We'll do the right eye first," he continued. "Ready?"

"I guess it's too late to stop—"

"Thirty, that's twenty, that's ten, that's five, four, three, two, one," said Dr. Reynolds, counting down the seconds until he shut the laser off. He switched quickly to the left eye, completing the same procedure.

"That's it," said Dr. Reynolds. "You're finished."

"I've had pedicures that lasted longer than that," said Josie.

Dr. Reynolds glanced at Josie with a weary expression. "She's finished. Take her home."

Carla had dark patches taped to both eyes as Josie led her to the Saab.

"Think you can deal with the top down?" asked Josie.

"Let's do it," said Carla. "I can't see a thing anyway."

So with the roof open, the car screaming down the freeway, Carla had looked up, seeing nothing through the patches on her eyes, but imagining the bright September sky, cloudless and free. She yelled thank you to Josie, as loudly as she could.

Chapter Thirty-Seven

By the time *The Bear That Saved Christmas* went into pre-production in late January, the Writers Guild had already conducted an arbitration procedure on behalf of Joshua King. Joshua had joined the union in August, at the instigation of his agent, Shep Adams, and thus was protected when the guild determined that Carla Trousse would receive no credit for rewriting the screenplay. Studio X and NJTF were unable to fight for Carla as they were signatories to the guild. Joshua King would receive sole writing credit for the script.

Carla was upset, but she had no recourse except to join the guild herself. She was mollified by the fact that her new spec screenplay, *Clive* had been submitted wide by her new agent, Eddie Cleveland. The buzz around town was that it was the "hottest script to go out since *The Bear*."

"I have lots of ideas," Carla told Josie afterwards. "If my whole career consisted of this one rewrite, I should give up now."

Esther Rodriguez-Rabinowitz had been very close to telling Henry and Carla about her secret identity in January, when her newest novel had blossomed into a thousand-page epic story about a family of Italian farmers, and for the first time ever, the pressures of her family, her producing job, and her secret life as a novelist became almost over-powering. But the crisis passed, and by the time principal photography on *The Bear* began, Esther was happily working on her next novel in secret, and producing *The Bear* in public.

Nadine Dillenberger had come over to NJTF from TGC, bringing with her Laura, her assistant. Her boyfriend, Ernie, had written and directed a digital movie that had been accepted by Sundance. Carla, Danny Cohen, and Nadine were all making the trip.

Heather Kavakos had gotten married to Andreas in December, and had moved to Gstaad to work as a ski instructor.

Tess Johnson was certain that Joshua King had no idea why he was having such difficulty being hired. But she remembered in great, vivid detail the way that Joshua had looked at her well-maintained thirty-six-year-old body, and thought that he was doing her a favor.

No one—especially a person who misunderstood the film business as fundamentally as Joshua King—would be permitted to sleep with Tess and think it was a favor. She bashed him all around town, and enjoyed it.

Gerry Simpson quit working for TGC to begin his own manage-ment company, called SFC, which he said stood for Studio Friendly Cinema. Industry insiders knew the truth: Star Fucker Central was Gerry's company, and he was proud of it.

Roland Starr remained at the helm of TGC, mostly because Kirk Gordon was too busy to hire anyone else.

Henry Antonelli had promised his wife, Cecilia, that he would take a real vacation after filming of *The Bear* was completed. Cecilia didn't even pretend to make any arrangements; she was too busy attending all of Christopher's tennis matches, piano recitals, soccer games, and Grandparents Day Activities.

Phillip and Samantha Giberson celebrated their tenth wedding anniversary by spending two weeks in Portofino, Italy. Christopher moved into Carla's new apartment when his parents were away.

And Mike O'Leary and Eve Marvell announced their engagement

in January, six months after they'd met. Mike had proposed in Eve's hometown of Cambridge, Massachusettes, dropping to his knee during the course of their jog around the trail at Fresh Pond. Mike called Josie himself with the news.

Part Four

Chapter Thirty-Eight

"What about therapy?" Carla suggested. "It helped me."

"Fred Segals helped you," said Josie, looking at her erstwhile student. Carla was wearing a Marc Jacobs outfit, and a pair of Jimmy Choo sandals. She wasn't skinny at all, but she was healthy and very, very chic. Carla was now an avid exerciser, and, with the help of Samantha, had hired a stylist to help her dress. "Therapy's a New York thing," Josie continued. "I don't feel frantic—I just feel tired."

After the machinations of last September, Josie had applied herself to her job at NJTF with renewed energy. She no longer refused to write coverage, and she pioneered NJTF's canvassing of area colleges' writing programs to find new talent. But she felt dogged, not passionate. At the creative meetings over *The Bear*, she had felt especially estranged. Carla had devised an ingenious third-act device for the movie—she had Carrington Clark III investing in a start-up company that had found the cure for male pattern baldness, thus bringing in the billions of dollars needed to save the Santa Claus franchise. Everyone had been thrilled, complimenting Carla on her ingenuity. Josie was happy too, for Carla and the project, but was tormented by the way she had sat on the sidelines, empty of creative ideas, unable to contribute in the meetings when everyone else was brainstorming and confident.

After the script was locked, Tess, Esther, and Henry had spent hours discussing all the potential wardrobe choices, the casting options, and the people who would find the production designers. Josie had been involved in all of the meetings, and she had even learned the difference between a Key Grip and a Sound Mixer. Her social life had dwindled down to brief get-togethers with Rebecca and her family twice a week, or with Carla and her new family. Her old friends called her, but she was notoriously lackadaisical in responding to them, and eventually they stopped trying to reach her. She knew something was truly wrong when she read in the trades that Priscilla Pickering had been caught stealing a script from a young writer. Josie didn't even care.

"Are you going on Monday?" Carla asked her. It was the last day of pre-production; filming was scheduled to begin on Monday, commencing with a 6:00 A.M. crew call. "I'm getting my own chair. It's their way of making up for the fact that I'm not getting credit."

"You can keep the chair forever," offered Josie.

"Like that's a fair exchange," said Carla. "But it's okay. Next time."

Besides her new look, which was undeniably more consistent with society's norms, Carla had adopted a decidedly more confident tone.

"Do you know Jonathan Sachs?" Carla asked Josie. "He keeps talking to me directly about a project. I keep telling him to call Eddie, that that's what agents are for. Now he's saying I should talk to him directly because he's a friend of yours."

"Don't call him," said Josie.

"I'm not like you, Josie," Carla said. "I call everyone back within a day. People take me seriously that way."

"You're perfect for this business," Josie said. "Talent and a killer instinct—unstoppable."

"I figured that out long ago," replied Carla. "With your help, of course. I give you full credit. But what about you?"

"Don't worry about me," Josie said. "I'm all right. Just figuring things out."

The rest of the day Josie tied up the final loose ends of the movie: She discussed the final budget for the art department, and whether they should use fake snow falling on a soundstage in the Valley, or move the production for three days to Manhattan (and risk a possible real snowstorm). She strategized with the casting director about ways to entice Renée Zellweger to book a cameo in the film, and she approved the hiring of the accountant. Her last appointment was with the wardrobe designer, where Josie advised him that his conception of Wall Street chic was completely wrong.

When she left the production office that night, she intentionally did not say good-bye to anyone. One reason was that she was fearful that even a prosaic leave-taking would trigger this new welter of emotions that had recently begun to send her sprawling to her couch, sobbing, or lying awake in bed, staring at her skylight.

But the other reason was that on Monday afternoon, when everyone was at lunch break on the movie set, Josie would be on a plane with Rebecca. She was going to the Adirondacks.

"Yes, I know what I'm doing," Josie had said to Rebecca. "I want to go."

Rebecca had gasped. "You're kidding me, right?"

"Nope," said Josie. "Just promise me that Amelia will keep her fluids to herself."

Chapter Thirty-Nine

At the end of the first day of filming, Carla and Henry and Cecilia and Antoinetta and Phillip and Samantha and Christopher celebrated with a picnic outside of Henry's house.

Cecilia's nieces and nephews were there, as were all of Henry's extended family. Antoinetta had cooked everything, unwilling to leave anything in the hands of the California caterers who kept telling her that her pasta should be made of soy.

Glasses were clinked, dogs were chased, Frisbees were thrown. Carla sat back on her towel, looking at the Pacific, remembering her vision of herself on the beach when she was still in New York, almost a full year ago now, when the idea of being purged by the winds of the coast and the thrust of the waves had propelled her on this journey.

She could not be happier—she did not know, had never known, that this kind of happiness was even possible.

"By the way," asked Henry. "Who's Clive?"

• • •

Across the country, Josie followed Rebecca and her family through the woods of North Creek, New York. She was on cross-country skis, and she was clumsy and cold and sweating. She was also furious with Roman, who kept telling her "It's easy, it's easy, just put your knees together and bend down!"

Josie had fallen, at last count, sixteen times. She had urged Rebecca to go ahead, that she would catch up.

But now she was lost. It was completely quiet, and the trees were iced with that particular combination of snow and frozen water that looked like ice frosting for the gray, barren wood.

She plodded ahead through the thick, clumped snow. She smiled when she remembered what she had done on Monday morning, before the plane left. She had gone over to Studio X, with documents that were the official transfer of Josie's producer credit over to Carla. Josie had made the decision over the weekend, signing the papers in front of Seth and Phillip, making them promise not to tell Carla until she had left for her trip.

"You sure about this, Josie?" asked Seth. "No credit at all?

"I'm sure." And then she had signed the papers and left.

Now she was lost in the woods somewhere in New York State, and she was completely alone. She felt as if she were following a path, and continued moving forward, all the while worried that she should be turning around.

But then she came into a clearing, and with a few more pushes on her ski poles, she emerged onto a frozen lake, covered in snow, the mountains of the Adirondacks surrounding her in silence.

She pushed herself onto the lake, making the first tread marks into the deep snow. She had no idea what to make of this place—the snow, the silence, the solitude—but she felt as if she could keep going here, that no one was going to stop her or judge her or push her. No one, not even herself.

She stopped moving and looked up to the cold gray sky. She thought she heard a child's cry, but she was mistaken; it was the wind. She looked out again, at the lake, wondering, and then she felt her mind stop churning, and she inhaled deeply, and then breathed out, a fresh, cold burst of air.

All new, all by herself.

· · ·

In Santa Monica, Esther worked on her new novel late on Friday night, knowing she would not be disturbed because everyone else was on the movie set and Aram had the twins. When the phone rang, she answered it herself.

"NJTF," she said. "Esther speaking."

"Hello?" It was an old man's voice. "Who's this?"

"I'm sorry," said Esther. "This is a film company in Los Angeles. Who are you calling for?"

"This is Mark Alloway. I'm a lawyer in Florida."

"Is there something I can help you with?"

"Are you the outfit working on the film *The Bear That Saved Christmas?*"

"Yes."

"Now you listen to me. I've got to tell you, I'm sitting here in my home in Boca, and I'm reading about it in the paper, and I read the name of Joshua King and I almost—"

"Mr. Alloway? Excuse me? What are you calling about?"

"I wrote that script! The whole thing—the Wall Street trader, the Santa Claus franchise—you know what I'm talking about! I registered it with the Writers Guild in New York City—you'll be hearing from them. That punk kid took it from my desk in Boca after he walked my dogs! I'll tell you, I practiced law for forty-five years—I'm seventy-two years old—and I've never seen this kind of trick before. I'll sue him up and down the country, he won't know what hit him!"

Esther sighed as she looked out the window, toward the ocean she couldn't see. She put down her novel and pulled out one of her NJTF notepads. She picked up a pen.

"Let's start from the top, Mr. Alloway . . ."

Acknowledgments

The following people aided and abetted me during the course of writing this novel, providing in various doses criticism, inspiration and much-needed support:

James Adams, Liz Baird, Hilary Bass, Jennifer Besser, Andrew Bevan, Jonathan Burnham, Julie Cohen, Laura Dail, Mark, Lucy, Anthony, Jennifer, Roman and Mark DeMarco Jr., Laurie Horowitz, Steve Hutensky, Laura Knight, John Leguizamo, Jamie Levitt, Jane Lury, Robin O'Hara, Bob & Lynne Papinchak, Kristin Powers, Dean, Christopher and Barbara DeMarco Reiche, Alicia Sams, Jennifer Sanger, Kathy Schneider, Caroline Upcher, John & Sally Van Doren, Margaret Van Cleve and Diana Weymar.

Deserving special mention is Emory Van Cleve, who came up with the title of this novel. That he also puts up with me, encourages me even when I'm a pest, and unfailingly provides humor, kindness and love is a gift I'm not sure I deserve, but one for which I am overwhelmingly grateful.